DAVID GIBBINS has worked in underwater archaeology all his professional life. After taking a PhD from Cambridge University he taught archaeology in Britain and abroad, and is a world authority on ancient shipwrecks and sunken cities. He has led numerous expeditions to investigate underwater sites in the Mediterranean and around the world. He currently divides his time between fieldwork, England and Canada.

By David Gibbins

The Gods of Atlantis

DAVID GIBBINS

headline

First published in Great Britain in 2011 by
HEADLINE PUBLISHING GROUP

First published in paperback in 2011 by
HEADLINE PUBLISHING GROUP

3

Cataloguing in Publication Data is available from the British Library

ISBN 978 0 7553 5400 9 (B-format)
ISBN 978 0 7553 5815 1 (A-format)

Typeset in Aldine 401 by Avon DataSet Ltd,
Bidford-on-Avon, Warwickshire

Printed and bound by CPI Group (UK) Ltd, Croydon, CR0 4YY

Headline's policy is to use papers that are natural, renewable and
recyclable products and made from wood grown in sustainable forests.
The logging and manufacturing processes are expected to conform
to the environmental regulations of the country of origin.

HEADLINE PUBLISHING GROUP
An Hachette UK Company
338 Euston Road
London NW1 3BH

www.headline.co.uk
www.hachette.co.uk

Acknowledgements

I am very grateful to my agent, Luigi Bonomi of LBA, and to my editors, Martin Fletcher in London and Caitlin Alexander in New York; to Emily Griffin for helping to get this book into production, and to Jane Selley for her skilled copy-editing of this and my previous books; to the rest of the excellent team at Headline, including Aslan Byrne, Darragh Deering and Jane Morpeth; to the Hachette representatives internationally who have done so much to promote my books; to Alison Bonomi, Amanda Preston and Ajda Vucicevic at LBA; to Nicky Kennedy, Sam Edenborough, Mary Esdaile, Jenny Robson and Katherine West at the Intercontinental Literary Agency; to Gaia Banks at Sheil Land; to my film agent John Rush; and to Harriet Evans, my former editor at Headline, whose huge enthusiasm for my first novel *Atlantis* led me to think of writing the sequel that has become *The Gods of Atlantis*.

I am grateful to my mother Ann Verrinder Gibbins for casting a critical eye over many draft chapters and manuscripts; to my brother Alan for diving with me in lava tubes off volcanoes, for his photography and video work for my website www.davidgibbins.com and for his expertise as a pilot, greatly benefiting the flying chapters in this book; and to Angie Hobbs for her unrivalled knowledge of Plato.

Among many others who have provided helpful comments on my books I am especially grateful to Professor Paul Cartledge of Cambridge University. The research behind the first part of this book owes much to former professors and colleagues at Bristol, Cambridge and Liverpool Universities, where I was fortunate to study and to teach in institutions that have been at the forefront of research into the Neolithic in Anatolia; I would especially like to thank James Macqueen, who introduced me in riveting fashion to ancient Near Eastern civilization when I was an undergraduate at Bristol, and to the British Institute of Archaeology at Ankara for first enabling me to visit the site of Çatalhöyük in Turkey in 1984.

Finally, to Angie and our daughter Molly, to whom all of my books are dedicated with much love.

Map of the Mediterranean region

ATLANTIC
OCEAN

see inset

Herculaneum

The Pillars of Hercules — Lixus

Carthage

Cape Juby

0   kilometres   1000

0   miles   1000

0   kilometres   500

0   miles   500

BLACK SEA

Istanbul

GREECE

Troy

TURKEY

Çatalhöyük

Göbekli
Tepe

Mycenae

Crete

MEDITERRANEAN SEA

Alexandria

Jericho

EGYPT

In 1934, Heinrich Himmler – the second most powerful man in Nazi Germany – bought Wewelsburg Castle, a medieval stronghold perched high above the valley of the River Oder in Westphalia. Himmler associated the region with the mythic origins of the German nation, and saw the castle's triangular shape as a 'spear of destiny', pointing north. The castle had a sinister history: legend held that thousands of accused witches were tortured and executed there, and an inquisition room still survived in the basement. But nothing in its past could equal the plans that Himmler had for it.

He set about transforming Wewelsburg into the 'order-castle' of the SS, the ideological centre of the Nazi cult. Slave labourers were brought to a new concentration camp near the castle, and over a thousand of them were worked to death quarrying and transporting stone. A circular chamber was created, the 'SS Generals' Hall'. In the centre of the floor was a twelve-spoked sunwheel, leading out to twelve pillars and twelve window niches. Directly below lay another chamber, a domed vault based on the tombs of the Bronze Age Mycenaeans, and a semi-mythical ruler Himmler admired – Agamemnon, the Mycenaean conqueror of Troy. At the zenith of the dome was an ancient symbol that had been found on pottery at Troy and on golden decorations at

Mycenae, a symbol the Nazis appropriated for their own baleful ends – the 'crooked cross', the swastika.

What went on in those rooms may never be known. Wewelsburg became a focus for Nazi archaeological research, to fulfil Adolf Hitler's desire to 'return to the source of the blood, to root us again in the soil, to seek again for strength from sources which have been buried for 2,000 years'. Yet Hitler himself never visited the castle. It was to remain Himmler's preserve, central to his obsession with prehistory and the occult. From there, the Ahnenerbe – the 'Department of Cultural Heritage' – sent expeditions to Tibet, to Peru, to Iceland, to places still unknown today, searching for Aryan origins and for the greatest prize of all, the lost civilization of Atlantis. Underlying everything lay Himmler's racial theories, and Wewelsburg became a springboard for some of the greatest crimes against humanity ever conceived. It was there that he began to formulate the 'Final Solution', the mass murder of the Jews. And it was there in 1941 that he assembled his top SS generals for ideological strengthening before the invasion of Russia, the most destructive military campaign in history – one foretold to Himmler in a legend of a final battle between West and East, and fuelled by his doctrine of Aryan racial superiority over the Slavic peoples of Russia.

Yet even while these terrible events were unfolding, Himmler continued to be obsessed with the symbols and artefacts of the past. He envisaged Wewelsburg Castle within a huge semicircular complex, the 'Centre of the New World', its plan reminiscent of the circular prehistoric monuments that he associated with mythical Aryan forebears. He planned a huge archaeological collection at Wewelsburg, to make it part of SS indoctrination. The placing of the sunwheel and the swastika in the Generals' Hall and the vault below show how he drew power from ancient symbols, and incorporated them into the very core of Nazi *ideology. And just as he saw those prehistoric monuments as evidence of a new order, of a new race arisen, so he saw his new world as one where the only gods were the gods of the Nazis, the gods they themselves had become.*

Nobody knows how close Himmler may have come to realizing his dream, and what artefacts may have been brought there. Deep within the castle lay another chamber, Himmler's private vault, but when American soldiers captured Wewelsburg in 1945 they found it empty, its contents unknown and seemingly lost forever to history.

One artefact might have been at Wewelsburg, an artefact of extraordinary power that could have unlocked the greatest obsession of all: the dream of the lost civilization of Atlantis, and of Atlantis reborn . . .

Then, as dawn first glimmered, from the horizon rose a dark cloud, and Adad the storm god was raging within it. Then Nergal, god of plague and war, wrenched out the boats' mooring poles; Nunurta, god of the earth, made the dams overflow; and the Anunnaki, dread gods of the underworld, their torches brandished, shrivelled the land with their flames. Desolation from Adad spread over the sky, and all that had been bright was turned into darkness. Like a bull he charged the land; he shattered the land like a vessel of clay; for a day the raging winds flattened the land, and then came the flood. Like a tide of war it swept over the people. A brother could not distinguish his brother; from heaven the people were not to be seen . . . For six days and seven nights it raged, the wind, the storm, the flood; it flattened the land. On the seventh day the wind abated, the storm that had ravaged the land like a war; the sea was lulled, the gale was spent; the flood ended. I looked on the day, and all sound was stilled; all the people had turned to clay. All around me the waters were flat like the roof of a house. Then I opened a hatchway in the boat, and on my cheek streamed the sunlight. I bowed down and wept, my cheeks overflowing with tears. I gazed into the distance, to the furthest bounds of the ocean, and saw land arising. On the mountain of Nisir the boat ran aground; the mountain of Nisir held the boat fast, and would not release it . . . I brought an offering and made a sacrifice, and I poured a libation on the peak of the mountain . . . so it was that the gods took me and caused me to dwell in this place, at the ends of the earth . . .

The words of Uta-napishtim to Gilgamesh from Tablet XI of *He who saw the deep*, the Babylonian version of *The Epic of Gilgamesh* (late 2nd millennium BC Akkadian, but derived from a story first written down in Sumerian in the 3rd millennium BC and probably originating millennia earlier)

Prologue

The Voyage of Uta-napishtim

The man gripped the edge of the boat and squinted at the western horizon, trying to see past the blinding glare of the sun. Earlier he had sensed a flickering in the sky, a strange smell in the air, but he no longer knew whether it was real or a dream, after weeks of wallowing in this weed-choked sea. He tensed his hands and heaved himself up, then leaned over the side and stared into the depths. His knuckles were raw and bleeding from sunburn and salt, but he no longer felt the pain. Ever since they had been marooned in this windless sea he had taken to staring down, pulling his tattered leopardskin cape over his head to shade the water, letting it form a cover that had stiffened with the salt.

The sea was deep blue, and he could see far down, to where blue became black. He glimpsed flashes of silver, and sparkles

1

of light. He knew that something was down there, shadowing them, a shape that lurked on the edge of the underworld. If only he could fix it with his eyes, then he would be able to draw on the power of its spirit. He had spent hours looking, days. Even his brother Enlil no longer called him by the nickname they had used as boys, Noah, but now addressed him, half mockingly, by his shaman name, Uta-napishtim, 'he who sees the deep'. The others in his boat were too far gone to help him look, only four of them now, paralysed by thirst and hunger and fear. But he was their spirit traveller, their shaman. They might see the earthly form of the monster, but only he could touch its spirit.

He picked up his obsidian knife and ran his thumb along the blade, feeling it cut into his skin. He remembered going with Enlil and their father Ra Shamash deep into the volcano to find the sacred black stone, and watching the old man make the rippled flat of the blade by pressing off tiny flakes with a piece of antler. Noah had a cache of blades here now, in a basket under the thwarts, but this knife made by his father was the most sacred. That had been the day their father had taken them for the first time to the spirit cave and given them their shaman names, and taught them to inscribe their names into the rock using the ancient symbols, beside the paintings of bulls and leopards and vultures. But their father had gone to the spirit world years before, and now only Noah could give the others in his boat the strength to raise the paddles and seek out the shore he knew lay somewhere ahead. Three cycles of the moon ago, as the flood waters rose up the walls of their city, before he had completed the last bull sacrifice and they had taken to the boats, his dying mother Nisir had closed her eyes and seen it in a vision: a thunderbird flying towards her, then twin peaks on the edge of the western sea, lofty like those of the sacred mountain of Atlantis that had been drowning all around them. And now he was sure he had seen it too, through a crack in the horizon the day before, framed by distant breakers like those that skirted the last land they had sighted weeks ago, the great cape that jutted out from the desert shore. If they could survive this malevolent spirit that would drag them down, if he could tame the beast and ride it into the spirit world, then they might reach that shore. *Atlantis might be reborn.*

A man's voice came over the water. 'Noah Uta-napishtim, my brother.' Noah put down the knife and shielded his eyes. He saw the raft of seaweed they had drawn in from the sea, tendrils of green and yellow filled with small crabs and fish to sustain them, until they had consumed them all. His eyes moistened in the glare, and he lifted a finger to them, wiping his eyelids and licking it, and then put his thumb on his lips, feeling the wetness of the blood that had been drawn by the knife. They had swallowed the last of the fresh water days ago. That morning his cousin Lamesh had drunk seawater and the malevolence had entered him, and they had lashed him down over the crossbeams at the front of the boat. Lamesh had consumed the lifeblood of the underworld, but before appeasing the spirits with the knife, Noah knew he must see the malevolence himself, must fix with his own eyes the monstrous shark that lurked below them.

Now he saw his brother's boat, shimmering in silhouette, a pair of carved wooden leopards facing each other on the pointed upswept prow. Theirs were the last two boats of the flotilla that had set out from the drowning city, the ones that had carried on past the cataract that was flooding their sea and reached the safety of Troy, their outpost on the edge of the Middle Sea. For one full cycle of the moon they had paddled on, past rocky islands and great stretches of desert shore, until they had reached another narrowing of the sea and a towering rock the local people called the Pillar of Herakleos; then they had been on the western ocean. They had raised sails of deerskin, and the wind and current had taken them south along the desert shore. Before the great cape that had been their last sight of land they had alighted at Lixus, at the Garden of Hesperides, where the priestesses called the Ladies of the West had fed them with golden apples and honeyed almonds, where Noah's brother had fallen under their spell and been tempted to stay and found their new citadel.

But just as they had done at Troy, they inscribed a pillar with their names in the ancient symbols and sailed west, over a vast open ocean with no landfall in sight. When the days were overcast, Adad the navigator had stood in the bow of his brother's boat and held up the crystal sunstone; it too had come from the volcano, prised from the spirit cave generations before, and used many times by Adad and his forefathers to navigate the spirit lines of their own sea. Its light had dazzled Noah's eyes, as if it were drawing in the rays from the dawn, leading them on over the ocean. And at night Noah had traced the line of the Great Bear to the pole star, keeping it on the right, just as he had watched his father do when he had aligned the pyramid of Atlantis to the rising and setting of the sun: his father Ra Shamash, he who gave the light, sun shaman, whom they had laid to rest in the chamber inside the pyramid, surrounded by the sacred obsidian blades and ironstones from the sky that had been brought across the ice by their ancestors. But Noah need hardly have bothered to chart the heavens. It was as if they were on a river on the ocean, being swept inexorably west, a river like those of his dreams in the cave that had become the flow of his own spirit journey.

The planks in their boats had held, their sewn seams caulked with boiled animal fat. The sweet foods of the Ladies of the West had sustained them, along with the flying fish that leapt into their boats. But then they had been beset by fearsome storms and mountainous waves. Six boats had become four. And finally they had entered this flat ocean, where there was no wind to fill the sails. They had paddled on until they were exhausted. Men desperate for food had scraped and licked the animal fat from the seams, and the boats had leaked and wallowed. They had made fire with flint and boiled their deerskin sails for broth; Enlil alone had insisted on keeping his sail. They had gnawed the boars' teeth they wore as necklaces, and scraped the marrow from the bulls' horns that adorned the prow of Noah's boat. That had kept them strong enough to fish, using nets made of twisted seaweed. But even that had proved too much. They had sickened, their gums swelling and bleeding and their teeth falling out, and they had become listless. Then they had begun to die.

Noah saw his brother clearly now, heaving on the cord that lashed the two boats together, compressing the floating weeds in between. Enlil stopped, panting and coughing a terrible dry cough, and then tottered upright with a club in one hand and a spear in the other. He was unrecognizable as the muscle-bound giant who had once guarded the holy of holies, the chamber in Atlantis where they had kept their most sacred objects. Now he looked like one of the scarecrows they had made together in their father's fields, naked except for the tattered remnants of his lionskin cloak. Like Noah's, his skin was peeling off in blistered layers, his face a puffed mass of sores surrounded by matted hair and a beard. He stared across, trying to lick his lips, and then shook his spear. 'Noah Uta-napishtim,' he croaked again.

'Enlil, my brother,' Noah replied, his voice cracking. 'If you call me that, I will call you by your shaman name, Gilgamesh, "he who would stand above men".'

Enlil slapped the club, then dropped it and stumbled, trying to stand upright, holding himself with the spear. His boat tilted, revealing the repairs they had made after the last storm: thick bulls' skins taut over the wooden frame, hemp rope sewn through the planks and lashed around the hull. Enlil had taken care of his boat. Noah saw the other matted and blistered bodies inside, men whose skin was grey beneath the sunburn, whose eyeballs had shrunk into their sockets, whether dead or alive he could not tell. Enlil went down on his knees against a thwart, still holding the spear. 'My brother,' he said hoarsely. 'Your animals are all gone.'

Noah turned to look at his own boat. Enlil was right. They had left with breeding pairs of animals: goats, sheep, boar and aurochs, the giant cattle that had lived in the marshland near the shore where they had grown up, animals he and Enlil had corralled as boys and fattened for the blood sacrifice. But now the animals had all died, and they had devoured the flesh. The bull had been the last, killed as it lay on the thwarts bellowing with thirst and hunger. Noah had plunged the knife into its chest and drawn out the heart as he had done with bulls many times before, on the altar of their ancestors outside the spirit cave. Its hooves were still tied to the cross-beams, and the skull lay in the scuppers of the boat beside him, stripped of every morsel of flesh, the bone plastered over and painted in red ochre with the horns facing the bow. They had fed on the bull in a great feast after they had passed through the storms, and had drunk its blood in huge gulps. But that had been half a cycle of the moon ago. Since then there had been nothing more to eat. Only a few of those who had feasted then were still alive now.

'My brother,' Enlil croaked again. 'You seek strength in the spirit world of our ancestors.' He shook his head, then rattled the spear. 'This is my strength, the metal that made this spear strong, the spear that has given us food.'

Noah squinted at the copper spearhead glinting in the sun. He remembered that day in the volcano as boys when they had searched for the obsidian. Enlil had gone further than any among the shamans had dared to go before, into the deepest chamber where the red-hot molten rock seeped out of the underworld. He had seen a golden stream flow among the molten red, and had watched it blend with silvery rock and form a hard metal. He had sworn Noah to secrecy, had not even told their father; only Enlil knew where it was to be found. And then, years later, as a man, he had emerged one day from the volcano and stood in front of the people, brandishing weapons of metal that made his shaman name seem like a prophecy: Gilgamesh, he who would stand above men, *he who would be a god*. Now, on this voyage, the spear had brought down a great bird, its wingspan three times a man's reach, and had jabbed and killed a turtle. And then a whale had circled them, one bigger than they had ever seen before, blowing spray high into the sky. The fishy smell from the whale's blow had left them ravenous. The old man Naher in Haran's boat had slipped into the water with a spear tied to a pig's bladder, and had used all his strength to drive it into the whale's head. Haran had lashed his boat to the carcass, and Noah as shaman had been given the first strip of oily skin. But then the blood in the water had attracted the sharks, more numerous and fearsome than they had seen before. The sharks had gorged themselves in a frenzy, ripping the whale to pieces, and then the great monster had reared up from the depths, leaping out of the water with its teeth bared. It had crushed Haran's boat and consumed them all, Haran and the old man and the others, dragging them down into the underworld, to the blackness Noah had seen in the depths below. He narrowed his eyes at his brother. *That was what spears of metal had done for them*.

Enlil swayed, leaning on his spear. 'And we have no women.' Noah felt his chest tighten. *No women*. It had been a week since sweet-voiced Ishtar had died a terrible, rasping death in the bottom of the boat, taken by the malevolence that now stalked them. The sea had seethed and sparkled, and then a vast welter of bubbles had erupted on the surface, swallowing Ishtar's boat and leaving her floating unconscious, wrapped around with the thin, glistening tentacles of the blue jellyfish that infested these waters, filaments that tingled to the touch and sent agonizing jolts through the body. They had hauled her into Noah's boat still alive, and after she had died he covered her in red ochre and laid her on a raft of seaweed.

She had worn her boar's tusk necklace, and held her wooden staff with the vulture skull on top, its eyes made from the sacred blue rock the hunters had brought from the mountains far to the east. Ishtar was to have been their mother's successor, trained as a shaman, but then she had been swayed from the old ways by Enlil and his followers, those who had set up idols in the shape of men, gods they fashioned after themselves. Noah had stared at her body in the knowledge that he was now the last shaman of Atlantis, the last who knew the rapture of the spirit journeys and how to spill blood on the altar of sacrifice.

He had watched the birds swoop down, tearing off strips of flesh from Ishtar's body, just as the vultures had done in Atlantis where the dead had been exposed in the stone circle above the city. After two days he had severed her head, filled her eye sockets and covered the sinews of her face with plaster he kept in a pot in the bow, placing cowrie shells in the hollows where her eyes had been pecked out. Her skull was there now, embedded in plaster below the prow, half in and half out of the spirit world. Noah had told his brother that the birds were the spirits of their ancestors taking her amongst them. Enlil had replied that the birds were hungry. Enlil had lost touch with the spirit world, spending all of his days in Atlantis inside the citadel. Noah had still walked past the fields their fathers had learned to cultivate, and had lived in the forest where their grandfathers had hunted, at one with the animal spirits. He had only ever entered the citadel to mount the steps up the volcano and perform his duty as sacrificing shaman, a duty that Enlil and the others had come to scorn.

Noah remembered the monster of the deep, lurking below, what it had done to Haran's boat, how it enslaved them with fear. Out here, the spirits of the beasts still ruled, not the gods that Enlil and the others thought they themselves had become, wielding their spears of metal.

Enlil banged the thwart again. 'There is no land ahead.'

Noah raised his arm to the west, pointing. 'But my brother, I saw it. Through a gap in the storm clouds before the great calm. Twin peaks on the horizon, exactly as our mother Nisir prophesied, the mountain she called Dû-Re. I saw distant breakers, and I felt a change in the rhythm of the waves. We will go there if we summon all our reserves and paddle west. We will find new animals, new pasture. We will find women.'

'Your visions are mere dreams. The flat sea is like the desert. The sun reflects off it and blinds you to reality, creating phantasms on the horizon. And for half a cycle of the moon, since the storms ended, we have seen nothing.'

But Noah knew what he had seen. And two nights before, there had been another sign. He had succumbed to hunger, and had devoured the strip of whale skin that had been given to him when they had cut into the carcass. Eating it had given him terrible sickness, as if the spirit of the whale were punishing him. But when he awoke, the sickness had passed and the torpor had lifted. His mouth had stopped bleeding, and the swelling of his gums had receded. It had been a sign of what he must do next. Now he squinted at Enlil. 'I must offer blood to the spirits.'

Enlil waved his arm dismissively. 'If you pour blood into the sea, the great shark will come for you. He is hungry, like those gulls.'

'Then you can kill him with your spear of metal.'

Enlil snorted. 'I would not waste it. This spear and others like it will make us gods amongst men. When they escaped the deluge, our cousins Adad and Nergal and Ninurta and Annunaki set forth south over land to the great rivers beyond the mountains, and Ishmael and Sethi and Minos sailed through the islands south from Troy, towards the far shore where the great river rises through the desert and waters the oases along its banks. They will found new citadels in those places. But I am the only one with the secret of the new metal, of the alloy that creates the strong copper.'

'You swore that you would never reveal it. I warned you of its dangers. Men will use it to kill each other.'

'As long as I alone have the knowledge of the metal, others will bow towards me. I will use that strength to keep peace among men.'

Noah looked at Enlil. He remembered how his brother had seemed a pillar of strength in his lionskin, its torn head and tattered mane now hanging over his shoulders. Herakleos, the Ladies of the West had called him, after the great rock that marked the edge of the Middle Sea, as they showered him with adulation that Noah feared would go to his head. For all Enlil's bravado, Noah knew that his brother was afraid of what might lie before them, afraid because he had spurned the ways of the shamans who saw the ocean in their spirit journeys, for whom the unending horizon brought not terror as it seemed to bring Enlil and his followers, but instead the rapture Noah felt in the journeys of the mind he took in the spirit cave, journeys where he floated towards the world of their ancestors. 'We are close,' Noah said. 'Look to your own signs. The crystal lights the way forward. The palladion has become heavier, just as our mother prophesied. When the spirit bird flies out from Dû-Re towards us, when the palladion becomes as heavy as it felt in the spirit cave in the volcano, there we will find our new Atlantis.'

Enlil put down his spear and lifted a package from the floor of his boat, swaddled in a bearskin. He struggled to hold it, then raised one leg on the thwarts and rested the object on his knee. He pulled a lump of quartz out of a pouch on his belt and held it up, averting his eyes from the glare. 'The crystal shines because it draws in the sun's rays through the clouds, and when the sun is setting in the west the crystal shines on that side,' he said, shoving it back in the pouch. He pointed at the swaddled package. 'The palladion fell from the sky and was brought from the snows of the north by our ancestors. It becomes heavier now because we are approaching the edge of the world, where the earth meets the heavens. Soon it will become so heavy that it will sink my boat.'

Noah remembered what his mother had told him about the days of their ancestors when the glaciers had reached down almost to the shore of their sea. The palladion was the most sacred of the ironstones they had found on the surface of the ice. Noah remembered seeing Enlil disappear with it into the secret place in the volcano where he had learned to work metal, emerging with it days later in a shape that seemed to copy the circle of stone pillars with lintels that he and his followers had forced the old shamans to erect outside the spirit cave. Enlil had taken the most sacred artefact of their ancestors and made it his own. Now he unwrapped the skin, and Noah saw the crooked cross, its surface smooth and polished. Enlil raised it into the air. 'I will meld the ironstone with gold to lock the strength within. Then the others will know that I am destined to hold its power.' He nodded towards Ishtar's severed head in the front of Noah's boat. 'You have your own idols. And you believe your destination is just beyond the horizon. If you know the way, you no longer need the crystal or the palladion to guide you.'

'Throw the palladion into the sea, my brother. It belongs with the shades of our ancestors, not in your new world. Placate their spirits, and we may yet fulfil our mother's prophecy.'

'I will tell your story far and wide, Noah Uta-napishtim, the story of one who had no animals because he had sacrificed them all, and no women.' Enlil wrapped the palladion back in the bearskin and placed it out of sight, then stood up again with his spear. 'I will tell how a star of heaven fell from the sky, but it was too heavy for you, and only I could lift it and use its power; and how I wandered through the wilderness in the skin of a lion and crossed the waters of death, how with my own strength I lifted the vault of the sky that covers the abyss. I will tell how the heavens roared and the earth roared too, how daylight failed and darkness fell, lightning flashed, the clouds lowered and rained down death. I will call the great fish Humbaba, "toothed monster", but I will make him a bull-man of the mountains; when he roars, it will be like the fury of the storms we have sailed through, his breath will be like the fire of the volcano and his jaws will be death itself. I will tell how I, Enlil Gilgamesh, slew the beast and rid the world of the spirit demons that your kind had nurtured for so long.' He stomped the spear. 'And as for you, my brother, I will tell how I led you to the ends of the earth, the last of the shamans, how I cast you away in darkness, to the place from which none who enter ever return, down the road from which there is no coming back. I will call your mountain not Dû-Re, but Nisir, after our mother, as it is for her memory that I have kept you alive and brought you this far, and because this mythical mountain is her creation.'

Noah realized with a sudden empty feeling that his brother had been intending to leave him all along. Enlil had saved him from Atlantis, from horror and death, and had brought him far from the reaches of his vengeful followers who would extinguish all of his kind. 'On our voyage from Atlantis,' Enlil continued, 'I let you carve the old symbol of Atlantis on my pillars, set up where we landed; but when I return, I will topple them, and they will be buried in the earth, and new statues will arise, gods fully formed in the shape of men.' He heaved up the skin containing the palladion and unwrapped it again. 'The old symbol will die, but the new one I have fashioned in the palladion will endure through the ages to signify the coming of the gods.'

Noah looked at Enlil. 'These are brave words, my brother, but perhaps in your story you will come back to seek me again, and I will tell you from my new spirit cave in the mountain the truth about what you have become, that believing you have become a god does not save you from the certainty of death and the spirit journey we all must take.'

Suddenly there was a white flash in the sky. Noah looked down at the water between the clumps of weed. *Something was different*. He could no longer see into the depths. It was as if the cusp of the underworld had risen up, as if they were now floating on it. He glanced at the sky. A darkness had come, a strange pall, as if they had been cast into shadow. Perhaps Enlil was right; perhaps they had reached the end of the world. Then he looked to the western horizon and saw a towering bank of cloud, billowing and shadowy, streaked with black. The surface of the sea, dead calm for so long, began to shimmer. He felt something they had not felt for days, something coming from the west, ruffling the water. *It was wind.*

A flash lit the sky again, and a whiteness sped across from a central point like an expanding corona. Noah watched in astonishment as the palladion seemed to catch the light and burn at the edges, a flickering blue aura that pulsed around the ironstone. Enlil swayed back, then gripped the palladion with both hands as the phantasm disappeared. 'That must be my sign,' he shouted hoarsely. 'I will go.' He put the palladion out of sight in the scuppers and quickly cast off the rope that held the two boats together. He staggered over to the bipod mast lying on the thwarts and heaved it up on its rope. One of the other men crawled over to help him. The mast came upright, and the tattered deerskin sail billowed out. The wind had already strengthened and the boat wallowed away, leaving the mat of weed behind. The sail cracked, taut and full. Enlil shouted across at Noah. 'We will be blown back to Lixus, and to the pillar at the edge of the Middle Sea. I will topple the stone we left at Lixus to show your passing from the world of men. You have no sail, and you cannot follow. You will remain forever outcast here at the edge of existence, Noah Uta-napishtim. Farewell, my brother.'

Noah watched the boat recede. Low black clouds advanced

towards him, constricting the horizon, the spindrift shimmering in tendrils of white over the waves. The wind raised the stiffened mass of his hair, and tugged at his beard. This was not like the dry wind that had come off the desert weeks before. This wind was moist. *There would be rain.* He lurched over to a basket in the centre of the boat and drew a bleached animal skin over it, pressing it down to catch any rain that fell. As he did so, he saw the faded colours of a painting he had made on the skin: a mass of buildings, joined together with ladders on the rooftops, and behind them the triangular form of the pyramid his father had built; above that was the long-feathered figure of the bird spirit, and behind it the peaks of the volcano shaped like a bull's horns, the place where Enlil and the others had walled up the spirit cave of their ancestors. He remembered his vision of twin peaks on the horizon ahead. He felt his cracked lips with his tongue, then drew his thumb again over the obsidian blade, bringing the wetness of blood to his lips. He looked at the emaciated body of Lamesh tied down in the front of the boat. *Soon there would be more blood in the offing.*

A violent gust tilted the boat, whining and howling over the sea, flattening the wave crests and streaking the water with foam. Lightning forked on the horizon, and he heard the dull rumble of thunder. Enlil's boat was already far to the east, a speck on a foaming crest beneath racing clouds, and beyond that was the same wall of blackness. Noah twisted around. The blackness was on every side. His heart pounded. Shadowy streaks moved in the clouds at frightening speed, gyrating around him in one direction. Now he knew why there had been no ocean swell: he was in the eye of a great storm. The waters that were surging round the horizon would soon reach him. It was a storm that had been set in motion when they had lured the malevolence from the deep, a storm that would encircle and engulf them like the ring of fire he had once lit around the altar of sacrifice, a fire that burned fiercely until all that was left of the bodies was the red-hot embers blown upwards by the exhalations of the underworld.

The boat lurched sideways, then pitched into the water with a mighty crash. A huge wave crest rose high above the trough, and the boat tilted and yawed. He saw another shape ahead, a great swell, sucking them along in its wake. Then the shape swung round, and he saw a giant fin cut the water. The shark rolled, its white belly upwards and its jaws gaping. In a flash, the huge rows of serrated teeth reared up at him, and he stared the monster in the eye. Then it was gone, sweeping the stern of the boat with its tail. *He had seen it. He had taken in the spirit power of the beast. Now it was time.* He turned quickly and reached into a jar beside Ishtar's skull, taking out handfuls of red ochre powder and smearing it all over his face and body. He picked up a polished stone mace and lurched towards Lamesh. They had tied him on his back, over a shallow stone basin, his feet and hands lashed to the rails, and drugged him with the resin of the poppy. Noah saw the fin of the beast circling, menacingly. He raised the mace, but his arm was too weak. He dropped it, then picked up the obsidian knife and put both hands on the grip, holding it tight, shaking.

He remembered the last time he had held the knife like this. It had been in the spirit cave, where they had exposed the bodies of the dead for the hooked talons of the spirit birds to rip the flesh and take it to the world beyond. It was there that

Noah had tied down the bulls and cut their hearts out, giving the meat to the people and letting the blood gush into the stone basins for the old shamans to gaze into the world beyond. But with their spears of copper, the new priests had forced the shamans to build a wall over the sacred cave, to block it off except for a small entrance to the mountain, and then to cut huge pillars in the quarry and struggle up with them, heaving them into a circle. They had chiselled their new symbols over the old. And then Enlil himself had ripped the plaster-covered skull of their ancestor Anu from the ground, gouging out the cowrie-shell eyes and placing it atop the first of the pillars; he had carved hands into the lintel of the pillar, while the others of the new priesthood, those with braided hair and beards, began to rub and chisel away the sacred paintings on the cave wall and hack off the ancient symbols of their ancestors, leaving only those that Enlil and Noah had incised on the wall that day their father had told them their shaman names.

And then the flood waters had begun to rise. Enlil and the new priesthood had assembled the people and blamed the shamans, ordering them to go to the cave to appease the spirits. But once inside, the shamans had been blocked in, Noah among them, sealed inside a flickering world of shadows and red embers from the fire that was always kept alive in the inner recess. The old shamans had tossed the sacred leaves on the fire and taken the milk of the poppy to ease them on their journey to the spirit world, but fear had tainted their visions. Those who had once floated in water in the dream voyages of the mind were now terrified of drowning. Their visions took them on a journey of horror, to darkness and fire coming from within the mountain. An old man seized with terror had carved an image on a pillar, a swirling face that seemed to be caught in a scream. Noah himself had been half crazed, seeing men and women tearing at their hair and tossing their heads around and around. And then they had asked him to bring out the knife, to do what only he could do. *The basins had filled with blood once again.*

He remembered what an old woman had said as she lay back over the basin, her eyes milky-white with blindness, her hand holding his and pressing the knife against her heart. *You now have the bloodlust, Noah*, she had whispered. *You will never lose it, and you will doom all around you by your greed for it. In the times of our ancestors, when we were driven to seek the spirits on a river of human blood, he who spilled it was forced to kill himself to save the people from his bloodlust. You must kill yourself too, or be cast out for ever from the world of men. Your brother Enlil knows this too, as I taught him the old ways.* When she pulled the knife in, Noah had tasted the blood that spattered from her mouth, and he had felt the exultation course through him. She had been right. *He had wanted more.* They had come willingly, the men and the women and their children, the boy with the flute. The knife had plunged in over and over again, and the stone basins had filled with human blood, overflowing and smearing the skulls of the ancestors still embedded in the floor around them.

And then Enlil had broken through the wall and come for him, unable to leave his brother behind in that chamber of death. He had forced the others who remained alive to a dark recess in the cave and had rolled the boulder in front of them, even as they screamed for Noah to kill them too. Noah had gripped a basin and stared into the blood-filled pool. In his desperation to break the spell, Enlil had taken out the palladion from a pouch and dropped it into the basin, drenching Noah with blood. Noah had seen only the reflection of the pillar with the skull on top, advancing towards him in repeated visions, swirling round and round. He had fallen backwards, wide-eyed and panting, just as the first water from the sea had surged into the chamber. Enlil had pulled the palladion out of the basin and put it in his pouch, then held Noah upright and hissed in his ear: *Atlantis is finished. We new priests will go to the four corners of the earth and found new cities. You, my brother, the last of the old, I will take beyond the Middle Sea to the place where earth and sky meld, to where you and your spirit ways will be beyond the world of men.* Enlil had dragged him outside to the boats, but for days afterwards as they paddled away, Noah could hear the screams of the shamans in his mind, and see the blood he had been unable to wash from the cracks on his hands and under his fingernails.

Now the storm clouds swirled around the boat. Noah tried to stay his hand as he held the knife. He was trembling not with fear, but with anticipation. He had crossed the boundary in that cave, and now there was only one river of blood he could ride.

Now the spirits would be appeased.

He plunged the knife into Lamesh, deep and hard, drawing it savagely round, feeling the warmth of the blood as it gushed out. He reached inside, grasped the still-beating heart and pulled it out. He took the knife and sliced into Lamesh's neck, sawing hard at the bone, and then held the matted hair with one hand while he severed the head from the body. He dropped the knife and raised the head high, feeling the rivulets of blood pour down his arms and face. The storm was closing in now, twisting and swirling, the lightning flashing and the thunder cracking deafeningly. He dropped the head and scooped up blood from the wound, drinking it in great slurps, slaking his desperate thirst. He saw where the blood had poured into the small stone basin below the thwart, filling it to the brim. He stared into it, searching, seeing only the rippling concentric circles where the blood dripped off his face and fell on the surface of the pool. And then there was a flash in the sky and he saw it in the blood: twin peaks spouting fire, the fabled mountain Dû-Re, appearing over and over again as the blood rippled with the motion of the boat. He looked up, letting the rain pour over his face. *The spirit of the beast had answered him. The river of blood had flowed to the realm of the ancestors.*

Suddenly giant waves were upon him. The roar of the wind drowned out the thunder, and the sea heaved the boat upwards as if it were being forced up the ridge of a mountain, driving it far away from the circling fin of the shark. Noah clutched the thwarts, swaying, feeling the sweeping sheets of rain that blew in from the east. He suddenly realized what that meant. *The wind had turned. The boat was being blown west again.* They were on the crest of a towering wave, hanging still. There was another flash, and sunlight appeared through a hole in the darkness ahead. He blinked the rain and blood from his eyes, then followed the rays of the sun to where they lit up a narrow strip of sea to the west. A bird came into view, blown towards them on some eastward eddy of the storm wind, a bird with long trailing feathers like nothing he had seen before, coloured like a dark rainbow. *A thunderbird, but a bird of the land, not of the sea.*

Then he saw it on the horizon. A raging line of surf, and beyond that, the twin peaks jutting against the blackness of the sky.

The prophecy had been fulfilled.

Atlantis would be reborn.

PART 1

1

South-eastern Black Sea, present day

'Jack, you're not going to believe what I've just found. It's gold. *Solid gold.*'

Jack Howard twisted round and stared at the orange glow of the headlamp from the other diver below him, the form almost completely obscured by the swirling black cloud of sediment that filled the tunnel. He dumped air from his buoyancy compensator and dropped down, flexing his knees to prevent his fins from scraping the jagged lava wall, then angled sideways to avoid becoming entangled in the cable that snaked up to the submersible on the sea floor above them. He injected a blast of air into his suit to reacquire neutral buoyancy, catching a glimpse of Costas' face through his visor as he finned sideways to let Jack take his place. Costas was staring intently at the tunnel wall in front of him, aiming his headlamp at one spot. Jack followed his gaze, edging forward, keeping his breathing shallow to maintain his depth in the water, staring into the swirl of sediment. Slowly the particles settled, and he began to make out the wall beyond. He could see the twisted black lava from the eruption five years ago, its friable surface broken and exposed by the boring drill that had dug through the solidified flow the day before to create the tunnel. But then he saw something different, embedded in the lava, a smooth rock surface cracked and mottled by the searing heat of the eruption. He peered at the polished surface, his heart suddenly pounding with excitement. There was no doubt about it. He was looking at a pillar, on some kind of plinth. *A pillar carved by human hands.*

'Yes.' He punched his fist in the water, then turned to Costas, speaking into his intercom. 'I'd begun to wonder whether this place really existed at all, or if it was just a figment of our imagination.' He turned back to the pillar, seeing where the plinth had been carved out of the natural tufa. He had a flashback to the moment he and Costas had first seen archaeological remains at this site five years ago from the Aquapod submersibles, watching in awe as the veils of silt dropped and the walls and roofs of the ancient city appeared, the most exhilarating moment to that date in his career as an underwater archaeologist. Revisiting scenes of past triumph was sometimes a strange experience, recalling emotions and high drama long gone, but this time it was different, like entering a completely new world. The volcanic eruption that had engulfed the site and forced them to leave five years ago had created a totally unfamiliar environment, a seascape as barren and devoid of life as the surface of the moon. He turned to Costas. 'This is the first proof we've had it was all real. You're right. It's archaeological gold.'

Costas tapped his shoulder, and aimed his headlamp midway up the wall above the plinth. 'Jack, I meant *real* gold. Have another look.'

Jack followed Costas' beam and took a deep breath, holding it for a moment to rise half a metre in the water. The beam lit up a final swirl of volcanic particles that obscured the pillar, and Jack put out his hand and wafted them away. He let his hand drop, and then gasped in amazement. 'Well I'll be damned,' he whispered.

'See what I mean?'

Jack stared, wondering whether his imagination was playing tricks on him. The object in front of him was remarkably similar to one they had found five years ago, the object that had first led them to this place. He saw the reflected shimmer of gold on the inside of his visor, and he closed his eyes for a moment, half expecting it to be a phantasm, to be gone when he opened them. But it was still there, a golden disc about a hand's breadth across embedded in the pillar, the sheen of gold almost blinding him in the reflected glare of the headlamp. He reached out and carefully pressed the fingers of his glove against it, feeling the solidity. *It was real*. He felt the adrenalin course through him, and turned and grinned at Costas. 'Now I *really* believe it.'

'That's the Atlantis symbol, isn't it?'

Atlantis. It was the first time either of them had uttered the word since leaving *Seaquest II* in the submersible two hours before; as if to say it would risk the site closing up on them again. Jack stared, searching with his eyes, seeing nothing but the golden reflection. 'Where are you looking?'

Costas turned his head to move his beam away. 'Use your own headlamp, angled down, low beam. You should get more shadow.'

Jack reached up to his helmet and activated the twin halogen lamps on either side, then ramped them down. Suddenly a symbol appeared on the disc, its lines deeply impressed into the gold. He stared in astonishment, his mind racing back to the extraordinary events of five years ago, to the excavation of a Bronze Age wreck in the Aegean Sea at the start of their quest. They had found a golden disc impressed with this symbol, alongside other symbols Jack had recognized from an ancient pottery disc found a century before at the Minoan site of Phaistos in Crete. The Phaistos symbols had baffled archaeologists for generations, but the disc from the wreck contained parallel symbols in the Minoan Linear script, an early form of Greek, which allowed the Phaistos symbols to be translated.

What they had revealed was astounding, the greatest revelation from an ancient text in the history of archaeology. One word had stood out, a word that had bedevilled archaeologists since time immemorial, a word spelled out in the syllabic script of the Minoans and represented by the symbol in front of Jack now: *Atlantis*. That had been remarkable enough, but then his colleague Maurice Hiebermeyer had made another discovery deep in the Egyptian desert, a fragment of papyrus showing that the story of Atlantis told by the Greek philosopher Plato had not been a myth but was based on hard reality, on an account given to a Greek traveller by an Egyptian priest who had inherited secret knowledge stretching back thousands of years before the first pharaohs. Together the papyrus and the disc contained clues that had brought Jack and his team to the south-eastern corner of the Black Sea, searching a shoreline submerged when the Mediterranean had cascaded over a land bridge at the present-day Bosporus and filled the Black Sea basin, the last and most catastrophic event in the sea-level rise caused by the great melt at the end of the Ice Age twelve thousand years ago. For Jack, it had been the perfect archaeological quest, a marriage of textual clues, hard science and intuition, and it had brought together all the skills of his team. They had revealed nothing short of the most dramatic archaeological site ever discovered, surrounding the twin peaks of a partly submerged volcano. It had been a spectacular vision of human ingenuity and achievement at the beginning of the Neolithic, when people had built monuments that equalled those of the Egyptians and the Sumerians and the Mesoamericans thousands of years later.

Jack traced his glove over the symbol on the disc, up the central axis to where two symmetrical patterns extended outwards like garden rakes, each terminating in a series of parallel lines. The text on the Phaistos disc had instructed them to follow the shape of the eagle with outstretched wings, and they had realized that the symbol was also a map, a plan of the submerged tunnels and chambers they had discovered under the peak of the volcano. Five years ago they had passed through extraordinary wonders: a huge chamber full of ancient cave paintings of the Ice Age, then a tunnel with carvings showing latter-day priests of Atlantis with conical hats, and then the holy of holies, the place where the tunnel

29

ahead of them now might be leading. Yet that chamber with its huge statue of a mother goddess had been freshly carved shortly before the flood, and Jack was convinced that somewhere inside the tunnels and chambers lay other secrets, something that would link the holy of holies and the priests with those ancestral images from the Ice Age: perhaps an inner sanctum that would reveal how the belief system of the Ice Age hunter-gatherers had transformed into a religion of priests and gods and worship. The most likely location, the complex of tunnels ahead of them now, was a place they had only just begun to explore five years ago when the North Anatolian Fault had shuddered and the volcano surged to life again, forcing them away from the site seemingly for ever.

Jack pressed his hand against the surface of the disc, wishing he could remove his glove and feel it against his skin. He had found gold before: gleaming coins of the Roman emperors, dazzling cups and jewellery on the Bronze Age wreck, gold fit for a king. But this disc was extraordinarily old, at least as old as the flooding of Atlantis more than seven thousand years ago. That was three thousand years before the earliest site elsewhere to produce worked gold, at Varna in Bulgaria. The gold in the disc could have come here with the first hunter-gatherers who had sought shelter in the caves on the slopes of the volcano during the Ice Age, who had painted the rock with images of mammoths and fearsome lions and leopards: a band of humans of precocious intellect and vision who had travelled south from the retreating glaciers with their most precious belongings. Their talent with metals was clear from the finds five years ago, their ability to collect and work copper and then to make an alloy to produce bronze, thousands of years before bronze technology re-emerged and became widespread in the ancient world. They could have brought the gold with them from the nearest rich source, the gold-bearing streams of the Caucasus Mountains to the east, laying woolly mammoth skins in the water and collecting the precious flecks just as the Greek myths had Jason and the Argonauts do with the Golden Fleece. And they could have smelted and fashioned the gold into a disc bearing their sacred symbol, perhaps at the time they were transforming their world – moving beyond the natural caves in the volcano to cutting their own passageways and chambers in the rock, then fashioning mud-brick and lime and volcanic ash into the walls of houses, creating the world's first civilization.

To Jack, the golden disc represented everything that was fascinating about this place: the symbol of a people on the cusp of the greatest revolution in human history, a symbol that allowed them to look forward to a new world and yet also back to the time of their ancestors. He wanted to feel what they had felt, to see the world as they had seen it, to look far back in prehistory to the time before the memory of the deep past had become clouded by the foundation myths that followed the first cities and the first dynasties; and he wanted to look forward to where these people were going, to under-stand what motivated them as they poured all their energy into creating this place and then fleeing the oncoming flood. If he could see those things, then he would have found the greatest treasure of this place. He wanted to discover their past. Above all, he wanted to find out about their beliefs, how these people saw their existence at the dawn of modern religion. *He wanted to find the gods of Atlantis.*

Costas tapped Jack's helmet. 'You happy?'

Jack drew his eyes away from the symbol and looked at Costas, his form now visible as the sediment cleared. Beneath a tattered boiler suit filled with tools, Costas was completely encased in white, like an astronaut. His helmet bore the anchor logo of the International Maritime University, partly obscured by a laser range-finding device that he had spirited up in the engineering department, one of numerous gadgets that always festooned him when he went diving. Underneath the white outer layer they were both wearing e-suits, Kevlar-reinforced drysuits with integrated buoyancy systems, back-mounted oxygen rebreathers and dive computers with readouts visible inside their helmets. But the famed environmental resilience of the e-suit did not extend to diving in near-boiling water inside an active volcano, so they were entirely encased in thermal protection developed at IMU from the latest NASA and Russian spacesuit technology. Jack had to remind himself that they were not inside some lunar simulator, but under the Black Sea off Turkey, more than thirty metres below a solidified lava flow and heading for a place that made outer space seem distinctly congenial by comparison.

He tapped the intercom on the side of his helmet. 'Happier now I know we're on target. Lucky that pillar wasn't crunched by the borer.'

'I was driving it, remember? Rule number one. Never trash the archaeology.'

'You mean you got lucky.'

'We used the 3-D terrain map of the site from five years ago, and put the borer dead on the entrance to the chamber leading to the holy of holies.'

'I've lost all sense of direction. My compass has gone haywire.'

'Did Lanowski mention the magnetic anomaly?' Costas said. 'We noticed it yesterday when we did a magnetometer run over the site. The readouts showed some pretty spectacular spikes, centring over the likely location of the magma chamber. The Turkish geological survey guy with us said he'd recorded a similar anomaly at several other places along the North Anatolian Fault, though nowhere as spectacular as here. You get anomalies like this at a few other places in the world where an upsurge in magma has a localized effect on the earth's magnetic field – along the Puerto Rico Fault in the north Caribbean, for instance. The guy said there's a lot of variation in how magnetic materials react to these field changes, but they'd noticed that meteoritic iron is the most dramatic. Several samples they had from one meteorite impact site in Siberia felt twice as heavy as normal at one place along the North Anatolian Fault where they tried them, and he reckoned it might even be more marked here.'

'Sounds like fodder for the fringe theorists,' Jack replied. 'The people who still think Atlantis could only have been built by extraterrestrials. The truth is, everything we saw here is paralleled elsewhere in early sites, only on a lesser scale. And we only have to look at the Egyptian pyramids or Stonehenge to see that doing things on a colossal scale was never as much of a problem in the past as the fringe theorists seem to believe.'

'Man makes himself,' Costas said. 'Isn't that the famous Jack Howard byline? Everything he builds, and all his ideas, come from within.'

'And then he sometimes unmakes himself,' Jack said. 'That's what I really want to find out here, whether these people were the first to take hold of their own destiny and see the potential within themselves, and the danger. That's what seems to have fascinated Plato about Atlantis when he used the story to warn the Athenians about hubris, about flying too close to the sun. Call it the Icarus factor.'

'My objective is to see whether little baby ROV will work inside a volcano,' Costas said cheerfully, patting his over-sized torso. The Michelin Man effect of the suit was compounded by the cargo Costas was carrying: a miniature remote-operated vehicle the size of a toaster, which he had zipped up inside a protective bag on his chest, like a kangaroo with a pouch. Costas was one of the world's leading submersibles experts, and his passion was miniaturized ROVs, the focus of endless happy evenings tinkering in the engineering complex of IMU's main campus at Cornwall in south-west England.

'So how's Little Joey doing?' Jack enquired.

Costas held up the tethering cable that hooked the ROV's battery to the submersible at the entrance to the tunnel, and checked a monitor on his wrist. 'Only a few minutes more now.'

Jack turned again and stared at the golden disc. 'Odd that we didn't notice this pillar the last time we came this way.'

'Jack, we were a little preoccupied, remember? You were having a gun battle, and I was about to be executed by a Kazakh warlord who was going to hurl me into the magma chamber.'

Jack stared ahead pensively, casting his mind back five years.

There had been a dark side to the discovery of Atlantis, and a cost to himself personally that had preyed on him again since returning here. Five years ago they had made another discovery, one that had turned the archaeological hunt into a modern-day race against time. At the end of the Cold War, a renegade Russian captain had taken his submarine full of nuclear warheads towards a secret rendezvous with a buyer in the Republic of Georgia, but had struck the uncharted submerged flank of the volcano and sunk. When Jack and his IMU team had stumbled across the submarine, the middleman had returned with a vengeance, seeking his merchandise. In the ensuing battle, the original *Seaquest* had been sunk and they had lost one of their team, Peter Howe, the IMU security chief. Peter had been a close friend of Jack's from their schooldays and time in British Special Forces, and had been persuaded to join IMU when Jack had set it up soon after completing his doctorate at Cambridge. In the five years since his death, Jack had been driven by a feeling of responsibility to the dream he had shared with the original few – with Peter, with Costas, with Maurice Hiebermeyer – a dream that had seen them chart discoveries far more extraordinary than they could ever have imagined when he had founded IMU. But there was still a shadow over this place: the discovery of Atlantis had come at a price, one he never wanted to have to pay again.

Costas peered at him. 'We could call it a day, Jack. This is going to be a dangerous dive, and we've got a spectacular result now with that disc. It's hardly as if IMU activities have been out of the spotlight for the last five years, but when you decide the time is right to reveal this to the media, it'll boost public interest big time. And we're not even supposed to be here at all. It's your call.'

Jack took a deep breath. Costas was right. They had returned to Atlantis on a wing and a prayer. Two weeks ago they had been in *Seaquest II* off the ancient site of Troy in the northern Aegean Sea, excavating the remains of a galley from the time of the Trojan Wars in the late second millennium BC. At the citadel of Troy itself, his oldest friend Maurice Hiebermeyer and their Cambridge professor James Dillen had been in charge of clearing an extraordinary underground chamber they had found beneath the ancient palace, searching for clues to support Jack's theory that Troy had been founded at the time of the exodus from Atlantis four thousand years before the Trojan War; that it was a staging post for the diaspora of people who had taken their language and knowledge of farming south and west across the Mediterranean at the dawn of civilization.

At Troy, his mind had never been far from Atlantis, only a few hundred miles east of the Bosporus in the Black Sea, but the chances of a return had seemed remote. Then, two weeks ago, the Turkish and Georgian surveillance team who monitored the Atlantis site had requested IMU assistance in boring a sample shaft into the volcano. Several months previously they had recorded a fall-off in seismic activity, and for the first time in five years a limited intervention for geological purposes seemed feasible, though it was still deemed too risky for diving. The main concern was to understand better the seismic characteristics of the North Anatolian Fault, the huge rent in the earth's crust that ran west under the southern shore of the Black Sea to the Bosporus Strait, threatening Istanbul. Jack had seized on the chance and offered *Seaquest II*, which had the right sub-sea boring equipment and could sail immediately from the excavation site at Troy. Costas and their brilliant if quirky engineering genius Jacob Lanowski had spent several sleepless nights downloading all the survey data from five years ago so that they could position the boring tunnel exactly where Jack wanted it to go, towards an unexplored entranceway he had seen five years before; at the same time, the priority remained to get the tunnel into the upper magma chamber to satisfy the geologists' needs.

After heated discussion with *Seaquest II*'s captain, Scott Macalister, Jack had won the day, and Macalister had agreed to allow a dive, on the condition that Jack himself arrived from Troy only the day before and then left as soon as he had off-gassed enough nitrogen to allow him to fly. He and Costas had departed that morning in the submersible under cover of darkness, from *Seaquest II*'s internal docking bay. It was a covert mission in every sense of the word, and went against many of Jack's better instincts. The international protocol following the eruption five years before had been to leave the site undisturbed until improved technology and seismic conditions allowed further research, with IMU acting as the overseeing agency and the Turkish navy enforcing a no-dive zone to deter looters. The site was beyond the twelve-mile territorial limit and the protocol was therefore not protected by law, but Jack knew that any attempt openly to dive at the site would upset the agreement and might make the Turkish authorities think twice about continuing IMU's permit to excavate at Troy. He had weighed it all in his mind over and over again, but he knew that the chance to be where they were now might never come up again in his lifetime. Anything they found would have to be reported as incidental to supposed emergency repair work on the boring equipment, and his own presence in the tunnel – which could only have been for archaeological exploration – kept strictly hushed up.

He turned to Costas. 'You know my answer. I've taken too much of a risk with IMU's reputation getting here to bail out now. And I want more than gold. I want to find the inner sanctum of Atlantis.'

'You remember what Macalister said?'

Jack recalled Macalister's briefing just before they set out in the submersible. Although Jack was archaeological director of IMU, Macalister as captain of *Seaquest II* had the final say over anything that might affect the safety of his ship and crew, and one of those concerns was holding position over an active sub-sea volcano that might burst forth at any moment. 'He said don't push this place. We've seen what it can do.'

'You remember what else he said?'

'Just the usual.'

'He said no frigging about. Do not let Jack Howard see something else that intrigues him and disappear off alone down some tunnel. He knows you pretty well, Jack. We go in, we take pictures, we come out. Full stop. He told me if needs be, tie a rope to your ankle.'

'And you said?'

'I said nobody ties Jack Howard down. I said I trusted you.'

Jack grinned. 'Trusted me to do what?'

'Trusted you to look after me, to look after yourself and to think of your daughter Rebecca and how much she needs

38

her dad, alive and well. Remember what happened six months ago.'

Jack was silent. He remembered all too well. During their search for the treasures of Troy, Rebecca had been kidnapped, the worst forty-eight hours of Jack's life. It had ended in an explosion of violence that had frightened even Jack, showing him how far he would go to protect his own. It was still unresolved business, with the mastermind behind the kidnapping still at large, but the important thing was that Rebecca was safe and being watched over by the best security people available. She had needed all her friends at IMU afterwards, but she was young enough to feel that it was also a huge adventure, and she had shown a toughness and resolve that proved to Jack that she had inherited a certain ability to look after herself.

'It was hard enough keeping her from joining us. She'd have been halfway down the tunnel ahead of us by now.'

'Like father, like daughter.'

'Anyway, what about Costas Kazantzakis, always stuck down a hole in the seabed fiddling with some malfunctioning gadget, oblivious to the world around him?'

'My gadgets don't malfunction. And I don't fiddle. Anyway, when have I ever let you down?'

Jack grinned through his visor at Costas. 'Never.' He lifted his right hand with the palm out, and Costas did the same, pushing them together. 'Buddies.'

'Right on.'

Jack turned back to the stone pillar, now clear of silt, with the golden disc reflecting luminously in his headlamp. He flipped up the protective cover of the pod on the front of his helmet and activated the control board on his right wrist, using the pod to take a series of flash photographs and then a video sequence panning up the pillar and focusing on the symbol on the disc. He closed down the visor and pushed himself off from the pillar, hanging in the water alongside Costas in the middle of the tunnel. Costas patted his tool belt, an impressive array of wrenches, jacks and other gear that went with him everywhere, strapped and Velcroed to the tattered grey remains of a boiler suit he wore over his spacesuit, and then gestured at the golden symbol. 'You don't want to grab it and bag it?'

Jack shook his head. 'I think that thing belongs here.'

'You getting superstitious?'

Jack shook his head again. 'You remember the golden disc from the shipwreck five years ago, how we realized it was a key to getting into the door in the rock face? It's just a hunch, but this thing looks like some kind of opening device too. If we can make an obverse of that symbol and use it as a key, then that disc might turn and activate something else. A job for the IMU engineering lab.'

'I'm on to it. We'll need a laser scan of that symbol.'

Jack tapped the pod on the front of his helmet. 'Just done it.'

'One of my malfunctioning gadgets?'

Jack grinned. 'Okay. My apologies. It's just something for the future. We'd need another window in the seismic profile for Macalister to let us down here again.'

'We've waited five years for this window. We can wait again.'

Jack stared ahead. For once he felt more comfortable in a tunnel than in the open sea. Years before, he had nearly lost his life diving in a mineshaft when his cylinder valve had jammed, and had only been saved by Costas buddy-breathing with him to the surface. Since then they had dived together thousands of times, but whenever they were in confined spaces that incident was always lurking just beneath his consciousness, forcing him to keep focused. Yet here the thought of the sea outside was more daunting. Below about a hundred metres' depth, the Black Sea was virtually devoid of life, a toxic soup of hydrogen sulphide caused by decaying organic matter with not enough oxygen present. Thousands of metres beyond that, in the abyssal depths, the water was like brine, a legacy of the time before the Atlantis flood when the Black Sea had been cut off from the Mediterranean and had nearly dried up, leaving salt lakes in the deepest reaches. Jack had seen photographs taken by Russian deep-sea probes of ancient wrecks with human bodies encased in salt, sepulchral forms still chained to galleys half swallowed in the brine. And he remembered his escape from the wreck of the first *Seaquest* five years ago, his desperate climb in the ADSA advanced deep-sea anthropod pressure suit through a bed of volcanic vents spewing plumes of smoke into the darkness. He had sworn he would never dive there again, and he had meant it. He remembered what Macalister had said. *Don't push this place.*

He glanced at the digital time readout inside his helmet, and looked at the tether behind Costas. In a few moments they would be ready. He stayed calm, keeping his breathing measured, checking his instruments one last time.

'I know what you're thinking,' Costas said. 'You're thinking there's nothing to worry about. You've got the best possible equipment, and the best possible buddy.'

'Not that. I'm imagining a tropical island, snorkelling on a reef, then cocktails on the shore.'

'And women?'

'All you want. Of course, I'm spoken for.'

'Katya, or Maria?'

Jack coughed. 'Tough call. So I was thinking of taking Rebecca, for her school holiday. Last chance for some father–daughter bonding. She'll be having boyfriends soon.'

'Jeremy's been seeing her, you know.'

Jack turned to Costas. 'Jeremy Haverstock? You must be kidding. You must be *joking*.'

'He's a good guy. The best. Helped me a lot with building Little Joey.' He patted the bulge over his stomach again. 'Anyway, we all thought you knew.'

'I thought they were just friends. Colleagues. Rebecca stayed on at Troy to study the pottery, to help Jeremy record the inscriptions.'

'Rebecca? Spending months recording potsherds? The action girl who makes Lara Croft look like a wimp? I don't think so.'

'She's only seventeen.'

'Come on, Jack. It's all part of being a dad. Face reality. Anyway, when?'

'When what?'

'When am I going to this tropical paradise?'

'Well, you'll need some R and R after this.'

'You always say that.'

'I promise.'

The amber light on Costas' wrist display changed to green. He patted the ROV pouch on his belly. 'Time to rock and roll.'

'Let topside know before you unhook the tether.'

Costas tapped the external intercom button on his helmet. 'Mission control. Do you read me? Over.'

A voice crackled through the intercom. 'This is *Seaquest II*. We copy you. Over.'

'Houston, we're go for landing.'

There was a pause, and then another voice came on line. 'This is Macalister. Gentlemen, just remember which planet you're on. You're diving in the Black Sea, not landing on the moon. Acknowledge.'

Costas grinned at Jack. 'Houston, that's a big wide smile.'

The first voice came on line. 'Repeat that. We do not copy. Over.'

Costas raised his eyes. 'Acknowledged. We're divers, not astronauts. Over.'

Macalister came on again. 'Be safe. Remember the briefing. We'll look out for your radio buoy from the submersible in one hour. Over.'

'Roger that. Little Joey's all juiced up. We're going in hot,' Costas said.

'Don't say that,' Jack replied.

Costas turned to him, grinning through his visor. 'Afraid of a little lava?'

'Check your temperature readout. It's already seventy degrees Celsius. You could poach an egg in this water.'

'Anything over a hundred and thirty degrees, you abort the mission,' Macalister said.

'Roger that. Houston, we are signing off. Over and out.' Costas reached back and unhooked the tether from his suit, then let it go. They watched it snake and slither out of sight

43

up the tunnel, towards the hazy smudge of green more than thirty metres away that marked their entry point from the sea floor, where they had left the submersible. They were now completely cut off from outside support, dependent entirely upon themselves and their equipment, facing a challenge fraught with as much risk as they had ever faced before. Jack turned and looked into the swirling darkness below them, reducing his headlamp beam so his vision was not dazzled by the reflection of light from particles in the water. He saw the hazy outlines of the tunnel walls ahead, and the blackness beyond. He felt his breathing tighten, felt the apprehension, and then took a deep breath and relaxed as the adrenalin coursed through him. He was in his element, where all his training and ambition had led him, an underwater explorer about to enter the most extraordinary archaeological site ever discovered. Right now, there was no better place in the world to be. Costas turned to him, his visor reflecting an image of Jack like a photograph of an astronaut in space, then gestured down the tunnel. 'Good to go?'

Jack steeled himself. *They were about to dive into a live volcano.* He raised his hand, then pointed into the void. 'Good to go.'

2

Jack stared down into the narrowing void ahead of him, keeping part of his mind on the smudge of light he knew lay some thirty metres behind them at the entrance to the tunnel. It was like a flash imprinted on his retina, and he tried to hold it there as a reminder that they had an escape route. He looked over at Costas, remembering their shared experience in the mineshaft many years before. They had let all their training and experience kick in, working the rescue methodically from the moment he had jammed his tank valve on the timber and his air had cut off. The problem for Jack was the reflection, years later: what if Costas had not been face to face with him at that moment, when he had struck the timber and dropped their only torch, plunging them into darkness?

Jack had worked hard to turn the nagging uncertainty to his

advantage, convinced that it made him a better diver, more alert to danger, but always for a few moments before a dive like this one he had to go through a ritual. He shut his eyes tight, thinking about nothing, deliberately slowing his breathing, remaining spread-eagled and neutrally buoyant. After a moment he took a deep breath, opened his eyes and looked at his wrist readout, checking the depth and temperature. He felt a nudge beside him, and heard Costas' reassuring voice. 'You done?'

'All set. You lead, or me?'

'It'll have to be you, Jack. I don't think I could get around you now, with Little Joey hitched to my front. I'll be about five metres behind.'

'Roger that. I'm about to begin my descent.'

'Watch your external temperature gauge. Remember, it should read no more than a hundred and twenty degrees. We have about sixty metres more in the tunnel before we reach the area we passed through five years ago, on the way up to the inner sanctum.'

'You mean the magma chamber, full of red-hot lava.'

'At least we won't have to use our torches.'

A few years before Jack had been in an IMU submersible off the Kīlauea volcano in Hawaii, watching lava pour over the seaward cliffs and roll down the underwater slopes in a glowing orange mass until it had congealed. He had found it a disconcerting experience, with all his instincts telling him that the water around the lava should have boiled and vaporized, and he had wanted to reverse the submersible to avoid falling into the vacuum he felt sure would appear above the flow. And now here he was, not in a submersible but in the water himself, about to swim into the same scenario. He flexed his fingers, looking at the bulbous white Kevlar that was the only barrier between himself and whatever fiery mass lay ahead. He glanced at the readout inside his helmet, seeing the green light showing that the small electric motor running the air-conditioner unit inside his suit was functioning. He pressed his intercom. 'Cross-check internal temperature readings.'

'Twenty-two degrees Celsius,' Costas replied.

'Seems a little hot. Mine's twenty.'

'You're a Viking, remember? I'm Mediterranean. And I'm keeping myself in training for that tropical island you promised.'

Jack glanced down at the clear plastic tube inside his helmet beside his mouth, leading to a freshwater bag inside the rebreather console on his back. 'Just make sure you keep hydrated,' he replied. 'Remember, the more you sweat, the more likely you are to get the bends when we go back up.'

'My thermostat's set at twenty-two max. And I have no intention of being a boil-in-the-bag meal for whatever fiery denizen of the deep lives down here.'

Jack glanced one last time at the stone pillar to his left with the golden Atlantis symbol embedded in it, then manually expelled air from his buoyancy compensator before angling down to follow the slope of the tunnel, kicking forcefully with his fins. He could hear the hiss of the automated buoyancy control bleeding air into his suit, maintaining his buoyancy at neutral. The lamps on either side of his helmet illuminated the tunnel ahead to a distance of at least fifteen metres, showing the ragged edges of the lava where the borer had dug through and a trail of debris on the bottom where the conveyor had taken the broken material up the tunnel and out on to the flank of the volcano. Back up the tunnel the lava had mostly been *pāhoehoe*, billowy and ropy shapes where the molten rock had quickly cooled on contact with the water, whereas in the tunnel ahead it looked like Hawaiian *'a'ā* lava, stonier and more clinky, a result of slower cooling that had left it denser and less aerated. Where the borer had cut into the harder lava, Jack could see a spiralling pattern extending down the tunnel, making it seem like a vortex. As he swam on he began to see tiny bubbles rising from the depths ahead of them, swirling up like a twisting veil.

'That's boiling-hot carbon dioxide and sulphur dioxide, the volcano off-gassing,' Costas said from behind him. 'That's the stuff that makes it poisonous to be anywhere near an eruption like this topside without breathing gear.'

Costas had swum up close behind him, and Jack saw his form reflected in the edge of his helmet. The glass visor was a flat surface set on a slight curve where it closed against the helmet, using external water pressure to make the strongest possible seal; after almost a decade using the e-suit, Jack had got used to the centimetre or so of distorted vision it created around the periphery of the glass plate. But now, seeing the elongated form of Costas' helmet, it seemed like an optical illusion, as if the distorted image around his visor rim had become part of the walls of the tunnel beside him. He began to see multiple images as if he were looking into numerous reflecting mirrors, shifting as Costas moved his headlamp and the reflection changed. He closed his eyes, then opened them again, trying to focus on the tunnel ahead. 'Tell me I'm not hallucinating,' he said. 'For a moment I was seeing multiple images of you on the edge of my visor, as if they were spiralling around the tunnel.'

'It's called polyapsia,' Costas replied. 'Lanowski's been telling me about it. It's a common altered-consciousness vision.'

'You mean a psychedelic trip. That's the last thing I want down here.'

'You were just seeing multiple reflections, set against the apparent swirl of the tunnel ahead of us. Your mind was playing tricks on you. Lanowski thinks that's what prehistoric people were doing in places like this, in caves and tunnels: having altered-consciousness experiences. What you've just seen shows how easily they could have done it. And they wouldn't have been able to rationalize it as we can.'

Jack blinked and stared ahead, seeing the cut marks made by the titanium bit of the boring machine, then shifted his head so the reflection of Costas was no longer visible. 'It was disconcertingly easy to fall into it.'

'Look at it this way. You wanted to return to Atlantis, to get inside the prehistoric mind, right? To see what these people were seeing. Well, you're doing it now. This isn't exactly a time machine, but it's a way of getting into their perceptions. Imagine we're going through a kind of rocky interface like those Stone Age caves, towards the spirit world ahead of us. Being in a tunnel's a common hallucination during near-death experiences, too.'

'I was wondering when you were going to say that. From now on, reality rules, okay?'

'Roger that. Now let's get on. We're down to eighty-five metres absolute water depth, and we don't want to linger at these depths any longer than we have to.'

Jack felt a surge of adrenalin, suddenly excited at what might lie ahead. He checked his computer readout. Sixty-seven degrees external temperature. The slew of bubbles increased to a fizzy mass, his headlamp beams reflecting off them in a confusing maelstrom of light and colour that refracted through the bubbles, creating images that folded and unfolded. There was more width to the tunnel now, and Costas edged up along his left side, just as the tunnel gave way to a wider natural opening. Costas put his hand out into the bubbles, moving it round. 'They're like swirling images of animals, like those prehistoric cave paintings,' he said. 'I wonder if Stone Age people saw something like this in pools of water above the magma chamber, bubbles that might have reflected light coming from lava.'

'They might also have been poisoned by the gas,' Jack said. 'These would definitely have been malevolent spirits.'

'Check this out.' Costas paused beside the left-hand wall of the tunnel, and panned his light up and down a thick streak in the lava that shone a golden colour. 'This might explain a thing or two. It's copper sulphide. If this is common in the lava here, then we've just found the source of copper for the people of this place. Those brave enough to come close to the lava might even have seen it melting.'

'Fantastic,' Jack exclaimed, putting his hand on the copper seam. 'That ties up another loose end. If the source of copper was within the volcano like this, then the elite could easily have controlled it. That first spearhead or sword made of copper would have been a huge milestone in prehistory. Priest-king becomes warrior-god.'

They pushed off and swam forward, Costas now in the lead. 'We must be on the edge of the magma chamber,' he said. 'All I can see is reflection off the bubbles. If there's any lava activity ahead, we should see it with our lights off.'

They switched off their headlamps in unison. For a moment, all Jack saw was blackness, and then he became aware of little flashes in front of him, the bubbles now appearing like tiny polychrome drops of oil lit through by some distant source of light. As his eyes adjusted, he saw a hazy presence somewhere beyond, a wavering red glow that suffused the background ahead of them.

'Holy shit,' Costas said quietly.

'That's lava, isn't it?'

'A whole lake of it,' Costas exclaimed, swimming forward to the lip of the tunnel. Jack followed behind and stared out at one of the most extraordinary and terrifying vistas he had ever seen. It was a vast underwater cavern, at least forty metres across. In the dark recesses above them he could see the roof of the chamber, an ugly mass of solidified lava that looked as if it had been blown upwards to harden over an empty space, leaving appendages that dripped down like malformed stalactites. But it was the scene below that was so mesmerizing. The bottom of the chamber was a seething cauldron of lava, oozing up to the surface and then solidifying quickly on contact with the water, leaving pillow-shaped undulations with lobes and toes that disgorged from the cooling crust. Jack peered directly down, through a yellow-brown haze that lay in the water like a miasma above the crust. He watched a crack open and molten lava ooze into solidifying folds resembling arms and legs, like some protean being, half human, before another surge of lava swallowed it back into the cauldron. It was as if he was looking at the birthplace of the gods, at the very fount of creation itself.

Costas pressed the control panel on his wrist to activate the video camera in front of his helmet, and moved his head slowly around to take in the scene. 'The yellow-brown stuff is suspended glass fragments from the lava. That's the other thing that makes it lethal to be near an eruption. You don't want to breathe any of that in or get it sucked into your equipment. Thank God for the closed-circuit rebreathers. I make it seventy-nine degrees Celsius where we are now. We're probably looking at over a hundred degrees down there, with the gas plumes at a hundred and fifty degrees when they hit the water.'

'At least hot water rises, so we're not going to fall into it.'

'It's those gas plumes I'm worried about, the carbon dioxide and hydrogen sulphide. Look, there's one over there.' Jack watched as a spectacular white mass erupted like a geyser on the far side of the chamber, followed by a glowing lava fountain that cascaded sideways and seemed to melt part of the wall of rock on the side of the chamber. 'That's a solid mass of bubbles, more gas than water,' Costas said. 'I've seen plumes like that over sub-sea vents in the mid-Atlantic. Some Bermuda Triangle fanatics think that's what causes ships to disappear. If you swam over one of those plumes, you'd drop like a stone into the lava. And did you see the wall? We're inside the caldera of a live volcano, Jack, and it's collapsing in on itself. It's like those holes you dig in sand by the seashore, where the water undermines the sides. That's what the lava's doing underneath us now, rising even in the time we've been watching it.'

'How long do you think we have?'

'I don't even want to think. I feel like one of those mythical heroes, finally having reached the edge of the underworld and wondering whether going on from here means no turning back.'

'We've got to make a decision fast.'

'Let's do the geology first. It's mainly basaltic, but I can see streaks of rhyolitic lava, viscous, silica-rich stuff that's come from deep within the magma. That's a major warning sign, something the vulcanologists couldn't have known without us being here. And whatever the geologists thought about the seismic activity falling off, it looks like a lull before the storm. There's clearly a major event brewing under the North Anatolian Fault, something that could easily extend as far west as the Bosporus and Istanbul. What we're looking at here is enough to put the whole of northern Turkey under evacuation orders.'

'Good enough,' Jack said. 'Let's get out of here.' He fixed his mind's eye again on the smudge of light at the entrance to the tunnel far behind them, and turned away from the hellish scene in the cauldron. But then he caught sight of something below. A plume of bubbles had risen along the wall to their left, clearing away the brown silicate material that had obscured the rock face. Suddenly he saw a rock-cut stairway leading from below the lava up the side of the chamber. He followed it with his eyes, his heart pounding, and then saw another entrance in the wall ahead of them, twenty, maybe twenty-five metres away. He grasped Costas by the arm and pointed, his voice hoarse with excitement. 'We've been here before, five years ago. That's the original rock wall from the time of Atlantis, and that's the entranceway I remember passing. It was surmounted by the Atlantis symbol. That's what I came here to look for, Costas, to see what's inside. '

Costas followed his gaze, and then turned to look at him. 'This is the only chance you'll have to see what's there. We can't go away and wait for things to cool down. That lava's going to destroy everything here, all of the archaeology. Whatever's inside that entranceway will be lost for ever.'

'What are the odds for a look?'

'What's your predicted gas supply?'

Jack glanced at his computer readout. 'At current consumption and depth, about thirty-five minutes.'

'Mine's thirty. That gives us half an hour to get over there, take a look, and then return here and get back to the submersible. There's no radio link with *Seaquest II* until we're out of the tunnel. If we go out now to give them the geological rundown, we'd never get back in. Look at the rate of rise of the lava. That entrance probably won't be there in half an hour.'

'Will an extra half an hour make any difference to the speed of the earthquake-response team?'

Costas paused. 'The Turkish authorities are already on Category A alert, with evacuation plans on full standby. What we've got to say will push them to activate, but there'll have to be top-level government meetings in Ankara. It's a huge decision to make. Millions of people will be disrupted.'

'The odds for us?'

Costas swam forward and peered over the edge. 'There's a lot of plume activity just where we want to go. And the lava's rising. But when have the odds ever been in our favour?'

'What's your call?'

'I haven't had a chance to test Little Joey yet. I couldn't face Jeremy and say I hadn't tried.'

Jack stared at the ancient entranceway, the stairs in front of it now lit up in the orange glow of the lava that was lapping the base of the rock. It was now or never. He thought about what Costas had said. Half an hour might make no difference. But that calculation depended on them escaping alive. If they never made it out and nobody knew what they had seen, that activation might never be ordered. Millions of people on standby might become millions of dead and injured and homeless. He might be about to make the most momentous decision of his career. *Of his life.* He stared at the ancient rock-cut entrance, his vision narrowing to a tunnel again, one that seemed to draw him forward over the burning pit in front of them.

'Okay,' he said. 'Let's do it, and then let's get the hell out of here.'

3

Jack swam to the edge of the tunnel and looked at the underwater magma lake, watching the yellow-brown haze that seemed to undulate over the lava as plumes of bubbles rose through it and shimmered towards the ceiling of the cavern in the darkness far above. He knew that to swim from the ledge over the lava would be like walking on quicksand, with the rising bubbles pulling on his buoyancy and the plumes acting like sinkholes in the water. Far out in the middle he watched a spectacular geyser of molten rock arch upwards, its surface speckled with bubbles of gas. He turned back, checking the gauge readout inside his helmet. They were eighty-five metres beneath the surface of the Black Sea, at least twenty-five metres below the outer flank of the volcano, and he was down to the final third of the air mixture in his rebreather. He had twenty-five minutes left at this depth, no more, before going on to his reserve supply. There would be no chance of an emergency ascent from this depth to the surface and *Seaquest II*; their only option was to stick to plan and return up the tunnel to the submersible. Getting to the ancient entranceway and then coming back here would be cutting it fine.

He turned to Costas, who had reached down and opened a Velcroed Kevlar flap on his left thigh, pulling out a tube about the length of his forearm. One end was attached to a spool of what looked like heavy-duty fishing line. He clipped the spool to a carabiner on the chest strap of his rebreather backpack and then twisted the tube, causing a handle like a pistol grip to fold out below. Another twist further up and a metal rod with a point like a harpoon snapped out of the front. He wrapped his right glove around the grip and put his other hand further up the tube. 'I haven't had a chance to show you this yet,' he said.

'Odd place to go spearfishing,' Jack said.

'It's something I've been playing with since we were here five years ago,' Costas replied, eyeing the rock face ahead of them. 'You don't tend to think that getting through submerged caverns would be an issue because you can swim through them, but thinking about volcanic activity made me wonder what it would be like if some force were dragging us down, exerting a pull on buoyancy exactly like those gas eruptions would do now.'

'Got you,' Jack exclaimed. 'It's a grapple gun.'

Costas pressed his wrist control panel, and Jack saw a thin shaft of light from his helmet where a laser rangefinder penetrated the gloom. 'Twenty-six metres to that ledge,' Costas murmured. 'The grapple spear has a lead core to increase weight and the shaft is as narrow as possible for minimal water resistance, but even so its effective range is only about twelve metres. It'll go further but you need good force of impact for the head to explode.'

'Explode?'

'The first ten centimetres of the shaft contains a joined matrix of rods made of titanium with a magnetic ferrous core. The head impacts the rock and detonates a small C-5 charge, and the rods shoot into every nook and cranny for ten centimetres or so around the point of impact. Then they're locked tight by an electromagnetic pulse I fire down the wire from the gun.'

'And then you reuse it?' Jack pointed across the canyon. 'We're going to need two lengths.'

'Once it's wedged into the rock and magnetized, it won't come out. But there's a second head below the first on the shaft, and you can detach the line from the fired head and put it on the second. It's a gamble, Jack. The total distance is several metres beyond the specs.'

'How do we get back?'

'That entranceway is about five metres higher than we are here. We'll have to free-swim back, but if we launch ourselves with maximum buoyancy we could swim in an arc and land back here without being pulled down.'

'Okay. Let's get going.'

'Move behind me. This thing fires a substantial black powder cartridge.' Costas clicked on his laser rangefinder again and aimed at the jagged crevice he had been eyeing on the wall, then pulled the trigger. There was a violent shudder and a jet of bubbles and the spear shot off from the tube, pulling the line behind it. The spool abruptly stopped reeling and Costas was pulled forward, just holding himself in time from being yanked off the ledge over the rising bubbles. He pulled hard on the line, then looked back at Jack. 'Okay. It's held.'

'What's the drill?'

'I stay here, you swim along the line. You get there, I swing off this ledge and follow you.'

Jack leaned over the void. 'That line's ten metres long, and the lava's what, eight metres below us? That puts you in the soup.'

'That's where you come in. As I swim out as fast as I can from here, you reel in the slack. That way if I'm pulled down, the line will hold me high enough above the lava.'

'Roger that,' Jack said, pushing himself off and grasping the line in front of Costas. 'You secure?'

'Go for it.'

Jack finned forward over the lava, watching the streaks of red in the cooling lobes and nodules directly below him. At about the halfway point he was suddenly surrounded by a miasma of bubbles escaping from the lava below, a silvery mass that seemed to waft around him, bathing him in refracted light. He lost all points of reference, and seemed to be falling precipitately, a feeling that made him want to let go of the line and spread-eagle himself like a skydiver. His hand jerked on the line and he twisted sideways. It was no illusion; he really had been falling. He began pulling himself along, his buoyancy computer continuously adjusting to compensate for the effect of being dragged down in the vacuum created by the bubbles. He reached the grapple, checked that it was locked securely into a crack and then turned to look for Costas, who had crouched down on the edge of the tunnel opening, holding the line. Jack held on to the rock face with one hand and put his other out in the diver's okay signal, his forefinger and thumb joined in a circle, and then transferred both hands to the line. He heard Costas' voice crackling on the intercom through some kind of interference, the broken sounds briefly becoming distinct. 'You ready?'

Jack wedged his body as much as he could into the rock. 'Roger that.'

Costas launched himself forward in a slow-motion dive, his bulky suit making him look like an astronaut. As the line went slack, Jack hauled on it, looping it quickly around a rock protrusion behind him. It suddenly went taut as Costas was sucked down by a gas plume and disappeared out of sight. The line went slack again, and for a horrible few seconds as he frantically pulled on it Jack thought that Costas might have impacted with the lava. Then the crackling came on the intercom again, and Costas appeared out of the plume and ascended a few metres below him. He reached the ledge beside Jack, then wedged in an elbow and took the grapple gun out again from his pocket, unhooking the line from the carabiner on his chest and feeding it back into the tube. He glanced at Jack through his visor. 'That was close.'

'Your boiler suit looks like glue.'

Costas grunted, reached into the crevice to disengage the line from the grapple, then pressed a control on the tube to re-spool the line and hook it back into the second grapple, ready for firing. He wrapped his hand round the grip again and peered at their objective, the rock-cut platform in front of the ancient entranceway some fifteen metres away. 'Twice lucky?'

'Go for it.'

There was a jolt as he fired the device again, and Jack watched the grapple arc over and disappear into a fold in the rock about a metre below the ledge. Costas pulled hard, and the line went rigid. He leaned back and Jack swam over him, taking the line in one hand and kicking out above it. This time he quickly made it to the opposite side and Costas followed, swimming forward while Jack hauled, not bothering to loop the line but letting it drop down below. Costas reached the rock beside him and hung on, breathing heavily on his regulator, then he grasped the line near the grapple and let go of the rock to release the carabiner. As he did so, Jack saw a white expanse of gas billow up below them, and at the same moment the rock holding the grapple broke free under the tension and tumbled off the face, dropping down below Costas into the fomenting mass of bubbles now rising up around them. Jack wedged one hand into the rock and reached down with his other to grab Costas under one arm, holding tight as the plume rose through them. For a split second it seemed as if they were dangling in air, and Jack was holding Costas' entire weight. Then the plume dispersed above them and Costas hit the manual on his buoyancy control. Jack twisted round and looked up, seeing the carved lintel shape above the doorway, straining to look for the ancient symbols he desperately wanted to see.

Just as he relaxed his hold, there was a jerk and Costas' arm slipped away. Jack twisted back and saw a horrifying sight. Costas was at least five metres below him, his arms flailing, descending fast. Jack slammed his buoyancy control to dump the air inside his compensator and swam downwards. The chunk of rock with the grapple still inside had pulled Costas down like an anchor, and was now embedded in the lava near the edge of the chamber, sinking in and pulling Costas with it. Jack reached him with only a few metres to spare, pulling his chest strap with one hand and releasing the carabiner with the other, then injecting air into both of their buoyancy compensators. He watched the line snake away and disappear into the molten mass below them, and turned Costas round to face him. 'You okay?'

Costas was wide-eyed, his visor fogged up around the edges from his exhalation. Jack had a sudden sickening feeling. They had just lost their one lifeline, and they had expended more air than they had bargained for. Costas returned his stare. 'I think that's twice very lucky,' he said hoarsely. 'Let's get up there, do what we have to do and get the hell out of here.'

As they swam upwards, Jack turned to look out over the lava lake. A surge was rising in the middle, then moving along as if something were swimming just beneath the surface like some ancient spirit monster. Suddenly the mass rose in a giant bulbous dome and split open, disgorging a huge bubble of gas into the water. A second later there was a blinding flash and Jack could see the pressure waves in the water surging towards them. Costas clung to him, pressing his visor against his. 'Brace yourself!' The shock wave pushed them violently towards the rock face, and then they were pulled back again over the lava lake by the implosion. Jack held on to Costas with one hand and finned with all his strength back towards the rock-cut door. He seemed to be getting nowhere, as if this were a bad dream, the door impossibly beyond his reach. Then the sucking force of the implosion miraculously relented, and they came to the ledge below the door.

'What the hell was that?' Jack said, panting.

'Phreatic explosion.' Costas' visor fogged up as he struggled to regain breath. 'It happens on land when lava flows over pockets of water, superheating it. Somehow that big bubble of gas under the surface of the lava must have had the same effect, sucking in water, encasing it and boiling it up.'

Jack stared up at the carved lintel above the doorway in front of them. Costas followed his gaze, panting, then he saw what Jack had seen. 'Symbols. Ancient writing. Is this what you saw before?'

'It's fantastic.' Above the doorway was the rectilinear Atlantis symbol, with other symbols on either side, familiar from the syllabry they had discovered five years before but not yet translated. They looked freshly carved, as if done just before the flood, and several looked only partly completed. Beneath them Jack could make out other symbols, very eroded and clearly much older, some of them looking as if they had been partly chiselled away. He activated his camera. There was no time for detailed recording now. He was jittery with adrenalin, and checked his computer readout. Fifteen minutes of breathing gas left at this depth. He was conscious that the danger had made the reflective part of his mind shut off in the focus on survival, on dealing with each new threat as they encountered it, and that he needed to maintain an awareness of the bigger picture, of just how close they had come to never leaving this cavern alive. He stared at the entrance. He would need five minutes, just to look. With the lava rising inexorably, it was the last chance before whatever lay inside there was lost for ever.

'Jack, you've got a problem.'

'What is it?'

'Check your internal temperature readout.'

Jack looked sideways inside his helmet, scanning the digital readout. 'Twenty-six degrees Celsius. I thought it was getting a little warm. I'll adjust the thermostat.'

'Don't do that yet. Wait till you really need it. You'll blow the system.'

'What do you mean?'

'It must have been the heat when we were close to the lava. You've got a leak from your coolant reservoir, Jack. You can't afford to be that close to extreme heat any more, as you'll soon have no way of cooling down.'

Jack shut his eyes, trying to control his breathing. For a moment he felt nauseous, a flutter in his stomach, the sickening feeling of the walls closing in. Part of him wanted to swim up and dump his air against the ceiling, to create a pocket where he could rip off his helmet and be free, but he knew that to do so would only be a brief illusion of normality in an air space that would feel far more confined than the water below. He swallowed hard. *Keep focused*. He sucked on his water tube, then looked into the doorway and tried to ignore the lava, which was rising up the rock face below at an alarming rate. Costas had already unzipped his front pocket and disgorged the ROV, which he was testing like a remote-controlled helicopter. Jack realized where the nickname Little Joey had come from. It looked like a miniature robotic kangaroo, with hind legs, a swivelling video aperture for a head and a tethering cable for a tail, leading to a spool on Costas' chest. The robot craned its neck around and peered at Jack with its single video eye, and then jetted back to Costas, hovering in the water in front of him. Jack swam ahead to the door entrance, then switched on his helmet lights. 'I'm going in. Five minutes, no more.'

Costas put a hand on the ROV's neck. 'Little Joey will be following you. He can send back remote signals, but I'm keeping him on the tether in this place. If you see anything, hold him like I am and put him on to it. Remember, I'm seeing what he sees on the screen inside my visor. Just point and I'll drive him forward. Then you come out, pronto.'

Jack stared at the ROV, its single camera eye encased in a sphere of glass. It angled its head around and looked at him, the black lens cap half-down like an eyelid. He realized that he was cocking his own head in the same way, as if they were querying each other. He shook his head in disbelief at what he had just done and looked away. The ROV *was not alive.* 'Roger that.'

'Remember what Macalister said. No disappearing down holes.' Costas' voice crackled. 'That electromagnetic inter- ference is increasing again. There must be a lot of ferrous material in the lava here. I may be out of contact with you.'

Jack surged forward, passing through the entrance and finning down the rock-cut tunnel. After about ten metres the tunnel became a T-junction. Jack stopped and checked his remaining time. Four and a half minutes. It had to be one or the other. The ROV came up alongside him and angled to the right, illuminating the passage. Costas' voice crackled on the intercom. 'Jack, give me a confirmation on what you see. I think I'm looking at another entranceway.'

'That's an affirmation. But there's one on the opposite side too.'

'Little Joey's pointing the way. Left would take you to the surface of the volcano, now under tons of lava. Right would take you towards the location of that open-air platform we saw five years ago, a more likely place for some kind of sanctuary.'

Jack heard crackling as Costas tried to say more, and then a low hum. Whatever it was that was causing the interference, this place was the epicentre. He had no time to weigh up the options. He swerved right and followed the ROV into the passageway, kicking hard to get beyond it. He swam about ten metres further, then followed the passageway as it veered left. Ahead of him the tunnel was partly blocked with rough-hewn squared stones that looked as if they had been hastily assembled. Whatever it was that had been beyond there on the eve of the flood seven thousand years ago, somebody had wanted it cut off. An aperture still remained, big enough for someone unencumbered to crawl through, but not big enough for a diver with gear. Jack rolled sideways to fit the hole and shoved his head through, his headlamp angled upwards. It was a chamber, maybe eight metres across. He could see jagged protrusions of lava from the eruption five years ago, visible beyond another wall of crude masonry that blocked what must have been the open front of the chamber, clearly a cave in the face of the volcano. He twisted to the left, lying on his back, and saw that the opposite side was natural rock, a wide opening that extended inwards. Big multifaceted crystals of quartz were visible in the wall just to his right. He flicked on his helmet video camera, moving his head from side to side to ensure maximum coverage, then struggled to twist around until he was lying on his front. He strained to raise his head up, angling the lamp as high as he could, then he froze with horror.

He was staring at a human face. It was a skull, embedded in the floor of the chamber. The bone had been plastered over and was partly covered with a rough calcite accretion that must have formed underwater after the flood. One eye socket was open, and the other was filled with plaster and a cowrie shell, as if the skull were staring at him through the slit. Jack instinctively recoiled, his breathing coming in short rasps, and then he forced himself to raise his head higher and look beyond. It wasn't just one skull. There were dozens of them, all embedded in the floor and facing him, all of them plastered over in the same fashion. The accretion as well as the anoxic conditions of the water must have preserved them. Then he saw another skull lying on its side, unplastered, with the jawbone hanging away, and shapes on the floor covered with accretion. Beside the skull nearest to him was a stone basin about half a metre high on a plinth. He reached out his left arm and put his hand inside, scraping the interior, then pulled his hand away and stared at his glove. It was smeared in a thick, viscous substance that seemed to have lined the bottom of the bowl, some kind of residue. He brought his hand under his headlamp beam and stared at it, his heart pounding. The substance was a deep maroon colour.

He was not only looking at the people of Atlantis. *He was touching their blood.*

He propped himself up on his elbows, straining his neck up as far as he could. His beam flashed on the interior wall of the cavern. To his astonishment, he saw the shadowy outline of paintings on the rock, ibex, leopards, great horned bulls, faded and ancient. In one part he thought he saw where they had been erased, the rock scrubbed clean. He strained up further, and then he froze again.

Towering above the floor were giant pillars, twenty or more of them, their tops extending outwards in a T-shape. They looked freshly cut, with sharp edges; and had not been hewn out of the living rock but hauled here from somewhere else. The arms were carved with outstretched hands, and other relief carving adorned their sides: swirling abstract forms, parts of human bodies, leopards and bull's horns, scorpions, a vulture. One swirling circular shape might have been a human face, but he could not be sure. As he looked around, he realized that the outer pillars formed a circle about eight metres across, with pairs of pillars within the circle. His mind reeled. *A stone circle.* The pillars confronted him like the skulls, ghostly sentinels from the past. Jack felt a shiver down his spine. Were these pillars statues of men, or were they gods?

In a flash, he remembered what he had come here to see.

The birth of the new religion.

The death of the old.

The threshold of a new world order, seven thousand years ago, at the dawn of civilization.

His time had run out.

He struggled backwards, grabbed the ROV and shoved it into the hole, leaving it sitting on its hind legs with the camera aimed inwards. He ripped a small tube out of his sleeve pocket and quickly took a scrape sample from the floor of the chamber. Little Joey's head turned and eyed him, cocked sideways, and then swivelled back to look into the chamber. Jack disentangled his fins from the tethering line and crouched into a ball, rolling round and extending his legs so that he could fin back along the passage. He pulled hard with his hands at first, anxious not to dislodge the ROV, and then he powered ahead towards the T-junction. As he did so, the low hum and crackle in his intercom suddenly became shouted words. 'Jack! Get out of there now!'

He surged forward and veered into the main tunnel facing the entrance to the magma chamber, where Costas should have been visible. What he saw instead was an image from hell. A surge of lava was lapping towards him, five metres or more into the tunnel. All his instincts told him to go back, to seek some other way out, but he knew he had to go forward and swim over the lava to where he could now see Costas' beam shining at him no more than ten metres away.

He finned frantically, following the tethering line for the ROV. After five kicks he was over the lava, almost within touching distance. He was being pushed against the roof of the tunnel, and realized to his horror that the boiling water above the lava was rising and forcing him upwards. He remembered his failing coolant system. He was beginning to overheat. The sweat dripped off his face on to the interior of his visor, and he could see the outside of his suit crinkling and turning brown. *He was being cooked alive.* Suddenly there was a yank on the tether line and he held on, feeling himself being pulled. He turned upside down and clawed his way along the ceiling, but then remembered his cylinder and air pack. He might survive the Kevlar on the front of his suit being scorched, but not his breathing gear. He turned over again, drew himself up into an upside-down crab crouch and pushed his feet and elbows against the rock, hopping forward a metre or so each time, trying to keep his helmet away from the lava. The sweat in the inside of his visor began to boil like spatters of water on an oven hot ring. He pushed one last time and was free, rocketing up into Costas in a tangle with the tethering line. He was dimly aware of Costas unhooking the line and fumbling with his wrist control panel, and he saw that the thermostat had been turned down to its lowest setting, ten degrees Celsius. Costas spun him round and stared him in the face. 'There may be enough juice in that thing to give you a burst of cool air before it packs up. Can you feel it?'

Jack felt the sweat drip into the corners of his mouth, and then he sensed the coolness. He opened his eyes, blinking the salt out, then reached with his lips for the water tube and sucked hard, grateful that he had not tried to come out upside down and cooked the water reservoir on his back. He spat out the mouthpiece after a few gulps, then gasped hard for a few moments while Costas looked him over. 'I don't see any sign of leakage in your e-suit. But the heat-resistant outer shell and the Kevlar is melted from your elbows and knees. You're not going anywhere near lava again and surviving it. Which is a good thing, because as of about a minute ago, that option closed on us anyway.'

'What option?' Jack gasped. 'What do you mean?'

'I mean the option of going back the way we came. The option that would have taken us close to the lava again. Take a look.'

Jack floated free of Costas, kicking a loop of the tether cable away, then looked down. It was a terrifying sight. The lava below them had risen at least five metres in the time since they had exited the tunnel. He suddenly realized what Costas meant. He looked over to the tunnel entrance, where the borer had broken through into the magma chamber, their entry point. A great surge of lava flowed up into it, and then another. He spun around to Costas. 'What are the options?'

'When Lanowski and I took the submersible over the volcano, we saw a number of places where gas was escaping into the sea. Mostly they were pinpricks, but there was one really big flow. I took a GPS fix on it and I've just been trying to relate that to all the directional data I've got from our dive. I think it's one of those two caverns above us.'

Jack looked directly up, and saw two distinct areas of blackness in the rocky ceiling of the chamber some ten metres overhead. 'Which one?'

'We'll have to take pot luck.'

There was a heave in the water, and Jack looked down. To his horror he saw that the entire lava lake had surged upwards, and a great bulge like a wave was rippling towards them from the far side of the chamber. 'Up! Now!' he shouted. He finned hard, remembering to breathe out as he did so, then stopped and flipped round, heading back down. Costas was struggling with the tether cord, which was caught around the strap of one fin. Jack reached behind his breathing pack, whipped out his knife and pulled the serrated edge as hard as he could against the cord, sawing the knife against the metallic cable inside. The cord snapped and he pulled Costas' foot away, smearing himself with the melting rubber of Costas' fin. He finned frantically upwards, grabbed the cord at the back of Costas' pack and yanked it to fill the emergency flotation wings in the shoulders of the e-suit. He exhaled forcefully to avoid an embolism and prayed that Costas was doing the same. The lava surge passed only a few metres below them, and seconds later they hit the ceiling of the chamber, jarring against the lava. Jack still had his knife in his hand, and he stabbed it into Costas' buoyancy aid to expel the air, watching as the bubbles from the torn fabric disappeared up into the darkness above. Costas pushed off, looking down at the melted remains of his fin, and then at Jack. 'Phew. That was close.'

Jack felt himself close to boiling point again. He took a slurp of his water, now unpleasantly warm, and looked down. The lava was surging up all round them, rising at a horrifying speed. 'I think what we've got here is a major volcanic event,' he said hoarsely.

'No kidding. It's called an eruption. And with the lava pressing up into this space, the volume of water inside the chamber is decreasing and boiling up. There'll be a flashpoint and another phreatic explosion and everything will vaporize, including us.'

A lava fountain licked the bottom of the divide between the two caverns. 'See that?' Jack said. 'We haven't got any choice. It's going to have to be this cavern.' He pushed off the wall, and they both began swimming up. Jack glanced at his gauge. They were sixty-five metres below sea level, which put them about ten metres higher than the point on the outside of the volcano where they had left the sub. He looked at Costas. 'Does that magic program of yours tell us how far away the sub is?'

'The system's crashed in the heat. But I think we've come in a curve, so not as far as we've swum. Maybe fifty metres from here, a bit more.' They reached the top of the chamber, a jagged ceiling of solidified lava that looked like malformed stalactites, with deep cracks and crevices between. The upper recess was about five metres wide. Costas flicked on both of his headlamp beams and swam a circuit on his back, staring up, before returning to Jack's position. 'There are three possibilities. How much air have you got?'

'Almost on reserve. Fifty-five bar.'

'Okay. You vent carbon dioxide from your rebreather into one chamber, I'll do mine in another. You've got about ten bar more than me left in your breathing gas, so for the third chamber vent some air straight from your tanks.'

'Roger that.' Jack followed Costas to the first hole and pressed the button that vented the accumulated carbon dioxide from his rebreather. They watched the bubbles ascend in the beam of Costas' headlamps, and Costas peered hard while Jack looked down at the lava surging below them. 'I can see where the gas is pooling against the ceiling,' Costas said. 'Nothing's escaping.' They moved to the next spot and repeated the process. An arc of lava shot up in the water to within a few metres of them. Costas looked at Jack. 'Same story.'

'You sure?'

'Yep.'

'This is it, then.' They looked at each other, then peered down. Jack realized that the lava was rising with greater speed now because the cavern had narrowed, forcing the molten material upwards. 'We've just run out of time.' An upwelling of gas enveloped them and they both caught hold of a lava protrusion just in time to prevent themselves from falling. They finned together up the last five metres, face to face, until they hit the ceiling. Jack saw something, twisted sideways and switched off his headlamp. It was a patch of green light coming down around a hanging pillar of lava about five metres away. He pulled his way over and peered at it, then looked upwards, his heart pounding. *They might make it*. He had a sudden thought, and turned to Costas. 'You got any detonator cord?'

'Never leave home without it.' Costas quickly reached down into the Kevlar pocket on the waist of his suit. 'What's the plan?'

'This rock isn't part of the ceiling, it's a dislodged chunk of lava that must have been blown up here during the eruption five years ago. You can tell because it's wedged upwards, not downwards. A little help and it might go.'

Costas clipped the detonator into the two-metre section of cord he was trailing, and wrapped it into gaps around the rock. 'You ready?' Jack gave the okay sign and swam back five metres to the other side of the recess, followed seconds later by Costas. 'Turn your back to it and press your visor against mine.' Costas held Jack tight. 'Three. Two. One. Fire in the hole.' There was a sharp bang, and Jack felt the shock wave ripple against his back; he was thankful for the Kevlar pressure suit. They both turned just as the lava chunk fell in a tumble of smaller pieces, splashing into the molten lava below them and exploding into fiery fragments that quickly melted and sank. Jack pulled Costas over to the hole and they looked up. There was a crack about a metre by half a metre wide, and above that he saw the open ocean.

'There's no way we're getting through that opening with all this gear,' Costas said.

'We'll have to ditch it and swim for the sub.'

'This is a one-way ticket, Jack.'

'But you'll be there waiting for me.'

'No. You first.'

'No way,' Jack said. 'I need to see that you can get though that hole. You're wider than me.' In a few moves he stripped off Costas' backpack, holding it in front of him with the air hoses still attached. Costas did the same for him, and they both floated under the crack. Jack felt the heat of the water searing into his elbows and knees where the thermal layer of the suit had melted. 'Okay?' he said. 'Relax, take six long, deep breaths, then hyperventilate for four. Give me the okay signal when you're ready.' He heard Costas breathe fast and hard and hold his breath, and then saw him put his forefinger and thumb together in the diver's okay signal. He quickly disengaged the hoses from Costas' helmet and heaved him upwards, watching him disappear in a welter of bubbles. He breathed in deeply, then looked down. *This was not happening.* A huge ball of fire was surging towards him, an explosion of lava that would rip right through the crack and erupt on the surface of the volcano. He had no time to hyperventilate. He took one huge breath and held it, then pulled out his hoses. On a second's impulse, he held the pack down and knocked open the safety release valve on the main tank, causing gas to rip out at high pressure. He held it for as long as it took to rocket through the crack into the sea above the volcano, then he let it spiral away. He finned frantically sideways just as the lava shot up in a geyser behind him, the force of the displaced water pushing him further. Below him the magma chamber imploded, the roof dropping into the space where they had been swimming only minutes before, now a fiery mass of molten lava.

He spun around, disorientated, seeing the plume of red fall back into a slick mass on the seabed. He could see no sign of the submersible, nor of Costas. He sensed the shadow of *Seaquest II* far above, but ignored it. He would never make it to the surface. Then he saw a yellow smudge down the slope of the volcano. It was the light from the submersible's lamp array that could be activated externally. *Thank God. Costas had made it.*

He forced his vision to narrow into a tunnel, to exclude all sense of his surroundings other than his destination. He began to swim hard, ignoring the tightening in his chest, the feeling at the back of his throat that was his body's first attempt to stop him breathing in water and drowning. He was eighteen metres, maybe fifteen metres away. He could see the submersible clearly now, a yellow cylindrical form about ten metres long, raised above the seabed on retractable legs, allowing divers to enter via a hatch in the floor. He saw Costas beneath it, frantically twisting something. The hatch swung open and Costas pulled himself upwards, his head out of sight, then dropped back down into the water, facing Jack. His helmet was gone, but he was wearing the black safety mask they kept as a backup in a pocket on their legs. Jack was ten metres away now, eight, focusing on Costas' beckoning hands, trying not to black out. He felt his diaphragm heave upwards as his body counted down the final seconds to unconsciousness. The tunnel darkened, and his limbs felt impossibly heavy. Then he was grabbed and heaved upwards in a cascade of water. Costas slammed the locking points on either side of his helmet and the visor sprang open, flooding him with air.

Jack settled back in the water in the open hatch in the floor of the submersible, breathing in great gulps, his arms draped over Costas' shoulders, his eyes dazzled by the fluorescent glow inside. He reached his left arm up to the camera pod on the front of his helmet, detached it and lowered it in front of his face, then pressed the record button. The little LCD screen lit up and showed a video image, at first a scatter of reflected light from particles in the water and then a sharp view of the chamber in the volcano. It was all there. *It had been real.* He saw the skulls, the basin, the paintings on the cave wall. The image zoomed in to his final discovery, the extraordinary pillars, and then it went blank. He carefully placed the camera pod on the floor of the submersible, then shut his eyes with relief and slumped back over Costas' frame, breathing deeply, letting the energy return to his limbs.

'Jack.'

'What is it?'

'The bear hug.'

Costas' forearms were up on the edge of the floor, entirely supporting Jack's weight, and his head was wedged sideways against Jack's helmet. Jack gave a half-hearted kick, then slumped back. 'Can't,' he gasped. They remained still for a moment, locked together, and then they both began to laugh uncontrollably. They kicked and heaved, and Jack pulled himself up until he was sitting on the edge of the hatch. He reached out to help as Costas clawed his way up on the other side and sat down heavily. They stared at each other's dripping forms, and then reached across the water and slapped hands. Jack closed his eyes.

They had come here on a wing and a prayer.

But they had done it.

They had returned to Atlantis.

4

The Taklamakan Desert, western China

The man felt himself being pushed out of the vehicle, and then being held roughly by one pair of hands while another untied his wrists from behind his back. He flexed his fingers, trying to bring back the circulation. His blindfold was yanked off, but he had the sense to reach into his overcoat pocket to find his sunglasses, putting them on before opening his eyes. Even so the glare off the desert was blinding, and he blinked hard a few times before beginning to discern anything of his surroundings. He glanced at his watch and saw that he had been in the Toyota for a little over two hours, from the time when the helicopter from Kashgar had left him at the appointed place, a remote location where a branch of the southern highway that skirted the desert had come to an abrupt end. The desert track beyond had been spine-jarring, little more than the natural rocky substrate cleared of sand, and the four-wheel drive had been engaged for most of the way. Yet the secrecy had been a charade. The one he had come here to find was already aware that he knew the location of this place. The discomfort of the past two hours had been to make a point. He was in someone else's territory now.

An arm appeared from behind him, pointing ahead, and his driver spoke in a heavy Chinese accent. 'Follow this track until you reach the fort. Wait there.' The car door slammed, and the Toyota roared off in a cloud of dust. The man put his hand over his nose and mouth against the dust and walked forward as instructed, keeping slow in the searing heat. After a few minutes, he had descended from the dunes to a hard surface of compacted dirt that looked as if it had been deliberately cleared of sand. A few long-dead tree stumps surrounded a crumbled well-head, and beyond that he saw a water-tanker truck in front of the settlement, a motley collection of prefabricated single-storey structures. It had clearly once been a small desert oasis, one of numerous pockets of humanity that thrived in the Taklamakan at the time of the Silk Road, but had since been extinguished by the howling winds that pushed the dunes over everything in their path.. The houses were typical of forced modern settlements in the desert, attempts by the Chinese authorities to stake their claim in a region that was one of the least hospitable on earth yet contained huge untapped mineral and oil reserves. He reached the first house and continued walking, passing men and women who seemed intent on some unknown business. It was odd that they ignored him completely, a European in a fine suit and overcoat striding out of the dunes and walking through their midst, but then he remembered that this place was not what it seemed.

Ahead, beyond the houses, he saw what looked like eroded rocky outcrops sticking out of the sand, but as he got closer he realized that they were the crumbling towers of an ancient desert stronghold, probably abandoned a millennium or more ago when the trade routes dried up. The road changed to a rough track covered with fragments of old pottery as it took him under a precarious-looking stone gatehouse. Inside was an ancient timber door, wind-worn and rent with cracks. He peered through, seeing a desolation of ruins surrounding a domed structure half buried in the sand, once perhaps a mosque or a Nestorian church. He pushed the heavy iron latch, to no avail, and then stood back, protected by the tower roof from the sun and the blowing sand. Suddenly there was an electric hum, and the entire surface around him began to lower, an elevator platform large enough to take a small truck. He had expected something like this, but even so it took him by surprise. As it dropped below head height, another platform slid over to close the opening, and he was plunged into darkness. Then all movement ceased and a fluorescent light illuminated the elevator chamber, showing three tunnels leading off in different directions. Doors slid down over two of the entrances, and the elevator platform turned so that he was facing the remaining one. He paused for a moment, touching his tie and brushing the sand off his legs, and then walked forward.

After about a hundred metres, another door slid down behind him and he was in darkness again. He stopped walking, and felt the ground beneath him moving, some form of escalator. It came to a halt, and he was left in utter stillness. There was a curious scent in the air, jasmine perhaps, and he sensed that he was in a larger space. Then a shaft of light came down from high above and lit up a leather chair a few metres in front of him, facing away. Another shaft lit up a large table in front. A man with Chinese features was sitting behind the table, his face looming out of the shadows, the outline of a computer monitor to his right. The man in the suit walked up to the chair, then carefully smoothed his overcoat beneath him and sat down.

The man behind the desk stared at him for a moment and then spoke in English, his accent a mixture of refined British and American. 'So. You found out how to contact me, and now you have discovered my fortress. Normally anyone who comes within fifty kilometres of this place without my invitation is liquidated by my men, but for you I have made a temporary exception.'

The other man said nothing, but crossed his legs and looked casually at the ceiling, then to his left and right. It was as if his gaze had activated a lighting system, and the dark recesses of the chamber filled with subtle shades of colour. He saw that he was within a domed structure, seemingly extending off into infinity. Above him was a dazzling representation of the night sky, projected on to the inside of the dome as if they were in a planetarium. To his left was a long rectangular pool, its water dark and utterly still, surrounded by long-legged ibises, some with their necks up and others bent down with their bills close to the water. But the most striking apparition was the rows of warriors on either side, hundreds of them, identically armoured and holding long poles terminating in elaborate bronze dagger-axes. They seemed alive, staring at him, their eyelids occasionally flickering, a slight rustle and rasp of movement in the background. Beyond them the sky appeared to be swirling, like a desert dust storm, the illusion of movement enveloping the chamber as if they were in a tunnel about to be sucked with the warriors down a vortex into the eye of the storm.

He let his gaze fall back to the man behind the desk, and then spoke. 'A representation of the interior of the third-century BC tomb of the first Chinese emperor Shihuangdi, based on the *Records of the Grand Historian* by Sima Qian.' He spoke quietly and precisely, his English impeccable but with a hint of a French accent. 'The tomb chamber, of course, remains undiscovered beneath the great mound at Xian, though the terracotta warriors and the bronze birds from the pits surrounding the mound are real enough. I hosted a reception at the British Museum at the opening of the travelling exhibition last year. The weapons are more varied than the classic Qin dagger-axe you present here, but then you surely know that. It is a small point.' He gestured up at the stars. 'Outside this chamber, I imagine, you can see this very view at night, in the desert sky unpolluted by the modern world. But you would be deathly cold, and the sand would sting your eyes. In here, you have the illusion of control over the cosmos. That was the conceit of the First Emperor too. It was a conceit that began when Stone Age men first turned their backs on the world of nature, the world they could not control. To some, it made them think they were gods. But such fantasies are just that. The First Emperor remains dead in his hole in the ground, surrounded by crumbling illusions.

Adolf Hitler came to a squalid end in a ditch outside the Führerbunker.' He waved his hand dismissively at the room. 'In my world, power does not come from computer-generated fantasies.' He took off his gloves, laid them on his knee and folded his hands over them. 'I have come to discuss a business arrangement.'

The other man stared at him, then tapped a keyboard set into the table. The entire phantasm disappeared, the warriors and the ibises and the night sky, and the two shafts of light returned. He swivelled his chair and looked at the computer monitor. 'Jean-Pierre Saumerre. Born in Marseille of Algerian Muslim background, but one grandfather French. Educated at the Sorbonne and Cambridge University. After completing a doctorate in econometrics, worked for his family company Arancho, a conglomerate with numerous interests across Europe, Africa and the Middle East. Eight years ago relinquished his role as CEO to enter European Union politics. Meteoric rise through the corridors of power in Brussels, becoming Director-General for Business Affairs eighteen months ago. Board member of the European Central Bank, and presently up for election to vice-presidency of the European Commission.'

He peered at Saumerre over the screen, and then sat back on his chair with a cold smile on his face. He picked up a vicious little knife and pressed the end of the blade gingerly with the tip of one index finger. 'A man very close to holding the purse strings in Brussels, the biggest black hole for tax money in the world. Perhaps, Dr Saumerre, you did not relinquish your family business interests after all.' The man licked the tip of his finger where he had drawn blood, raised the knife with his other hand and suddenly flicked it past Saumerre's face to the wall opposite, where it buried itself to the hilt. He put his hands palm-down on the table and stared at Saumerre, the smile gone. 'You talk of a business arrangement?'

Saumerre waved his hand in the air where the knife had passed as if whisking away a fly, then reached into the breast pocket of his overcoat and extracted a brown envelope, pulling a sheet half out. 'Shang Yong. Born into one of the oldest clans in China, tracing their descent back to the warriors of the First Emperor. A computer-simulation expert, educated in Hong Kong and at boarding school in England, then at UCLA and MIT. After graduating, he disappeared back into China, where he re-emerged as head of the Brotherhood of the Tiger, an ancient secret society that has developed lucrative business interests on the back of the Chinese economic boom. Front companies in Hong Kong and Shanghai, but suspected of operating from a secret base somewhere in the Taklamakan Desert, aiming at virtually feudal control over the frontier region of western China. A megalomaniac who is ruthless to those who stand in his way and responsible for numerous murders in China and around the world. After the usual terrorist suspects, about the top name on Interpol's most-wanted list.'

Shang Yong smiled, and held his arms wide. 'Perhaps Dr Saumerre feels that as he is a god in Brussels, he has some kind of divine power in the Taklamakan too. Are you here to arrest me?'

'I have come alone. At the moment, nobody else knows I am here.'

'Yet I think you are trying to threaten me, Dr Saumerre.'

'We are all being held to ransom. That is the balance of power in our world, is it not? That is why I am here. If you help me to remove one who is threatening me, then the file on you is shut. It will never be reopened, because from then on we will be business partners, to huge mutual advantage.'

'You say *our world*. What do you mean? I think you and I live in different worlds.'

'Not so different. Did you not wonder how I discovered this place? Satellite surveillance shows only a bustling little town, one of many being built by the Chinese in an attempt to colonize the desert and quash local Uighar resistance. Nothing out of the ordinary here, not even the ancient Silk Road fortress, one of many ruins half swallowed and forgotten in the desert. You have to go underground to see what's really here, and to get there you have to pass through a security perimeter that the First Emperor himself would have admired.' Saumerre leaned forward. 'When I say underground, I don't mean this hideaway. I mean deep underground, the oil-bearing shales beneath us. I have known about the Brotherhood of the Tiger for years, and admired your handiwork. The best assassins for hire anywhere, if one can afford them. But then two years ago you took an enormous hit when your key underworld links in the US and Hong Kong were exposed, after you became involved in an operation that stepped over your usual careful boundaries. I know this because you have been putting out feelers. Your plan had been to develop the Taklamakan as your own private fiefdom, to channel all of your income into boring and pumping the oil reserves in secret, then to present the Chinese government with an offer of partnership they could not refuse. After all, the Peking politburo contains two members of the Brotherhood, does it not? Names you would not wish exposed, as that partnership is central to your plan. But you have no capital reserves any more. You have no money to make the oil flow. So your dwindling band of agents in Europe and America and the Far East have been desperately seeking investors.'

Shang Yong stared at him. 'How do you know this?'

'I will let you in on a little secret. In the 1930s, my grandfather was a small-time gangster in Marseille. He was arrested and did time in a French penal colony in the Caribbean, which hardened him. By 1940 he was back in Marseille, but he was arrested again, this time by the Vichy police and the Gestapo for attempting to steal a vault-load of gold and precious stones confiscated from wealthy French Jews. It was an audacious scheme that demonstrated his potential, and his gaolers at a succession of concentration camps in France and Germany showed him grudging respect. He escaped from his final camp near Belsen just before the Allies arrived, returning to his old Marseille haunts penniless but with plenty of secrets, including the location of works of art stolen by the Nazis. He decided he needed a legitimate front for his business. He called it Arancho, after a tattoo of a spider he had acquired at the penal colony in Antigua.' Saumerre lifted his left forearm and unbuttoned the cuff, pulling it up to reveal a smudged dark spider on his arm. 'I bear it too.'

Shang Yong pulled up the sleeve of his loose-fitting robe and revealed his own tattoo, the grimacing face of a tiger. He let the sleeve drop, and beamed at Saumerre. 'So. We really do inhabit the same world. And your political career in Brussels is, shall I say, part of the family business?'

A flicker of a smile passed Saumerre's lips. 'I leave that to your imagination.'

'You wish to invest in our prospecting scheme? That is why you are here?'

Saumerre shook his head. 'I have no interest in your oil. I wish to employ your organization to follow a man, to get from him what I want and then to kill him. The fee I will pay you will be greater than any investment money you will find in the underworld.'

'And who is this man?'

'An archaeologist by trade, but he meddles in a world far bigger than he realizes. His name is Jack Howard.'

Shang Yong went pale. He bunched his fists, then tapped the keyboard and swung the monitor round so that Saumerre could see. It showed the home page of the International Maritime University website, with an anchor logo in the top left corner and a photograph of two men in diving suits holding an ancient amphora, one of them tall with a tousle of dark hair and the other smaller and swarthier, both of them smiling at the camera. Shang Yong pointed at the taller man, then bunched his fists again, his voice contorted with rage. 'Two years ago, in Afghanistan, this man shot and killed one of my best operatives, my own nephew. We were on the trail of a treasure he too was seeking, a jewel from the tomb of the First Emperor that would have given me what I crave, the jewel that made the First Emperor a god. It was Howard who was responsible for shutting down my operations in Hong Kong. Because of Howard I am trapped in this place. Ever since then I have been plotting revenge.' He held his breath, his fists still clenched, then exhaled slowly, relaxing his hands and flexing them. He was still for a moment, then looked at Saumerre shrewdly. 'You knew this name would enrage me. You have tried to find my weakness. I do not need you to exact my vengeance on Howard.'

Saumerre stared stonily at him. 'You have been plotting revenge, but with each passing day your empire shrivels, my friend. You have fewer than a dozen skilled operatives left, men and women who can operate internationally, who can kill and get away with it. Ever since Howard exposed the Brotherhood, they have been hunted down, and when one is killed or arrested there is no longer anyone trained as a replacement. Your face is known to every security service in the world. Even here you are safe only as long as the Brotherhood retains influence in Peking, but that is only two men, two elderly uncles of yours, two names I could give to Interpol right now. Everything hangs in the balance. Turn away from me, and the Brotherhood will fall. Come with me, and the Brotherhood will rise again, and you will truly have the wealth and power of the First Emperor.'

Shang Yong tapped a finger on the table, and continued to look at Saumerre through narrowed eyes. 'Give me more. Prove yourself.'

Saumerre paused. 'For years I have been on the trail of something my grandfather knew about, a lost ancient treasure excavated by Heinrich Schliemann in Greece in the nineteenth century, hidden by him and then rediscovered and hidden away again by the Nazis. It is called the palladion, and my grandfather knew it would unlock untold Nazi secrets. Six months ago, Jack Howard and his team began excavations at the site of Troy, scene of another of Schliemann's triumphs, and got wind of my quest. I found it expedient to have Howard's daughter detained to try to force him to give me the palladion when I thought he had found it. I used a Russian organization my family has employed before, but they let me down. They did not have the quality of the Brotherhood of the Tiger.'

Shang Yong slammed his fist on the table. 'We are the best.'

'That is why I am here.'

'The Russians failed, where my men would have succeeded.'

'Howard's security people uncovered what I have told you about my family past. If he had exposed me, I would not be here now. But he suspected that I knew more, that through my grandfather I could have knowledge of secret Nazi weapons that might fall into the wrong hands, that to expose me might persuade me to trigger a course of events that could lead to a terrorist attack or start a war. Howard and I have a stand-off. Any hint of my taking retribution against him or his people would lead to instant exposure of my criminal activities. So you see, this is personal for me too.'

'Why do you choose to act now?'

'His security people, and I am sure their contacts in the British secret service, have been waiting for a chink to appear in my armour, for something to prove that Howard's suspicions were correct. I have been waiting for what I knew was only a matter of time. They have begun to excavate a site that was uncovered last year, a Nazi bunker near the last concentration camp where my grandfather was imprisoned. I no longer have need of the palladion to open what my

grandfather knew was there. Howard an...
job for me. I have people in my pay who...
what I want.'

'And you will have what they find?'

'As you said. In Europe, I am a god. The bu...
Europe. I will find a way.'

Shang Yong bunched his fist. 'Howard can be killed now.'

Saumerre shook his head. 'To do that would lead to instant
exposure. I will wait until he has discovered what I want. He
will then be irrelevant to my plans. Other forces will have
been set in motion, and my charade in Brussels will no longer
be of consequence. Eliminating Howard will simply be a
matter of personal satisfaction for me and for you.'

Shang Yong tapped the table again. 'Tell me something,
Saumerre. Your mother was Algerian. You are a practising
Muslim, yes?'

'You have read my profile. As a politician I have huge
support among the Muslim community in France, and I can
always count on backing from the Middle East and Gulf
states. I am the only European politician of my stature who
is perceived to be a Muslim, and it has helped my rise
immeasurably. The utopian fools in Brussels think that the
solution to Islamic fundamentalism is to encourage more
Muslims into positions of high political power, and I am seen
as the trailblazer.'

'You say they are fools. So you think the path of the
fundamentalists is an irrevocable one?'

'I think there are many paths to the glory of Allah.'

Shang Yong looked at him shrewdly. 'The Brotherhood of
the Tiger does not heed that call. If you are set on that path,

you have come knocking on the wrong door. I can get my revenge against Jack Howard another way.'

Saumerre paused, tapped the envelope on his knee to drop the sheet back inside, then pushed it back into his overcoat, stopping halfway. 'So be it. But you are missing an opportunity. I am offering you a flat fee of five hundred million euros, half wired to your account now, half when I have Howard's head on a platter. And if I discover the prize I am after, then I will cut you in on half of a ransom I will demand of the world, a ransom they will have no choice but to pay and which will make your fee look like small change. But if you are unwilling to do business, then I will leave now.'

'You will not get past the door.'

Saumerre looked at his watch. 'If I am not back at my desk in Brussels by 0930 tomorrow morning, an automated sequence will cause a little red light to flash in the Pentagon in Washington. A top-secret protocol will be activated regarding verified and actionable information on known terrorist hideaways. The file that will open under my authority as a European commissioner will show that Shang Yong and his Brotherhood have financed fundamentalist terrorist attacks on Western targets as a way of furthering their own business interests. You see, you may speculate about my activities, but I know about yours. The file will contain GPS co-ordinates for this chamber we are standing in now. By 1000 hours an executive decision will have been taken in the White House, and by 1015 a massive cruise missile strike will have been launched from the carrier battle group presently in the Sea of Japan, with the secret connivance of those members of the Chinese government who would also like to see your operations destroyed. By 1215 everything here will be obliterated, whether I am still present or not. The countdown to this scenario only stops if I deactivate the sequence. It can be reactivated at any time.'

Shang Yong was silent, his face set in stone. Suddenly he got up, clapped his hands together and walked over to Saumerre, his face beaming. 'We are cut from the same mould. I think the play-acting is over, yes? Of course we can do business.' He switched up the light, dimming the fantasy world around them, put a hand on Saumerre's shoulder and gestured towards the computer monitor behind his desk. 'You can make the wire transaction here. You have a wish list? It will take me two days to prepare a team. Come with me. I want to know what it is they are searching for in that bunker. And I want to plan the execution of Jack Howard.'

5

South-eastern Black Sea, off Turkey

'So what went wrong?'

Scott Macalister strode into the operations room on *Seaquest II* and shut the door behind him. Jack swivelled his chair from the computer monitor on the central table to face him, and Costas looked up from his tablet computer beside Jack. Macalister was immaculately turned out in his reserve naval officer's uniform, the four gold bands of a captain on his sleeves and a row of ribbons on his jacket from his years of service in the Canadian Navy and Coast Guard before joining IMU. He stood square in the centre of the room, his white officer's cap tucked under one arm and the other arm behind his back.

'What went right,' Costas replied, 'is that we collected more data on the volcano than we could ever have got using remote sensing. You've seen some of the images already, and the lab guys are processing the rest now. My immediate assessment of the danger level went straight to Lanowski to put in his report for the Turkish authorities as soon as I'd finished it in the recompression chamber about an hour ago.'

Jack leaned forward with his elbows on his knees, and looked up at Macalister pensively. 'What went wrong was that we took a big gamble, and escaped by the skin of our teeth. If it hadn't been for the crack in the rock that allowed us to escape, we'd still be down there now. You'd be having to explain our disappearance and what I was doing here. My presence would be seen by our colleagues on the international monitoring committee as a direct contravention of the agreement not to dive on the site for archaeological purposes. I know you've done everything you can to be shipshape for the monitoring team and they're due here any time. I'm sorry to have put you through this.'

Macalister stood still for a moment, then relaxed his arms and tugged his beard. 'The important thing is that Costas is right. The data on the lava flow are exceptional. The Turkish geologists already know we've bored a tunnel and sent down a submersible with sensing equipment. I can tell them we tried to use an ROV, and that would explain Costas' presence. Everyone knows that IMU does not send a state-of-the-art ROV anywhere in the world without Costas Kazantzakis attached to it by an umbilical cord. That'll also explain the departure of the Lynx this evening, carrying Costas back to the underwater excavation at Troy where Jack Howard urgently needs his help to raise the Shield of Agamemnon.'

He turned to Costas. 'I take it the ROV is still down there in the volcano?'

Costas looked crestfallen. 'Afraid so.'

'As for Dr Howard, who officially isn't here, he needs to be spirited away on the helicopter before then. We need the helipad to be clear by late afternoon for the arrival of the inspection team, and we need all available space to accommodate them.' He eyed Jack sternly. 'You okay with Mustafa Alkozen taking your cabin?'

Jack nodded. 'We've done it before. He and I rotated bunk space for a month in a submarine during a joint exercise in the Mediterranean, when he was the boat's weapons officer and I was a seconded diver from the Royal Navy. And he is IMU's Turkish representative, so he should have the best bunk.'

'Okay.' Macalister pulled on his cap, turned to go and then tapped his watch. 'Sixteen hundred hours on the helipad, right?'

Jack nodded. 'Roger that.'

Macalister stared at him for a moment, then shook his head and gave a wry smile. 'A wing and a prayer, Jack.'

Jack took a deep breath, then exhaled forcefully. 'A wing and a prayer.'

'I saw some of the images. Those rock carvings. Pretty fantastic stuff. You can show me the rest when this is over.' Macalister walked through the doorway and was gone, leaving them listening to the hum of the fluorescent lights and the whir of the computer fans.

'Phew,' Costas said.

Jack swivelled his chair back to the monitor. 'That reminded me of my first term in the Royal Naval College at Dartmouth, after Cambridge,' he said. 'I was always getting into trouble for stepping out of line. For taking too much initiative, I told them. My Howard seafaring ancestors were always mavericks. We're not really designed to take orders.'

'I've noticed,' Costas said.

'It was lucky the special forces guy at the college spotted me, otherwise I'd have been politely told to pack my bags.'

'Macalister has got a point,' Costas said.

Jack took another deep breath, and nodded. 'Of course he has a point. And he's the best damn captain we've ever had. I intend never to put him in that position again.'

'You know what they say, Jack. Once you've taken that extra step beyond the boundary, you'll only want to do it again.'

'Then it'd be time for me to stand down. I can't let my personal ambitions impede IMU's other projects, not least ones with a major scientific and humanitarian outcome like this one. If Macalister hadn't told us just now that our data on the volcano had made it worthwhile, I'd seriously be considering vacating my cabin for good.'

'Don't tell Rebecca that.' Costas grinned. 'She's waiting on the sidelines ready to jump in.'

'That's the other factor. Every time I have a near-death experience underwater, I think of Rebecca. She's already lost her mother.'

'But you wouldn't be the same person for her if you didn't take the risks. It's all part of the tapestry you've woven for yourself, Jack. What was it Othello said? "There's magic in the web of it."'

Jack gave a wry smile. 'Well then I just need to keep that

web from unravelling. We need to stay on the edge, not stray over it. Copy that?'

'Whatever you say.'

'My buddy.' He slapped Costas on the shoulder. 'And by the way, thanks for saving my life.'

Costas waved his hand. 'I thought it was the other way round.'

'Let's get back to our images from this morning. I want as much of this wrapped up as possible before I have to leave.' Jack turned to the computer screen, arched his back and stretched his arms. He seemed to feel every sinew and muscle in his body, and stretching released a sensation that coursed through him like a drug. He and Costas had just emerged from four hours in the recompression chamber breathing pure oxygen, but even so his system was still working overtime to flush out the excess nitrogen from their dive. His body was willing him to go up to his cabin and lie down, but he knew that the adrenalin that was still coursing through him would keep him alert. And he knew that if he did try to rest, his mind would only return to that moment when he and Costas could have safely returned after having discovered the pillar with the golden Atlantis symbol. *What was it that had driven him on, driven him to risk everything?* He put the thought from his mind, and refocused on the screen. The important thing was that they had less than two hours now to process the imagery from their dive, and if they let that opportunity slip, it might be weeks before they were together again on *Seaquest II* or at the IMU campus in England. Jack had seen astonishing things today, as astonishing as anything he had seen in his archaeological career, and he wanted those images to be in the forefront of his mind as the excavation at Troy wound down. He had gone back to Atlantis with questions, and they were still burning. Who were these people? Where had they gone? *Who were their gods?*

'Jack, this is incredible. Lanowski's just finishing his 3-D CGI map of the site. The final version should be streaming online in a few minutes.'

Costas turned back to his screen, and Jack continued staring at the image he had called up on his monitor before Macalister had come in. It was a still from the video he had taken with his helmet camera inside the volcano that morning; below it he had arranged a line of thumbnails of other Neolithic sites in the Near East that he had pulled up for comparison. The image from the morning was raw, unrefined, the foreground still specked with white where the light from his headlamp had reflected off particles in the water. But seeing it like that made it more vivid, as if he were still caught in the amazement of that moment when he had first entered the chamber. It showed the pillars standing like sentinels, three-metre-tall monoliths carved out of volcanic tufa, each one rising to a T-shape a metre or more wide. He could see animals carved in shallow relief on the pillars – lions, wild boar, scorpions and spiders, leopards and bulls. On the back wall of the cave he spotted something he had not seen on the dive: a bull's skull fixed into a hole in the rock, half in and half out, the bone plastered over and the horns painted red. Above it was a painting of vultures swooping down on a headless human body, shaped crudely in outline; beside that were the spectral remains of painted animals, visible where they had not been hacked away and smoothed out. Not only the pillars but also the carvings on them seemed to have been freshly chiselled, sharply delineated. *Out with the old, in with the new.* Archaeologists had begun to talk about the Neolithic as a time of religious transition, a time when humans first conceived of gods with human characteristics, gods who were to play out all the human capacity for cruelty and greed in the mythologies of Mesopotamia and the Near East. Jack stared at the pillars. Was this where it had all begun? *Was Atlantis the birthplace of the gods?*

He held the mouse and dragged the image up to see the floor of the chamber. The lab analysis of the sample he had taken had just come through, showing that the stone floor had been covered in layers of terrazzo, burnt lime. Embedded within the lime was the most extraordinary sight of all: the plastered human skulls that seemed to be emerging from the ground in the same way that the bull's skull was emerging from the rock wall. He scrolled over the other skulls, the ones without plaster, some of them fallen alongside the three stone basins he could now see, each about half a metre high and carved out of the living rock. The scattered skulls and the basins were partly covered with the calcite accretion that had settled over the floor since the inundation. It was a haunting, ghostly scene, with the pillars like rough-formed bodies standing in the background, towering over the toppled skulls. Jack tried to retain a professional detachment, but it made the hairs stand up on the back of his neck. *What had been going on here?*

Costas slid his chair alongside, minimized the image and tapped a key. A three-dimensional lattice appeared on the screen, angled as if they were viewing it from the upper right-hand corner. The terrain mapper had been designed to project a holographic image on to the miniature screens inside their e-suit helmets, to help them navigate over seabed features in poor light conditions, using GPS, sonar, photogrammetric and other data previously fed into the computer, but here it was being used to build up a flat-screen isometric image of the site. As they watched, the grid lattice disappeared below a contoured image of the Black Sea bathymetry, zooming down to the abyssal plain in the centre of the sea and then rising up the slope towards the Turkish shore and their present position some fifteen nautical miles off the border with the Republic of Georgia. Jack saw the twin peaks of the volcano just below the surface of the sea, and then the slope where the flow of lava and other volcanic fallout had buried the ruins of the ancient city five years ago, in a terrifying eruption that had nearly cost them their lives.

'I'll pause it here,' Costas said, tapping a key. 'You remember when we left this place five years ago we thought the eruption would have destroyed pretty well everything of the lower town?'

Jack nodded. 'You said you'd need a sub-bottom profiler that could see through lava to find out what was left. A powerful low-frequency echo sounder. The stuff you've been tinkering with in the engineering workshop at IMU for the last five years.'

'Not tinkering, Jack. Perfecting.'

'Okay. Perfecting.'

The image sharpened, showing details of rock outcrops and fissures on the slopes. It was like looking at an aerial view of Mount St Helens in Washington State after the 1980 eruption, a scene of utter devastation. Along the seaward slope, where

Jack remembered five years before seeing dense pueblo-style buildings, all he saw now was a great slick like a frozen mudslide, completely burying the original rocky substrate and all of the ancient structures. His heart sank as he saw the scale of the destruction. 'It's much worse than I feared. Those were mud-brick buildings. The lava must have destroyed everything.'

'Well, prepare to be amazed.'

Costas tapped a key and the image transformed. The wide beds of lava constricted to narrow flows down the side of the volcano, like frozen rivers. In between Jack saw ghostly rectilinear outlines covering the slope. Costas pointed at the upper part of the screen. 'You're right, the lava would have destroyed all the mud-brick structures in their path. Where we dived this morning was through one of the solidified flows from five years ago, and the only structure that survived was that stone pillar with the golden Atlantis symbol. But the lava flows are much narrower than we thought. When we were boring the tunnel yesterday, I used the submersible to take some core samples further down the slope, and I've just had a look at the results. Most of it is not lava but pyroclastic flow, solidified mud and ash. It looks as if the volcanic ash hardened with lime into a kind of hydraulic concrete, like the stuff we know the people of Atlantis used to make waterproof walls. Where the flow was pyroclastic, it didn't destroy Atlantis. It actually preserved it.'

He tapped again, and the image sharpened further. Jack let out a low whistle. 'Well I'll be damned,' he said. It was as if the flow had been peeled away to reveal intact structures beneath, a vast complex of flat-roofed buildings that seemed to have been built organically, reaching three or four storeys high and spreading up the slope of the volcano. Jack stared, shaking his head. 'It's fantastic. It's like jumping back five years to when we first saw Atlantis from our Aquapods. I never thought I'd see that again.'

'Well, we won't be excavating it in a hurry. Even if the volcano goes quiet and we can get down there again, it'd be like mining on the moon. Roman Herculaneum was covered by pyroclastic flow from Vesuvius, and they've only excavated one fifth of the site in two hundred and fifty years. And Herculaneum's not under a hundred metres of water poisoned by sulphur dioxide.'

Jack was still stunned by the image. 'More so than anything we saw five years ago, this view is incredibly similar to Neolithic houses found elsewhere.'

'That place on the Konya plain? Çatalhöyük?'

Jack nodded. 'About three hundred kilometres south-east of here.' He reached over and tapped one of the thumbnails, revealing an artist's impression of a town rising out of a plain, the structures built together like an Indian pueblo in the southern United States. 'Do you remember I took a few days off from the excavation at Troy last month to go there? A friend of mine is leading an expedition into the Taurus mountains to the south, looking for caves that might contain paintings and other clues to their Stone Age ancestors. The excavations at Çatalhöyük in the 1960s gave the world an image of what the first Neolithic towns looked like.'

'It dates to the same time period as Atlantis?'

Jack nodded. 'Early Neolithic, the first period of settled farming after the end of the Ice Age, beginning about eleven thousand years ago. Atlantis was inundated by the Black Sea in the late sixth millennium BC, but the radiocarbon dates we took from timbers in the buildings five years ago show that some of these structures date at least two millennia before that. Çatalhöyük flourished in the eighth millennium BC. But there were even earlier Neolithic sites.' He touched another thumbnail and the scene transformed to an image of a Near Eastern tell, an ancient city mound cut through by old excavation trenches with ruined walls protruding from the sections. 'That's Jericho, in the Jordan Valley, just north of the Dead Sea,' he said. 'You know the Old Testament story of Joshua leading the Israelites into the Promised Land, and coming to Jericho?'

Costas screwed up his eyes for a moment, then recited: '*So the people shouted when the priests blew with their trumpets: and it came to pass, when the people heard the sound of the trumpet, and the people shouted with a great shout, that the walls fell down flat.*' He turned to Jack ruefully. 'The benefits of a Greek Orthodox background, and then a boarding school in New York where we had to memorize passages from the Bible.'

Jack grinned at him. 'You never cease to amaze me. Is that how you got your interest in poetry?'

'Nope. That was the Dead Poets Society, after school. We had to join something, and I hated sports. It meant I could hide in the back row and doodle submarine engine-room layouts.'

'Some of the poetry must have washed off on you.'

'That's what Jeremy says. You know, he can declaim whole passages of Shakespeare. We do it when we're alone in the engineering lab. That's how I got that Othello quote.'

Jack shook his head. 'Well, I just hope some of the poetry goes into the submersibles.'

'Exactly what Jeremy said when we finished Little Joey.' Costas sighed. 'Little Joey, who has made the ultimate sacrifice.'

Jack put a hand on Costas' shoulder. 'I really am sorry.' He turned back to the image on the screen. 'The excavations at Jericho during the 1950s revealed a perimeter wall around the city almost four metres high, as well as an eight-metre-high stone tower. The conventional Biblical chronology puts Joshua about the middle of the second millennium BC. But the walls of Jericho didn't date anywhere near that time. They dated a staggering six millennia earlier, to the eighth or even the ninth millennium BC. So the archaeology tells a far more fantastic story than the Bible. The excavations at Jericho were the first to put the early Neolithic on the map, and showed that collective endeavour to make large monuments like walls and towers was possible right at the dawn of civilization, at a time when most humans still lived as hunter-gatherers.'

Costas whistled. 'And wasn't Jericho the site where the first of those plastered skulls was found?'

Jack nodded. 'Just like the ones in the inner sanctum we saw today. There was a connection between these early communities across this region, a connection in their religion, their belief system. But Jericho's at the periphery of that early Neolithic world, at the south-west tip of the so-called fertile crescent that extended up to Anatolia and down through Mesopotamia. I believe that the true heartland lay here, along the Black Sea coast before it flooded, and down into Anatolia further south. And I'm not just talking about Çatalhöyük.

Two other sites have revolutionized our picture of early-Neolithic religion.'

He touched another thumbnail, and Costas' jaw dropped. 'Holy cow,' he exclaimed. 'Those pillars. They're almost identical.' It was as if the underwater sanctum from Atlantis had been lifted out of the cave and on to dry land, and sunk in a depression in the ground to make it semi-subterranean, like a crypt. The photograph showed a partially excavated oval structure about ten metres across, with T-shaped pillars placed at intervals around a coarsely built wall. On the nearest pillars they could just make out low-relief carvings of animals and vultures, and what appeared to be a human arm.

'That's at Göbekli Tepe, about two hundred kilometres south of here on the Anatolian plateau,' Jack said. He touched another thumbnail, and a similar image appeared showing a group of pillars arranged in rows within a chamber, sunk into the ground but rectilinear in shape. 'And here's Nevali Çori, the second site. There's also another pillar with an arm, and a sculpture in the round showing a human head with a vulture on it.'

'So this is why you were so excited when you saw that chamber today.'

'It fits into a pattern. These are among the most extraordinary archaeological discoveries ever made.'

'What's the date?' Costas asked.

'That's what makes these discoveries so earth-shattering. The Göbekli Tepe complex dates to at least 9000 BC. *That's eleven thousand years old.* Before the first evidence for agriculture, before the first settled towns. Even before Jericho. This place was built by hunter-gatherers. They're even calling this the world's first temple, the Garden of Eden. But there's something not right about that. Temples imply worship, and that's a modern concept. Look at the vultures, the skulls. I don't think anything was worshipped here. I think this was a place for ceremony, for ritual, but more like an access point to the spirit world.'

'Like the idea of an *axis mundi*, a portal between hell and heaven.'

'Except that our idea of the underworld, of hell, may be an invention of the developing religions *after* this period, something to frighten people into compliance. It's from then on that priest-kings began to shape religion to their own purposes, invoking human-like gods that melded in the eyes of the people with the priest-kings themselves and were worshipped as one.'

Costas gestured at the pillars. 'How long did this place last?'

'That's what's so fascinating. Göbekli Tepe wasn't transformed into a later religious complex. Some time around 8000 BC, it was deliberately buried. Thousands of years later, the same thing happens to henges and burial mounds in prehistoric Europe. In some places it may have to do with ancestor worship, with the idea that ancestors who were first venerated in these places had become too old and distant and needed to be parcelled away, to be buried to make way for the new. But I don't think that provides the full explanation. I think we're looking at the eclipsing of a whole belief system, one that was somehow still threatening enough for the new priests to order the destruction of the ancient ritual places, for those sites never to be used again. I believe the turning point came with the development of the first towns and cities, with the rise of priest-kings. They came at a time of new gods, gods that were beginning to emerge in the final period at sites like Göbekli Tepe when those pillars with the arms like humans were erected.'

'And at Atlantis maybe the same thing was happening,' Costas suggested, tapping a thumbnail to recall the underwater image from that morning. 'This sanctum was once open-air, on the flank of the volcano. It was once a cave with paintings, but it looks as if all that old stuff was being upgraded, with those pillars and new carvings. At the end, there was only a small entranceway through a masonry wall, and then that was blocked off. Someone was trying to obliterate it.'

'Exactly,' Jack enthused. 'And all of this involves planning and manpower, whether you're creating the site or destroying it. It doesn't take a race of supermen to build a complex like this one, but it does take plenty of toil and organization. If this was the Garden of Eden, it wasn't a place to lie around in and eat apples. There was a lot of quarrying involved to make those pillars, using primitive stone and antler tools. They were free-standing monoliths: they'd been quarried and dragged into position. The biggest of them is thought to weigh at least twenty tons. *Twenty tons.* That was my point about the walls of Jericho. Hundreds of people were brought together to work on these monuments, persuaded by some authority to carry out back-breaking and dangerous labour.'

'So how does the date fit with Atlantis?'

'I think what we found today is really early, older than anything else. The cave paintings in that Atlantis sanctum are Palaeolithic, at least twelve thousand years old. And five years ago we found the other cave deep in the mountainside, the one we dubbed the Hall of the Ancestors, with organic paint pigments we radiocarbon-dated back at least thirty-five thousand years, as old as the earliest cave paintings anywhere in the world. This volcano was a site of religious significance way back into the Ice Age. Shamans must have come here from miles around to go deep inside the mountain and try to access the spirit world.'

Costas nodded again at the image. 'So at the beginning of the Neolithic, say eleven thousand years ago, you've got a new group arriving?'

'I'd suggest new ideas from within, even from the shamans themselves, a new generation perhaps who could see how the world around them was changing and wanted to maintain control over it. They were people with a new religious power they could impose on the local population. People with the drive and vision of the original settlers at the site, who could translate that energy in a different way. A group whose influence soon spread far and wide over Anatolia and the Fertile Crescent, to places like Göbekli Tepe and Çatalhöyük and Jericho.'

'You said they had power over the local population, Jack. Is that how they built this place? Did they enslave the population?'

Jack pursed his lips. 'It's possible. Remember, the original people here were hunter-gatherers, the ones who found these caves and made the paintings. It's even possible that organized agriculture was forced on them by the new priests as a way of having settled labour available to build religious monuments. That's the kind of radical idea archaeologists started to play with when the temple at Göbekli Tepe was found, a temple older than the settlement around it, older even than the first evidence for agriculture. If we can pin that idea down, corroborate it, then Atlantis is an even bigger revelation than I could have imagined.'

'So what's going on at the time of the Black Sea flood?'

Jack paused. 'When I was researching our discovery of Atlantis, I looked at all the original flood myths: the Greek myth of Deucalion, the Old Testament account of Noah, the ancient Mesopotamian epic of Gilgamesh. There was no doubt in my mind that they all originated from the same natural catastrophe, the sea-level rise at the end of the Ice Age, and more specifically the flooding of the Black Sea over the Bosporus in the sixth millennium BC. A date in the Neolithic is even hinted at in the stories. The account of Noah taking breeding pairs of animals matches what we know happened when early farmers spread from Anatolia to the islands of the Mediterranean such as Cyprus, where the excavations of Neolithic sites produce bones of animals that were not indigenous to the islands.'

'You're talking about domestic animals?'

Jack nodded. 'Goats, sheep, cattle, tied down in longboats and rowed across from the mainland.' He stared at the image of the carvings on the pillars, showing leopards and bulls. 'But for this very early period, when animals were just beginning to be domesticated, we have to keep an open mind about that. Our focus is too often on finding an economic rationale: you take domestic animals with you because they provide food and clothing. But look at these carvings. You see bulls, yes, but are they bulls for food or bulls for ceremonies, to help shamans enter a spirit world? Were wild bulls first corralled and herded for *that* purpose? Did animal husbandry for food only arise later, after people had settled around these sacred sites and the corralling and breeding of animals acquired a new purpose?'

Costas leaned back, thinking. 'I remember that the palaeoecological study done by IMU five years ago showed an abundance of wild animals in this area, plenty for hunter-gatherer groups just after the Ice Age. If you've got enough meat that way, why try to domesticate animals?'

'That's the point,' Jack said. 'And when there's no economic rationale, you look to other explanations. That's where religion comes in.'

'So what about these pillars?' Costas asked.

Jack paused. 'The most intriguing group of texts I studied were the early Babylonian flood and creation myths, first written down on clay tablets in the third millennium BC in Mesopotamia. They name gods, like Enlil the all-powerful and Ishtar, goddess of love, and it's just possible that those names originate in this period of the Neolithic. The flood story in the Epic of Gilgamesh seems to derive from an earlier story, called the Atrahasis, meaning "When the gods were men". The Atrahasis and the other early creation myths contain a group of gods called the Annunu, and sometimes another group, the Iggigi. Later they take on more character and become an established part of the Mesopotamian pantheon, but to begin with they're nameless, faceless, like inchoate beings. They're like these pillars, which seem to have a human form within them, half in and half out of the spirit world.'

Costas leaned forward, staring at the image. 'The famous

cave paintings at Lascaux and the other Palaeolithic sites sometimes show human hands, created in outline by the artist pressing his hand on the wall and flicking paint around it. Look at the hands on those pillars. It's as if the sculptors had rarely represented humans before, and these are like blanks for statues, roughly shaped, with just the hands appearing, the only part of the human form they were used to representing.'

'Maybe it wasn't that they'd never represented humans before,' Jack said quietly. 'Maybe they'd never represented *gods* before.'

'But you talked of the bulls as sacred. Weren't they gods?'

'Not worshipped, but used as a conduit by the shaman to travel to the spirit world, real flesh-and-blood animals that could become spirit animals.'

Costas narrowed his eyes. 'So you're suggesting that the concept of god was a Neolithic invention?'

'It's been nagging at me for five years. I knew the story here was more than just a fabulous archaeological discovery, a dazzling view of the foundation of civilization. There's something here that should make us question ourselves, question the very basis of the belief systems that have kept people going for the last ten thousand years.'

Costas let out a low whistle. 'And this all begins here.'

'The earliest Babylonian creation myths tell how agriculture and animal husbandry were brought from a sacred mountain, a place called Dû-Re, the home of the Annunu.'

'The sacred mountain of Dû-Re,' Costas repeated slowly. 'Are you thinking what I'm thinking? Atlantis?'

Jack took a deep breath. 'The Babylonian creation myths always seem to look north beyond the mountains towards the uplands of Anatolia, to the places where we know cereals were first cultivated and wild animals first tamed. It was in Mesopotamia that agriculture first took off in a big way, along the arid riverbanks of the desert where irrigation and cultivation really were an economic rationale, crucial to the expansion of population where there were few wild resources. But I don't believe those ideas just trickled down from the nearest early farming communities in Anatolia like Çatalhöyük. Big ideas don't trickle, they move quickly. And I believe those ideas could have come with a wave of refugees from the flood on the Black Sea, with a priesthood who were on the verge of obliterating their Stone Age past, who brought with them their new gods and their new ability to control people. As for the Annunu of Babylonian myth, I think we may just be looking at them right now.' He pointed to the pillars on the screen, then tapped his fingers on the desk. 'I want to find out where else they went. I want to find a place where we don't have to look back at these people through their ancestors, through all the accreted layers of later civilization, in Anatolia, the Aegean, Egypt, Mesopotamia. I want to find a place away from the cradle of civilization where some of the old priesthood may have gone, the shamans, where they may have tried to found a new Atlantis.'

Costas pressed one of the thumbnails showing a map, and stabbed a finger at the eastern part of the Black Sea, at the site of Atlantis. 'What about this for an idea? Before the flood seven-and-a-half thousand years ago, Atlantis was the most prominent volcano in the region, a classic symmetrical cone with the distinctive twin peak where the caldera had collapsed in some ancient eruption. The level area between was built up as a ceremonial platform in the early Neolithic, leading to the entrance to the cave complex that became the inner sanctum you saw this morning.' He moved his finger down towards the southern border of Turkey. 'Now to Çatalhöyük. I remember reading the geological report, which showed that obsidian knives and blades found there came from the nearby extinct volcanoes of Göllü and Nenezi Dag. The obsidian had some kind of ritual significance, right?' He reached over and picked up the large hardback volume that had been lying beside the computer, Jack's report on the discovery of Atlantis five years before. He pointed at the image on the cover, a Neolithic wall painting that seemed to show a complex of structures below a mountain. 'And from Çatalhöyük we have this, a painting that may show Atlantis, with the twin peak of the volcano behind the town. All of this suggests the significance of volcanoes, and especially the one here.'

Jack nodded. 'By choosing that cover, I wanted to show that Atlantis was not unique, but was part of a pattern, though one we didn't fully understand five years ago. And it was an image of Atlantis as the people themselves saw it, the people whose minds I want to get into now.'

'Okay. Then we move to that Babylonian story of the mountain of Dû-Re, the home of the gods,' Costas continued. 'The most prominent mountains in the region to the north of Babylonia are all volcanoes.' He shifted his finger to the Aegean Sea to the left, between Turkey and Greece. 'And here's the island of Thera, the volcano that blew its top in the second millennium BC and destroyed Bronze Age civilization on Crete. Five years ago we thought that some of the priests of Atlantis could have escaped to Thera millennia before, where they may have established another sanctuary on the upper slopes of the volcano, trying to emulate what they had been forced to leave at Atlantis. You get my drift?'

'We should be looking for more volcanoes.'

'Not just natural volcanoes. Man-made ones.' Costas reached for his tablet computer, ran his finger over the screen and handed it to Jack. 'I was doing this as Macalister came in. Running a few alignments. It was just a hunch, but the similarities are striking.' Jack glanced down at the screen. On the left was a classic volcano cross-section, showing a magma chamber coming up from the earth's mantle with an eruption above it. On the right was a cross-section through a triangular structure, showing a horizontal passageway leading into a central chamber and above it a narrow vertical chute to a structure on the top. 'Not just volcanoes, Jack. Pyramids.'

Jack stared at the image. 'The Mayan pyramid of Palenque, in the Yucatán?'

'It's the best representation of what I mean.' The ship's phone beside the door rang. Costas walked over to it, spoke for a minute and then returned to Jack, sitting down and peering at him. 'What's eating you? I know that look.'

Jack stared at the screen a moment longer, his brow furrowed in thought. 'There's something momentous here, something that upsets our whole picture of the rise of civilization. It's tied in with the origins of human conflict. Wild man versus civilized man. And I think it could have been all due to religion. At the dawn of the Neolithic, men began to turn against their ancestral ways. Until the gods won out, there must have been conflict. I've been thinking about the Garden of Eden again, Costas, and I've been seeing terrible bloodshed. To the first priest-kings, the old religion may have been a far greater threat to their power base than rival states. Religious war may be as old as civilization. And the cause was the newly created gods.'

'What do you think happened here?'

Jack shook his head. 'I don't know. We have to try to understand Neolithic religion. What it was that frightened the new priests about the old.'

'Well, this should help. Jeremy's just arrived in the Lynx from Troy. Officially he's come to do some radiocarbon dates in the lab on the ship. He thinks they've found a really old layer at the site, possibly Neolithic. But he's actually here to see us. At the moment, IMU's best imaging facility is in the excavation house at Troy, so I sent him some of our raw video data from this morning to process. He's hopping with excitement. Says you've got to see it.'

Jack glanced at his watch. 'Okay. We've got a couple of hours until Macalister boots me out. A couple of hours to solve the mystery of this place. Maybe to rewrite the origins of civilization.'

'I'm just a simple submersibles expert, Jack. All I want is to build another ROV.'

Jack shot him a penetrating look. 'This may be bigger than any treasure we've ever hunted, Costas. We're talking about the origin of the gods.'

'So what do I say to Jeremy?'

'Call him in.'

Costas got up to go back to the phone, then turned. 'Oh. I forgot to say. Lanowski's coming too. He's going to try something at the ROV monitor station. It's Little Joey. There's a chance he might still be transmitting.'

Jack put his hand on Costas' arm. 'You've got to let it go.'

'I'm being serious. You remember when we drove the submersible up after the dive this morning? We could see where the caldera had imploded, but I've looked at the mapping data that Lanowski and I did yesterday, and I reckon that the new rim lies just inside the point where you entered that chamber. It's possible that the ROV is still intact. The volcano's rumbling away, and the chances are the next little hiccup will take the chamber out, but it's worth having a go.'

'How could you get a signal from under all that lava?'

'There might be a crack somewhere above the chamber. I remembered the electromagnetic disturbance we experienced and wondered whether that had clouded a signal. That's where Lanowski comes in.'

'Just as long as it doesn't cause you more pain than gain.'

'There's a reason I'm doing this, Jack. When I was still tethered to the ROV while you were escaping from the chamber, I glanced at the screen inside my helmet. As soon as you cut the tether, all of the recorded imagery was lost. That's a fault Jeremy and I need to get right for the next model. But I swear I saw something at the back of the chamber. It wasn't cave paintings or those pillars, it was something else. If Little Joey hasn't gone walkabout from where you left him, he might still be seeing it.'

'Okay. Good. Do what you can.'

'And Lanowski's got something else he wants to show you.'

'Not with his trusty portable blackboard, I hope. We haven't got time for three-hour explanations.'

'Something about going back to first principles. About not seeing the wood for the trees. About how if we want to find out where the last shamans of Atlantis went, we need to go back to what got us to Atlantis in the first place. The evidence. The clues. How it's been staring us in the face all the time.'

'Sounds a little too straightforward for Lanowski.'

'Wrong. He thinks it's too complex for the computer. He's going to have to do the analysis in his head.'

Jack raised his eyes. '*That* sounds like Lanowski.' He turned back to the screen and clicked the mouse to zoom in on one of the pillars they had seen that morning, a white monolith rising starkly in front of the cave wall, the T-shaped arms extending outwards. He remembered five years ago in the flooded tunnels of Atlantis seeing lines of priests and priestesses carved in low relief on the walls, solemn, hieratic figures with braided beards and hair, wearing conical hats and carrying staffs, marching confidently forward. They had been freshly carved just before the flood, like the carvings on these pillars, and they had seemed familiar, a vision of the future, figures that would not have been out of place in Babylonia or Egypt or Bronze Age Europe. But what had happened to the old order, to the shamans who had painted images of animals in caves, a spirit world that seemed utterly at odds with those priests?

Then he remembered the swirling shape he had seen that morning near the top of one of the pillars, crudely carved where older images had been chiselled and abraded away, yet itself fresh, done even as the flood waters rose. He moved the cursor to the top of the screen, found the carving and zoomed in. It seemed like an image from the past, from the deep prehistory of caves and shamans, yet he was convinced now that he had been right and there was a human face in it, a frightening visage like a dream image from a whirlpool. Had this been carved by those new priests to show the dark side of the spirit world, the grim tunnels that voyages of the mind could take; was it a warning to those who might wish to return to the old ways?

Or was it a cry for help, an image carved in the face of death, in moments of terrible overwhelming fear?

Jack felt his head reel, and closed his eyes. For a moment he had an extraordinary vision. The stone pillars no longer seemed like some ill-formed attempt at the human form, something abstract. Instead they appeared as figures half complete, as if that chamber had been inundated in the final act of transformation, as if those plastered skulls were about to be wrenched from the spirit world and placed atop the pillars, ancestors becoming gods. He saw a sudden act, a sweeping away of the past. He saw the spectral forms of those braided and bejewelled priests in the chamber, chipping and carving, erasing the old, and in the background the shadowy shapes of the shamans crouched against the cave wall, floating in and out of the rock like spirit animals. Then they disappeared and he saw the pillars complete, leering, terrifying: gods who now had faces, but instead of being born from the earth like those shapes in the lava, they arose from a seedbed of blood and fear.

It was one of the most remarkable images that archaeology had ever thrown at him, but also one of the most disturbing. *What had gone on inside that blocked-up chamber in those final desperate hours as the flood waters rose?* He took a deep breath, then leaned back in his chair and stretched his legs and arms out. He was dog tired after the dive, but he was determined to use every moment they had. He shook his head to clear the image and then looked at Costas. 'Okay. We need the best possible people here to brainstorm this one. Call them both in.'

6

Near Bergen-Belsen, Lower Saxony, Germany

Maurice Hiebermeyer stared at the image on his iPad, moving it around so that the overhead light hanging from the tent roof caught the ancient Greek lettering on the papyrus to best advantage. His technician in the excavation house at Troy had worked long hours with Jeremy Haverstock to refine the image, taking advantage of IMU's state-of-the-art computing facilities before Hiebermeyer and his Egyptian team had decamped from Troy at the end of the season to their home base at the Institute of Archaeology in Alexandria. Hiebermeyer had never been part of an IMU diving team – he was an Egyptian tombs man, not a shipwreck explorer – but Jack was his oldest friend and sparring partner, the two having first met as boys when Hiebermeyer had been sent from Germany to boarding school in England, where they had discovered a shared fascination with archaeology. After having been at Cambridge University together, they had gone their separate ways, Jack to found IMU and Hiebermeyer to Egypt eventually to found the institute in Alexandria, but Jack had made him an adjunct professor of IMU and they still met to tick off discoveries and plan future projects, just as they had done as schoolboys all those years ago.

He looked up from the iPad for a moment, feeling a surge of satisfaction at the work his team had done at Troy. His first major excavation outside Egypt in association with IMU had been a dig at Herculaneum in Italy four years ago in search of a lost Roman library, looking for clues to early Christianity after Jack and Costas had found the shipwreck of St Paul off Sicily. But the last five months at Troy had been the longest time he had ever spent excavating outside Egypt. Both Herculaneum and Troy had been redeemed in his estimation by the discovery of Egyptian artefacts, in the case of Troy by spectacular New Kingdom sculpture that showed the extent of Egyptian influence in the late Bronze Age Aegean. He had been looking forward to some time off in the institute's castle headquarters alongside Alexandria harbour, time to reflect on his theory that the last kings of Troy were Egyptian, relishing the heated debate that would cause with Jack and their old Cambridge mentor, Professor James Dillen, who had been excavating with them and could counter with spectacular evidence for Mycenaean Greek involvement, for Agamemnon himself having been at Troy.

Then Hiebermeyer had received a request from the most bizarre quarter imaginable. Jacob Lanowski, IMU's resident genius, a man who had never seemed to acknowledge

Hiebermeyer's existence let alone shown the slightest interest in anything Egyptian, had sent him an email requesting an urgent scan of the Atlantis papyrus. At first Hiebermeyer had baulked, reluctant to remove the centrepiece of the Alexandria museum from its case, but then he had looked again at the multispectral scans done on the papyrus fragments from Herculaneum and relented, realizing that the imaging lab at Troy provided a ready facility for processing a new scan using technology that had been unavailable when the Atlantis papyrus had been discovered five years before. Lanowski had flown out to Turkey from the UK to be on board *Seaquest II*, and his email had come just before the ship had sailed from Troy for the Black Sea and Atlantis; a day later – yesterday morning – Jack himself had slipped away from the wreck excavation at Troy and followed in the helicopter. Before he had left, he had taken Hiebermeyer aside and told him of his plan to dive into the volcano. Whatever Lanowski's reasons, resurrecting the papyrus that had started the search for Atlantis nearly six years ago meant that Hiebermeyer was part of that extraordinary project again, one that he was always privately pleased to think had begun not in the Black Sea or the Aegean but in Egypt: in the Egyptian desert with an Egyptian papyrus found in the wrapping of an Egyptian mummy.

He shifted uncomfortably and looked down at the bulky white suit half up his legs, remembering where he was. A little over an hour earlier, he had arrived by German military helicopter from Frankfurt, having flown in from Alexandria the night before. The sky had been overcast as the helicopter came in to land, with fog reducing visibility to less than two hundred metres. He had been taken from the helicopter by jeep to a large Portakabin that seemed to loom out of nowhere on the edge of the runway. As two German Bundeswehr military policemen escorted him to the entrance, he had seen a form behind the Portakabin like a grounded airship covered in camouflage netting. When he had been briefed about the bunker on the phone, he had been told about the pressurized tennis-court bubble that had been put over the excavation, sealing the outside world from any possible contamination. In the fog the place had seemed unreal, disconnected from any known points of reference, like an image in a dream.

He had to remind himself that six months before, only a handful of people still alive had known about the bunker: Hugh Frazer, a wartime British army officer; a nameless Jewish girl who had survived the adjacent concentration camp unable to speak, and who still lived in a care home near Auschwitz in Poland, the place where her parents had been gassed; and the EU commissioner and criminal mastermind Jean-Pierre Saumerre, whose grandfather – a Marseille gangster imprisoned by the Gestapo – had worked in the camp kitchens and escaped after liberation with knowledge of a secret Nazi bunker in the nearby forest, the place under excavation now. After the war, Hugh Frazer had become a classics teacher and had taught Jack and Maurice's Cambridge professor, James Dillen. It was Dillen's memory of something in the teacher's possession years before that had led him and Jack's daughter Rebecca to Frazer's flat in Bristol late last summer; there Frazer had told them the full story of what he had experienced in the concentration camp on that terrible day of liberation in 1945, and the disappearance of his close friend Major Mayne and an American officer somewhere in the forest nearby while they were searching for hidden works of art stolen by the Nazis, shortly before the forest was destroyed by massive Allied aerial bombing.

Hiebermeyer had spoken to Dillen at length about Hugh Frazer the evening before at Troy, where Dillen and Jeremy Haverstock had been left to close down the excavation. Dillen had run through the events of last year, and their lead-up, to prepare Hiebermeyer for what he might find in the bunker. The spark had been a drawing he had seen as a schoolboy in Frazer's room, a drawing he and Rebecca learned had been made by the Jewish girl in the camp and given to Mayne on that fateful day in 1945, a drawing of an extraordinary and terrifying shape she had seen in the bunker: a reverse golden swastika that might have been the ancient Trojan palladion. By chance, Frazer had recognized the image from his student days before the war digging at Mycenae in Greece. There he had been told by an elderly foreman of an artefact sounding remarkably similar that had been taken at night from the grave of Agamemnon by Heinrich Schliemann and his wife Sophia more than fifty years before, a treasure that had been concealed and that may have fallen into the hands of the Nazis in their search for ancient artefacts they associated with the revered warrior-kings of antiquity.

Yet the discovery last year of the existence of the bunker – and the possibility that it contained not only stolen works of art, but also the greatest lost antiquities of Troy – had also drawn in Saumerre, whose grandfather had seen enough to guess that the palladion was associated with another purpose of the bunker, its most dreadful secret. For years the grandfather and his son and grandson had waited, hoping that the NATO airbase built over the camp site after the war would be decommissioned so that they might search for the bunker. Saumerre's conviction that the palladion itself lay in another secret Nazi storage site – deep in a flooded salt mine in Poland – had led him to kidnap Rebecca to force Jack and Costas to use their diving expertise to search for it. They had found only an empty container, but the outcome for Saumerre had been a showdown between his henchmen and Jack and Costas at Troy, where Rebecca had been rescued and Saumerre's power to harm them further had been checked by Jack's threat to expose his criminal empire, something Jack would only do once they were certain that Saumerre's ability to hold others to ransom had been neutered. For decades Saumerre's organization had been deeply involved in the search for hidden Nazi weapons, and there was no certainty what he might already have found. Hiebermeyer remembered what Jack had impressed on him in their final phone conversation yesterday, after he had spoken to Dillen: the only certainty was that Saumerre would now be watching this place with eagle eyes, and would be seeking any means possible to infiltrate the excavation to get his hands on what might lie inside.

The months since the bunker site had been discovered last year had seen a protracted process as Jack passed his knowledge to the British secret service, eventually leading to the site being opened up a week before by a specialist British army team under NATO authority. The situation, with Saumerre still in a position of power in Brussels, seemed extremely precarious to Hiebermeyer, who had never before been so closely involved in the present-day implications of one of

Jack's projects. Apart from an IMU geophysics team who had surveyed the airfield to determine where the camp lay, he was the first IMU representative at the bunker site. Yet his family home had been less than twenty kilometres away, and what had gone on here and in many other places like it during the Nazi period had shaped his own life and his passion for revealing the truth about the past, in this case with a personal family significance that had weighed on him over the last few days as the time for his visit had drawn nearer.

He pressed the icon to email the image of the papyrus to Lanowski, put the iPad on the trestle table in front of him and then fed his hands into the arms of the suit, pushing them through the wrist seals into the attached gloves and pressing his head through the neck seal, finishing by zipping up the front of the suit until it completely encased him. He was inside a tent at the back of the Portakabin that served as a kitting-up room for those entering the bunker, with suits like the one he had been struggling into hanging in a row along one side. He stretched his neck to left and right, feeling the discomfort of the rubber latex seal against his Adam's apple. 'It's a little tight, but I suppose that's necessary,' he grumbled.

The British Royal Engineers sergeant who had helped him into the suit finished wiping off the chalk powder he had used to ease Hiebermeyer's head through the neck seal, and then yanked the chest zip to make sure it was closed. He spoke with a strong Welsh accent. 'It has to be that way, sir. This is the latest-generation chemical, biological, radiological and nuclear suit. We used to call them NBC suits – nuclear, biological and chemical – but they added radiological because of the terrorist threat from dirty bombs. The CBRN suits are more like astronaut suits than the old NBC gear.'

'What happens if I need to relieve myself?'

'That's why we asked you not to drink for two hours and to use the toilet just now. There's a one-hour limit for each shift inside the bunker. If you feel claustrophobic, tell Major Penn and he'll get you out. We've done a few of these old Nazi bunkers before, and they can be pretty grim. There's a diaper with a urine bag if you need it.'

'Sergeant Jones, I am *not* wearing a diaper,' Hiebermeyer said firmly. 'This suit is bad enough as it is.'

'Okay.' Jones slapped his back. 'You're good to go. I'll do the helmet once Major Penn has briefed you.' He handed Hiebermeyer his glasses, then picked up a towel from the table. 'How bad's your eyesight?'

'Gets blurry beyond about two metres, but I don't need them for reading.'

'Then I recommend you don't wear them inside. The helmets can get a little warm, and if you sweat from the face, spectacles can fog up. It's a small glitch in the air circulation system we're working on.'

'There always seem to be glitches with equipment,' Hiebermeyer grumbled. 'My diver colleagues at IMU are forever burning the midnight oil in the engineering department trying to fix things.' He stretched his neck again, grimacing. 'Myself, I'm just an old-fashioned dirt archaeologist. All I need is a trowel, my desert boots, my trusty shorts and a decent hat.'

'I've seen you on TV,' Jones enthused. 'I've watched you with my kids. They think you're the star of the show. Those old khaki shorts flying at half-mast, somehow staying up? Pretty hard to forget, if you don't mind me saying so. It was a programme about Atlantis, and you were in Egypt unwrapping a mummy to show how you'd revealed an ancient papyrus. There was an Egyptian woman with you, really good at explaining it all. I couldn't work out which of you was in charge.'

'That would be Aysha,' Hiebermeyer replied. 'In answer to your question, I was, but now she is. We got married about a year after that film, and now she's six months pregnant.'

'Congratulations. Your first?'

Hiebermeyer gave him a doleful look. 'It wasn't part of my plan.'

'You'll love it. It'll change your life. I've got three, myself.' He nodded towards a bag on the table. 'Sure you don't want to try the diaper? Could be good training.'

Hiebermeyer glared at him. 'Don't push your luck.'

The sergeant grinned, and then swivelled him towards a full-length mirror leaning against the side of the tent. 'The final part of the drill is to do a complete visual inspection yourself. I've got to nip out, but Major Penn will be here soon. He'll be pleased to see you to talk some history. We've got a European Union Health and Safety official here in an hour, due to go into the bunker with me on the next rotation. The man's been before and I've watched Penn having to restrain himself while he was treated like a schoolboy. That's what makes a good officer. I'd have been at the guy's throat.'

Hiebermeyer took the proffered towel, wiped his face and the balding top of his head and put on his glasses. He had heated up already with the exertion of getting the suit on. He stared at the image of himself in the mirror. The suit looked similar to the new thermal-resistant diving oversuits that Costas had shown him at IMU headquarters a few months ago, the ones that Costas and Jack would have worn on their dive into the volcano today. He glanced up at the clock hanging on the tent wall. It was 12.30 p.m., one hour behind Turkey. They should have finished the dive by now, but he knew Jack would not want to hear from him until there was some news from this end. The excavation of a Second World War bunker was not like the other times, not like uncovering the mummy in Egypt or breaking into the lost Roman library in Herculaneum, when Jack would have felt just as Hiebermeyer did now about the return to Atlantis, itching to hear what they had found. This time it was as if the pall from those terrible days in 1945 were still here, something they all desperately hoped that the excavation of the bunker today would dispel.

Hiebermeyer had insisted on coming here in Jack's place to evaluate any antiquities that might be among the looted treasures found inside. He had grown up with the legacy of Germany under the Nazis, and had used that to persuade Jack that he should be the one to go into the bunker. To Hiebermeyer's eye as an archaeologist, every Nazi site revealed – every bunker, every sunken U-boat – added clarity to the events of that time; keeping the artefacts of the period visible was the best way of ensuring that people did not forget. He hoped fervently that the possibility that this place might contain a dark secret – something more than stolen art – would prove wrong, but they would not know for sure until every inch of the bunker had been exhumed. But his line with

Jack had another purpose, something he had discussed with Costas. They had seen the effect on Jack six months earlier of searching for Heinrich Schliemann's lost treasures from Troy, a search that had brought them face to face with the horrors of the Holocaust. The future of IMU operations depended on the charisma and driving force that came from the top, and both he and Costas had been concerned that Rebecca's kidnapping and the events of her rescue – twenty-four hours that had propelled Jack from a desperate underwater fight in a mineshaft to the final showdown beneath Troy, where he and Costas had rescued Rebecca from Saumerre's men – may have taken a toll on Jack that he had not fully acknowledged.

Hiebermeyer thought of Jack and Costas again, diving into the side of an underwater volcano. A brief shadow of doubt crossed his mind. He hoped that keeping Jack away from this place would not have the opposite effect, leading him to make reckless decisions, overcompensating as a way of dealing with an issue he could not confront head-on. But then Hiebermeyer hardly knew of a project where Jack and Costas had not stretched the envelope about as far as it would go. He thought back to when he and Jack had been at boarding school together, carving out the undiscovered treasures of the world between them, his on land and Jack's underwater. Hiebermeyer had sworn he would never dive, and he had stuck to it. Like Jack, he had an almost superstitious belief in his own ability to ferret out archaeological finds, and part of that certainty involved sticking to a ritual. He had been down plenty of dark tunnels and squeezed into plenty of lost tombs in his time, but never wearing more than his trusty khakis. He had told

Jack that the mere idea of diving equipment clouded his thinking. He held up his arms, flexing his fingers in the white gloves. This was the nearest he had ever got, and it was stretching his own envelope. He picked up the towel and wiped his forehead. And it was making him unpleasantly hot.

'Dr Hiebermeyer? David Penn. Royal Engineers.' A small, fit-looking man in his early thirties came into the room, wearing a camouflage smock with a major's star on his epaulettes.

Hiebermeyer held out his gloved hand. 'Maurice.'

Sergeant Jones returned and quickly went over to the CBRN suits on the racks, selecting one and checking it over. Penn took off his beret and boots and Jones helped him into the suit as he talked. 'I understand that Jack Howard won't be here?'

'He's diving, in the Black Sea. But he's on standby to join us, depending on what we find. I'm planning to call him after I've seen inside.'

'I spoke to him on the phone at length last week when my team arrived here. I understand you have a personal connection with this place?'

'Not this place exactly, but my father's family home was about twenty kilometres north-west of here. My grandfather was a merchant seaman and then a naval officer, a U-boat captain lost with his vessel in 1940, and my grandmother and father and his two younger sisters remained here for the rest of the war. In April 1945 they were among the civilians taken by British troops into Belsen to see the horrors there. My father was only nine years old but was very badly affected. They were made to stand beside a truck while former SS guards loaded corpses. For the rest of his life my father couldn't stand the smell of raw meat or rotting garbage. The British officer who conducted them into the camp said that what they were about to see was such a disgrace to the German people that their name must be erased from the list of civilized nations. He said it could only be restored when they had reared a new generation amongst whom it was impossible to find people prepared to commit such crimes. My father was a very responsible nine-year-old who saw himself as head of the family after his father had been killed, and he took those words to heart and interpreted them literally. He believed the officer was saying that he, a child, was forever guilty, because he had been born before the war. Even after my father had grown up and realized that the officer had not meant that, he told me that because he had spent his childhood and teenage years after the war believing in his own guilt, it would never escape him. He said that the only hope lay in my generation and beyond. So I grew up with this legacy too.'

Penn picked up a pointer and tapped a plan of the airfield pinned to the wall. 'Then you'll know that there was a labour camp here, an *Arbeitslager*, a satellite of Belsen. Its remains lie mostly under the northern end of the airfield. We've done one excavation there I'll need to explain to you, but let's leave that until we've been into the bunker. Did your father know anything about this place?'

'He said his father and uncles used to hunt in the forest before the war. My father remembered the night when this sector of the forest was destroyed, a massive orange glow on the horizon.'

Penn nodded. 'The twenty-fifth of April 1945, only hours

after the camp was evacuated. A five-hundred-bomber Lancaster raid was diverted from Bremen to destroy the forest. The British 21st Army Group had been concerned that pockets of SS would stage a fanatical resistance there and hold up the Allied advance. The bombing obliterated the camp and buried the bunker under tons of earth and felled trees, which is why it remained unrecorded when the NATO airfield was built over the site after the war.'

'Nobody in 21st Army Group knew about it?'

Penn shook his head. 'Few of the SS camp guards survived. The British SAS who liberated the camp shot a number of them, and others who fled into the forest were hunted down by the more able-bodied inmates. I've seen the file with all the information that Jack and his daughter amassed last year from interviewing Captain Frazer, the British officer who was in the camp. So we know that his friend Major Mayne and an American officer, a Colonel Stein, had been here looking for stolen Nazi treasures, but that the two men disappeared. My assumption is that they went into the forest looking for the bunker and got caught out in the bombing raid, or fell foul of guards still stationed here. There's no evidence for them in the bunker yet, but we've only cleared half of it. No word of its existence got back to 21st Army Group headquarters.'

'How did it survive the bombing raid?'

'It's a remarkable piece of engineering,' Penn enthused. 'I'll brief you as we go in. Construction was my speciality at the School of Military Engineering, but because there's not much call for this kind of thing these days, I volunteered for the NBS clearance unit, now CBRN, which would at least give me a chance to examine these places. There's a lot of redevelopment and construction work going on in Germany now, and a lot more underground sites are being found. I read that article you wrote last year about the archaeology of the Nazi period in *Der Spiegel*, and I completely agree with you about making these places scheduled monuments like any other archaeological site. It's going to become a big political issue in Berlin, because major pipeline and utility works are planned in the centre around the Tiergarten, and there must be an enormous amount to be discovered there.'

'An old friend of mine is a stalwart of the Berlin Second World War archaeology group, a voluntary organization that has been lobbying for more resources to do proper excavations there,' Hiebermeyer replied. 'There are also major refurbishments planned at the Berlin Zoo on the edge of the Tiergarten, on the site of the huge flak tower that was once there. That's where the Schliemann treasures from the Berlin prehistory museum were stored, where the Russians found them. My friend believes there are tunnels from there to the site of Gestapo headquarters and the Reichstag. They're actually doing some more exploring this week, and I'm hoping to go there after this for a quick visit.'

Penn looked at him intently. 'Fascinating. I'd like to collaborate. There are a couple of sites in Berlin that need our expertise, possible chemical and biological production sites. It's frightening how little is known about these places and what went on inside them. Many were deliberately hushed up, part of Allied policy. We cleared a newly discovered part of the Sarin II nerve-gas production bunker at Falkenhagen near Berlin a few months ago, a really grim place that looked as if it had been abandoned only days before.'

'It must feel as if you're still fighting the Second World War.'

Penn's head briefly disappeared from view as he ducked into his suit and pushed through the rubber neck seal. He struggled out, shaking his head in a cloud of chalk powder, and then stretched his arms out to pull the flaps tight over his chest for the zipper to be shut. 'Sergeant Jones here calls us bunker-busters.' He staggered backwards as Jones yanked the zipper. 'But we do real war too. We're due to fly out to the Panjshir valley in Afghanistan in two weeks. We get called out every time they find a cave complex with weapons caches that might include the bad stuff. I mentioned it to Jack during our phone call, and was amazed to hear he'd been up the valley two years ago, at the site of the old lapis lazuli mines. Something about a shady Chinese mafia group who were after the same thing as he was. It must be more of a free-for-all in northern Afghanistan than we realize. Jack told me he'd been on the trail of a Royal Engineers ancestor of his, a colonel who died up there during the time of the Raj. Who'd have thought British sappers would be back there in the twenty-first century.'

Hiebermeyer nodded. 'It was a big thing for Jack, finding that place. Unfortunately that mafia organization is still ticking over. You can emasculate them, but they grow back.' Hiebermeyer remembered Saumerre, Rebecca's kidnapping last year, the eyes that would be somewhere on them now, watching for any hint of a discovery that might bring the worst of those groups back to haunt not just IMU but the entire world. He glanced at Penn. 'The security here is pretty tight? I don't mean the biological containment, but security against infiltration?'

Penn pulled sideways as the sergeant secured his zipper. 'My sapper guard detachment go through special forces training. You saw the Bundeswehr military police outside, and there's another cordon around the airfield perimeter. This place is well and truly locked down.' He picked up his helmet, and Jones took Hiebermeyer's. 'You ready? We don our oxygen kit in the next room, immediately abutting the bunker wall. Then we wait for the previous pair to signal that they're ready to come out, about ten minutes from now. There's an overlap so four are inside at any one time. We run the shifts with military precision. We don't want too many in there at once in case there's a contamination incident.'

Penn walked through a hanging plastic partition and Hiebermeyer followed, with Jones behind. They were inside a polyurethane tunnel between the Portakabin and the bunker structure, a grey mass of concrete that had been partly dug out of the earth in front of them. Above it Hiebermeyer could see the dome of the bubble that encased the site, a strange, disconcerting scene, as if he were walking in a see-through tunnel through an aquarium, watching shapes appear and disappear in the polyurethane as the air movement inside the bubble flexed the plastic, creating a muted drumming noise as if someone were banging to get in from outside.

Immediately in front of them was a structure about the size of a portable toilet, sealed to the concrete surrounding the entrance to the bunker. 'That's the airlock,' Penn said. 'Beyond that we have no contact with the exterior atmosphere.' Sergeant Jones picked up a compact backpack that Hiebermeyer recognized as an oxygen rebreather, with a cylinder protruding from the top and a hose on either side. Penn took another one, and glanced at Hiebermeyer. 'You'll be familiar with these from Jack's kit. We use rebreathers because they're completely self-contained, with no chance of contamination through an exhaust valve.' Hiebermeyer felt the sweat on his brow, and took a deep breath. He felt hemmed in and suddenly wanted to be outside. He closed his eyes and took another couple of deep breaths, wiping his brow with his hands.

'You okay?' Penn asked, shifting his shoulders to ease on the rebreather and tighten the straps, peering at him. 'It's normal to feel spooked. One of my corporals said it's like a tunnel into a nightmare, as if the real history of this place is just beyond that plastic membrane and has never gone away. I know that's hardly reassurance, but if you're feeling something like that, you're not the only one.'

Hiebermeyer tried to relax. 'I've been down tunnels before in Egypt and come face to face with some pretty nightmarish apparitions. It's wearing the suit and being inside this bubble that takes a little getting used to.'

Jones finished tightening Penn's straps and lifted the rebreather on to Hiebermeyer's back. 'Before we put on our helmets, I'll give you a quick rundown on the structure,' Penn said. He glanced at the red light that was shining above the door, then at the watch strapped around his left arm. 'We should be ready to go in five minutes.' He pointed to a plan on a small clipboard hanging from his neck. It showed a long, rectangular building with an entrance passage lined by small rooms on either side, then a large central chamber and a further area at the far end of the bunker, shaded over in pencil. 'It's like a large Nissen hut, a massive corrugated-iron tunnel, a classic bomb-shelter design,' Penn said. 'You said your grandfather was a U-boat captain? Then you'll be interested to know that the concrete outer shell is based on the design of U-boat pens. The roof is built using a Fangrost bomb trap, concrete beams about a metre apart laid over support beams on the roof, creating space where the blast from bombs detonating against the upper beams would dissipate sideways. That's how the U-boat pens survived everything the Allies could throw at them, and that's how this bunker survived the raid on the forest on 25 April 1945.'

'It seems incredible overengineering, in an obscure place in a forest where they could hardly have expected an attack,' Hiebermeyer said.

'Some of the paperwork survived in the front office of the bunker. The place was built by Organisation Todt, the Nazi state construction agency run by Fritz Todt, and specifically by the naval construction department, the Marinebauwesens. The naval department had the greatest expertise in bombproof bunkers, as they built the huge U-boat pens at places like Brest and Lorient. The bunker would have been built using forced labour, of course, and the Organisation Todt had its own Polizei regiment as well as dedicated Schutzkommando who would have been perfectly at home supervising slave labour next to their fellow SS thugs in the camp. We think the labourers were Soviet prisoners of war, and that those who didn't die on the job were executed to make sure that as few people as possible knew about this place. I mentioned an excavation in the camp, and you'll see what I mean.' Penn paused, glancing down. 'Every time I look at these places and get wrapped up in the technology, I have to force myself to stand back and remember that everything the Nazis created, *everything*, had a cost in lives and blood. We've been brought up to think this was all about ruthless efficiency, about the expediency of employing people the Nazis regarded as subhuman. But there was more to it than that. It's as if the Nazi bosses fed on the terror, as if the blood were an opiate. You see it in the eyes of those Nazis in the photographs, crazed and hungry for more. Every time we excavate one of these places, I feel as if we're unlocking the ghosts they created who have been screaming ever since, and that we're releasing them from the nightmare.'

Hiebermeyer swallowed hard. As an archaeologist he had often thought about whether he was violating the dead, not in a spiritual sense but in terms of his own receptivity to the past: whether he was breaking a bond more important than the richest grave goods, whether by walking through a tomb entrance he was severing his empathy with people who had invested so much in sending their dead to the afterlife in tombs that were meant to be sealed for all time. But in this place, where the ghosts had not been laid to rest, where they seemed so close, it felt different, unnerving, as if he could sense the emotions, the terror, but also the most horrifying thing to him of all: the demonic certainty of the perpetrators that they were on a righteous path. It was like nothing he had felt before in all those tunnels of antiquity. He remembered the silhouettes of hands he had seen with Jack on a visit to the Lascaux cave in southern France when they were students, prehistoric hands that seemed in the flickering torchlight to be pressing out from inside the rock, spirits whose faces lay just beyond their vision. Here, looking at the shapes in the plastic, he felt the same, as if the swirling images he saw were faces caught in a scream, pressing against the membrane that had kept them locked in terrible torment.

He shook the image from his mind, and forced himself to concentrate on the plan on the clipboard. 'Albert Speer took over Organisation Todt, didn't he?'

Penn nodded. 'From 1942. But that's the odd thing. None of the paperwork was signed by Todt or by Speer. All we found were three sheets in a partly incinerated folder on the floor of the front office, beside a brazier. Someone had clearly been trying to burn it all, but must have left in a hurry. They were the usual Nazi foolscap order papers, with minutiae of costings for materials: concrete, steel girders, electrical and other equipment. But it was bizarre. Each of them had been approved and signed by the Reichsführer-SS, Heinrich Himmler.'

Hiebermeyer froze. 'You're sure of it?'

'I know his signature. When I was studying Nazi construction design, I looked at some of the surviving documentation for Wewelsburg Castle, his SS headquarters in Westphalia. It reveals the same personal involvement and obsession with detail that Himmler showed with the Final Solution. Wewelsburg was Himmler's private fiefdom, really nothing to do with Hitler, actually owned by Himmler himself since the early 1930s and as much his private fantasy as Hitler's mad dream for his new capital at his home town of Linz in Austria. The papers we found in the bunker would fit perfectly within the archive for Wewelsburg, the same kind of thing. Though why Himmler should have had a personal involvement with a secret bunker in an obscure part of Lower Saxony is anyone's guess.'

The light above the door went green, and Penn picked up a phone hanging on the wall, waiting for a response. Hiebermeyer felt a chill course through him. *Heinrich Himmler*. The image of that pasty face, the boyish grin, the nervous movements, seemed to be imprinted on his mind. As a student, Hiebermeyer had made a special study of the Ahnenerbe, Himmler's Department of Cultural Heritage, and had read everything he could about its expeditions to uncover evidence of Aryan roots, expeditions that took Nazi scientists around the world as well as deep into German prehistory. It had been the only time that Hiebermeyer's fascination with Egyptology had taken a back seat; it became a moral crusade he later recognized as a young man's attempt at expiation, at combining his archaeological fascination with a need to grapple with the Nazi past that was part of his own heritage as a German. He had wanted to reveal all he could about artefacts and sites uncovered by the Ahnenerbe, to discover what was worthwhile. But in the end he had found it impossible to disentangle reality from fiction, the real archaeology from the monstrous edifice of lies and fantasy, of twisted racial theory that made the archaeology an inextricable part of the story of hate and murder.

And behind it lay the man who more than all the other Nazis saw himself as a living god. When he viewed those newsreels and photographs, Hiebermeyer saw Himmler not as Hitler's faithful acolyte but as absolute master of that world, as if all that was needed was a trick of the mind to create an alternative Nazi reality run by Himmler rather than by Hitler. For Hiebermeyer, the end of his project had come when he had interviewed a former Wehrmacht officer who had known

Himmler in Berlin. *Behind this man*, the officer had said, *one realized that there was something horrifying*. By then Hiebermeyer had known that there could be no expiation, and that the version of the past created by this monster was a far bigger lesson from history than the stories that he might have been able to tease out of artefacts wrenched for ever from their contexts and incorporated into the fabric of Nazi ideology.

Penn put down the phone, then looked at Hiebermeyer. 'Okay. They're almost ready.' He paused. 'Himmler wasn't obsessed with art like Goering, so it's hard to believe that this bunker was built primarily as a private vault to secure a cache of paintings. That wasn't like him. And there was something else, really curious. The folder we found with those papers had been marked *Streng Geheim*, "Top Secret", odd enough for a group of construction order forms. But odder still was a strange symbol, a reverse swastika in red, and some words I'd never seen before. I know Himmler was obsessed with ancient heroes and kings, and Jack said that some of Schliemann's lost treasures from Troy might be here. That's what really got me. It was the name of the most famous king of the Greeks, from the Trojan Wars. They said *Der Agamemnon Code*.'

Hiebermeyer stared at him. '*Mein Gott*. When did you find this?'

'About two hours ago, during my last shift in there. You're the first outside our group to hear about it.'

Hiebermeyer remembered the whole horror story that might lie behind this bunker: the fear of a *Wunderwaffe*, a wonder-weapon; not some deranged Nazi fantasy, but something real, a terrible weapon that may have lain unused for all these years. *A doomsday weapon*. He glanced at Penn.

How much had Jack told him? Six months ago, they had learned that the Agamemnon Code was an activation signal for a covert Nazi scheme in the final months of the war, a scheme that they could only guess about but which was linked with this place. He remembered all the evidence they had marshalled last year, all the speculation, and he had a sudden cold thought. 'Tell me something,' he asked quietly. 'Those order lists. Did you see there anything out of the ordinary? Any strange equipment?'

Penn hesitated. 'There's a guy in there now, our translator. He's an expert on Nazi documents. We can't risk taking anything out of this place and exposing it, so we have to do all of our work inside. I just had a quick word with him on the phone. He knows you're German and wants your opinion on his translation. But the third sheet does contain something out of the ordinary. Something pretty bad, I'm afraid.' He paused, again pursing his lips. 'It's laboratory equipment: Bunsen burners, test tubes, refrigerators, a centrifuge. That's worrying enough, but there's equipment not just for a lab, but for a *medical* lab: syringes, chloroform, metal gurneys with restraining straps, huge quantities of lime. It's what we always hope we won't find in these places, but it's why all of these precautions are necessary.' He looked at Hiebermeyer. 'You can bail out now. Works of art are one thing, but this other stuff is way beyond your remit. We could be walking into a chamber of horrors.'

Hiebermeyer shook his head and took off his glasses, blinking to get used to the blur. Sergeant Jones came up behind him and placed the helmet on the sealing ring around his neck, locking it in place and hooking up the hoses from the oxygen tank. He was closed off again, in another kind of tunnel. He heard the suck and rasp of his breathing on the oxygen regulator. He felt the sweat drip down his nose and over his lips, and he blinked it out of his eyes. He knew he was not sweating from the heat. He was sweating from fear.

'All set?' Penn's voice sounded peculiar, tinny, through the earphones inside the helmet. Hiebemeyer looked across, and gave him a diver's okay sign.

'If you need to come out, you tell me. Otherwise we have one hour.'

'I'm following you.'

Penn opened the door to the airlock chamber and Hiebermeyer followed him inside, squeezing into the confined space. Sergeant Jones slammed the door behind them, and he could hear the cross-bolt being dropped. They were in total darkness, and all he could hear was the hiss of their oxygen regulators. Then the inside door swung open, and Hiebermeyer walked into his worst nightmare.

7

South-eastern Black Sea

Jack turned in his chair as the door to the operations room on *Seaquest II* opened and two men entered. One had long, lank hair swept to the side, and was unusually neatly attired in trousers and a pressed shirt that must have been dug up especially for the visit by the inspection team. Dr Jacob Lanowski was one of IMU's most unusual assets, an engineering genius from Caltech and MIT whose capacity for lateral thinking was matched by his eccentric character. He had the pale face and shadowy eyes of someone who spent most of his waking hours hunched in front of a computer screen, whereas the tall young man beside him was bronzed and fit, wearing old army trousers and a khaki T-shirt that was still streaked with the dust of Troy. Jack had first met Jeremy Haverstock four years earlier at the Institute of Palaeography in Oxford, where Jeremy had been completing a doctorate on early-medieval scripts supervised by Jack's old girlfriend Maria de Montijo, director of the institute. After their first project together researching Viking exploration, Jack had persuaded Jeremy not to return to an academic career in America but instead to take up a position with IMU, and since then he had gone from strength to strength. Like Lanowski, he was an expert in his field but had diverse talents, exactly what Jack looked for in a team member, in Jeremy's case a boyhood fascination with robotics engineering that had quickly cemented his friendship with Costas.

Jeremy took a portable hard drive out of his pocket and pointed to one of the computer workstations. 'I need to get the program running,' he said, veering off and sitting down in front of a console.

Lanowski went straight to the ROV monitoring station on the other side of the room and clamped the earphones to his head with one hand, quickly tapping the keyboard with his other. He put down the earphones and walked over to Jack and Costas. 'I'm running a system diagnostic. It should take about fifteen minutes. Any more noise from the ROV?' he said, peering through his little round glasses at Costas.

'Nothing since we spoke, but I did what you said and shut everything down. I want to see how you reboot the system.'

Lanowski knelt down, reached under the table and extracted a portable blackboard, then propped it up on a chair and pulled a piece of chalk out of his pocket, tossing it in the air and catching it. He pushed up his glasses and gave Jack a lopsided grin, his eyes burning with anticipation, then cleared his throat and turned to the board.

'Oh no you don't,' Costas said firmly, standing up and moving the blackboard back under the table. 'Not the blackboard. Not the chalk.'

'Just a little diagram to show how electromagnetic interference from a magma upsurge in the earth's crust might be causing the problem with the ROV. To help you redesign the equipment so that next time it actually works.'

'Not now, Jacob.' Costas stood defiantly in front of the blackboard, his arms crossed. Lanowski sighed, tossed the chalk again, caught it and put it back in his pocket, then drummed his fingers on the chair beside him until Costas reached over and put his hand over Lanowski's, stopping it.

Jeremy pushed his chair back and loped towards them. 'Okay, that's loading. Might be about the same time frame, fifteen minutes or so.' He stood in front of them, as tall as Jack, and smiled broadly. 'Boy, am I glad to see you two. From what Costas said on the phone, it sounds like you really did it this time. Diving inside a live volcano. Hard to beat that.'

'Watch this space,' Jack said, smiling. 'You know that officially it didn't happen?'

'Captain Macalister collared me on deck as soon as I got out of the Lynx, and gave me a rundown.'

Costas reached over and slapped Jeremy on the back. 'How's my favourite ancient linguistics and submersibles technology expert?'

'Excellent,' Jeremy replied. 'I'm really pleased with our final days at Troy. I left Professor Dillen in charge, after Maurice and his team had departed for Egypt. It was great to get Hugh Frazer out there, wasn't it, before he passed away? It was heart-breaking when we took him to that care home in Poland to see the old lady with the harp, still sitting with it as he remembered her as a girl in that concentration camp in 1945. But he was really thrilled to be at Troy and see the wall painting Dillen discovered of Homer with his lyre. I think it brought back the joy of his time excavating with his friend Peter Mayne before the war, the strength of that friendship, their love of Homer. He and Dillen stayed up on the walls half the night declaiming passages in ancient Greek, and drinking wine from the golden cup of Agamemnon that Jack found in the shipwreck.'

'You let them do that?' Costas said, eyeing Jack. 'You've just gone up even higher in my estimation.'

'Far better than consigning it to a glass case,' Jack murmured, turning to Jeremy. 'Anything more on that Egyptian statue Maurice found?'

'I think you'd better let him tell you about that,' Jeremy replied. 'He says he's only going to reveal it when it's cleaned up, but it'll change our whole view of prehistory.'

Jack grinned. 'Maurice always says that when he finds something Egyptian outside Egypt.'

Jeremy looked at Costas with concern. 'I meant to say. About Little Joey. I'm really sorry for your loss. All those hours we spent together in the engineering lab over the winter, working on him.'

Costas looked to one side, swallowing hard. 'I keep saying to myself that the fun's in making the toy, not in playing with it. But it doesn't ease the pain. Lost for ever, entombed inside a volcano. I can't even bear to say his name.'

'But he did good work.'

Costas nodded; his voice was hoarse with emotion. 'He did good work.'

Jack looked at Jeremy. 'And how's my favourite daughter?'

'Sends her love. To Uncle Costas too.'

Lanowski was peering at Costas, and put a hand clumsily on his shoulder. 'About the ROV. I've been thinking. What you need is children.'

Costas looked down at the hand, and then at Lanowski. 'Did I hear you right? I need what?'

'I said you need children.'

Costas gently removed the hand. 'Of the many strange things I've heard you say over the years, that's just about the strangest.'

'I was only sharing that passion this morning with my girlfriend.'

Costas' jaw dropped. 'Your *what*?'

Lanowski reached into his shirt pocket and tossed out a picture of a raven-haired beauty. 'She's Brazilian. Models for *Vogue*. That's how she paid her way through college. She's got a PhD, of course.'

'Of course,' Jack murmured, scratching his chin.

'And she hit on you, just like that,' Costas said incredulously. 'A Brazilian *Vogue* model with a PhD. You've kept that well under wraps.'

'Well.' Lanowski coughed, moved his long, lank fringe from his forehead, then pushed up his glasses again. 'We haven't actually met.'

'You haven't *met*.'

'Well, not as such. Not hands-on.'

'How do you know she wants children, if you haven't actually met?'

'Her profile says she wants children, and my profile says I want children. Do the math.'

'Ah,' Jack said, putting his head down to hide his expression.

'Ah,' Costas echoed. 'You've got an *internet* girlfriend. Have you, um, sent her your picture?'

'That's why I was getting you to take a photo of me in the submersible yesterday, at the controls.'

'I was wondering what that was all about.'

'I just mentioned to her that submersibles were my latest thing, with my friend Costas, and she jumped on it,' Lanowski said. 'That's the great thing about internet dating. You learn right away about shared passions.'

Costas nodded sagely. 'Could have taken you years to find that out.'

'The picture might do the trick,' Jack murmured.

'Well, my friend,' Costas said, slapping Lanowski on the back, 'you know where to find me if you need a best man.'

Lanowski looked at him gratefully, then at Jack, not batting an eyelid. 'I'll remember that. Now for the ROV program.' He turned and walked quickly back to the monitoring station, sat down and put on the headphones.

Costas turned to Jack, speaking quietly. 'Was he being serious?'

'Lanowski's got a brain about the size of Jodrell Bank observatory. He can spot you coming a mile off.'

'But maybe?'

'Maybe. Look out for the virtual-reality engagement ring.'

Jeremy ruffled his shock of blond hair. 'About Rebecca. I knew you couldn't make it back to Troy to see her off because of your covert diving operation here, so I went with her in the Lynx to Istanbul airport. She sent me a text as soon as she landed at JFK in New York. She's back in school now. Her mother's friends – her foster-parents, I should say – met her at the airport, Petra and Mikhail. Rebecca really looks forward to going back to see them, you know, to tell them about this whole new life she has with you.'

'They're great people,' Jack said, sitting back. 'After Elizabeth sent Rebecca away from Naples for her own safety as a little girl, they looked after her for almost fifteen years, until Elizabeth was killed in the Mafia hit and I learned that I had a daughter. I owe them a lot. I spent a week with them last summer after returning from Troy, on their farm in upstate New York. It was really interesting to hear for the first time about Mikhail's background. He trained at the elite Moscow State Institute for International Relations. Officially he's a research professor at Columbia, but he's been on the payroll of the CIA since his defection. He's a specialist in the early Cold War period, and we talked a lot about the Soviet conquest of Berlin in 1945. He thinks there's more to be found out about the treasures from Troy that were taken from Berlin to Moscow after the war, and he was going to look into that for me. Rebecca wants their place in the Adirondacks to continue being her main home while she's still at high school, using the apartment in New York City during termtime, and I'm fully behind it. All that matters to me is her happiness wherever she can find it, especially after her mother's death. And last summer, being out in the fields and in the woods at the farm, I could see where she developed her independent streak.'

'Maybe a bit of genetics in that too, Jack,' Costas murmured.

'It's a brilliant place,' Jeremy enthused. 'Completely cut off by the forest. The lake at the back's great for canoeing and fishing, isn't it? You can camp on the island. Perfect.'

Jack raised his eyes in surprise. 'You've been there too?'

Jeremy shrugged. 'I thought you knew. You're always running between projects, Jack. Kind of hard to pin down over the last six months. Rebecca told Mikhail and Petra I was going back to the States last autumn to spend some time with my folks. Their place is only a couple of hours away.'

'Huh. She didn't mention it. I suppose I've been a bit preoccupied. I really wanted to get the Troy excavation wrapped up by now, to clear the decks for what lies ahead. Coming back to Atlantis has been a dream of mine, but it definitely wasn't on the cards.' Jack paused, pursing his lips. 'Maybe I've had my foot pressed a little too hard on the accelerator. After Rebecca's kidnapping last year, I thought the best thing for both of us would be to submerge ourselves in work, to get on top of the Troy project and tie up the loose ends before we took some off-time together.'

'Some pretty big loose ends still out there,' Costas said quietly. 'Have you heard from Maurice yet?'

Jack took a deep breath, then shook his head. 'Not yet. But he should be at the bunker in Germany by now. Last week I spoke on the phone to the British army officer in charge of the excavation, which is being carried out by a NATO nuclear, biological and chemical team because of the risk of what might lie inside. The excavation is top secret and under a massive security cordon, exactly what we insisted on when I first approached my secret-service contact in London six months ago and told her what we knew. There's a full MI6 team in charge of the Saumerre case. Officially Maurice is there to provide expert guidance on any stolen art and antiquities that might be inside the bunker, but we all know there's more to it than that. We got in pretty deep last year, and Saumerre is playing his waiting game with us, not with the security services.'

'What about Rebecca's safety?' Costas asked.

'Saumerre won't go anywhere near Rebecca again or anyone else in IMU as long as I threaten to expose him, but that could change if he thinks we've discovered what he wants in the bunker and he decides that he's got nothing to lose.'

'You know Ben Kershaw was with her on the flight?' Jeremy said. 'I had no idea until I spotted him boarding the aircraft at the last minute.'

'He *is* our security chief,' Jack said grimly. 'After what happened last year, Ben told me he wasn't letting her out of his sight until Saumerre was history. Ever since he took over IMU security following Peter Howe's death out here six years ago, Ben has really come into his own. There are two others already on the ground in New York to provide round-the-clock surveillance, one ex-SAS like Ben and the other a serving MI6 agent provided by our case officer in London. Petra and Mikhail are fully aware of the situation. Mikhail was a Soviet officer in the Afghan war before he became an academic and defected with Petra, one of the reasons why Elizabeth thought he'd be a good guardian for Rebecca when her family's Mafia connections in Naples became too much of a threat. I think he's enjoyed turning their farm into a temporary armed compound. It doesn't mean I rest easy, but it means I know she's being looked after by the best people, and my presence would only be an interference as long as the security is ramped up. It means I can focus on the archaeology now.' He paused, then looked at Jeremy quizzically. 'Speaking of which, how did Rebecca do in the potsherd cleaning programme at Troy?'

'Brilliantly. She discovered at least a dozen more sherds painted with the reverse-swastika pattern. It firms up your theory that it really was the symbol of ancient Troy. She stuck with it far longer than I expected, even turned down a chance for some impromptu training in the Lynx. I kept her under close supervision all the time.'

Costas coughed. 'I'm sure you did.'

'She's seventeen,' Jack said to Jeremy firmly. 'Lots to learn. And you're what, twenty-six?'

Costas glanced at Jack, then waved his hand breezily. 'A year or two from now, the age difference won't mean a thing. And as you said, Jack. Happiness wherever she can find it.'

Jack narrowed his eyes at Costas, then turned back to Jeremy with a resigned smile. He got up, put a hand on the younger man's shoulder and guided him to a seat. 'Okay. Let's talk about Atlantis.'

'Macalister asked me to remind you that the Lynx is fuelling up for your departure. The Turkish geological team is due in at 1600 hours, and the helipad needs to be clear by then.'

Jack glanced at his watch. 'That gives us just under two hours.' There was a sudden whoop from the far side of the room, and they all turned to look. Lanowski had moved from the ROV station to one of the computer consoles, its screen facing away from them. He was talking to himself, occasionally chuckling and leaning back in his chair, then leaning forward again and staring. He suddenly went ramrod straight. 'Eureka,' he exclaimed. '*Eureka.*'

'Uh-oh,' Costas said quietly to Jack. 'The girlfriend?'

Jack raised his voice. 'What is it?'

Lanowski looked up. 'Something I've been working on. Something I have to thank Maurice Hiebermeyer for.'

'*Hiebermeyer?*' Jack exclaimed. 'I wasn't aware that the two of you had ever exchanged a word.'

'Email. He's my new friend. My new *best* friend.'

'What about me?' Costas muttered.

'Looks like you've been knocked off your pedestal,' Jack replied, looking with concern at Lanowski. 'Are you going to share with us?'

'Of course, I've read everything Hiebermeyer's ever written, and I've even donated two of my books to his institute in Alexandria,' Lanowski said more to himself than to anyone else, looking at the screen as if he were talking to it. 'Egyptology's always been a fascination of mine. Engineering problems, mathematical problems. Pyramids, mummies, papyrus. Codes.' He stared at them, his eyes gleaming. 'Yes, gentlemen. Codes.'

'What on earth is he on about?' Costas whispered.

Jack spoke firmly. 'What about the ROV, Jacob, what you're actually here for?'

Lanowski kept his gaze on the monitor, but waved one arm behind him. 'It's running itself. If it's still transmitting and anything shows through, it'll appear on the big screen above the ROV station.'

'Okay,' Jack said. 'We're at Atlantis, not in Egypt, and we haven't got all day. While we're waiting for Jeremy's image to upload, I want to talk to you about altered consciousness.'

Lanowski continued staring at the screen, then suddenly looked up. 'About what?'

'Altered consciousness. Costas said that neuropsychology was another one of your fascinations.'

Lanowski tapped a key and got up, then pushed back his chair and walked over to Jack, staring at him. 'Yes?'

'I had a couple of interesting experiences on the dive today. First in the tunnel going down into the volcano, a strange sensation of being in a vortex. Then in the final seconds before reaching the submersible, when I was out of air. Looking back on it, I remember more of what I sensed. The instant I knew I was about to black out I saw sparkly lights all round me in a kind of lattice pattern, and then a tunnel with a light at the end that I seemed to be drifting towards, with a face appearing and multiplying all around me. The face was Costas, of course, leaning out to pull me in, and the light was the open hatch of the submersible, but the closer I swam towards it, the further away it seemed. I wanted to relax and let it draw me in.'

Lanowski nodded. 'Anoxia, dopamine, adrenalin, fear, survival instinct. A common feature of altered-consciousness experiences is the sensation of floating underwater. And you were in a high-stress situation, and experiencing sensory deprivation. Odd thing is, it can feel good. Addictive. Diving must tap into something hard-wired in our brains. I've been trying to work out what makes you guys always want to go deep. It's not just nitrogen narcosis, is it?'

'There's something to that,' Jack said, leaning back again. 'But for me it's always been cognitive, by which I mean how my own sense of observation and analysis is ramped up by being underwater, and that's something I relish and want to experience whenever I can. I've always seen diving as an interface between present and past, as if putting on the equipment and getting underwater puts you into a different state of awareness, more acute, with the pressure on time making you think quickly and opening up lots of avenues in the mind. Maurice Hiebermeyer says the same thing about going down tunnels, opening up tombs. Being in that state for only a few moments can give those critical insights that don't always come from hours of patient excavation on land. But my experience today was a different kind of altered consciousness and made me think about the Neolithic. What I'm really interested in now is putting myself in the minds of those shamans who went down tunnels in their minds, who perhaps saw visions that we can understand in terms of neuropsychology but they interpreted as manifestations of a spirit world.'

Costas shook his head in disbelief. 'So when you were having your near-death experience and I was saving your life, you had a blinding flash of inspiration about the Neolithic? Archaeologists never cease to amaze me.'

Lanowski flicked away his fringe and pushed his glasses up his nose. 'When I was a first-year undergraduate at Princeton, I worked evenings in the neuropsychology lab. I needed money, and I signed on as a guinea pig.'

'Uh-oh,' Costas muttered. 'This is about to explain a few things.'

'Don't worry,' Lanowski said cheerfully. 'Only a few mild opiates, and some marijuana. Far less than most students were consuming around me. And the beauty of it was, I didn't need it. I could put myself into an altered state of consciousness without drugs.'

'Why does that not surprise me?' Costas said.

'If you really believe in the world of your visions, then the mind can easily take you there,' Lanowski continued. 'That's the essence of religious experience. There's little difference in that respect between a shaman having visions in front of a cave wall and a worshipper in a church transfixed by a statue of the Virgin Mary. Neither of them needs hallucinogenic drugs to get there. Or as in my case, you can really believe in the power of your own mind and your ability to control it.'

'This lab you worked in,' Costas said. 'Let me guess. You did most of their analytical work for them too?'

'It came out as a paper in the *Journal of Cognitive Archaeology*. My name isn't in the author list because I wasn't officially part of the team, being merely a guinea pig.'

Jack stared at him. '*That* paper? That was your work?'

'I was in the lab one evening and saw the garbled manuscript they were working on, so I rewrote it until it actually made sense. It was sent off the next day with each of the authors assuming the others had fixed it up. They were hardly on speaking terms anyway. My first publication, anonymously.'

Jack turned to Costas. 'That paper's become the launch pad for exactly what I've been pondering, the mind-state of people in the late Stone Age.'

Jeremy pulled a battered old book out of his pocket. 'I'm not a neuropsychologist, but I do like poetry,' he said. 'What you're describing, the religious experience, we tend to think of as rapture in the face of God. But you don't have to believe in a god to experience rapture, to have the same sort of visions and pleasure as the believer contemplating the Virgin Mary. In deep prehistory, the experience of rapture may have been the preserve of the shaman or seer. In the West today, I'd argue that the shaman's role is largely taken by the poet and the musician and the artist. In fact, you could say that the mark of a true gift in a poet, the poet as shaman, is whether we can see rapture in the process of creativity, and whether we can experience something of that when we read the work.'

He flipped through the book and found a page, and Costas leaned over to look. 'Ah. "The poet who had drunk the milk of paradise".'

Jeremy nodded. 'Samuel Taylor Coleridge, his poem "Kubla Khan". And for milk of paradise, read opium.'

Costas glanced at Jack. 'While we were working on the ROV, Jeremy and I went through his undergraduate dissertation on Homeric imagery in the poetry of W. H. Auden. There's all that dark imagery of the fall of Troy and modern war in "The Shield of Achilles", and for relief we went for some eighteenth-century romantic euphoria. That meant Coleridge. This poem's good because of the watery imagery, and I can relate it to the experience of diving in the way you were just describing.'

'Coleridge wrote the poem one night in 1797 after what he described as a "sort of reverie" brought on by two grains of opium,' Jeremy continued. 'So in this case, drugs were used, but it's the effect we're interested in, and that fits closely with what you're talking about. Coleridge had just been reading an account of the Tartar emperor Kublai Khan's pleasure palace by the sea, and that seems to have made him think about creative power that works with nature and creative power that doesn't. That's also what made me think of the poem, the idea of a tension between two Neolithic belief worlds, the one of the shaman and the one of the gods, the one attuned to nature and the other to man. But just now I also thought of Coleridge's dream images, and how they were like the ones Lanowski was describing. A lot of them have to do with with rivers and the sea.' He read from the page:

> 'In Xanadu did Kubla Khan
> A stately pleasure-dome decree:
> Where Alph, the sacred river, ran
> Through caverns measureless to man
> Down to a sunless sea.'

Costas followed from memory:

> 'Five miles meandering with a mazy motion
> Through wood and dale the sacred river ran,
> Then reached the caverns measureless to man,
> And sank in tumult to a lifeless ocean.'

Jeremy put his finger on some handwritten notes under the poem. 'Coleridge wrote a letter to a friend of his, John Thelwell, about the same time he composed the poem. Listen to this: "I should much wish, like the Indian Vishnu, to float about along an infinite ocean cradled in the flower of the Lotus, and wake once in a million years for a few minutes." And then he writes: "My mind feels as if it ached to behold and know something great – something one and indivisible."' Jeremy paused. 'The metaphor of flowing water as a vehicle for the imagination is pretty widespread, and images of water are common among the Romantic poets. But this is one case where we can talk in neuropsychological terms about altered consciousness, because Coleridge tells us himself that he'd taken opium.'

'Coleridge himself called the poem a "psychological curiosity",' Costas added. 'He also writes of a mighty fountain, spewing out huge fragments, spoken of almost as if it's a volcano: it comes from a deep chasm, a savage place. The poem's like a cosmology of the earth and the underworld combined with visions that come from an altered state of consciousness, visions that are familiar to us because they're hard-wired into our brains just as Lanowski suggested.'

Jeremy shut the book and pocketed it. 'I think it's another way of understanding what we're looking at in early prehistory. For too long archaeologists have assumed that ancient belief systems are somehow beyond their reach. Many early archaeologists were dogmatic about their Christianity, and shamanistic religion was regarded as the least accessible of all, a primitive, ill-formed system of spiritualism that existed before God revealed himself. But I'd argue that's precisely where we need to go if we are to understand the origins of religion today, to look at neuropsychology. And most fascinatingly, what Coleridge was describing shows how that experience could have been intense and rapturous without the worship of gods.'

'It's not just in modern poetry,' Jack said thoughtfully. 'You get the same kind of imagery in the earliest literature of all, in the Babylonian Epic of Gilgamesh, where long voyages are taken over water and there's that same juxtaposition of the world of nature and the world of men. And the Epic of

Gilgamesh may preserve an actual memory of the spiritualist world of the early Neolithic, a world just before the gods came into being.'

Lanowski got up, put the blackboard resolutely back on the chair and whipped out his piece of chalk. He drew a spiral on one side of the board, then turned back to them, his eyes gleaming. 'Here you see the vision of a tunnel, a vortex. It's the most common altered consciousness vision, and also the most common early Neolithic symbol. You find it everywhere, from the megalithic tombs of Ireland to Atlantis. The vortex can be surrounded by animal images, like Jack's image of Costas repeatedly on the edge of his vision, but here it's empty. You could call it a vision of pure rapture. But then something changes.' He flourished the chalk, then drew two circles beside the first, the same size but without the spiral. 'Think of Stonehenge. Think of the Neolithic temples. They're circles. But what do they have inside them?' He slashed a T shape and a pi shape on the top of the board. 'What you've got, gentlemen, is gods. That's what the trilithons at Stonehenge are. That's what the T-shaped pillars of Göbekli Tepe and Atlantis are. And how do you depict this new type of temple, this new religion, as a symbol?' He put the chalk in the centre of the second circle and drew a series of straight lines radiating out, turning each line sharply to the left. He swivelled back to them, his arms held out questioningly.

'The *Sonnenrad*,' Jack said quietly. 'The ancient sun symbol, used by the Nazis as the SS symbol.'

Lanowski flourished the chalk. 'The old vortex, hijacked. Now you see not a swirl, but the walls of the tunnel lined with these images of gods.'

'And there's another ancient symbol,' Jack said quietly.

Lanowski turned and drew inside the third circle, this time only four lines intersecting, the ends turned left. Jack stared at it. *The swastika.* But now he saw it not as a cross at all, but as a symbol of the ascendancy of the gods; the gods who had taken over the old religion ten thousand years ago. *And a horrifying modern symbol, a symbol of gods reborn, not in the depths of prehistory but in the cauldron of Europe eighty years ago.*

Lanowski tossed the chalk, pocketed it and marched back to his computer workstation. 'Just a little more time, Jack. Then I've got something more to show you.'

Jack looked to the ROV screen, which was still blank, and Jeremy glanced at the monitor where he had left his program loading. 'Okay,' Jeremy exclaimed. 'We're in business. This is going to completely change your view of Atlantis.'

Jack and Costas followed Jeremy, who sat down in front of the monitor and glanced at Jack. 'As soon as you surfaced from the dive, Costas emailed me the photos from your helmet camera, the ones you've already seen as raw images. The beauty of that camera pod is that it incorporates a miniature thermal-imaging device and GPR, ground-penetrating radar, allowing us to see beyond the visuals. It's going to revolutionize underwater archaeology, because it'll enable nearly instant transfer of the processed images into the diver's helmet monitor, allowing a kind of X-ray vision. A few glitches, but Costas and I are nearly there. Meanwhile, look at this. What you'll see is what Jack actually saw when he poked his head into that chamber, minus the reflections from his headlamp off suspended particles, which I've removed.' He clicked the mouse, and an extraordinary image came on the screen, taking Jack back to that heart-pounding moment in the depths of the volcano only a few hours before.

'Holy shit,' Costas murmured. 'It's like a charnel house. Like something out of an Aztec nightmare.'

It was the image of the human skull Jack had been looking at before Jeremy and Lanowski arrived, visible in sharper detail so that they could clearly see the finger marks of the ancient sculptor in the plaster that had been formed over the bone. But behind it were rows of other skulls, far more than Jack had seen before. Jeremy opened up a toolbar and sharpened the contrast. 'I count at least twenty-five. About half are deliberately plastered like these ones, and the rest only look as if they are because they're covered in calcite precipitate that formed over them after they were submerged. The anoxic environment of the Black Sea accounts for the amazing preservation. Our osteologist at Troy thinks the plastered skulls are mostly older people, men and women who may have lived a full lifespan and died naturally, some of them very old. They're perhaps the skulls of venerated elders. But the other skulls are widely varied, adults of different ages, teenagers, children. The plastered skulls are all upright in the floor, set in a layer of burnt lime. The other skulls are scattered around as if whatever ritual was happening here was abandoned partway through, as the flood waters were rising.'

Jack stared at the image that had been inches away from him underwater, seeing how the plaster had been moulded to form high cheekbones and bedding in the sockets for cowrie-shell eyes. He could see how the plastered skulls had been carefully sunk up to chin level in the lime floor. He remembered the most striking images from the Neolithic town of Çatalhöyük, of bulls' skulls embedded in house walls, almost as if they were caught at the moment of coming through. In the cave paintings of the Palaeolithic the animals seemed to be emerging from the walls, sometimes floating in front of them, alongside haunting imprints of human hands; the plastered skulls here seemed the same, as if they represented bodies emerging from a chthonic spirit world, emissaries between the world of the living and the world of the dead.

Costas tapped Jack's shoulder. 'You said plastered skulls like this had been found at other sites?'

'At early Neolithic Jericho in Palestine,' Jeremy interjected. 'I was researching it on the way here. A famous skull found by Dame Kathleen Kenyon in her excavations in the 1950s.'

'And at Çatalhöyük,' Jack added. 'They're usually interpreted as evidence for a cult of the dead, for ancestor worship. But I worry about that. Worship is the wrong word, a modern word with misleading connotations. To me, this image from Atlantis suggests that they should be seen in the same way as the bulls and the other animals, as travellers between our world and a spirit world, a world entered through the rock of the volcano, through caves, through house walls. Maybe the ancestors could do this if their remains were properly treated. They were venerated, just as elders would have been when they were alive, but I don't think they were worshipped. I don't think the ancestors were seen as gods: that's an idea I don't see any clear evidence for in prehistoric hunter-gatherer societies.'

Jeremy nodded. 'The ancestor theory fits in with what our bones lady thinks. The plastered skulls are all disarticulated, right? There are no neck bones attached. There's no evidence of trauma injury. These skulls were taken from bodies that were already skeletonized.'

Jack reached for his tablet computer, dragged his fingers over the screen and showed it to Jeremy. 'There's a lot of vulture imagery from Atlantis and the other Neolithic sites. Look at this one: a painting of a vulture pecking at a headless corpse from Çatalhöyük. And here's a vulture from Atlantis, from one of those stone pillars above the skulls, another image taken by my helmet camera. You can see a carving of a great bird of prey with a human arm clutched in its talons. It looks like a Mayan thunderbird, a spirit bird, but is probably meant to be a real bird of prey. I'm convinced we're looking at evidence for sky burial – for excarnation – with bodies being exposed to be consumed by vultures like Zoroastrian sky burial today in India. That sanctum at Atlantis was originally partly open to the air beside a platform on the flank of the volcano, and I believe that sky burial was one of the functions of these temple sites before the pillars were erected. The birds may have been seen as spirit birds, and by consuming human flesh they may have been able to transport the spirits of the departed to the other world. Seeing this now, I think the Atlantis symbol may not have been an eagle as we supposed, but instead a vulture, a spirit bird.'

Jeremy nodded. 'Now for that X-ray vision I was talking about. Prepare to be amazed.' He zoomed in, tapped a key and sat back, and they watched while the screen repixellated. 'This is a composite CGI of what you just saw, using the GPR data.' The screen transformed into an image showing far more than was visible with the naked eye, shapes and artefacts that were buried beneath the lime encrustation. Costas whistled, and Jeremy pointed at the skull in the centre of the image, one that had been visible only in vague outline before. 'This is one of the unplastered skulls, a child about nine or ten years old. Look closely and you can see that four of the neck vertebrae are still attached. You wouldn't get that if you'd taken the skull from a properly skeletonized body, with all the ligaments gone. And then look over there, beneath the lime accretion on the floor.'

'Holy cow,' Costas exclaimed. 'It's a complete skeleton.'

'Nearly complete,' Jeremy corrected. 'And that wasn't just dumped there. Look, you can see dark rings where the wrists were lashed together, probably copper wire. There's a little reed flute in one of the hands. This was a fully articulated fresh corpse, with musculature and sinews intact when the waters rose and it was encased in lime. I said *nearly* complete. The head's missing. And it isn't another body. It's the *same* body. The number of missing neck vertebrae match those on the child's skull.'

Costas looked at Jeremy aghast. 'Do you think this child was killed by being beheaded?'

'That's what I thought at first. But then I emailed this image to our bones lady. She zoomed in on the skull, and pointed this out. You see? It's been bashed in on one side. And look at the shapes of the objects buried in the lime just below it. There's some kind of mace, a stone-topped wooden hammer. And that leaf-shaped thing in the foreground is a chipped stone knife, ripple-flaked, almost certainly obsidian. You see what I'm getting at? What Costas said about the Aztecs might not be that far off the mark.'

'That child was sacrificed,' Costas whispered.

Jeremy zoomed out from the skull to reveal a panorama of the chamber, showing the circle of pillars and the stone basins rising up between the skulls. 'Look at the relationship between the skeleton and the skull and that stone basin. It makes sense of the basin, don't you think? It was an altar. A sacrificial altar.'

Jack wondered whether the basins were windows into the depths, into the underworld, some kind of visionary device. He remembered the dark red stain on his glove when he put his hand into the basin. 'We know they sacrificed bulls, because we found the remains of one five years ago spread over a large stone table at an entrance chamber into the volcano. But this is a revelation. It's horrifying. *Human* sacrifice.'

Jeremy leaned back. 'I think that child was killed by being bludgeoned with the mace. Then it was bled from the neck into the basin, and the knife was used to behead it. Separate the head from the body, and maybe you dispatch the soul to the spirit world. Maybe the blood in the basin was a conduit, a river, fitting in with those altered-consciousness visions we were talking about. Maybe the sacrificer also travelled that river, a portal to the spirit world opened up by the act of sacrifice.'

'With implements specifically designed for the purpose,' Jack murmured. 'Obsidian blades like that one have been found in caches in houses at Çatalhöyük, and have long been suspected to have symbolic significance. And those stone basins look much older than the pillars, carved out of the living rock. They were part of the ancient function of this chamber way before the flood.'

'Wasn't there a tradition of child sacrifice in the Near East?' Costas said. 'I mean the Old Testament account of Abraham and his son Isaac. And the Phoenicians, and their successors in the west Mediterranean, at Carthage. When we've been at the IMU museum at Carthage I've often walked around the tophet, where the children were supposedly sacrificed.'

'But we know child sacrifice may have been exaggerated by the Romans,' Jack said, staring pensively at the image. 'It may only have been in times of extreme duress, in the case of the Carthaginians when they were faced with annihilation by the Romans.'

'But isn't that what we're seeing at Atlantis?' Costas said. 'I mean, extreme duress? The flood waters rising, and no way out?'

That was it. *And no way out.* Jack remembered the walled-over chamber, the pillars freshly carved and the old paintings erased. Had this been a newly refurbished temple, on the verge of being revealed as the flood waters came, but instead used as a dungeon for the last remaining shamans, their death chamber? He stared at the skeleton. Had those people been driven in desperation to take human life, when the blood of bulls had no longer been sufficient?

'It wasn't just children,' Jeremy said. 'The osteologist reckons there are at least twelve other trussed-up bodies in there, all of them articulated skeletons and all of them decapitated. They seem to be of widely varying ages, adults and younger, probably male and female. Visionary ability is often perceived to be passed down in a family, isn't it, from parent to child? That's what I think we've got here. I think we've got entire families being locked in this chamber. It's a really chilling image, like those Jewish families trapped at Masada by the Romans. It's as Costas says: people driven to it by extreme duress.'

'You mean driven to sacrifice?' Costas said.

'Call it sacrifice. Or call it assisted mass suicide.'

They were all silent for a moment, staring at the image. Costas coughed, and then spoke quietly. 'So let me get this right. In this Garden of Eden, at the dawn of civilization, you've got vultures picking away at dismembered corpses. You've got a new order of priests that make the Jesuits of the Inquisition look like angels, forcing people to hack out limestone pillars and drag them up the volcano to make this temple, a temple to themselves, the new gods. And you've got an old order of shamans, off their heads on some kind of psychedelic trip, trapped in this death chamber and performing human sacrifice. And all of that while the flood waters are rising, and their world is being annihilated.'

'The old order swept away, the new world about to dawn,' Jeremy murmured. 'If you look at the Old Testament account and the Epic of Gilgamesh, the flood is represented as an act of God, an act of divine punishment. Maybe that idea was created by the new priests and became the myth. And maybe the flood was actually propitious timing for the new priests, the new gods, who were ready for the diaspora to leave and found new cities and civilizations around the ancient world.'

'In which case,' Costas said, 'who was Noah? A shaman survivor?'

Jeremy paused. 'In the Epic of Gilgamesh, Uta-napishtim is cast up on a mountain far across the waters, cut off from the world of men and their gods.'

Jack stared at Costas, his mind racing. 'It's possible. Maybe one of them did survive. Maybe the annihilation wasn't complete.'

'Maybe he was a vacillator,' Jeremy said. 'Maybe he had been unsure whether to stay with the old order or go with the new.'

'Maybe he was guardian of the animals, of the bulls the shamans corralled for sacrifice, and the new priests needed him to tend those they were taking with them.'

Jack focused on the image on the screen. 'If I could get into that chamber this morning, then someone could have got out. That hole in the wall had been made deliberately, by pulling the stones from the outside. Maybe someone dragged him out, at the last moment.'

Jack cast his mind back again to his image of those final hours. Had the shamans been sealed in, blamed perhaps for the flood, told to use all their powers to stem the waters? Or had that been a lie, and it had truly been a death chamber of the new priests' devising? In the absence of bulls to sacrifice, sealed in that chamber and realizing they were facing certain death, had they crossed the boundary and committed the ultimate act of sacrifice? *Had the new gods forced them to unspeakable horror?*

Lanowski came bounding up to them, rubbing his hands. 'Okay. I'm ready.'

Costas looked back at the wall. 'But the ROV monitor's still blank.'

'I don't mean that. I mean what I've been working on at the computer.' Lanowski peered at the image on the screen. 'Oh. I nearly forgot.' He reached into his pocket and handed Jack a crumpled slip of paper. 'The lab technician gave this to me as I was coming in. The test results on that red stuff on your glove.'

Jack smoothed open the paper and read the report. It was exactly as he had thought. *It was human blood*. It had been on his glove, in the cracks and crevices, clouding the water as he rubbed it off, the seven-thousand-year-old blood of that child, perhaps, of its family, blood that had fed the pool in that basin that someone was using desperately in an effort to get into the spirit world, to escape the horror of drowning as the flood waters began to lap the chamber. For a moment Jack wished he had pulled himself further inside, up over the basin, so that he could peer into it, to glimpse what the one with the bloodied mace and the dripping knife had tried to see. But then he knew he would only have witnessed a reflection of that circle of pillars looming over the basin, radiating in the circular shape of the bowl like the spokes of the *Sonnenrad* in Lanowski's drawing, flickering in whatever firelight they had left in the chamber, a fiery image of the new gods leering through the spent blood of the old order.

He glanced again at the three circular shapes Lanowski had chalked on the blackboard, from spiral to *Sonnenrad* to swastika. He suddenly remembered the palladion, the symbol of ancient Troy they knew had taken the swastika shape: a sacred meteorite forged and hammered into the crooked cross and melded with gold, stolen by the Greek king Agamemnon from Troy and then found by Heinrich Schliemann at Mycenae and secretly taken by the Nazis to Germany. He stared at the image of the swastika. 'The star of heaven,' he murmured. '*Of course.*'

'Come again?' Lanowski said.

'The star of heaven,' Jack repeated, his heart pounding with excitement. 'It's been staring us in the face all along. It's in the Epic of Gilgamesh.' He picked up his tablet computer and called up the text of the Babylonian epic. 'It's on the first tablet, "The Coming of Enkidu". Gilgamesh has a dream, and tells his mother, the goddess Ninsun. Listen to this: "I walked through the night under the stars of the firmament, and one, a meteor of the stuff of Anu, fell down from heaven. I tried to lift it but it proved too heavy. All the people of Uruk came round to see it, the common people jostling and the nobles thronging to kiss its feet; and to me its attraction was like the love of a woman. They helped me, I braced my forehead and I raised it with thongs and brought it to you."'

Jack put the tablet down. 'It's incredible. I'm convinced that's the same story as the Trojan foundation myth, which recounts the origin of the palladion as a meteorite. I think both stories hark back to Atlantis: the Epic of Gilgamesh from the perspective of northern Mesopotamia, the Trojan myth from the viewpoint of those who fled Atlantis to the Dardanelles and actually took the palladion with them. The "star of heaven" was the palladion after the meteorite was forged and hammered into the shape of the swastika. Ninsun tells Gilgamesh that in the dream the star was an analogue, that in fact he was dreaming of the coming of Enkidu, the wild man he will tame and make his brother: the story may represent the tension between the first civilization, represented by Gilgamesh himself, and the ancient wildness that still survived from prehistory. It puts the palladion in a whole new context. No wonder it had such power through history, revered and feared, hijacked by the first priests of Atlantis as their new sacred symbol, and then rediscovered and given a terrible new lease of life almost ten thousand years later by the Nazis.'

Jack sat back, remembering the start of their trail six months before, a trail that had hinted at the devastating truth about the palladion and its new symbolism in a currency of evil played out in the Second World War. He looked down, staring at his palms. Six months ago he had had other blood on his hands, the blood of those who had died violently in their quest for the palladion, lives Jack had taken in his attempt to protect those closest to him. He thought of Maurice Hiebermeyer and the Nazi bunker, and a cold shiver ran through him. The swastika on the blackboard suddenly seemed to be swirling, drawing him into a different kind of history, one of horror and immolation that those first priests could scarcely have imagined. He tore himself away, and looked at Lanowski. 'You were going to tell us something?'

Lanowski peered back, his face flushed and his eyes burning with fervour. 'You want to know where the last shaman of Atlantis went? Where Noah went with his Ark? You want to find the new Atlantis?'

Costas and Jeremy peered at Jack. He glanced at his watch, exhaled forcefully and then looked at Lanowski. 'Okay, Jacob. Give us what you've got.'

8

Near Bergen-Belsen, Germany

Maurice Hiebermeyer tripped over the step into the bunker and stumbled forward, putting his arm out to catch himself on an upright metal pole that loomed in front of him. He fell into it heavily, wincing as his wrist took his weight, then lost his footing and twisted round on to his back, jarring his head and losing his grip as his hand slid down the viscous exterior of the pole. Major Penn caught him and heaved him back on to his feet, holding him upright while he regained his balance. Hiebermeyer panted hard, his heart pounding, his ears filled with the suck and pop of the diaphragm in his regulator as he drew hard on the oxygen in his backpack. He tried to calm himself, staring through the glass visor of his helmet at the mottled patch of concrete wall that was all he could see ahead. For a moment he felt disorientated, and then he realized that he had twisted around and was facing the entrance they had just come through into the bunker. The slight blurriness was a consequence of following Sergeant Jones' advice to remove his glasses to avoid having them fog up as he perspired. It seemed to make little difference now, as the sweat on his face had already made the glass plate of his helmet seem opaque.

He breathed slowly, trying to catch his rising claustrophobia. He knew he could ask to leave and could be out of that door and back into some semblance of normality within minutes. He shut his eyes tight, then opened them again as his heart rate stabilized. A patch had cleared in the centre of his visor, allowing him to see the metal grid of the walkway in the beam of his headlamp.

'Are you all right?' The tinny voice through his earphones came from Major Penn, now visible beside him in his bulky white CBRN suit.

'I'm fine,' Hiebermeyer replied, his voice sounding oddly muffled inside the helmet. 'A twisted wrist, but I can live with that.'

'I've checked over your suit, and there's no obvious damage,' Penn said. 'The worst-case scenario would be any kind of tear. Even the chance of contamination would be enough to put you in the quarantine chamber in the Portakabin for a month.'

'No thanks,' Hiebermeyer replied.

'I forgot to mention that it can be a little slippery in here, like that pole. There's not much dust because there have been no people in here for more than seventy years, so no dead human skin. But there's a thin layer of old fungal growth over everything. The forensics guy thinks that something decayed in here and putrefied a long time ago. It's on the floor too, so watch your step.'

Hiebermeyer stared at the yellow-brown smear on his glove from the pole. *Something decayed in here*. He felt a wave of nausea, swallowed hard and wiped his hand against his leg. He swung around, his headlamp beam traversing indeterminate shapes and shadows as he turned back towards their objective, the main chamber of the bunker, visible through an open door at the end of the entrance passageway. He walked forward, following Penn. The halo of condensation around the edge of his visor made it seem as if he were in a tunnel, almost moving in slow motion. Penn stopped, clicked off the intercom button on the side of his helmet and activated the external link that allowed him to communicate with the phone in the Portakabin. It was strict procedure to activate it only when absolutely vital, to keep workers inside the bunker from being distracted, and even the other two men in the chamber ahead of them would only be included in their intercom audio loop if necessary. Hiebermeyer could see that Penn was talking in an agitated manner. After about a minute he clicked the side of his helmet and his voice crackled again inside Hiebermeyer's headset. 'That was Sergeant Jones in the kitting-up room,' he said, sounding annoyed. 'The EU inspector Dr Auxelle has arrived ahead of schedule. He's forced Jones to let him come into the bunker now. Auxelle knew I was in here already, and Jones doesn't have the authority to stand up to him. Auxelle probably threatened him, though Jones is too professional to tell me that. It's all completely unnecessary. Auxelle could have waited twenty minutes as the schedule dictated, so that he and Jones could have gone in as planned and the turnover worked smoothly, keeping the maximum number in the bunker to four. But he knows the pair ahead of us are making the first entry into the laboratory at the back of the main chamber, and he wants to be in on the act. It's always like that with these people. We have to deal with EU Health and Safety nabobs all the time. They like you to think they're in charge, and you have to go along with it or risk being blacklisted.'

'It sounds as if I'm the one who's arrived on your doorstep at the wrong time,' Hiebermeyer said. 'If you hadn't been in here with me, you could have dealt with it and made him wait.'

'Auxelle and Jones are in the double-lock chamber already, so there's nothing I can do about it. And it was my call to slot us in the schedule now. I promised Jack Howard that I'd personally escort you and get you in and out as fast as possible. He said that he'd been against you coming here and that you had other priorities at the moment.'

'I'm seeing this through.'

'Okay. With Auxelle and Jones directly behind us, we've got to move more quickly. I'm going to take you directly to the storage crates, and then that's it. I want to be in the scrubbing room waiting for Auxelle when he comes out. I think the time has arrived for a showdown.'

'Sounds like a little suspicion on your part that he might have picked up some contamination wouldn't go amiss.'

'I wish. That's one area where he can't override my authority. A month in the quarantine chamber would certainly get him out of my hair.' He grinned at Hiebermeyer through his visor, then put a hand on his back. 'You okay? Let's try to do this within twenty minutes. We'll be using our headlamps all through. The old electrics in here still work, powered by a huge U-boat battery that we think was here mainly to keep some kind of refrigeration unit going in the laboratory, something they wanted guaranteed long-term. But we're not risking the old electrical system. We always work with our own power supply. We should know what the electrics were powering soon enough, as the two sappers ahead of us will be at the lab door by now. I've asked them to hold off reporting unless there's urgent need so that we can focus on those crates, but to give me a situation report at 1420. That's eighteen minutes from now. I've just warned them on the intercom about Auxelle and Jones coming in.'

Hiebermeyer cautiously followed Penn along the metal grid on the floor. On one side his headlamp caught the window of a small room, the glass covered with the yellow-brown layer and reflecting a strange unearthly glow. Further ahead a machine gun sat on its tripod on the floor, an old German MG-42, the receiver still closed over a cartridge belt that linked to an ammunition box below. Beyond that lay the opening to the main chamber of the bunker. He followed Penn through, their beams traversing the walls. Two headlamps bobbed at the far end of the chamber, evidently the sappers at the entrance to the laboratory. He saw a small jet of intense orange flame and a shower of sparks. 'They're using an oxyacetylene torch,' Penn said. 'Before now we'd only seen the laboratory door over the crates. We work methodically, inch by inch, and that's as far as we'd got. We knew the door was slightly ajar, and we suspected it might be rusted on its hinges. Let's hope they get through within fifteen minutes.'

They walked further on. With only his single beam stabbing into the gloom, Hiebermeyer found it difficult to get a good sense of the dimensions, but he began to see how they fitted with the plan that Penn had shown him of a structure about the size of an underground railway station, as if a huge section of corrugated culvert pipe had been half buried in the ground. The interior seemed to be glowing yellow-green, and he realized that everything was covered with the same viscous layer he had encountered in the entranceway. He stumbled slightly, and the shadows of the crates loomed large on the wall, elongated on its concave surface. He saw Penn's form in exaggerated silhouette as if it were advancing towards him, an unnerving image from a distant childhood nightmare, a story an older boy had told him of the trolls that lurked underground in these parts, waiting for boys like him. It had seemed frighteningly real, in the land where trolls and goblins had been invented and had then come hideously to life in the dark days of the Third Reich.

His breathing quickened, rasping and sucking through the regulator, and he stopped to calm himself. Penn veered left between two rows of wooden crates of identical dimensions, each about a metre and a half high. They looked unopened and sealed up except for one at the back, its lid slightly ajar. Hiebermeyer followed, his heart pounding. *It could be an absolute treasure trove*. Penn had told him about a crate he had seen containing what looked like paintings, and now they both stood in front of one isolated from the rest and narrower, with no cover. Propped up on the back was a panel that looked as if it might have been the lid, but made up of a single board rather than joined planks. Penn pointed inside. 'I saw this on the way out this morning. Looking at it now, they're definitely paintings, their frames removed and the canvases encased in plywood.' He jerked his thumb at the propped-up panel. 'That one's a portrait. Someone must have taken it out to have a look in 1945. You can just make out the image, though I think there's been some kind of reaction between that mould and the oil from the paint, which has oozed out. It looks irrecoverable, I'm afraid.'

Hiebermeyer could see what Penn meant. The colour definition had gone, as if someone had squeezed all the paints into one bowl and then applied the resulting mess without mixing it together properly, leaving streaks of individual colours through the layer of yellow-green. As he stood back and angled his beam, he could just make out a portrait, like a shallow relief carving, as if the form within were pressing through the panel. He looked hard, mentally checking the image against dozens of lost masterpieces that he had worked through in a catalogue before coming here, in preparation for a moment like this. He shook his head and turned away, then turned back. Still nothing. He tried again, closing his eyes this time.

'Let's move on,' Penn said, pointing at the crate with the lid that was slightly ajar. 'Whatever that painting was, it's history now. And my guess is these bigger crates are what you're going to want to see, more likely to contain antiquities.'

Hiebermeyer stayed rooted to the spot. Suddenly it clicked. *He recognized it.* 'Mein Gott.'

'What is it?'

'It's the *Portrait of a Young Man*, 1516, stolen from the Czartoryski Museum, Krakow, Poland. It's so famous that I hadn't even bothered to look at it again when I was researching lost art before coming here. It's *ritratto di Raffaello*, meaning either by Raphael or of Raphael, or both. Nobody knows for sure, because it's been impossible to study the original using modern analytical techniques. It was one of the most exquisite portraits of the Renaissance and until now the most important painting still lost from the war.'

'Well you can tick that off the list, in more ways than one. I don't think there's any chance of restoration. Another legacy of the Nazis. Come on.'

Hiebermeyer stared at the panel, trying to see what he had remembered from those pre-war photographs of the painting: the sensitive face, the long hair and rakish beret, the languid, confident pose of the young man, the luxurious fur shawl draped over one shoulder. If those two Allied officers really had got inside the bunker – Major Mayne and Colonel Stein – he wondered whether they had stood where he was now, and had seen the painting in its original glory: whether it had given the American, Stein, an art historian at the Courtauld before the war, a thrill of recognition and a shaft of hope before they went on to whatever darkness lay ahead, or whether they too had seen an image forever tainted by the Nazi horror they must have witnessed in the death camp in the forest. Hiebermeyer suddenly lost the image of the young man in his mind's eye and saw only a mess of colour streaked with red, rivulets of paint at the base of the panel where oil had oozed like blood. He remembered years before when he'd realized that resurrecting the artefacts collected by the

Nazi Ahnenerbe would never be possible, that they were best left as part of the ghastly history that Himmler had created for them. The image he saw now seemed to vindicate that, but he had not expected it to be so visceral, as if what this painting had become was more than just a lesson from history; rather an excrescence that could never heal.

Penn went forward to the unopened crates and knelt down, wiping a painted label on the side with the back of his glove and then doing the same to the next two crates. Hiebermeyer knelt down beside the first. One word stood out: *Ahnenerbe*. For a moment all he heard was his own breathing, as if it were disembodied. All those years he had dreamed of searching for these treasures, they had been here under his very nose, only a few kilometres from where he had grown up. He felt light-headed, as if the regulator were no longer giving him enough oxygen. He reached out to one of the crates to steady himself and then withdrew his hand at the last moment, remembering the awful smear of decomposition that had stained his glove when he had slipped at the entrance.

Penn came back to him. 'That's it, all of the crates. They look like identical markings.'

'It all makes sense,' Hiebermeyer murmured. '*It all fits*.'

'You'd better explain.'

Hiebermeyer remained squatting. His long conversation with Dillen and Jack the day before about the events of 1945 was still fresh in his mind. He peered at Penn. 'Those two officers in 1945, Major Mayne and Colonel Stein, they're the key. Stein was in the Monuments and Fine Arts section, a genuine art expert, but the MFA was really a cover for a unit searching for Nazi secrets. Major Mayne was in 30 Commando

Assault Unit, a deliberately misleading name for another one of those outfits. These two men only came together in the last hours on the way to this place, after Captain Frazer had returned from his visit to the camp and tipped off his friend Mayne at British HQ that there was something worth investigating here. We pieced all this together after Jack and his daughter talked to Frazer last year. A Jewish girl in the camp had drawn Frazer a picture. She'd been tortured and raped in the forest, in this bunker, but had managed to escape in the final days and was back in the camp immediately after liberation under the care of British nurses. The picture showed something she'd seen in the bunker, a golden reverse swastika that Frazer recognized as a lost antiquity from Troy. He and Mayne had excavated together at Mycenae before the war and had heard from an old Greek foreman the story of how the object had been found by Heinrich Schliemann and his wife Sophia in the Tomb of Agamemnon, and then secretly taken back to Germany. Frazer and Mayne were convinced it was the lost palladion, the sacred symbol of Troy taken by Agamemnon after he had defeated the Trojans. And now, knowing what is in these other crates, I understand,' Hiebermeyer murmured. 'It makes sense that the palladion should have ended up here. *Absolute* sense.'

'Go on,' Penn said. 'These inscriptions?'

'Look at the dates on these crates.' Hiebermeyer pointed at the stencilled lettering and stamps where Penn had revealed them. 'They're all the same: 13 April 1945. That's only two weeks before the Allies arrived here. *Two weeks*. We know that in the final months of the war Hitler ordered the treasures of the Berlin museums to be taken to secret storage outside the city. Franz Bormann went to the Zoo flak tower in Berlin and took away most of the crates stored there. A lot went to Austria, to the salt mines at Merkers, well away from Allied bombing and where the salt provided a good atmosphere for storage. So I ask myself the question: if there were still much better storage sites accessible, what on earth were the Nazis doing sending art and antiquities to this place, to a bunker in Lower Saxony, in early April 1945, right into the path of the Allied advance?'

'Maybe into the eye of the storm,' Penn suggested. 'Maybe that was the calculation. Send them to the least likely place, and they might have the greatest chance of surviving undetected. When the Nazis built this bunker in 1942, they went to extraordinary lengths to conceal it. We think the entrance tunnel was rigged to self-destruct, but in the event, the British bomber raid on the night of 25 April did it for them. The self-destruct button may have been a final measure planned by someone who'd actually intended to remove this stuff beforehand and wanted all evidence destroyed. Take a look beyond the final crate. There's a row of heavy-duty suitcases on the floor. I think someone may have been about to break down the contents of the crates into manageable packages, but events overtook them and the Allied front line moved faster than they'd expected.'

'Or maybe whoever it was had expected a ceasefire, an armistice.'

'Are we talking about Hitler? Surely by April 1945 a few crates of art would have been the least of his concerns?'

Hiebermeyer shook his head. 'There are other markings on the crates. They say Ahnenerbe, the Department of Cultural

Heritage. And you can see the *Sonnenrad* sun symbol of the SS, and then the word Wewelsburg. You told me you'd studied the architectural plans for that place. The order castle of the SS, run by the man who signed the papers you found in this bunker. You see what I'm getting at?'

Penn gasped. 'Of course. Himmler. *Heinrich Himmler.*'

'The second most powerful man in Nazi Germany, who maybe wanted to be the most powerful.'

'*Himmler,*' Penn repeated. 'Didn't he try to negotiate with the Americans, and then got excommunicated by Hitler for it?'

Hiebermeyer nodded. 'If I'm right about this, then maybe that's where his gamble went wrong. A truce would have allowed him to clear this place out. I'm certain that the crates contain the lost treasures of Wewelsburg Castle: antiquities brought by the Ahnenerbe in the 1930s from around the world, hijacked by Himmler to fuel his fantasy of an Aryan prehistory, of a master race including the kings of ancient Greece, Agamemnon himself, and even the rulers of a mythical Atlantis. I've spent half my lifetime yearning to know what happened to these artefacts.'

Penn had moved along to the side of the crate with the lid ajar, and rubbed the side of it. 'Look at this one. The lettering's different.'

Hiebermeyer followed him up the narrow space and squatted down again, his suit crinkling and bulging as he did so. He stared at the lettering and numbers, his mind racing. 'That's it. That clinches it.'

'*Museum für Vor- und Frühgeschichte,*' Penn read out slowly. '*Troia.*'

Hiebermeyer's heart pounded. 'That's the Museum of Pre- and Proto-History in Berlin. That's where the treasures were displayed that Schliemann had taken from Troy and given to the German people in 1881. In 1941 they were moved from the museum and stored in the Zoo flak tower. I always knew there would be a third crate,' he said excitedly. 'A crate containing the secret treasures Schliemann never gave to the German people but concealed himself somewhere in his home town near the Baltic, where Ahnenerbe researchers under Himmler discovered them. Treasures that included the golden reverse swastika, the Trojan palladion, which Himmler made into his most potent symbol.'

'A third crate?' Penn said. 'Where are the other two?'

'When Bormann went to the flak tower to take the treasures to the salt mines, he left behind two crates, the ones containing the Troy artefacts from the museum. They were still there during the final Soviet onslaught and were taken to Moscow, where they resurfaced in the 1990s. When the Soviets arrived in the flak tower, the door to the storage room was guarded by a Dr Unverzagt, an Ahnenerbe Nazi who had been director of the museum. When the story of his role came out after the artefacts were revealed in Moscow, most archaeologists assumed that he had been guarding the greatest treasures of his museum to ensure that they weren't looted by Soviet soldiers and were captured intact; that he was doing it for the sake of archaeology and science. But I think they were wrong.'

'You think Himmler was personally involved in this?' Penn straightened up, and leaned over the half-open lid of the crate.

'Himmler was obsessed with the treasures of Troy,'

Hiebermeyer replied. 'And he was Unverzagt's boss. The Ahnenerbe worshipped Himmler, the man who had given so many failed and second-rate academics the job of a lifetime. Many of them were all too happy to go along with the racist poison, and plenty of them believed in it. Why did Himmler order Bormann to leave those two crates in the Zoo tower? Because he wanted them for himself. Why were they still there when the Russians arrived? Because Himmler's gamble didn't pay off, and he had no time to remove them. Why was Unverzagt still there guarding them fanatically? Not for the sake of archaeology, but in the vain hope that his god Himmler would return.'

'You should take a look in here,' Penn said. Hiebermeyer heaved himself up, wincing as he pressed his injured wrist against his knee, then aimed his headlamp over the side of the crate. He could see neatly stacked smaller wooden boxes inside, labelled with swastikas and the SS *Sonnenrad*, evidently from Wewelsburg. One of them had a line of symbols along the top of the label he recognized from Stone Age cave paintings. He followed Penn's beam. There was an empty space at the end of the crate, half filled with a lumpy yellow substance covered with mould. He realized that it had been straw, cushioning material. Then his beam crossed Penn's, and he froze.

'Is that what you were looking for?' Penn asked.

Hiebermeyer was speechless. It was the shape of a swastika, indented in the straw, about fifteen centimetres across. It had clearly been a heavy object, metallic, judging by the depth of the indent. He scanned quickly around, looking inside the crate. The object that had made the indent was nowhere to be seen. 'Is there any chance your people could have missed finding it?' he said, his voice hoarse with emotion.

'None of the other crates are open. I told them to leave this part of the room until you arrived and we could look at it together. Apart from this, every inch of the chamber has been inspected, up to the laboratory door. Nothing has been found. If this was that golden object you were talking about, the Trojan palladion, then it looks as if someone scarpered with it in 1945. Odd, though, that it doesn't seem to have been carefully packaged away like this other stuff, instead of just lying here in the straw.'

Hiebermeyer swallowed hard. *He had desperately hoped to find it.* He brought his beam back to the shape in the straw, and stared. 'That's because it was never in the museum collection in Berlin, and it can only have been here in the bunker for a short time. We believe that after the Ahnenerbe discovered the palladion in Schliemann's hiding place in his home town, it was stored in great secrecy in Wewelsburg Castle. We believe that Himmler imbued it with holy significance, perhaps involving it in some kind of initiation rite for a select few. It became a sacred symbol of the new creed, of the god Himmler had made himself. We know that it became the symbol of something called the Agamemnon Code, an activation code somehow tied up with Himmler's plans for a dark scheme in the final days of the Reich.'

'The reverse swastika on the letterhead of those order papers, marked Top Secret,' Penn said. 'Was that it?'

Hiebermeyer nodded. 'Himmler clearly envisaged a future for himself, rather than the self-immolation that Hitler and his cronies saw as their only way out. But before then, when the palladion had become like the Holy Grail, Himmler had it sent from Wewelsburg to a place of even greater secrecy. I mentioned salt mines? Well, Jack visited one of them last year on his hunt for this object. The man we now believe knows the use to which the palladion was to be put had blackmailed him into going there to retrieve it, by kidnapping his daughter. It had been put deep in the Wieliczka salt mine, in a shaft now flooded under almost a hundred metres of water, near the death camp at Auschwitz. All Jack found was a box containing an impression like this where the palladion had been stored. As the Soviets advanced towards that part of Poland, we believe the palladion was removed from the box and taken by another of Himmler's chosen few on the march with the last inmates from Auschwitz to the west, to Belsen and this place. Among them was the girl who drew that image for Captain Frazer.'

'And then someone took it from here, from this crate, in those final days.'

'Perhaps on Himmler's orders. Perhaps when the Agamemnon Code was activated.'

Penn was silent for a moment, then took a ruler from his tool belt, leaned over and quickly measured the impression. 'There is one place where I've seen a swastika shape like this, the same wide arms and distinctive cross. The more I look at it, the more I think it might be an exact fit. It's on the door to the laboratory. It's an indent just like this but within a roundel. We're fairly sure it's some kind of locking mechanism. Sergeant Jones thought it might be magnetic, but we won't know until we inspect it. The door's very slightly ajar. Maybe the palladion was a key to unlock what was in there. Maybe it unlocked other places like this, part of some scheme of Himmler's that never came to fruition.'

Hiebermeyer could barely breathe. Of course. *It was a key*.

'Major Penn.' A voice sounded through both of their intercoms. 'You need to come to the laboratory door, now.'

'Okay.' Penn straightened up. 'That's my two sappers. And I just saw Sergeant Jones and Auxelle come through the chamber. Let's move now.'

Hiebermeyer followed Penn from the crates on to the main walkway. He glanced back, seeing where the Raphael was propped up, the mottled colours lost in the haze of green. Listening to the rasp of his own breathing, he was reminded of film he had seen of Jack and Costas rising from an underwater site, features of the archaeology clearly visible and then suddenly lost in a green-blue haze, as if they had passed through some kind of lens in the water. He thought about the painting again. Whatever Himmler had devised, whatever ghastly wonder-weapon he had been developing, he had not been above collecting the choicest Old Masters for his own private enjoyment: not for some Nazi Valhalla, but for a real future that he envisaged for himself, perhaps a new Wewelsburg arising in his imagination like Atlantis reborn. Hiebermeyer now knew something with cold certainty. Himmler may have been a fantasist, but there was a ruthless calculating streak to him. All of this had been carefully planned, and had been thwarted only by a misplaced gamble at the end. And if Himmler had planned to hold the world to ransom with his wonder-weapon, that threat remained for others like Saumerre to find and use. For the first time

Hiebermeyer forced himself to face the reality of what might be in that laboratory ahead. He hoped that the nightmare would come to an end here and now.

'Major Penn.' The voice of one of the sappers came through their intercom. 'The inspector and Sergeant Jones have already gone into the laboratory. I couldn't stop them.'

Penn snorted angrily and made his way over. The door was now half open, and there were lights moving inside. Hiebermeyer saw the swastika in the roundel that Penn had described. As they came closer, one of the sappers stepped up and stopped Penn. 'Sir, you'll see there's a body in front of the door, mostly skeleton. We found it when we first arrived here twenty minutes ago, but he's long dead and we didn't see the need to disturb you. There was a smear of old blood on the door where we were cutting through. He was shot at close range in the back of the head, massive skull damage. You'll see more of the same when you go in through that door. Been a little life-and-death struggle here with no winner as far as we can see. This one's American, by the way.'

Penn went straight to the form on the floor and leaned over it. 'A lieutenant colonel's silver oak leaf on the lapel,' he murmured. 'No division or corps insignia on the shoulders. He's got a holstered Colt automatic, but he's wearing a dress uniform, not a field uniform. Not a combat soldier.' He peered at Hiebermeyer. 'Sounds like our Monuments and Fine Arts man, Colonel Stein, wouldn't you say?'

Hiebermeyer nodded, staring at the body, his head swimming. There was a sudden commotion from within the laboratory, and the sound of something falling heavily. A voice came over the intercom. 'Quick!' They heard the French accent of the inspector. 'Come and help! Sergeant Jones has collapsed!'

Penn pushed into the chamber, the other two sappers following and Hiebermeyer bringing up the rear. He saw two more decomposed bodies lying entangled together just inside the door, and Sergeant Jones in his white suit stretched out beside them. The nearest body was wearing tattered striped prisoner clothes, but the one beneath it, lying face-down, wore British battledress, a major's crown clearly visible on one shoulder. Hiebermeyer stared. It could only be Major Mayne. His revolver was still holstered, but his skeletal hand was behind his back, clutching a commando knife that poked up through the other man's ribcage. The man in the prisoner's uniform held a rusted pistol, a Walther, and there was a spent casing on the floor. Hiebermeyer saw a tattoo on a piece of skin that clung to the bones of the forearm. *It was the SS mark*. He barely had time to register it when Penn pulled his arm.

'We've got to get Jones out of here,' he said urgently. He looked angrily at Auxelle. 'How long has he been like this?'

'Only moments. But he had been breathing heavily. Maybe it was seeing the bodies.'

'That's not like Jones. More likely a malfunction with his oxygen. If that's the case, we've only got minutes.' He looked at the other two sappers. 'You each take a leg, Auxelle and Hiebermeyer take the arms. I'll support his waist. Let's move.'

Hiebermeyer lifted Jones' arm but had forgotten his own twisted wrist and slipped with the weight, twisting round and falling back against the wall, his other hand clutching a rail and slipping into something glutinous. He pushed himself up with his back against the wall, and as he did so he tripped the electric light switch. The bare overhead bulbs flickered and then came on with a sudden dazzling glare, blinding him for a moment. Then he saw walls of a sickly pale blue, like the colour of a hospital operating room. The layer of yellow-green was still there, but the light rendered it opaque, a bilious colour. He saw a small refrigerator in front of Jones' legs, its door ajar and the interior gleaming, empty. He stared at it, transfixed, his mind blank, and then he turned to look where he had put his hand.

What he saw was an image of unspeakable horror. Along the side wall of the room were five gurneys, metal trolleys with their upper surfaces formed like shallow basins. Four contained human bodies, naked but grotesquely adiposed, as if they had been covered with a layer of white plaster. The two furthest bodies were strapped down but horribly twisted, like the plaster casts of bodies from Pompeii preserved in their death throes. His mind reeled. He forced himself to look. These people must have been strapped down alive in this laboratory, and were still alive when they were abandoned here. The third and fourth bodies were older cadavers that had been decapitated and disembowelled, with autopsy tools half rusted on a tray in front. The fifth gurney, the one he was holding, contained two severed heads, wax-like and hairless, staring at him blindly through sockets closed up with fatty secretion, the skulls held in the clutches of a three-armed forceps like the severed talons of some bird. They seemed to be embedded in a congealed layer, the glutinous substance he had put his hand into. He lifted it out, tendrils of congealed white and yellow dripping from his fingers. His stomach lurched as he realized what it was. He had seen this once before, inside a two-hundred-year-old lead coffin that he had watched being excavated from a church crypt. The archaeologists had called it body liquor. *He had put his hand into decomposed human fat.*

He doubled over and threw up inside his helmet, coughing and retching as the oxygen from his regulator bubbled through the vomit. He clutched Jones' hand tight, but he felt other hands heaving him up, pushing him forward as he staggered over the two corpses on the floor. He kept his eyes shut and his mouth wide open, breathing in oxygen and vomit, coughing it out again, retching. As they staggered out of the laboratory and back towards the entrance, he fixed his mind on the refrigerator he had seen, its interior gleaming and empty. Something had been stored there, something the Nazi scientists must have extracted from those bodies, and something they had experimented with on the living. Something unimaginable. *But it was gone.*

He was conscious of only one thought.

He had to call Jack.

9

Costas took a last dejected look at the blank screen in front of the ROV monitor, and then swivelled round to join Jack in front of Lanowski's computer. The clock showed 1510 hours, less than an hour before Jack was due on the helipad to leave *Seaquest II* in advance of the arrival of the inspection team. A few moments before, they had felt the ship lurch as she repositioned herself, her new location visible on the digital wall map some two nautical miles north-west of the volcano and the site of Atlantis. Captain Macalister was clearly taking few chances after the images Jack and Costas had brought back with them from their dive into the caldera that morning, but he had agreed to keep the ship within range should a minor miracle happen and the ROV spring back to life. Costas pulled his chair up until he was between the other two men and then rested his elbows on their chair backs. Jeremy had left the room to deal on the phone with an urgent problem at Troy, a statue with Egyptian hieroglyphics that had appeared just as the excavation was winding down; with Hiebermeyer preoccupied at the bunker in Germany and out of contact, Jeremy had wanted to speak to Hiebermeyer's wife Aysha to see whether she could return from Alexandria to judge whether they should excavate now or rebury it for the next season. Costas nudged Lanowski. 'Okay, Jacob. I'm itching to know where you think the new Atlantis might lie. We're not getting anywhere waiting for Little Joey to reveal more about that inner sanctum. I think he's left us for good.'

Jack pointed at the screen. 'Remember this?'

Costas leaned forward and stared at the image, a torn brown scrap of papyrus with ancient Greek script that had been seen over the last five years by thousands of visitors who had stood in front of the original in the archaeological museum in Alexandria. 'The Atlantis papyrus,' he murmured. 'The tail end of the account written by the Greek traveller Solon at the temple of Saïs in the Nile delta, the part of the Atlantis story that somehow never reached Plato when he used Solon's account to write his version of the Atlantis myth in the fifth century BC.' He pointed to a word visible at the top of the screen, letters in Greek spelling out ATLANTIS. 'That's what Hiebermeyer and Aysha saw when they pulled this scrap from the mummy wrapping. I've never heard Maurice so excited by something that wasn't actually Egyptian. I can still remember the look on your face when we came up from the dive on the Bronze Age shipwreck and you took his call.'

Lanowski tapped the keyboard, then sat back and craned his head round at Costas. 'Gladstone. William Ewart Gladstone.'

Costas stared back at him. 'Huh?'

'British prime minister in the late nineteenth century. Does that ring a bell?'

Costas screwed up his eyes, then peered at Lanowski cautiously. 'The guy who was so fascinated with Heinrich Schliemann's discoveries at Troy, who helped push Schliemann to international fame.'

Lanowski nodded. 'Well, like a lot of the Victorian intelligentsia, Gladstone was also fascinated by archaeological discoveries that might illuminate the Bible, especially with the wealth of clay tablets being found at ancient Mesopotamian sites that were seen as part of the backdrop to the Old Testament. One of the most famous discoveries was the Epic of Gilgamesh.'

'It's what we were talking about,' Costas said. 'About the tension it represents between the wild and the civilized, and how it might derive from conflict between the old shamans and the new priests in the early Neolithic.'

Lanowski nodded enthusiastically. 'For the Victorians, the biggest revelation in the Epic of Gilgamesh was the story of a flood that paralleled the Biblical deluge. Gladstone attended a lecture in 1873 at the Society for Biblical Archaeology in London, where the tablet containing the flood account was first revealed. An obsessive genius named George Smith had been sifting through thousands of tablets from Nineveh in the British Museum, and when he came across the flood tablet, he was so excited he rushed about the room and stripped naked.'

'Don't get any ideas, Jacob,' Costas muttered.

Lanowski's eyes glinted. 'Don't worry. I've already had my eureka moment. What George Smith found was the flood tablet in the version of the epic written down in the early first millennium BC, but since the nineteenth century fragments have been found that are a lot earlier, dating to the first period of cuneiform writing in Sumerian and Akkadian in the third millennium BC. The fact that the story of Gilgamesh seems to have been well formed that early strongly suggests that it had been passed down orally for a long time before then, conceivably from as far back as the early Neolithic.'

'And it's the basis for the Old Testament deluge story?'

'Or a parallel tradition, deriving from the same historical backdrop. And for my money, the Gilgamesh story is a lot more intriguing, with more pointers to the early Neolithic. Uta-napishtim, the flood hero, is a more ambiguous character than Noah. For a start, he isn't the sole survivor of the flood, and he's actually presented as more of an outcast. After the flood, the gods grant him immortality, but he lives on the mountain where his boat came ashore, far from the rest of humanity. It's as if the gods' favour comes at a price: we'll grant you immortality and give you this mountain to live on, but don't ever come back to our shores again. As if they owe him something, even feel guilty about him, but he's a threat to the new world of men they lord it over and they don't want him around. And so Gilgamesh, half-god himself, travels a huge distance across the sea to find him, to try to discover the secret of immortality. It's then that Uta-napishtim tells him the story of the flood.'

Costas looked at him shrewdly. 'And you're going to suggest that this flood story contains something about a survivor from Atlantis?'

Lanowski beamed at him. 'The character of Uta-napishtim

himself could be a clue. An outcast. A shaman perhaps, the last of the old order? Gilgamesh goes a huge distance across the water to get to him. And Uta-napishtim lives on a twin-peaked mountain, called Nisir.'

'The mountain of Dû-Re was twin-peaked as well,' Jack murmured. 'That's where the oldest Babylonian myths locate the birthplace of the gods.'

'I think Dû-Re *was* Atlantis,' Lanowski enthused. 'Dû-Re was somewhere to the north, where the Babylonian scribes always placed their ancestors and the home of their gods, precisely where Atlantis and those other early Neolithic sites were located in relation to the early cities of Mesopotamia. But Nisir is a kind of alter-Atlantis, Atlantis reborn, a huge distance over the sea. The question is, was the sea simply a conceptual barrier, a barrier in the mind, or was it a real ocean, and if so which one?'

'And?'

'And that made me think of Jack's lecture at the Royal Geographical Society last December, on prehistoric voyages of discovery. About his title, "Voyages of the mind, voyages of the body".'

'I missed it, I'm sorry to say,' Costas said. 'Too wrapped up getting Little Joey finished in time for the sea trials.'

'Well, if I may,' Lanowski said, looking questioningly at Jack. 'The nub of his argument was this. We've had it all wrong. Great voyages of discovery didn't begin after the rise of civilization, with trade and colonization. They began before that. Way before, as far back as the middle Palaeolithic, fifty thousand years ago or more, when we know people went great distances by sea to get to Australia, for example. Ergo, hunter-gatherers in deep prehistory had boats capable of long-distance seafaring. Hunter-gatherers ranged over huge distances on land, so why not by sea as well? By the end of the Palaeolithic – at the end of the Ice Age – just as many people were living off the sea as off the land. But the advent of farming actually stifled exploration. People moved inland, settled in one place, turned in on themselves, were enslaved by agriculture as well as by new rulers who wanted to control them, to prevent them seeing the world outside their own narrow confines, a control maybe exerted using new religious beliefs based on fear.'

'So why voyages of the mind?' Costas asked.

Jack leaned back. 'That title was prescient, given what we've been talking about here,' he said. 'Now I know why Jacob was in the audience looking at me as Professor Dillen used to when I stumbled my way through a passage of ancient Greek. I'd already been doing some thinking about Palaeolithic religion, about shamanism and altered consciousness. I looked at all that in relation to seafaring in two ways. First, I read about the common altered-consciousness hallucinations of being in water, and I imagined that a real sea voyage, especially an arduous one, would be something like that. Altered states of mind are often most easily achieved under duress, right? It might have been particularly easy when the imagery of the real-life experience and the dream world seemed so close. And I wasn't thinking that Stone Age seafarers were floating around aimlessly in a psychedelic daze, but actually that they were purposeful and destination-conscious. They were doing what they did in those caves, navigating their way into the spirit world, but this time marrying it with a real-life voyage using the stars and even navigational aids such as quartz sunstones. I began to think that the idea of early seafarers being terrified of the open sea might be an inheritance from the establishment of sedentary living in the Neolithic. The sea wasn't the great unknown in deep prehistory. It *became* the great unknown when it suited rulers to stoke up the fear factor. Before that, sea voyages had given people with shamanic beliefs an experience that would have seemed familiar to them. I argued that they wouldn't have sailed off into the unknown in fear for their lives, but quite the opposite. They may actually have relished it, and looked forward with huge excitement to what they might discover in a spiritual sense as well as in reality.'

'And your second point?'

'Thinking about the prehistoric colonization of Australia led me to Aboriginal songlines, the dreaming tracks that were used to cross the outback. If hunter-gatherers could conceptualize land routes in that way, why not at sea as well? Memorized trackways are often the most practicable routes too, and that made me think about the predictability of ocean currents and winds. I ended my lecture with a picture of Thor Heyerdahl and his crew on the Ra expedition reed boat in the mid-Atlantic in 1969, showing how it would have been difficult to avoid being swept out to sea and towards the Caribbean once you'd sailed out of the Mediterranean and down the coast of west Africa. I argued that the sea isn't a barrier, it's a great complex of highways, and nowhere was that more the case than in deep prehistory. I quoted Heyerdahl's famous last lines from his account of the Ra expedition, that his theory about prehistoric maritime contact came about because he and his crew had actually sailed on the ocean and not on a map.'

'They'd tried it out rather than sitting in an armchair theorizing,' Costas said approvingly.

Jack nodded. 'And that gets us back to Atlantis. At the time of the Black Sea flood, the people of Atlantis may have been undergoing a religious revolution, but they were still not that far away from their Palaeolithic ancestors. If we've got it right, there were still shamans present in those final days before the flood, even if they were a beleaguered few. That knowledge of sea travel, that ability to sail off into the unknown, may not yet have been lost.'

Costas nodded. 'Makes a lot of sense.' He turned to Lanowski. 'So what's your big revelation?'

'Plato.' Lanowski laughed quietly to himself, pushed up his glasses, looked at Jack intently and chuckled again. 'Plato, Plato, Plato.'

Costas glanced anxiously at Jack, and then narrowed his eyes at Lanowski. 'All right, Jacob,' he said slowly. 'Let me guess. The Atlantis myth? Plato is the only surviving source. That is, except for the fragment of papyrus Maurice found in the desert that we're looking at on the screen right now, the bit by Solon about where to find Atlantis that never got to Plato.'

'Plato,' Lanowski repeated to himself, shaking his head as if he were in the throes of some private rapture. He suddenly stared at Costas. 'And Pythagoras.'

Costas held his gaze. 'Pythagoras. Let me see. Pythagoras is about geometry, right? Triangles, pyramids? Pyramids, early civilizations, Atlantis?' He shook his head. 'You've lost me.'

Lanowski beamed at him. 'We know from Aristotle that Plato was a follower of Pythagoras. What that means is that Plato believed there was a mathematical and even a musical structure behind everything. But instead of taking an interesting idea into hard science, the Greeks made it esoteric, using it in a mystical way and seeing Pythagorean logic in weird places. They also used it to create hidden messages of meaning. Some scholars have come to believe that Plato embedded codes in his writing to reveal his beliefs to other Pythagoreans. We're not talking about hidden messages as we might understand a code, but about arrangements of letters and words that had a mathematical logic or – in the case of letters – could be related to the musical scale. Other Pythagoreans might recognize them, like a symbol on a ring or a secret handshake.'

Costas looked puzzled, and jerked his finger at the screen. 'But if it's this papyrus you're on about, Solon wrote it about 580 BC. Isn't that a couple of decades before Pythagoras was even born?'

'Often the names we associate with a theory are not those who invented it, and there's good reason for thinking that ideas we call Pythagorean had their origins much earlier in Greece. If they were floating around already in Solon's time, then a clever polymath like him would have lapped them up.'

Jack stared at Lanowski. 'So you think Solon may have put some kind of code in his text?'

Lanowski pointed at the screen, his face flushed with excitement. 'Thanks to my friend Maurice Hiebermeyer, we've got a scan of the very papyrus in front of us. Usually what I'm talking about can only be revealed by stichometric analysis, taking the medieval texts that are our only surviving copies of ancient works and trying to reconstruct how they would have looked on the original papyrus, based on the regular length of lines ancient scribes used. But we've actually got an original papyrus, with the lines exactly as Solon composed them. Almost immediately I matched his layout to the twelve-note musical scale. Look, you can see where I've highlighted the text, the letters alpha to lamda for the musical notes in the first letters of a line of words running diagonally through that last paragraph. That was my eureka moment. I realized that Solon had been doing what Plato later did, that there was more to this papyrus than meets the eye. So now I've been looking at the letters along the right and left margins, and then at criss-cross patterns, and all the other obvious geometric possibilities, and then I've been applying basic cryptographic analysis using letter codes. I'm convinced there are words embedded in the text.'

'You know ancient Greek?' Costas asked.

'Yeah. Easy. Did it at school.'

'And?'

'I've tried about five hundred different letter codes.'

'In your head.'

Lanowski looked nonplussed. 'Of course. Computers can't actually think, you know.'

Costas leaned back. 'But surely all you're going to find is more patterns, more word games. Where does that get us?'

'That's what I thought at first. But then I remembered how easy it was for me to find that musical scale. Way too easy for an intellectual like Solon. I think he wanted some successor like Plato to see it and then look for what else was hidden, something we know Plato never had the chance to do because this fragment of papyrus was lost in the desert before Solon left Egypt, and he never replicated it. I love the idea that Solon might have been robbed of the gold he was going to use to pay the priest and that he suffered some kind of permanent amnesia, losing this part of his papyrus during the scuffle as well. But I think I'm taking up where Plato should have been, as someone who immediately recognizes that there must be something else hidden in the text.'

'That still doesn't explain how a hidden code could be anything other than wordplay, mathematical games.'

Lanowski looked at Costas. 'The technique *could* also have been used to conceal actual words, as a code in the way we might expect.'

'It makes sense,' Jack added. 'Why on earth would Solon bother to embed a word game in a script he's writing in the flickering torchlight at the foot of an old priest, telling him one of the most extraordinary tales he's ever heard? There must have been a particular purpose for concealment, and Solon wasn't a mystic like some of those later Pythagoreans.'

'There's geometry in that page,' Lanowski said, pointing at the screen. 'Not in the section at the top of the papyrus, where I think he was hastily copying down a dictation from the high priest, but in that final crucial paragraph. It's much more carefully written. Remember, Solon was translating from Egyptian into Greek as he was listening. So he was already thinking hard about language, about words. He was good at composing fast. I've really got to like the guy and I can see where he was coming from. He enjoyed making clever geometry out of his writing. It's really no different from the way a creative writer today uses metaphor and simile, alliteration and assonance. Only here I think the artistry had a special reason. Imagine this: the high priest is speaking slowly, carefully, giving Solon time to transcribe what he's saying. This was really important stuff, about the end of Atlantis, coveted information normally only passed from priest to priest. The high priest is taking a bit of a gamble telling him, perhaps induced by the promise of gold. But then he oversteps the boundary and tells Solon something really coveted, something sacred. Maybe he then regrets it and instructs Solon not to write it down.'

'But Solon finds a way,' murmured Costas.

'And maybe the high priest still doesn't trust him, and it was the priest who arranged for Solon to be robbed and knocked on the head after leaving the temple that final night.'

Costas shook his head. 'I still don't get it. We know from what's openly in the text that the priest told Solon a phenomenal story, something passed down over almost seven thousand years. There's incredible detail in the descriptions of Atlantis. What else could he reveal that might suddenly seem beyond the pale, too secret to tell Solon?'

Lanowski got up and paced in front of them, gesticulating. 'Let's imagine he told Solon where the Atlanteans went, something Solon wrote down at the end of the text in the corner of the papyrus that's been ripped off. We can pretty well guess what it would have said. Troy, Greece, Crete, the coast of the Levant, Mesopotamia, Egypt, where all the early civilizations subsequently developed. But then let's imagine there was another story. Something dark, a story of exile, of banishment. Something hinted at in later myth, but a truth that should not be told. Then I thought of the Epic of Gilgamesh.'

'I think I've got you,' Jack said. 'The idea of Uta-napishtim cast away, a pariah. To a place where nobody is supposed to follow.'

'And a place whose horror might have been exaggerated by the new priesthood of the early Neolithic, a priesthood which had already made people fear the unknown, the open ocean,' Costas said. 'Try to go there, and the ancient demons of the spirit world will arise again and haunt you.'

'And carry out appalling acts half remembered, take away the children and sacrifice them to satisfy their blood lust,' Lanowski said.

'So you think Solon heard what he should not have heard, agreed not to write it down but did so, in some kind of code?'

'I think the fear of that place and of the one who lurked there, a kind of nightmare shaman, may have still been felt by those priests of Egypt who were the last in the line to carry the actual story of what happened, a story that survived elsewhere only in the garbled accounts of the flood in the Epic of Gilgamesh and the Old Testament. Seven thousand years on, that last shaman and what he represented still struck terror into the hearts of Egyptian priests whose gods were supposedly all-powerful, yet who could not suppress that ancient fear of the old spiritualist religion and the threat it posed to the new world of the gods.'

'And?' Jack said. 'The code?'

Lanowski scratched his head. 'It's not quite there yet. I've narrowed it down to three possibles. It's what you say, Jack. A hunch. A gut feeling that I'm on to something.'

Jack stared at him for a moment, then nodded. 'Okay, Jacob. Email it to me when you've got a result.'

'Roger that.' Lanowski gave him a crooked smile, his face red with excitement, then sat back down in front of the screen and began mumbling lists of letters to himself, apparently oblivious to anyone else in the room. Jack drummed his fingers on the desk, feeling frustrated. Suddenly they were on the cusp of something big, and it was going to have to be put on hold. He tried to keep his mind on prehistoric exploration for a moment longer. The possibility of ancient voyages across the Atlantic had been a fascination of his during his student years, something he had married with Maurice Hiebermeyer's obsession with retracing the Nazi Ahnenerbe expeditions to see whether they were ever on to anything real. It had come to fruition years later when they had crossed the North Atlantic to Greenland and Newfoundland, following Viking explorers. But the other main route across the Atlantic, south from the Mediterranean and across from Africa, continued to be unexplored territory for him. The African route south had been taken by the Phoenicians, but there was no certainty that they had ever intentionally struck off west. And Jack had already begun to think much earlier than that, to early prehistory, the basis for his Royal Geographical Society lecture. Only he had never associated it with an exodus from Atlantis, until now. He could only hope that the trail that was beginning to form in front of them would set up some waymarkers soon.

'One final thing.' Lanowski turned and looked at him. 'If you want to work out where the Atlanteans went, get into the cave, Jack. And I don't just mean metaphorically. If we're looking for the last of the shamans, if we're looking for Noah Uta-Napishtim, we need to be looking for somewhere he can do his thing again, somewhere like that holy sanctum in Atlantis.'

'Just as long as it doesn't take us on a psychedelic trip into a cave of the mind,' Costas said. 'That transatlantic current dumps you in the Caribbean, right? Sounds good to me. I want a tropical island.'

Lanowski peered at him. 'My girlfriend says every man needs his cave.'

'And she wants to get into yours?' Costas asked.

'It's no different from the cave you disappear into every night in the basement of the engineering department at IMU, hatching mini-ROVs.'

'Don't. Little Joey. It's still too raw.'

Jeremy came back into the room, stopped before reaching them and pointed. 'Hey, Costas. Have you seen that?'

Costas glanced back at the ROV monitor. 'My God,' he said hoarsely. While they had been talking, the screen had come to life. He quickly got up, pushed aside the chairs and sat down at the monitoring station, his eyes glued to the screen. Lanowski came up quickly behind him and leaned over the control panel.

'There may be some electrical impulse still left that could knock the camera askew. Until we're sure this image is recorded, let's keep hands off the control stick.' He tapped the keyboard, downloading the video stream, and Jack stared in astonishment at the underwater image on the monitor. He could see tendrils like monofilaments in the water, the glassy discharge from phreatic explosions. He imagined a horrifying scene directly behind the ROV, a billowing wall of lava completely sealing the entrance to the inner sanctum where he had peered in only a few hours ago. Even at this remove the view seemed confining, claustrophobic. He concentrated on the stone wall visible in the background. Like the other parts of the cave wall, it had been smoothed down, but he could just make out the ghosts of older carvings, similar to the ones that stood out starkly in front of them.

'They're symbols,' Costas exclaimed. 'Symbols carved on the wall. And look,' he said in hushed tones. 'The video's live. You can see tiny bubbles rising in the water, gas from the lava.'

Jack stared at the symbols. They seemed to have been crudely chiselled, as if done in a hurry. There were two separate clusters, each surrounded by a circle. Altogether he counted sixteen symbols: little spirals, stick-figure hands, triangles, zigzags, open angles, half-circles, groups of dots. Some appeared in both clusters, others in one only. At the centre of one cluster was a cross like an X, and in the other a slash with lines going out from it like a garden rake, repeated twice. The symbols presented an extraordinary image, like nothing else they had seen in Atlantis, evidently carved in the dying moments of the citadel, yet almost immeasurably old to those last Atlanteans, originating far back in the Ice Age.

'I recognize these,' he said. 'They're found in Palaeolithic cave art. Some archaeologists have dubbed them the Stone Age code, but nobody really knows what they mean.'

'Look at that one,' Costas exclaimed. 'It's like a precursor to the Atlantis symbol.' Jack saw where Costas was pointing. Instead of the fully formed Atlantis symbol – the one that they had interpreted as the form of a spirit bird, an eagle or a vulture – this looked like one wing of a bird, a straight line with four parallel lines extending from it. The symbol appeared three times at the same sloping angle with the parallel lines going off to the left, and once the other way round with the lines going right.

'Isn't this up Katya's street?' Jeremy said. 'Prehistoric symbology?'

'In fact, isn't this whole thing up her street?' Costas said, looking quizzically at Jack. 'She was pretty well in at the outset five years ago, our expert palaeographer, then there was all the involvement of her father the warlord in trying to get those nukes off the Russian sub that sank beside Atlantis.'

Jack gave Costas a wry look. 'That's precisely why she's *not* involved. Her father met his end here, remember? But I've always left the door open for her. I called her yesterday evening before I flew here from Troy, and told her that if we found any more ancient symbols at Atlantis I'd let her know.'

'But *you're* involved, aren't you, Jack?' Lanowski said, pushing his glasses up his nose and peering at Jack like a doctor. 'It's common knowledge at IMU. That is, when you're not involved with Maria. Costas explained it to me.'

Jack narrowed his eyes at Costas, and then looked back at Lanowski. 'I'm glad to see that even the most unimportant things don't get past your radar now, Jacob.'

'Oh,' Lanowski exclaimed, shaking his head, peering furtively at the flashing email inbox message on his computer screen. 'Oh, but they are important, Jack. *Very* important. I find you just can't get away from them.'

Costas grinned. 'Back to prehistoric symbology, guys.'

'Where is she now?' Lanowski said with a smile, pulling a memory stick out of his pocket and plugging it into the console. 'I can email a still from this video to her.'

'I caught her in a taxi on the way from the Institute of Palaeography in Moscow to the airport, where she was flying to Bishkek in Kyrgyzstan,' Jack replied. 'She should be at the petroglyph site at Cholpon-Ata beside Lake Issyk-Gul by now. They're four hours ahead of us, so it'll be near the end of their working day.'

'She's still digging up those petroglyphs?' Costas said, shaking his head. 'It's been almost two years since we were out there.'

'That's archaeology for you,' Jack said ruefully, reaching for his tablet computer as Lanowski saved the image. 'There are thousands of boulder carvings beside the lake and many square kilometres still to be explored. Since finding the Roman legionary inscription that took us there two years ago, she's worked backwards in time searching for the oldest petroglyphs, back to the Neolithic and even earlier. The place wasn't just a Silk Road site, it was a major prehistoric migration point between East and West. I wouldn't be remotely surprised if one day she found evidence of a group of early Neolithic refugees from Atlantis heading towards China.'

He took the memory stick from Lanowski, plugged it into his computer and took out his cell phone as he emailed the image. He found a saved number and then put it up to his ear, waiting. 'During the summers, she's out there with an international team, really well resourced after our board of directors agreed to fund the project,' he said. 'But out of season like now, it's usually just her and Altamaty, like it was at the beginning.' He suddenly looked away, putting his free hand over his other ear. 'Hello? Altamaty? It's Jack. I can barely hear you. It must be windy. I've got something for Katya.' He strained to listen, and then took down the phone. 'He's digging out their laptop and getting the webcam up, and then he'll go and find her.'

Jack activated the webcam on his own computer and propped it behind the main console keyboard so they could all see. The webcam came on line, showing a shaky image and a pair of hands, evidently propping a laptop on a rock; then the image stabilized to reveal a bleak landscape of scrub and boulders with clouds racing overhead. A face appeared, a ruggedly handsome man with Mongolian features wearing a mountaineering jacket and a Kyrgyz woollen hat. After he had adjusted the position of the laptop again, they saw him lope off beside a tractor and wave, pointing back at the computer. A few moments later a woman appeared and walked towards them, taking off a pair of gloves. She was wearing hiking boots and jeans and a down jacket, and her long black hair was tied back behind her head. She came in front of the webcam, put down a trowel and brush, took a camera from around her neck, and then adjusted the screen. She had strong eastern features too, mixed with European, and dark eyes. 'Hello, Jack. I hadn't expected to hear from you so soon. It's cold and windy here, so let's be quick.' She had a deep voice and spoke with a slight American accent. She wiped her nose and rubbed her hands together, then smiled again at him. 'I can see you're on *Seaquest II*, in the operations room. Have you done the dive? I miss you.'

'I'm here with Costas and Jeremy and Jacob Lanowski, all

watching you just off screen,' Jack replied. 'We've done the dive, and we've just had an image from the ROV taken inside a cave we didn't see five years ago. It's pretty amazing stuff. Take a look at the attachment we've just sent you.'

She looked down to the side of the screen, evidently opening another window. Her eyes lit up and she stared for a few moments, then took out a notebook and flipped through it, holding the pages down in the wind. She stared again, and then looked back at the webcam. 'You probably recognize these symbols from the cave at Lascaux in France,' she said, angling her face away from the wind. 'I know you and Maurice went there as students, because he talked to me about it. The symbols date across the entire range of Palaeolithic rock art, from about thirty-five thousand to twelve thousand years ago. Finding these symbols in Atlantis is completely consistent with the animal cave paintings there. The symbols appear in various numbers and combinations in caves across Europe and in rock art elsewhere, as far away as Australia and South America. Some of my colleagues believe that outside the main area in southern Europe, the similarity of the relatively small number of symbols found is just coincidence, that they were mostly simple enough for people to have invented them independently. But I don't buy that. People moved around a lot in the Palaeolithic, and their shamans may have moved the most. If humans reached Australia by fifty thousand years ago, then they could have got anywhere else by sea, literally anywhere. To the Americas, for example, from Europe.'

'We've just been discussing that,' Jack replied. 'So what about the Atlantis symbol? It's fascinating. It looks as if that rake-shaped symbol is some kind of precursor.'

'It makes perfect sense that the Atlantis symbol should have derived from a Stone Age one. Interesting that someone seems to have been trying to erase them.'

'The big question,' Jack said. 'Are we looking at some kind of script? A code?'

'That's what I'm doing here now, at Cholpon-Ata,' Katya replied. 'Looking for rock inscriptions that might go that far back in prehistory. If the Stone Age symbols are a form of script, then it takes the history of writing back tens of thousands of years. I do think they have symbolic meaning, that they're ideograms that may somehow represent the rituals carried out in those caves. The big breakthrough would be to find clear patterns of association, repeated clusters of symbols in the same order. That's when this image from Atlantis could get really exciting.'

'What about the clustering?' Jack persisted. 'Words, names?'

'Possibly, but more as general ideograms or even mnemonics,' she said. 'There's an old shaman in Altamaty's Kyrgyz tribe who scratches simple signs like this into the sand or on a rock before he goes into a trance. The symbols by themselves don't mean a sound or a word, but in clusters they represent the name of an ancestor, the spirit the shaman is trying to reach. They tend to be descriptive of what that ancestor had done in life, and are regarded as spirit names: "She who held the torch", "He who would be a great hunter". They can become generic, so that one particular ancestor becomes representative of many, and the shaman only scratches out a few of these formulae before he sets to work. What's the context of your symbols? You said they're in a cave.'

Jack nodded. 'We saw animal paintings too, just out of sight. Mostly late Ice Age – leopards, bulls – rather than megafauna such as woolly mammoths, so my guess is a late-Palaeolithic origin, about twelve thousand years ago. It seems to have been some kind of open-air sanctuary with a cave backdrop.'

'You might expect to find more of these symbols, more clusters, if it was a place for shamanistic rituals.'

'On the screen here from the ROV we can see where other symbols, more deeply incised and clearly older, have been chiselled out and smoothed away on the surrounding rock. We think there was a religious transition going on, from shamanism to gods. It looks as if these two clusters of symbols you're looking at were done hastily, scratched rather than carefully chiselled.'

'Maybe as the flood waters rose,' Katya suggested. 'Some kind of desperate measure to evoke ancestors, perhaps. Shamans could have had those spirit names I was talking about while they were still alive, the names they were to be known by in death as their spirits were evoked. One can imagine the last shamans of Atlantis stuck in that place with the water rising and certain death ahead, knowing there would be no future shaman to call up their spirits and so scratching the symbols on that wall.'

Costas coughed. 'What about "Noah was here"?'

'What did you say?' Katya demanded.

He craned his head close to Jack so the webcam caught him. 'Noah was here. It's just a name we've been bandying about. Noah and his Ark, thinking of the people who escaped from Atlantis.'

'If Noah was a name back in the early Neolithic, it's more

likely to have been a proper name, even a nickname,' Katya replied. 'His real name – his spirit name – is more likely to have been something like Uta-napishtim, the name of the deluge hero in the Sumerian flood account in the Epic of Gilgamesh. The name Uta-napishtim is found in the earliest fragments of the flood story, dating from the dawn of Mesopotamian writing in the third millennium BC, as is the name Gilgamesh. Maybe Uta-napishtim and Gilgamesh were spirit names derived from a Stone Age language now lost to us. My favourite spirit name is Sha naqba īmuru, meaning "He who has seen the deep", the first line of the Akkadian version of the Epic of Gilgamesh. I think it's what I'd call Jack if I were a shaman. The Mesopotamian scribes might not have known it, but the names of their heroes may have had similar spirit-name meanings in early prehistory.'

'Wow, Katya, I wasn't really being serious about Noah,' Costas said.

Katya smiled. 'A long time ago, Jack told me always to listen to Costas, because, how did he put it, Costas is good at hitting the nail on the head.'

'Hey, that's just about the nicest thing he's ever said about me.'

'The wind's really picking up.' Katya's voice was nearly inaudible. 'Jack, give me a day or so and I'll check these symbols against my database.'

'That would be fantastic,' Jack said. 'Email me whatever you get. We're trying to piece something together here, where these people went. Not the priests, but the shamans. We want to know whether any of them might have survived to found a new Atlantis.'

Katya leaned forward. They could see the wind ruffling her hair, and she put up a hand to protect her eyes from the blowing dust. To Jack she looked utterly at home, her features at one with the landscape and the wind, and he remembered her Kyrgyz ancestry on her father's side. She raised her voice. 'I have to go. There's one of those winds howling in from the east. Speaking of shamans, that one from Altamaty's tribe calls these winds Genghis Khan's revenge. Altamaty says thank God you and Costas didn't actually go into that tomb under the lake two years ago, otherwise we'd have been blown to the Black Sea by now. When it's like this, you wonder if the shamans have a point. We haven't even got the yurt up yet. Thank Jeremy for the pictures from Troy. Rebecca's just emailed through the one showing her at the helicopter controls, actually flying it. Pretty cool. And my love to Costas. And to Jeremy and Jacob. See you.' She leaned forward into the screen and her hair came loose, swirling round and blotting out the view, and then the screen went blank. Jack leaned back, staring at it pensively.

'Phew,' Costas said. 'Love to you too, Katya.'

'Internet girlfriends,' Lanowski said abstractly, looking at Jack and then narrowing his eyes at Costas. 'They're the best.'

'You weren't going to show her what else you'd found?' Jeremy asked.

Jack shook his head. 'Katya's father died in that volcano five years ago, remember?' He jerked his head back at the computer monitor with the image of the skulls. 'He may have been a hated warlord and Katya may seem as tough as nails, but I wasn't going to show her that.'

'Good call,' Lanowski said thoughtfully.

'Rebecca's her number-one fan,' Jeremy said. 'Especially after Katya taught her to shoot a Kalashnikov.'

'She did *what*?' Jack exclaimed.

'Last summer, before we went to Troy, when Rebecca worked at Cholpon-Ata for a month. Katya and Altamaty took her hunting in the mountains. They forage for a lot of their food, you know. They think they saw a white tiger.'

'Jesus,' Jack muttered. 'She didn't say anything about that a few months later when Ben Kershaw very cautiously taught her to shoot a .22 on the foredeck of the ship, with full hearing and eye protection and under my watchful gaze.'

'She thought you'd be mad. But don't worry. The kidnapping changed her a lot. I think she'll tell you everything now. Katya really helped, too. She told Rebecca what it was like growing up as a woman in Russia around the kind of men her father dealt with, what you have to be prepared to do to hold your own. Rebecca really lapped it up. I think she's got a role model in Katya.'

'Who's Altamaty, by the way?' Lanowski said, looking at Jack with a hint of concern on his face.

Jack stared at him. 'What? Oh, he's in charge of the petroglyph open-air museum. It's a World Heritage Site now, a result of a little bit of extra lobbying from us. He's really climbed up the ladder in the last two years. He's also been doing some fascinating underwater work in the lake. He was a diver in Soviet special forces, and I made him a research associate of IMU. And yes, he and Katya are very good friends.'

'And you're not always around,' Lanowski said cautiously.

'Not always.' Jack stared pointedly at the screen. 'Now,

where were we? I think we're just about done.' He picked up his phone and saw that the message indicator had been flashing. 'I had this switched off while we were talking before I called Katya and someone's left a message. Just let me listen to it and then I'm off to the helipad.' He pushed the chair back and got up, stretching and feeling the aches from diving in his body again. He glanced back at the computer screen. It had been great to see Katya again. And secretly he was pleased to hear how much Rebecca adored her. Lanowski was right, too. His time management was out of hand. After this was over, he needed to sit on a mountainside somewhere and work out his priorities. Moving from one adrenalin-fuelled project to another was the life he was made for, but it was time to splice in some other kinds of excitement and make that a permanent fixture. It had been building up to this ever since Rebecca had appeared in his life. He needed to listen to his friends. He took a deep breath, then walked over to the other side of the room, one hand in his pocket, clicked the inbox and put the phone up to his ear. He stood still, listening intently, then slowly took the phone down, staring back at the other three. 'That was Maurice Hiebermeyer.' He felt numb, unable to move, as if he had just reached a tipping point. 'He wants me to go to the bunker site in Germany right away.'

'Any news?' Costas said, staring at Jack.

'He said he wasn't going to tell me anything on the phone. And I can't call him back, as he's spending six hours in decontamination.'

'Shit. That sounds bad.'

'He said it was just routine. They all have to do it. He said now he knew what it felt like when we had to go into the recompression chamber. But I've never heard him sound like that before. I barely recognized his voice.'

'It can't have been a good experience, whatever he saw.'

'I should never have let him take my place.'

'You can't be everywhere, Jack. And he insisted.'

Jack glanced at his watch. 1545 hours. 'Time I packed my bag.'

'How are you going to get there?' Costas asked. 'Maurice used the Embraer to fly from Egypt to Germany, and it's still at Frankfurt waiting for him.'

Jack waved his phone. 'I had a call last night from an old friend who's just about to finish his flying career in the Royal Air Force, Paul Llewelyn. He's spending the night at Incirlik airbase in southern Turkey, and he knew I'd been excavating at Troy. He gave me a call on the off-chance that we might hook up.'

'Didn't he go on your first expeditions when you were undergraduates?'

Jack nodded. 'A battered van, a home-made inflatable boat, an ancient compressor and cobbled-together diving equipment. Peter Howe was another stalwart. I always dreamed of something like this, *Seaquest II*, IMU, but I never imagined that the adventures we planned would attract the dark clouds we seem to be under now. Back then we didn't have the equipment to search for Atlantis, but those were days when the world seemed like our oyster.'

'The excitement's still there, Jack,' Costas said, peering at him. 'Bigger than ever. Don't lose hold of that. And the best projects are still to come. You've got a daughter to keep entertained, remember?'

Jeremy coughed. 'I think she might see it the other way round.'

'So what about Paul?' Costas said.

'He's ferrying a Tornado GR4 back from Kandahar in Afghanistan to the UK. For years he's been offering me a back-seat ride in a fast jet. The old NATO base next to the bunker site in Germany is still functional, and they've put in a skeleton ground team to deal with aircraft bringing in supplies for the excavation. The Lynx should be able to take me from here direct to Incirlik, and I'll see whether Paul can make a small diversion on his way back to England.'

'Sounds like fun,' Jeremy said.

'Fun's probably not the right word for where Jack's going,' Costas murmured.

Lanowski got up and put a hand awkwardly on Jack's shoulder. 'Take it easy, Jack.' He pointed at the image of the papyrus on his screen. 'I want you back here in this ship to find out where that's leading us.'

'Jacob's right,' Costas added. 'And remember, Saumerre can't make a move until he has the upper hand, and he'll only have that if he's got hold of the weapon he thinks lies in that Nazi bunker. There's no chance of that now, is there? The place must be locked down like Fort Knox. Once we find it and we're certain Saumerre is neutered, then the matter is out of our hands and we can let MI6 blow his network wide open and take him down. Then we can get back to the archaeology. This has been eating away at you for months, Jack, at all of us. Let's get it done.' Costas turned back, looked at the ROV monitor and idly tapped the control handle. The screen lurched. He hit the handle. It lurched again. 'Holy shit,' he whispered.

'What is it?' Jack turned, followed by the others.

Costas tapped the handle again. The image wobbled. 'It's not just the camera that's still working,' he said hoarsely. 'It's Little Joey. *He's still alive.*'

Lanowski quickly sat down beside Costas, tapping the keyboard and working the mouse. He nudged Costas' hand away and held the handle himself, gently tugging it in every direction. 'Okay,' he exclaimed. 'It's only the eye that's moving, the socket holding the camera, and we've only got movement in one direction, at about forty-five degrees on a three-sixty-degree compass, which will take us up the rock face to the right of those symbols. The computer says it'll only go up to an arc of forty degrees or so, which means it'll stop after about two metres up the rock face.' He let go and sat aside, staring at the screen.

Costas put his hand back on the handle and moved it slowly to the right. The image climbed away from the symbols, showing a smoothed section of rock wall, then a dark crack and a large protrusion with a crack on the other side. 'It's a boulder,' he said. 'Those cracks look like the edge of some kind of tunnel, and the boulder's been wedged into it. I can't push it any further to the right.'

'Try going up,' Lanowski suggested.

Costas did as he suggested, moving the stick carefully. Nothing happened. He pushed it to its maximum angle. There was a sudden blur and the image wobbled, as if the eye of the ROV were on a spring. A shimmer of bubbles and a cloud of brown filaments surged up from below, and the water wavered and blurred like heat rising in air. 'Something bad is happening,' Costas murmured. 'I think the lava has just entered the chamber and has pushed into the back of the ROV, and the water's boiling up. In that confined space there'll be a massive phreatic explosion. I think this really is the last gasp for Little Joey.'

'Don't give up just yet,' Lanowski urged. 'Take a look at that.'

The wobbling stopped and the image stabilized. The eye of the ROV had angled upwards to the top of the boulder, to a wider crack between its upper surface and the top of the tunnel. They all stared in stunned silence.

What they saw was a scene of horror. On top of the boulder were three human skulls lying at different angles, their lower jaws wide open. The skulls were covered in the same lime concretion as the bones of the sacrificial victims on the floor of the chamber, cementing them to the top of the boulder. But it was not the image of the skulls that was so horrifying. It was what lay behind and in front of them. The skulls were articulated with other human bones, ribcages caught in the crack behind, arm bones extending over the boulder as if some awful multi-legged creature had been trying to get out. One ribcage had collapsed and several of the arms were missing hands, but the rest of the bones were joined together, evidently cemented to the rock while the sinews were still in place.

Jack stared. *As if some creature had been trying to get out*. It was suddenly an image of shocking clarity. These people had been alive and struggling when the flood waters rose, their last screams caught in the contorted grimaces of their skulls. And this was no accident of fate. They had been forced inside that tunnel and sealed in with the boulder. He could barely imagine what lay in the darkness beyond.

What had gone on here? Human sacrifice, mass suicide, then the last of the shamans sealed inside, doomed to an agonizing and terrifying death. Had this been the final apocalypse, the end of the old order and the beginning of the new? He remembered those stark stone pillars standing in the chamber. Had they presided over this, those new gods, like statues half formed that now would be able to reveal themselves in their final shape, wherever those who had carried out this act were destined to find landfall and hold sway over men again?

Then Jack remembered Lanowski's chalk drawing on the blackboard: the crooked cross, the swastika, a shape that seemed to form in Jack's mind out of the swirling images of the deep past. Now he knew that the end of the old order had been a time of appalling violence. But he also knew that those who had vanquished the old, these new priests, these gods, had not come from somewhere else, like invaders sweeping in on a wave of destruction. They had come from within. He remembered Hiebermeyer's call, where he was going now, to a time when that cross had been resurrected to serve a new breed of gods. Suddenly the image of fear and desperation in those skeletons from seven thousand years ago seemed terrifyingly immediate.

There was a sudden jolt, and a blur. The camera appeared to move forward, as if the ROV were riding something underneath. Then there was a white flash and the screen went blank. A moment later the ship's klaxon sounded, and a red light went on above the control-room door. 'We're moving again,' Costas said. 'Macalister must have registered another seismic disturbance, and he'll be taking us further offshore.

My guess is that's the archaeology gone for good. That chamber's going to be entombed in lava, Little Joey too.'

Jack sniffed the air. He thought he caught a whiff of sulphur, whether some effulgence of the volcano drawn in by the ship's ventilators or a residue on their own bodies from the dive was unclear. Smell was the one sense he had been deprived of that morning; the dive had come to seem more like a voyage of the mind than reality. But the hint of acrid smell jolted him. Instead of a phantasm, an image now lost for ever to history, the vision of those people in their death throes now seemed shockingly real. He knew that where he had to go next, the smell of death was more than just a ghostly exhalation. He realized what had been troubling him for the last six months, what had led him to block off the world around him, to totter on the edge on the dive that morning. It was not only Atlantis that had come at a price, with the death of Peter Howe five years ago. Troy had come at a price too. Six months ago they had opened up another cave from the past, another chamber with a dark revelation. It was unresolved business, and he needed to confront it head-on now. He straightened up, clicked on his phone, nodded at Jeremy and Lanowski and gave Costas a steely look. 'Next time we meet in this room, it will be on the trail of a shaman of Atlantis who may have survived all this, a seven-thousand-year-old seafarer who might just have been called Noah. Until then, sit tight. You'll be hearing from me.'

10

Over Europe

Jack scanned the instrument panel in front of him and observed that the airspeed indicator and altimeter had shown near-constant figures since they had flown over the northern shore of the Adriatic Sea fifteen minutes ago. He checked his watch, noting that he was now beyond the high-risk period for flying following his decompression dive the day before. He was strapped into the rear ejector seat of an RAF Tornado GR4, and since their exhilarating take-off from Incirlik airbase in Turkey he had managed to put aside thinking about his destination and let himself enjoy the thrill of flying in a fast jet. They had flown low over Troy, allowing him a fascinating view of the ancient site, as well as the Dardanelles Strait where any prehistoric exodus from the Black Sea to the west must have taken place. Now he peered sideways through the canopy over the swept-back starboard wing, looking past the silvery nacelle of the long-range drop tank and seeing the snowy peaks of the Alps some twenty thousand feet below. He turned back to face the upper part of the instrument panel, which blocked his view of the pilot's seat in front, and spoke into the intercom. 'That looks like Innsbruck in Austria below us, Paul. What's our ETA?'

'I'm dropping from six hundred to five hundred knots in fifteen minutes and then finding a lower altitude. All going according to plan, we should be flying over Hanover in Germany and coming in to land in about thirty-five minutes.'

'Copy that.'

'You okay? Lunch still inside you?'

'I'm having the time of my life. I can't see how this kind of flying could ever pale.'

'That's the problem. It's a constant adrenalin kick. I've done thousands of hours in Tornados, including four big operational deployments – the Gulf War, Kosovo, Iraq, Afghanistan. I've had enough of war, Jack, but I still love the flying. I can't believe this is going to be my last official fast-jet flight.'

'Congratulations on the Distinguished Service Order, by the way. Well deserved.'

'Those things should go to the ground crews. They're the ones who keep these birds flying. The unsung heroes.'

'That's the way I feel about my diving expeditions. It's always a team effort.' Jack cast his mind back more than two decades. Paul Llewelyn had been one of his close-knit group of friends at Cambridge University, where they had shared college rooms in their first year; he was a fellow diver and had gone along with Jack on his first expeditions to the Mediterranean.

They had not seen each other for several years now, but Jack had spent an hour with Paul in the officers' mess at Incirlik while the air-traffic controllers worked on clearance for a modified flight plan to his destination in Germany and the aircraft was fitted with long-range drop tanks. He had sworn Paul to secrecy and told him about their Atlantis dive, then briefed him about the excavation at the bunker site in Germany and about Maurice Hiebermeyer, another mutual friend from Cambridge. He had outlined the security and contamination risk at the bunker and why Paul would not be allowed out of the aircraft when they landed at the old NATO runway next to the excavation site. Beyond that he had let himself enjoy the experience of flying, and being with an old friend. He spoke into the intercom again. 'Paul, do you remember the last time we flew together? In that rickety old Bulldog trainer in the University Air Squadron?'

'That time you were in the driver's seat. You actually got your wings just before I did. I'm still trying to live that down.'

'Learning to fly was just part of my toolkit. I wanted to get all the skills I could under my belt. I guessed I was going to have to fly at some time in the future, and I was right. But for you, flying and getting into the RAF was always your main passion, like diving was for me.'

'It's still there, Jack. All I ever wanted was to get inside one of these things. And here I am now, an RAF group captain, about to be booted up to one-star rank so I can fly a desk in the Ministry of Defence in London. I'll be like one of those mothballed planes in the Arizona desert, waiting for a reactivation everyone knows is never going to happen. All fast-jet jocks say the same when they reach my stage. It's as if we've gone beyond our sell-by date, but they can't quite bring themselves to scrap us.'

'Ever think of retirement?'

'I'd retire from the air force, but only to fly again. You?'

'Rebecca says I need more sabbaticals, and to stop taking all the best projects. She said IMU needs to get more expeditions going with other people leading them. People like herself.'

'I can't wait to meet her. Her mother's death must have been a terrible blow, but it's amazing how kids can weather storms. So Elizabeth disappeared back to Naples without telling you she was pregnant? I bet you can't believe you've only known Rebecca for three years.'

'Her kidnapping last year really brought it all home again.'

'*Kidnapping?* Jesus, Jack, what have you been getting into?'

'It was only for forty-eight hours. That was close to a lifetime for me, though. I found out a few things about myself, I can tell you. About what protecting your own will make you do. All I can say is I've got more blood on my hands than the last time we met. It's wrapped up with the bunker discovery, so the security issue is ongoing.'

'But she's all right?'

'Back at school in New York City after working with us at Troy. You met Ben Kershaw when you visited *Seaquest II* a few years ago? He heads up the IMU security team and is looking after her. Round-the-clock surveillance. And Rebecca's developing quite a few survival skills of her own. She's about to get her glider pilot's licence, you know. If she can fit it in with her advanced nitrox diving course. And her weekend co-op programme at the Metropolitan Museum of Art.'

'Christ, Jack. Sounds like a chip off the old block.'

'That's why I could never retire. She needs management.'

'Been there, done that. Remember, I have three teenage daughters. Trying to keep Rebecca under control is exactly what you *don't* want to be doing.'

Jack laughed. 'Advice taken. But back to retirement. My friend Costas jokes that there's an inner philosopher in me ready to retreat to some remote cabin and grow a long white beard like Charles Darwin, cogitating for my remaining years before producing the definitive tome on human prehistory.'

'You always were the thinking action man, but I really don't see it.'

'Nope.'

'I haven't met Costas yet, but I've seen him on the IMU films. Seems like a good guy.'

'He and I first met during my short-term commission in the Navy; you remember? Between graduating and my doctorate, before I founded IMU. Costas had been at MIT before going to the US Navy research establishment to work on submersibles, his métier. We actually met in the naval base at Izmir in Turkey, where I discovered he was a diver and cajoled him into doing some shipwreck exploration with me. He's in charge of the engineering department at IMU, but he's a lot more than that. I couldn't imagine doing an expedition without him. He keeps me on the straight and narrow. He's a rock.'

'Efram Jacobovich still pumps money into your foundation?'

'We had some pretty amazing friends at Cambridge, don't you think? I remember the first time I met Efram in the dining hall at college. He'd thought up the internet ten years before it was officially invented. He had software tycoon written all over him. I took him on a frigid dive in the English Channel that put him in bed shivering for a week, but something about the experience must have struck a chord for him to give IMU its endowment ten years later. He's been a fantastic friend and supporter.'

'And your father gave IMU your family estate in the Fal estuary? I remember my visits there when we dived off the south coast looking for that elusive Phoenician shipwreck. Perfect place for a maritime research campus.'

'It just seemed right. My father's family had been in Cornwall since Tudor times, when the estate was given to my ancestor Captain Jack Howard by King Henry VIII for services rendered against the Spanish. In Spanish history books he was a pirate, but in ours a glorious hero. Since then the family history has seen quite a bit more adventure on the high seas but also a gentle decline into aristocratic impoverishment. My own apparently exotic childhood moving around the world was actually as much about my father evading financial inconvenience as it was his bohemian life as a painter. Luckily there was a trust fund that paid for my boarding school, and another one that kept the Howard Gallery and its art collection from the debt collectors. My father was a great supporter of the idea of IMU, but it also came as something of a relief to him, because he could bequeath the estate to our foundation as a tax break.'

'I remember reading the obituaries. What was it now, eight years ago? I've got very fond memories of him, and your mother. How's she doing?'

'Still lives there and runs the place, really, in between

mountain trekking expeditions. She and Rebecca get on like a house on fire. Still has her huge garden and her dogs.'

'So what about old Heimy? You should be seeing him within an hour.'

'It's funny – that's what Rebecca calls him, too. Of course he got married last year, as you know.'

'Maurice Hiebermeyer, married. It beggars belief. I got an invite, but I was on deployment in Afghanistan. Amazing he remembered me, but I always knew there was a thoughtful and loving human being inside the fanatical Egyptologist. Lucky he found a woman who spotted that too. Makes my head reel to think of it. Does he still have those awful khaki lederhosen?'

'Still wears them at half-mast.'

'You remember our little escapade in Egypt that summer after graduation? You illegally scaling the Great Pyramid at Giza to spend the night on the top waiting with a camera, me flying Maurice in a dilapidated old Tiger Moth biplane for some dawn aerobatics over the Sphinx. It was something to do with re-creating a *National Geographic* picture Maurice had seen from the 1920s showing RAF biplanes over the pyramids. We just had to have a go, otherwise we weren't going to hear the end of it.'

Jack laughed. 'It was also a shrewd publicity stunt. Maurice had spent weeks camped outside the Egyptian Antiquities Authority, trying to get them to take his discovery in the Fayum desert seriously. If you remember how he looked in those shorts, you could see what the problem was. But our stunt got us hauled in front of the director-general himself, and Maurice instantly won him over with his knowledge of all things Egyptian. I can still see the two of them on their knees on the office floor poring over Maurice's sketch map of his discovery, the mummy necropolis that was to make his name. And now there he is, director of the Institute of Archaeology at Alexandria and arguably the world's foremost Egyptologist.'

'Seems a long way from that to unearthing a Nazi bunker in Germany.'

'He volunteered to take my place. His family home was not far from there, and he said he felt a personal responsibility as a German to address the past.'

'We're about to lose altitude now. Just in case you need it, the sick bag's in the pocket in front of you.' Jack felt his stomach lurch as the aircraft suddenly dropped out of the sky, hurtling at a forty-five-degree angle towards the patchwork of fields now visible below. They levelled out at three thousand feet, and Jack watched the wings sweep forward and the airspeed indicator drop to three hundred knots. Paul's voice crackled on the intercom. 'Okay, Jack? That's Lower Saxony ahead of us. We'll be over the airfield in a few minutes. I'm going to do several wide sweeps around so you can get your bearings.'

Jack swallowed hard, feeling his stomach return to normal. 'Do you know this area? I remember your first RAF posting was in Germany, in the late 1980s.'

'I was always fascinated with the Second World War. I spent a lot of my leave time travelling around, trying to come to grips with what happened in those final months in 1945. With the fall of Berlin and the confrontation with the Soviets, it was as if the history of that time was suppressed, almost as if there was a conscious effort by the Allied authorities to put a lid on it. Nobody in Germany wanted to dwell on the night-mare, and there was a desperate need to get people to look forward. But to me there still seemed an awful lot of unan-swered questions. There's plenty of unexcavated history here, just below the surface. With the end of the Cold War, I felt the lid might blow off. I know you can't really say more, but I'm guessing that's what this bunker excavation is all about.'

Jack looked out as the aircraft banked to starboard and saw runway lights in the haze ahead. Seconds later they swept over the airbase and the flat land beyond, a large area of low scrub and marsh punctuated by patches of plantation forest. Paul came on the intercom again. 'We're doing a wide turn to come in from the south. I did a stopover here once in the 1980s, and the Luftwaffe guys at the base told me a bit about the history. There was a large old-growth forest here, a former royal hunting ground. On the day the British liberated the camp at Belsen a few miles from here, this forest was the front line for the British 11th Armoured Division, part of 21st Army Group. On the other side of the forest, just about where we are now, remnant German forces including SS were about to establish defensive positions. Nobody on the Allied side wanted a repeat of the bloodbaths in the Hürtgen or Reichswald forests, so an RAF bomber raid was diverted here. Almost five hundred Lancasters, most carrying fourteen thousand pounds of high-explosive and incendiary bombs. My Phantom squadron at the time prided itself on being the descendant of a wartime pathfinder Lancaster squadron that flew on that raid, and then dropped relief supplies to the survivors of Belsen. I often wonder what it would have felt like for those bomber crews on what we would now call humanitarian missions, saving lives instead of destroying them. I don't think it would have been easy. It's hard to change your mindset from being an instrument of destruction to an instrument of salvation. It puts too much of what you might have done before into sharp focus. Anyway, they achieved their objective in that forest. What wasn't destroyed by blast was burned in the firestorm. The airbase was originally an RAF forward operating field built immediately after liberation, on land cleared of smashed trees by German prisoners of war.'

Jack looked out of the other side of the canopy as the aircraft banked in the opposite direction, beginning a wide turn to bring it head-on with the runway. He spotted a camouflaged dome like a tennis-court bubble off the west side of the runway, with further camouflage netting covering what appeared to be a large Portakabin with several vehicles parked alongside. He took a deep breath. *So that was it.* 'Is anyone else picking up our voices?'

'The radio's off-line. I was instructed to keep external chatter to a minimum by the intelligence officer when I was briefed on the phone about this landing. It was someone from the secret service, MI6. That's when I knew this was big, and it's why I haven't plugged you for more.'

'Okay. I'll bring you into the picture. There was another outcome to that bombing raid. Where the north end of the base now lies was a small *Arbeitslager*, a labour camp. The Allied troops thought it was a satellite of Belsen, but we now know it had another purpose. By April 1945 it was overflowing with Jews who had survived the death march from Auschwitz. A small British force liberated the camp the day before the raid, and cleared out the last of the survivors just before the bombing began. It pretty well obliterated the camp, and the remains were then buried under the concrete and asphalt of the runways.'

'Good God. A concentration camp here? I had no idea.'

'In all the publicity about the death camps that so shocked the world in 1945, this one was never revealed. In this vicinity, the world only knew about Belsen.'

'I take it the excavation site is under that camouflaged bubble?' Paul asked. 'But that must be a good two thousand metres from the northern perimeter of the base, well away from the location of the camp as you describe it.'

'The bubble covers the site of an underground bunker that lay deep in the forest, linked to the camp only by a concealed track.'

'How do you know all this?'

Jack paused. 'When we were excavating at Troy last year, we were on the trail of treasures dug up by Heinrich Schliemann that found their way to Germany and may have been hidden by the Nazis. You remember my old classics tutor at Cambridge, James Dillen? Well, the guy who had taught Dillen Greek and Latin at school had been a wartime British army officer, and was one of the first soldiers into this camp. That was what led us to this place. He'd done some archaeology in Greece before the war, and saw something here he recognized. But after the war he was one of those people who put a lid on it. The camp must have been a horrific experience. He talked for the first time about it to Rebecca and James when they visited him in his flat in Bristol last year.'

'Only last year? He must have been getting on a bit.'

Jack paused. 'His name was Frazer. Captain Hugh Frazer. He'd bottled it up all those years, and I think it was a great relief to let it out. Afterwards we took him to Poland to see one of the survivors of the camp. It was very moving, but you can never talk about closure. That's the hard truth of it. Hugh was already very ill, and he died six weeks ago.'

'Sorry to hear it. He was with 11th Armoured?'

Jack paused. '30 Commando Assault Unit. A forward reconnaissance outfit.'

'*Jesus*, Jack. I know all about 30 AU. They were part of T-Force, searching for Nazi secret weapons. This isn't just about stolen antiquities, is it? Take a look down there now. You don't usually get guys in full CBRN suits at an archaeological site.'

Jack saw two figures in white chemical, biological, radio-logical and nuclear suits disappear into the camouflaged enclosure in front of the bubble. 'All I can tell you is this. A lot of the Nazi propaganda about wonder-weapons was exactly that. As for the real stuff, some of the scientists located by T-Force were spirited away and re-emerged at the forefront of Cold War rocket and weapons technology, even in the technology of swept-wing aircraft design like the Tornado. That's been common knowledge for decades. But some secrets remained. You were right to wonder about the hidden truth of those final months of the war. But you shouldn't just have been concerned about history. You should have been terrified for the future.'

The Tornado levelled out at three hundred feet. 'Okay, Jack. I'm switching to VHF airband, so everything we say is now being overheard. There's a skeleton air-traffic-control crew in the tower. My orders are to land, power down, drop you off and fly out immediately. You copy?'

'Copy that, Paul. And thanks for the ride. It's been fantastic.'

The external intercom crackled. 'NATO XJ4, this is RAF Tornado fiver niner kilo seeking clearing to land. Over.'

'Fiver niner kilo, you are clear to land. Observe agreed protocol. Over.'

'NATO XJ4, this is Tornado fiver niner kilo. Roger that. Over.'

Jack felt the landing gear lock and the increased air resistance as the Tornado angled upwards for its approach. A few moments later they touched down with a screech of rubber on asphalt, and the reverse thrusters roared into life. The aircraft came to a halt less than halfway down the runway. Paul increased the throttle, swung the Tornado round and taxied it back down to the start of the runway, then pulled it round again so it was poised for take-off. The camouflaged dome was about five hundred metres to their left, and Jack could see two figures beside a jeep with its lights on, watching them.

Paul powered the engine down and popped the canopy so that it rose above them. Jack took off his helmet and felt the cool breeze coming down the runway. He realized that he had been bathed in sweat, and he ruffled his hair. He unstrapped himself and clambered out of the cockpit and down the steps on the side of the fuselage, then hopped off and struggled out of the pressure suit. He climbed back up and put the suit on the rear seat, then clambered down again and jumped on to the tarmac. He gave the fuselage a pat, then stood back, looking at the sooty streak on the tail fin caused by the thrust reversers, and the light grey camouflage that showed the effect of months in the punishing conditions of Afghanistan. 'She's a fine old warhorse,' he called up. 'Let's hope she finds a new master as good as the one she's got now.'

Paul raised his arm in acknowledgement, then clamped his visor back down. Jack walked a few paces away, then turned round again. 'Paul, I've been thinking. You flew helicopters once, didn't you?'

Paul raised his visor again. 'It's what stalled my promotion for so long. Instead of going to staff college when I should have done, I jumped on an RAF vacancy at the Army Air Corps helicopter school, and then volunteered for an RAF placement scheme with the Royal Navy. I spent six months flying a Lynx helicopter off a frigate in the Caribbean on drugs interdiction. It probably ruined my chances of ever becoming Marshal of the Royal Air Force, but I wouldn't have missed it for the world.'

Jack grinned. 'Well, if you ever get bored at that desk in Whitehall, there's a job for you at IMU. We've got an Embraer and three Lynxes, so there's always plenty of flying. I want to expand our aerial survey capability, with the new technology for archaeological site detection now available.' He paused. 'But I'd be looking for more than that. Someone with your experience of command and control and your international contacts could be invaluable. We seem to get ourselves involved in some tricky situations these days, far more so than I envisaged when I founded IMU. Far more than I want. But it's reality, and we need to beef up our security capability. Let me know if you're interested.'

Paul eyed Jack. 'Not just a charity job for a sad old fighter jock?'

Jack grinned. 'Not a chance. You might even get to fly Maurice around Egypt again in a biplane.'

'He still owes me for that little trip. He was going to take me to the Munich beer festival. Then he got distracted by some mummies.'

'Sounds oddly like Maurice. I'll remind him.'

'I wouldn't mind getting wet again either, you know. Only I'd be a little rusty.'

'We'd soon get you up to speed. Rebecca will probably have her instructor rating by then and can fill you in on all the latest diving technology since the 1980s.'

'The good old days,' Paul said, grinning. 'None of this nonsense about mixed-gas diving and rebreathers. Just good old compressed air, and a wing and a prayer.'

'A wing and a prayer,' Jack repeated. 'I'd forgotten it was you and Peter Howe who used to say that. The good old days indeed.'

'I've got great memories of him. We've got to hold on to that.'

Jack paused. 'His death has really hit me again, diving at Atlantis where it happened. That's why the good old days are exactly that. Things happen, and you can't go back.'

'Jack, seriously. I'm worried about you. This place, this bunker. This wasn't what you got into archaeology for. Remember what you said about my flying. It was my passion, and always will be. Your passion is archaeology and diving, what you've just been doing at Atlantis and Troy. That's the kind of adrenalin you thrive on, what makes you tick. Keeping that going is exactly what Peter would have wanted. The greatest discoveries are yet to come. Don't ever lose sight of that.'

He dropped his visor again, waved and lowered the canopy. Jack put his hands over his ears as the twin turbofans started up, and hurried off the tarmac to be away from the blast of the exhaust. The whine of the engines rose to a scream and the Tornado rolled down the runway, its jet exhaust distorting the air for the length of the airfield behind. It rose at a sharp angle just before the end of the runway, its twin afterburners roaring and crackling as it powered up into the sky and disappeared into the clouds.

Jack could still feel the vibrations as he turned to face the jeep that was now accelerating towards him. For a moment he relished the quiet, hearing only a whisper of wind on the grass, before it was disrupted by the jeep engine. He wondered what it had been like for those Allied soldiers who had come upon this place that day in April 1945. He remembered what Hugh Frazer had said, and he sniffed the air. The hint of sulphur on his body from the volcano had gone, overwhelmed by the smell of aviation fuel and jet exhaust that lingered in a layer of black smoke from the Tornado's departure. Hugh had talked of the terrible smell that day in 1945, a stench of squalor and decay, and the smoke rising from piles of fetid clothing that had been taken from the inmates by the emergency medical staff to be burned in pyres across the camp.

He stared along the line of empty concrete aircraft shelters and remembered pictures of Belsen, trying to imagine what the camp here had looked like, and then he looked at the camouflaged bubble over the bunker. This place was not just about the horrors of the Holocaust. It was about another crime that had been commited here, a terrible, calculated crime in the name of twisted science, a crime whose outcome might yet exact a terrible price from humanity. It had kept Jack awake at night in the six months since the bunker had been discovered, turning over in his mind his own role in the events now unfolding. And there had been another price in 1945. Two Allied officers had disappeared in the forest, one British and one American, the British officer a close friend of Hugh's whose death had haunted him for the rest of his life. For Hugh this place had come to represent the unbridled horrors of war, just as the burnt ruins of Troy had seemed to speak the same message to Jack when he had left them the day before his return to Atlantis.

He watched the two figures park the jeep on the tarmac and walk towards him. He thought about what Paul had said. This place was a long way from the archaeology he loved. Yet all archaeology was ultimately about understanding the present, and about truths that often had a dark side. Atlantis was about the foundation of civilization, when people had first learned to exult in the possibilities of the human condition, yet also had understood what the hunger for power could make men do. Troy had been about the descent into the abyss of war. And this bunker was archaeology too, but a new kind of archaeology, the excavation of a past almost within his own lifetime, but a past whose truth could only be revealed by the tried and tested techniques of archaeology, bringing all the forensic skills of his profession to bear. It was his job now, his responsibility, as much as the revelations of Atlantis or Troy. He took a deep breath and walked forward to meet the two men.

11

Lower Saxony, Germany

F ive minutes after leaving the runway, Jack hopped out of the jeep at the site of the Nazi bunker. In front of him was the large Portakabin with barred windows, and behind it the polyester bubble covered with camouflage netting that rose over an area the size of a tennis court. He could see where the edges of the bubble had been sealed to the roof of the Portakabin and anchored into a freshly dug perimeter ditch filled with concrete around the site, isolating the bunker from the atmosphere outside; beyond the Portakabin was a parked flat-bed truck containing an air compressor to keep the bubble pressurized, large carbon-dioxide scrubbers and pumps to clean the air and a filtration system to extract anything toxic from the outflow. The door to the Portakabin was guarded by two Bundeswehr military policemen carrying

Hechler & Koch G-36 assault rifles. Jack's driver spoke in German into his phone, and then turned to him. 'Dr Hiebermeyer has finished the decontamination process and will be with you in a moment. You are to wait here.'

Jack nodded in acknowledgement as the jeep drove off, and then turned back to the entrance just as the door opened and Hiebermeyer came out. He was wearing a spotless white shirt and pressed trousers, the first time Jack could remember since their schooldays not seeing him in dusty khaki excavation gear. His right wrist was bandaged and hanging in a sling. With his other arm he swept back his remaining strands of hair, still glistening from the shower, and pushed his little round glasses up his nose. Jack watched him close his eyes and breathe deeply a few times. His glasses had steamed up on leaving the Portakabin, and he took them off and cleaned them on his sleeve, then peered around and spotted Jack. His shoulders slumped with relief and he walked over, putting his hand on Jack's arm. 'I heard the jet take off. It's really good to see you. I read your email update on the dive on my phone in the decontamination room. It's like a sauna in there.' He wiped his face with his hand. 'Diving to Atlantis again. Pretty amazing stuff. Human sacrifice, you think?'

Jack pointed at the sling. 'Your wrist?'

'Just a sprain. It was slippery in there. Everything's covered in a sticky decomposition product, kind of yellow-green.' He rubbed his forehead with his sleeve, then pushed his glasses up again. Jack looked with concern at his pale face and red-rimmed eyes. 'Are you okay, Maurice? You look whacked.'

Hiebermeyer exhaled slowly, looked down at the ground for a moment and then nodded. '*Ja*,' he said. '*Mein Gott*.' He looked at Jack again, his eyes lacking their usual exuberance, and then angled his head upwards and took a deep breath through his nose. 'I can still smell it, Jack. That decomposition product. We were encased in CBRN suits inside the bunker, but as soon as I took mine off in the scrubbing room, the stench was overpowering. I'd already thrown up inside my suit in the bunker, and I'm afraid I did it again. Not impressive for the hardened Egyptologist used to rotting mummies, but Major Penn says it happens even to the toughest of his team.'

Jack pulled out a small bottle of water from his khaki trouser pocket. 'Have something to drink.'

Hiebermeyer shook his head. 'Not yet. I couldn't stomach it. Not until we get away from this place.'

'It was that bad?'

'I've been down some pretty unpleasant holes in my life, but nothing like that. Count yourself lucky you're not going in there.'

'What do you mean?' Jack said abruptly. 'I thought that was why I was here.'

'Come with me. Let's sit down.' Hiebermeyer steered Jack past the guards to a seating area beneath some bushes about fifty metres away, a place set up for the excavation team to relax. They were alone and out of earshot of the guards. Hiebermeyer sat down heavily on a bench and put his head in his hands, then took a deep breath and pressed his hands together, staring back pensively at the bunker site. Jack sat down beside him, and Hiebermeyer turned to him. 'I have to tell you about what we found in there. And about what we *didn't* find.'

Jack suddenly felt a yawning sense of apprehension. *What*

wasn't there. This was what had kept him up at night over the past months. 'Go on.'

'First, the good news. The bunker's full of antiquities and works of art. There was one open crate filled with paintings. Raphael's *Portrait of a Young Man*, for a start. It's incredible, though the Raphael had been left exposed and is probably beyond recovery. And there are crates of archaeological treasures. It looks as if most of them are from Himmler's collection at Wewelsburg Castle, the objects looted by the Ahnenerbe from around the world in the 1930s that I'd always dreamed of finding. The only crate we looked inside was already open, its lid prised off some time in those final days in 1945. Inside were carefully packaged boxes, all labelled. One of them had prehistoric symbols on it that I recognized from cave art, the kind of thing the Nazis would have interpreted as precursor Aryan runes. But many of them had been packaged more than fifty years before the war, evidently left unopened for some future occasion. I recognized Heinrich Schliemann's handwriting, Jack. *Schliemann's.* They must be the lost treasures from Troy that he hid away, possibly rediscovered by the Nazis somewhere in Germany or when they conquered Greece in 1941. I'd always wondered what lay beneath Schliemann's house in Athens.'

Jack's heart was pounding. 'The palladion?'

Hiebermeyer pursed his lips. 'It had been there, Jack. We found the impression of a swastika in the packing straw in one corner of that crate, a heavy object about two hands' breadths across. But someone had taken it. There's no sign of it elsewhere in the bunker. We already knew the palladion had been in that salt mine in Poland, right? Some time in the final months of the war it was brought here, and some time in the final hours before the forest was bombed it was taken away again.'

Jack closed his eyes, trying to contain his disappointment. *The palladion, the most sacred object of the Trojans.* He remembered his dive with Costas six months before in the Wieliczka salt mine near Krakow, and their desperate fight with three of Saumerre's men at the place where the palladion had been hidden. What did the Nazis want with it? Who had given the order to move it here, to this bunker? Six months ago they had worked out that the reverse swastika of the palladion had been the symbol of the Agamemnon Code, a secret Nazi code activated near the end of the war that was somehow connected with the purpose of the bunker. He turned to Hiebermeyer. 'You're sure it wasn't taken recently?'

'Not a chance. The bunker was sealed in by tons of fallen trees and soil after the Allied bombing raid in April 1945. Nobody's been in there since.'

'So that's the bad news?'

'Not all of it, Jack.'

'I didn't think so.'

Hiebermeyer put a hand on Jack's shoulder. 'I'm glad Hugh Frazer isn't with us any more. He'd lived his life since the war wondering what had gone on here, what had happened to his friend Major Mayne. I wouldn't have wanted to be the one to break it to him. It was a terrible sight, Jack. It'll stay with me always.'

'You found him?'

'And the American colonel, Stein. They'd both been shot at close range by a 9mm Walther P38. We know that because the pistol and the shell casings are still there. The pistol belonged to another body, with an SS tattoo on his arm. It looks as if he and Mayne were caught in a death embrace, with Mayne's knife in his ribcage.'

Jack swallowed hard. 'Where were the bodies?'

Hiebermeyer lowered his arm from Jack's shoulder, stared at the ground and spoke quietly. 'At the far end of the chamber with the crates was a sealed room, a laboratory. The American was found outside the doorway, Mayne and the SS man just inside. The door had swung to on its hinges afterwards, nearly but not quite shutting. What I saw inside, beyond those bodies, was a scene of even greater horror.' He put his hand to his forehead, and paused. 'There were badly adiposed bodies, Jack, naked and strapped into gurneys. They were partly preserved in their own body liquor. That's where the awful yellow-green slime came from. Thank Christ the Egyptians mummified their bodies.' His voice was hoarse. 'The forensic anthropologist with the army team reckons they were being used as guinea pigs, as live victims for research. She thinks they were being dissected alive, to ensure that the Nazi scientists could extract living viruses and bacteria from their organs. Two of them looked as if they'd been abandoned halfway through. They'd died horribly, in agony. And they weren't the only ones. You remember you authorized an IMU geophysics team to come over here last month and survey the site of the concentration camp? They thought there was nothing remarkable in the results, but then the forensics guy saw something unusual that has just been confirmed.'

Hiebermeyer took a crumpled sheet out of his pocket, his

hand shaking slightly, and passed it to Jack. It was the printout of an archaeological resistivity survey. Jack smoothed it out and put it on his knees. He could identify buried foundations, visible in the contrast of black-and-white features that showed where walls had been. It looked like the survey of a Roman fort, with long barracks buildings and an organized layout of smaller huts. Hiebermeyer pointed to several hazy areas that obscured parts of the buildings. 'That's new-growth forest, trees that grew on the bombed-out site. But look here, at the top right-hand corner.' He pointed to a long, rectilinear feature at least ten by thirty metres in area, like a wide section of boundary ditch. Jack looked up from the sheet to the bunker, traversing his eyes along the forest boundary beyond and trying to visualize the place before the airfield was constructed. Hiebermeyer pointed to a low line of bush to the north-west. 'The team crawled around in the undergrowth and found a track about a kilometre long between the bunker and that ditch, with impressed tyre marks from large vehicles. Yesterday the forensics lady had a hunch about the ditch. She put a borehole down, and came up with lime, lots of it. They pulled back immediately and sealed off the site behind a guarded perimeter. She said she knew instantly what she was looking at. She'd worked on mass-burial sites from the Balkans wars of the 1990s and was sure the lime had been used to slake corpses, put down here in such quantities because the bodies were contaminated. We think the people on the gurneys inside the bunker were only the last batch of victims, the ones left to die an awful death when the Nazi scientists abandoned this place as the Allied front line came closer in 1945. I can only imagine that Mayne and the

American saw those bodies, probably the last thing they ever saw after they'd made their way into this place. But the normal procedure had clearly been to take the corpses from the bunker to the ditch. The forensics lady reckons it could hold five thousand bodies, stacked ten deep.'

'*Christ*.' Jack looked away. He had expected that they might find evidence of Mayne and Stein, the two Allied officers who had entered the camp soon after its liberation and then disappeared into the forest. From talking to Hugh Frazer, he knew that they were both part of the forward reconnaissance teams searching for Nazi secrets, ostensibly looking for hidden caches of art but really seeking any form of secret weapons research: anything the Nazis might use to devastating effect in their final defence of the Reich. Now he knew that what those two officers had seen would have been their ultimate nightmare, the worst-case scenario they would have been briefed that they might find. It was human experimentation, a terrible disease being perfected. Jack felt a cold shiver down his spine. *A disease that may have been spirited out of the past, a past not ancient but within living memory, then refined for use once again, a disease that could take more lives than all those snuffed out in concentration camps like this one, more than were killed in the entire Nazi rampage of murder.*

Hiebermeyer continued talking. 'That chamber was like a sort of ghastly inner sanctum. A huge U-boat battery had been installed outside to provide electricity, and it was still working after all these years. Whoever constructed that place was taking no chances and had planned for this laboratory to survive the fall of the Third Reich. And I haven't told you the full horror of the bodies on the gurneys. Two of them were different, old cadavers that had been disinterred from somewhere else, both of them partly dissected. The heads had been removed and were sitting there upright, embedded in body liquor and looking like those ancient plastered skulls of the Neolithic, only with stainless-steel forceps clamped to them like the ones the Ahnenerbe used to carry out craniological measurements when they went on their expeditions in search of Atlantis. One of them had a hole in it where the forensics lady thinks they extracted rotting brain tissue looking for something. Putting my hand in what came out of the bodies was what really did it for me, and that's when I threw up.'

'So these were different from the other corpses?' Jack persisted.

Hiebermeyer nodded, and swallowed hard. 'Different vintage. The forensics lady thinks they must have come originally from sealed lead coffins. She could even work out the year of death, because she returned to the chamber after we'd left to take a sample and analyse it using her portable lab within the bunker. She found enough to pin down what she'd already suspected was the cause of death, and everything fell into place. She was convinced that those two bodies were there because of what they contained. Still living within them when they'd been disinterred had been one of the deadliest viruses known to man, a virus everyone in the 1940s thought had been extinguished a generation before.'

Jack froze. *The nightmare had become real.* 'You mean the Spanish influenza virus from the 1918 outbreak.'

Hiebermeyer gave Jack a grim look. 'We can only speculate on what was going on here, but the forensics lady and her team are convinced. They think it was refinement, a process of trial and error, mutating and selecting the virus according to its effect on the victims, finding the most lethal form. The other corpses on the gurneys were young men born since 1918 who would not have had the immunity of survivors of the 1918 outbreak. Whoever was doing this was planning something even worse than the Holocaust, Jack: mass murder on a global scale, totally indiscriminate.'

'Or planning to *threaten* the world with it,' Jack murmured.

'This was a true doomsday weapon,' Hiebermeyer said. 'A weapon of the apocalypse. The ultimate creation of Hitler's madness.'

'If it truly was Hitler who ordered it,' Jack said, pursing his lips. 'There were other architects of evil floating around him, others with egos that might have pushed them to create an insurance policy of their own if the whole Nazi scheme went belly-up.'

Hiebermeyer paused. 'And now for the really bad news.'

'It gets worse?'

'There's no evidence yet that the virus survives anywhere in the bunker. As you can see, every precaution is being taken. But there's a downside to that. A horrible downside.'

Jack felt a lurch in his stomach. 'You mean we actually *wanted* to find the virus. The refined virus. The weapon.'

Hiebermeyer nodded. 'There was a refrigerator safe in the laboratory, about the size of a microwave oven. The forensics team are certain that's where the result of all this horror was stored. The safe was open, Jack. There was a stand for some sort of small container like a test tube inside, and it was gone.'

'*Jesus.*'

'Someone must have taken it back in 1945. The SS man tangled up with Mayne was dressed in camp inmate clothing, as if he were in disguise, like the SS who tried to flee from Belsen and other camps that way. He may have been lurking near the bunker to keep prying eyes out, waiting for instructions. There may have been another with him, someone who got into that refrigerator and removed it.'

'If they were planning to take it anywhere more secure in those final weeks of the war, it would have to be towards the shrinking Nazi perimeter around Berlin.'

Hiebermeyer peered at him. 'That's the real reason I wanted you in Germany.'

Jack raised his eyebrows. 'Berlin?'

'I have an old friend who spends his free time with the Berlin Second World War archaeology group, exploring underground bunkers and tunnels of the Second World War in Berlin. When I knew I was coming to Germany, I called him on the off-chance. He told me about something they'd found just south of the Tiergarten at the site of one of the biggest bunkers of them all, the Zoo flak tower. I said I'd try to get there after this. And now because of something else we found in the bunker this morning, it's become imperative.'

'Go on.'

'My friend in Berlin discovered a buried corridor that had once been under the tower. He found a door with a symbol deeply impressed in it, a reverse swastika within a roundel. And there's something about the bunker I haven't told you yet. Major Penn's men also found a reverse swastika impressed within a roundel, concealed under a sliding panel on the door into the laboratory. Penn measured the impression of the swastika in the straw in the crate full of Schliemann's treasures. It was the same dimensions and shape as the swastika in the door. And there's more. The lock was embedded with a strong magnetic device, producing a very unusual signature. We think the palladion was magnetic; the ancient Trojan story that it had fallen from heaven, a meteorite? Whoever opened up that chamber of horrors used the sacred symbol of ancient Troy as a magnetic key.'

'Good God,' Jack whispered. 'And you think it's the same at the Berlin site?'

'I phoned my friend in Berlin while you were on the way here. He said he hadn't thought to mention it before, but the magnetic pull around the swastika symbol on the door in the tunnel was enough to lock his torch against the metal.'

Jack's mind raced. 'If that's the only lead we've got to go on, we need to jump on it. Remember there are still eyes watching this place. If Saumerre knew about this bunker, then he might know about Berlin too. Do we need an IMU excavation team? I can have people in Berlin by tomorrow morning.'

Hiebermeyer peered at him. 'It turns out that beneath the Zoo tower there was a huge reservoir, designed to keep the tower self-sufficient. *That's* why you need to be with me, Jack, you and Costas and your diving gear. The tunnel leads underwater.'

Jack held his breath, and then exhaled hard. He looked at the forest edge, squinting against the sun that was breaking through the mist. He knew that his only course of action now was to deploy all of his energy and resources to see this through. Somewhere out there was a weapon of unimaginable horror, and they might have the only clues to discovering it.

DAVID GIBBINS

He gave Hiebermeyer a steely look. 'You should get back to Aysha. I can take over from now on.'

Hiebermeyer put a hand on his shoulder again. 'I promised Costas I'd stay with you, and I'll do so until he arrives. The buddy system, he calls it.'

Jack hesitated for a moment, then relented. 'I guess we'll make a diver of you yet.'

'After that place?' Hiebermeyer looked towards the bunker. 'Not a chance. That's the last time I put on any kind of suit.' He took his hand down. 'Seriously, Jack. Costas told me everything that happened in the salt mine in Poland last year, when you were searching for the palladion. About your killing spree. We just want to make sure you're in control.'

'Those were Saumerre's thugs, and they'd kidnapped my daughter. I'd do it again without a moment's hesitation. Saumerre's still out there, and it's unfinished business. I want to bring him down.'

'We need to tread carefully. We need to maintain the balancing act you set up with Saumerre six months ago after your showdown with his men at Troy. He knows that his position in the European Union bureaucracy in Brussels depends on you keeping quiet about his underworld background. One word from you and he'd lose everything that allows him to operate freely across Europe. He wants whatever was inside that bunker, what's gone missing. Remember our briefing by the security people after you'd got your MI6 contact on the case? They think he's dangled the possibility of a Nazi wonder-weapon in front of his terrorist customers. Imagine it: the biggest underworld deal of all time, far bigger than the old Soviet fissile materials that MI6 suspects he's been feeding them for dirty bombs. It's been quiet recently on the international terrorist front. The big boys are biding their time, because they're expecting a delivery. But Saumerre knows that if we rumble him and he loses his credibility, he becomes a liability to them. If that happens, you may not even need to take him down. But we have to keep playing the game of bluff and counter-bluff as long as possible, to let him think we've found what he wanted in the bunker.'

'If we had found it, the game would be over for him. He'd know he could never get his hands on it. And that's when he'd become a liability for us. He'd assume we'd be about to blow his cover, and he'd have nothing to lose. He'd do everything he could to take us down with him.'

'Or he could play a game of bluff with us.'

'You mean take a risk that we were bluffing about having the weapon, and try to convince us that in fact *he* had somehow got hold of it? He could threaten to use it himself, but the bluff would last only as long as it took for his terrorist customers to realize he was stringing them along as well.'

Hiebermeyer took a deep breath. 'There is something else. Jack. Just a slight concern I've had, and it's been growing as I've been sitting out here thinking about the last few hours. Being in that bunker was a nightmare, and I'm only getting my thoughts straight now. It was a niggle, but now it's become a worry. If Saumerre did claim he had the weapon, there's just a chance he might not be bluffing.'

'What on earth do you mean?'

Hiebermeyer paused. 'Major Penn's operation is impressively tight, but there was one chink in the armour. They work in two-person teams. This morning things went slightly awry because one of Penn's men, a Sergeant Jones, collapsed in that inner chamber and we had to take him out. It's a big concern, because he's still not regained consciousness, but the doctor is with him now inside the bunker. Apart from me, the only one inside that chamber this morning who wasn't one of Penn's team was the man paired with Sergeant Jones – a European Union Health and Safety inspector named Auxelle. He'd foisted himself on Penn yesterday, arriving at the perimeter roadblock in an EU limousine with a police motorcycle escort. By all accounts he was arrogant and pompous, but Penn had him checked out by MI6 before letting him in and there seemed to be no question over his credibility. He came with the highest EU authority.'

Jack turned to Hiebermeyer in alarm. 'The highest authority in Brussels? Who was his line manager?'

'That's what I've just been wondering. I have a horrible feeling that one of Saumerre's departments might be Health and Safety.'

'*Shit*,' Jack exclaimed. 'But there's no chance of this man having removed anything from the bunker?'

'Everyone is body-searched before leaving the double-lock chamber at the entrance, to make sure that they haven't inadvertently got material on them from inside that might be contaminated. Each one of a pair is responsible for checking the other. But Sergeant Jones was down, and he was Dr Auxelle's partner. In the concern to get Jones out of the laboratory chamber and attended to by the medic, there might have been a slip-up. What worries me is that we're probably only talking about a test tube or a phial, very easily concealed in one of those suits. And Major Penn was completely preoccupied with Jones. They've worked together in a lot of bad places.'

Jack looked at Hiebermeyer intently. 'Do you remember anything else about that laboratory? Anything odd?'

Hiebermeyer looked down and then nodded, putting his hand up to his forehead. 'Something was lurking in the back of my mind, and I've just realized what it was. You remember I said the safe was open? All I could think about at the time – all I could think about until just now – was that whatever had been inside was gone. But there was something else. It should have rung a huge alarm bell at the time, but I wasn't thinking straight. I'd just been stumbling over dead bodies. I should have held the reins tighter. Poor show, as your dad would have said.'

'I'd probably have been worse,' Jack said. 'I'm not used to being in tombs full of corpses, like you.'

'It was the interior of that refrigerator safe, visible because the door was open. Everything else in the bunker was covered in that yellow-green layer, the decomposition product. But the interior of the safe was gleaming. *Gleaming*. I should have realized that meant it had only just been opened.'

'Were Jones and Auxelle in there by themselves?'

'For a few minutes before Jones collapsed and Auxelle called us in to help.'

'Okay. We need to have Auxelle detained. We need to get our contact in MI6 on to it and have him interrogated. And I don't care how high-up he is in Brussels. We need to take him down now.'

'Brussels won't be happy with that. A secretive NATO team, mainly British, arresting a top EU inspector? And there's another problem. The story would be impossible to contain, and it would blow this place wide open to police and journalists, exactly what Major Penn and his team are under the strictest instructions to avoid. Everything about this bunker needs to be kept top secret.'

'Then I'll find Auxelle and do it myself.'

Hiebermeyer eyed Jack shrewdly. 'I think we should bring Major Penn in and tell him everything we know, the stuff MI6 may have kept from him about Saumerre and the whole backstory. I mean *everything*. He has a full special-forces security team surrounding this place, and exerts more authority than his rank suggests. Top secret operations like this to find and contain Nazi scientific sites have been going on since the end of the Second World War and are given all necessary resources by the former Allies, one area where the EU does not hold sway. It's why MI6 are overseeing the operation. Just a hint of bacteriological contamination and Penn can lock down a site for miles around. He's a pretty useful man for us to have on board.'

Jack stood up and paced across the grass, took a few deep breaths and looked around. Maurice was right. He needed to keep his cool, not to let his blood rise, to play the game carefully. He turned back. 'One question's nagging me. If Auxelle did take what was in that refrigerator, then what happened to the palladion? You said the door to the laboratory was already ajar when Penn's men arrived there, and that the impression of the palladion in the straw in that crate was covered with the decomposition layer. Everything points to it being removed from the bunker in 1945. It must have been used to open the laboratory door some time before Mayne and Stein arrived, maybe somehow during the fight with the SS man. If it was the SS man who opened the door, then the palladion should have been found near his body. Yet there was nothing. Everything points to an accomplice, one who survived, though that still doesn't explain why the accomplice would have left without removing the contents of the refrigerator.'

Hiebermeyer nodded. 'Penn has a theory about that. We had two hours together in the decontamination room and mulled it over. He'd been headhunted by MI6 at university and had actually done several courses at GCHQ Cheltenham before opting out and joining the army instead. One of the courses was on "need to know", how to keep a network going while minimizing the number of people who are in on the whole picture. Like you he thought we might be looking at two operatives, but he took it further. Let's imagine that one of them knew about the palladion and was also tasked to retrieve the phial in the refrigerator, the most secret and important part of the whole conspiracy. The person entrusted with that task, to take the deadly weapon to its next destination, had to be a particularly fanatical follower of the conspiracy originator, perhaps unique. If he was somehow unable to perform the task, then the fallback might be for the originator himself to try to retrieve it. But for that to happen, the originator had to have the palladion to open the chamber door. So the second man in the bunker knew nothing of the refrigerator but had been tasked to retrieve the palladion if something happened to the first man before he was able to get inside.'

'So the first man is about to perform his task as Mayne and

Stein arrive,' Jack said slowly. 'He dies in the ensuing struggle, killing Mayne and Stein in the process. But perhaps just as he is about to kill Mayne, pressing him against that door, he uses the palladion to open it, intending to leave Mayne and Stein's bodies inside and lock the door behind him, concealing what had happened and keeping any other Allied troops who might enter the bunker away from the truth of that inner chamber for as long as possible. But Mayne kills the SS man with his knife as he himself is shot, and they both fall into the room together. The accomplice comes upon the scene and his only thought is his own specific task, to retrieve the palladion and take it to his master.'

'And my friend's discovery under the site of the flak tower in Berlin suggests that the palladion may have had more uses than opening this one door,' Hiebermeyer said. 'The forensics lady was in the decontamination room with us after she'd returned from sampling those corpses. She suggested that you could combine the flu virus with a bacteriological agent to make it particularly deadly, adding something that would weaken the immune system to ensure that the virus was always fatal. Maybe this bunker wasn't the only laboratory. Maybe there was another one, perhaps in Berlin.'

Jack pursed his lips. As he turned, he saw an army officer in a camouflage smock and beret approaching them rapidly from the Portakabin, followed close behind by a soldier. The officer wore a sidearm, and the soldier was carrying a rifle and swivelling round every few steps to survey their surroundings, talking into a headset. The soldier stood off to one side while the officer came up to them, his face grim. 'Major David Penn, Royal Engineers. You're Jack Howard. I recognize you from TV.' He shook hands quickly and turned to Hiebermeyer. 'I have some very bad news.'

Hiebermeyer stood up. 'Yes?'

'Sergeant Jones died ten minutes ago. He never regained consciousness.'

Hiebermeyer looked stunned. '*Mein Gott,*' he whispered. 'Dead? How?'

Penn gazed down for a moment, then looked up and cleared his throat. 'The team medics inspected his suit and his body. They found a tiny puncture in the upper right arm of his suit and a matching puncture in his skin. The puncture was from a syringe. Sergeant Jones didn't die of natural causes. He was murdered.'

Hiebermeyer lurched backwards and sat down heavily. Jack had a sudden cold feeling in the pit of his stomach. *Where was Auxelle?* The soldier with the rifle walked quickly over and whispered into Penn's ear, and after a few questions Penn turned back to them, undoing the flap of his holster and looking around. 'I know what you're going to ask. Auxelle left as soon as we exited the bunker. Urgent EU business back in Brussels. As soon as we spotted the puncture marks on Jones' arm, I sent a Humvee from our outer roadblock racing after him. My soldier has just given me an update. They found the EU limousine by the side of the road five kilometres away, about the spot where my soldiers at the checkpoint had heard the sound of a helicopter landing and taking off. Auxelle was nowhere to be seen, but the driver of the limousine was still there. He'd been shot at close range in the back of the neck.'

Jack shut his eyes for a moment. *So it begins.* 'In that laboratory in the bunker,' he said. 'You're sure that refrigerator safe was open when you first saw it after going in to help Jones?'

'Wide open and empty,' Penn replied grimly. 'I assumed that whatever had been inside was removed in those final days in 1945. But now I think those two Allied officers, Mayne and the American, actually stopped that happening. For more than seventy years, their actions prevented the world from being exposed to a weapon too awful to contemplate. But it looks as if I failed them today.'

'Nobody has failed them,' Jack said. 'There's an evil mastermind behind this. We had a run-in with him last year, and his existence has been plaguing me for six months. You could never have predicted what has happened.'

'We're finished here now,' Penn said, putting a hand on his holster and pursing his lips. 'From the forensic data on those exhumed bodies, we know there was a lethal biological agent contained in that laboratory, and that the corpses we saw on those gurneys had been the victims of experimentation. That means the agent might be present elsewhere in the bunker. Just before Jones died, I activated Protocol 15, which means that this place up to the perimeter of the airfield is out of bounds permanently. An SAS team and a full squadron of German military police are on the way to bolster perimeter security. The machinery we used to excavate the bunker will return this evening and begin widening the trench around the walls so it can be filled with thousands of tons of concrete, and after that's been built up, there will be at least eight metres' depth of concrete poured on the roof. This place will be buried like the Chernobyl reactor. I'm afraid that means those works of art and antiquities will never see the light of day after all. They probably wouldn't have escaped the taint of this place anyway. And we're going to have to leave Sergeant Jones' body in there. That pinprick through his suit meant that his body was exposed to the atmosphere inside, and we can't risk it.'

'He had three small children,' Hiebermeyer murmured, shaking his head. 'He was only telling me about them a couple of hours ago.'

'I'm their godfather. I'm going to have to break this to them.' Penn bunched his fists, his voice tight with emotion. 'I'd do anything to get my hands on Auxelle.'

Jack clicked open his phone. 'We have a dedicated MI6 contact. It's the same as the one overseeing you.'

'Done,' Penn said. 'I made the call the instant we worked out what had happened to Jones. I used our secure line, and gave a full situation report.'

'Good,' Jack said, clicking shut his phone. 'I'll use the same secure line before we leave, if you don't mind. Doubtless Saumerre will have disappeared from Brussels by now too. We have to let MI6 find him and Auxelle. They still won't want to put out a warrant for them, but if anyone's going to catch up with them, they will. We have to bide our time but stay on maximum alert. Meanwhile Maurice and I have an invitation to Berlin to visit a bunker site that may have a connection with this place and what was stored inside. We'd benefit from your expertise.'

'Maurice told me about it. I have to go to Wales to visit Jones' wife and children. But I don't want to let go of this. I'll call you.' Penn turned and began to walk back to the Portakabin, followed by the soldier. Jack thought for a moment, and then ran after him, catching up with him just before the entrance. 'David,' he exclaimed.

Penn stopped and turned around. 'What is it?'

Jack unzipped the pocket of his khaki trousers, carefully pulled out a presentation case and opened it. Inside was a Military Cross, the silver of the cross tarnished and the mauve and white ribbon faded, but pinned carefully into the case. 'I told you on the phone last week about Hugh Frazer, the army officer who'd been in the camp and was a friend of Major Mayne's. Before Hugh died, I promised him that if we found Mayne's body, I'd leave this with him. Mayne won it in North Africa when the two of them were together in the same unit, and Hugh kept hold of it when he dealt with Mayne's effects after he'd gone missing. He said Mayne was a bloody good soldier, the best. I was wondering whether you could leave this with Sergeant Jones. Hugh would have liked to know that a fellow soldier like you was putting this where it belonged.'

He handed the medal to Penn, who stared at it for a moment and then gently closed the case. Jack could see that his face was taut with emotion. Penn nodded, and then clicked his heels. 'I'll see to it.' He turned and walked up the steps and through the Portakabin door. Jack walked back quickly to Hiebermeyer, who was leaning forward on the bench with his head in his hands. Jack sat down beside him, put a hand on his shoulder and then stared forward himself, looking pensively at the bleak wasteland surrounding the runway. His dive to Atlantis seemed light years away, yet he remembered the extraordinary, harrowing image on the ROV monitor of that chamber in the volcano, and then Lanowski's remarkable ideas about the Atlantis papyrus, something he would show Maurice when they had got away from this place. He peered with concern at his friend. He would also tell him about the exciting discovery of the Egyptian statue at Troy, but not now; that could be kept in reserve. He knew they had to do everything to keep from being overwhelmed by a sense of foreboding, a worst-case scenario with Saumerre and the Nazi weapon that could be playing out at this very moment. They needed to keep lifelines to the archaeological prizes beyond the darkness Jack knew lay ahead. He opened his phone, and looked in his inbox. Still no word from Katya about the ancient symbols.

Hiebermeyer straightened up, took off his glasses and wiped them on his shirt, then looked at Jack. 'I've had an invitation from my Tante Heidi to visit her. She wants us to go to Wewelsburg Castle.'

'Himmler's SS headquarters?'

'I don't know why. But it was after I told her I was coming to the bunker. She insisted that she had something to tell me, and I called her from the decontamination room and told her you'd come along too. Okay?'

Jack gave him a tired smile. 'I need to make that phone call to our MI6 contact in London, and then there's a jeep waiting to take us off the airfield to a rental car I'd already got arranged in Bremen. We can drive from there to Wewelsburg. Are you all right?'

'I'm supposed to be the one watching out for you, not the other way around.'

'Now you see why I didn't want you to come here.'

They both stood up. Hiebermeyer winced as he tried to flex

his injured wrist, and then relaxed his arm in the sling. The jeep that had brought Jack from the Tornado was waiting again outside the Portakabin, and they walked towards it. Jack looked at the bubble over the bunker, trying to imagine what lay inside. Hiebermeyer stopped and stared at it. 'This place,' he jerked his head, 'this is what most people imagine the worst of war is all about. This is war spread beyond the battlefield to its worst excess, to genocide. But the place we're going to now, to the heart of Nazi Germany, we have a word in German for what went on there. We call it *Gesamtkrieg*.'

Jack nodded. He knew what that meant.

Total war.

PART 2

12

Berlin, the Zoo flak tower, 0930 hours, 1 May 1945

Oberstleutnant Ernst Hoffman put down his pencil and clapped his hands over his ears, waiting for the terrible vibration to pass. Each time the flak guns on the roof fired a salvo they sent a titanic groan through the structure, and then an aftershock that seemed to set on edge every iron bar in the thousands of tons of ferroconcrete that made up the walls. It had been just about bearable while the guns were doing the job for which they had been designed, firing up at the waves of enemy bombers that had pounded Berlin for months, but now that the barrels were depressed to aim into the city at the advancing Russians they were straining the tolerance level of the gun platforms. The engineers who had built the tower could never have imagined that the defence of Berlin would come to this. The tower itself might survive the onslaught, a gargantuan five-storey structure like a medieval keep, but for the thousands of desperate people cowering inside, survival could only mean a matter of hours, a day or two at most. Here in this chamber on the second floor, Hoffman was insulated from the worst of the vibration, but the noise in the open stairways was appalling, shattering eardrums and shaking the fillings from teeth. To those trapped below it must have seemed like the final act of the apocalypse, a ghastly orchestral denouement to the Third Reich.

They called it the Zoo tower because it stood in the grounds of the Berlin Zoo, now a scorched battleground on the edge of the Tiergarten, the huge park in the centre of Berlin. On the other side of the Tiergarten lay the Reich Chancellery, with the Führerbunker beneath it, and north of that the Reichstag and Gestapo headquarters. Together they formed the last bastions of the Third Reich. The Zoo tower even had its own water reservoir, dug deep into the bedrock, and secret tunnels leading out under the Tiergarten. The garrison commander had told him that the tower could last for weeks, even months. But his calculation had been based on the normal garrison of 350: the Luftwaffe flak gunners and the medical staff in the eighty-bed hospital on the floor above Hoffman. The hospital now held more than a thousand wounded and sick, and the lower floor and stairwells were crammed with more than thirty thousand civilians. Hoffman shook his head. *Thirty thousand men, women and children.*

He caught a glimpse of his reflection in the polished metal of the crate beside him. His face looked long, angular, distorted by a dent in the metal, almost as if he had taken on the features of the Stuka dive-bomber that had been his home for almost five years, from his first missions over England in 1940 to the flaming wreck in Poland six months before, from Blitzkrieg to Götterdämmerung. He had grown from youth to man in that machine, from innocent to killer. *A man becomes one with his weapon.* He shifted slightly, wondering if that reflection could really be him. His skin was pale beneath his swept-back hair, ghostly in this light. Ever since being grounded and arriving in Berlin five months ago, he had felt as if the blood had been sucked from him. He flexed his fingers, feeling their strength. At least he had not gone to pieces like so many of his comrades in his Stuka squadron. And there was still one final task to carry out.

He watched the shadows cast by the candle tremble on the walls. The room was large, sepulchral, the walls of stark concrete, in places flaked with paint that had been shaken loose by the vibrations. Directly in front of him a closed door opened on to a spiral staircase that led up to the gun platform on the roof and down to the seething mass of humanity below. When the order had reached him two days ago from Gestapo headquarters to report to the tower, they had offered him Goebbels' rooms next door, where the propaganda minister had briefly held court as Reich Commissar for the Defence of Berlin before running to hide in the Führerbunker. Hoffman had refused, on the grounds that Goebbels might return, but in truth he could not bear to have his command post where that monster had been. And he had all he needed here: a couple of crates and a few planks to make a desk, a box of candles, ledger books to write in, a folding army cot against the wall, a bucket in the far corner with a makeshift wooden cover over it.

The breakdown in sanitation had been frightful. Diehard Nazis had used the lavatories as places to commit suicide, barricading themselves inside and blowing their brains out amidst the squalor, their bloated corpses still there. And the food supply had dwindled to virtually nothing. Hoffman's orderly had brought him his last meal the night before: a bowl of *Wassersuppe* made from potato peelings and beetroot, along with half a bottle of schnapps. He looked at the bottle on his desk, still untouched. He needed a clear head for what was to come. And alcohol had been part of the scourge of Nazism. They were all drunk, the architects of this monstrosity, the gods of National Socialism, cowering in the Führerbunker. Alcohol had fuelled the self-pity, the rage, the fantasies of victory that had brought Hitler's dream of a thousand-year Reich to this frenzied climax of self-destruction and horror.

He heard the dull thud of a pistol shot through the wall, then another. He closed his eyes for a moment, steeling himself. He knew what was happening. Half an hour before, on his way down the stairs from the gun platform, he had stood back as two *Feldgendarmen* had appeared, the hated military police. They were dragging a man between them, his jacket painted crudely with the letter H for Hungary. The man was one of the foreign labourers who had been used to clear refuse from the tower, before that job became futile. The *Feldgendarm* colonel called them the wily Greeks, the warriors of the Trojan Horse, a concealed enemy who would reveal themselves as the Russians moved in. Some of the labourers had removed the clothing with the painted letters and disappeared into the mass of people below, but others had kept their identity, imagining that the liberating Russians would treat them as heroes. Now they were paying the price for letting the *Feldgendarmen* see that too. The door to Goebbels' office complex had been open, and Hoffman had seen the drawn pistols. He wanted to go in and scream at them: *The Führer is dead. Why more killing? It is over*. But to intervene would have been suicidal. And in truth it was not over, not yet. He had to keep his nerve for what lay ahead.

Another pulverizing shudder coursed through the tower. Hoffman pressed his elbows against the planks that formed his desk, trying to stop the vibrations from shaking them off the crates at either end. He peered again at the crate to his left, where he had seen his reflection in the metal. It was covered with stamps and inspection marks, with an inventory of the contents, all the usual evidence of Reich bureaucracy. He knew that this had been an official storage room for works of art, waiting for the time when Hitler's grand scheme for a Führermuseum in his home town of Linz in Austria would be realized. The room had been used since 1941 to house treasures from the Berlin museums, in one of the few places thought to be impregnable to Allied bombing. Several months ago, Reichsleiter Bormann and his henchmen had removed most of the treasures to a salt mine in Austria. Hoffman had snorted when he heard that. During his posting in Berlin over the last few months, he had got to know these people close-up. Bormann knew that Hitler's days were numbered and was undoubtedly securing his own loot. The three crates that remained had apparently been left on the express instructions of Reichsführer Himmler, who had ordered a museum official, a Dr Unverzagt, to watch over them. Hoffman had found the man camped out here with the crates when he had arrived forty-eight hours before. Unverzagt had been one of Himmler's stooges, a member of the Ahnenerbe – Himmler's absurd 'Department of Cultural Heritage' – and Hoffman had instantly disliked him. But the man had left with no protest and had disappeared into the throng of desperate civilians below. Hoffman could not imagine any treasure valuable enough to induce someone to linger in that hellhole, and he was sure that Unverzagt would have bolted from the tower while there was still a chance before the Russians closed in.

Hoffman had inspected the markings on the crates when he first entered the room. They contained the treasures from ancient Troy given by Heinrich Schliemann to the people of Berlin more than sixty years before. Hoffman himself had seen them as a schoolboy, in the Museum of Pre- and Proto-History. Exactly why these crates should have remained here was unclear. But Hoffman knew Himmler personally, and he knew enough of Himmler's psychology to guess at the reason. Himmler was obsessed with ancient artefacts, with mythical kings and heroes, with *Übermenschen* – supposed races of supermen – and with those he identified as Aryan forebears, and above all with lost civilizations. Perhaps these artefacts had some kind of mystical power for him. Perhaps they were meant to stay in Berlin in her hour of greatest need. Hoffman shook his head derisively. The artefacts had not saved Troy, and they would not save Berlin. It was irrelevant now; within a day, the Zoo tower and those crates would be in Soviet hands. Meanwhile they served as good bench-ends to rest the planks of his desk against the incessant vibrations.

Hoffman realized that the flak guns had stopped firing, and

he took his hands from his ears. Another sound was missing, the screech and rattle of the electric ammunition winch that brought shells up from the magazine. The generators must have failed yet again. The electricity had worked in fits and starts all night, and he had relied on candles for his writing. He watched the last one now, the flame still flickering and shuddering from the vibrations, barely casting enough light for him to read the open pages of his diary. Candles had served another purpose in the tower. Since the Soviet artillery had come within range, the thick metal shutters on the windows had been closed and the ventilation tubes sealed. Down below, the people crammed together in the stairwells used candles like underground miners to tell how much oxygen was left. When the candles on the floor went out, they lit them at waist level. When those went out, they held their children on their shoulders for as long as they could, hoping that someone above would take them. Already the bodies were piling up, and the hospital orderlies could no longer go outside to use the makeshift cemetery in the Tiergarten. The stench of decay was beginning to permeate the tower, along with the putrid odour from the hospital on the third floor above him, a charnel house where the wounded lay among piles of amputated limbs and shrouded corpses.

Hoffman closed his eyes, and rehearsed the plan he had devised with the flak-battery commander. At least he would not have to endure another night in this place, even if this day were to be his last. He glanced at his watch. *Twenty minutes to go*. At ten o'clock he would leave to find the battery commander. The evening before, two German soldiers captured by the Russians had arrived at the tower under a white flag with a peace offer from the commander of the Soviet division confronting them. The garrison commander had vacillated, terrified of the *Feldgendarmerie*, who had orders to shoot anyone who showed the slightest sign of surrendering, even the commanding officer. Hoffman and the battery commander had secretly decided to act on their own volition if the garrison commander still had not delivered his surrender to the Russians by this morning. They would muster men in the battery loyal to them, kill the *Feldgendarmen* and go out under a white flag. It was a desperate scheme, almost guaranteeing civilian deaths, but not on the scale there would be if no surrender were forthcoming. The *Feldgendarmen* knew they would be shown no mercy by the Russians, so would never surrender. Hoffman and the battery commander had decided to wait overnight for the garrison commander to change his mind, but the man had been intractable, shut in his room and probably drunk, and now the *Feldgendarmen* were preventing anyone from getting near him.

There were two guards outside Hoffman's door now, there to ensure that he did his duty as well. He clenched his fists and took a deep breath, almost choking on the acrid air. *His duty*. He was the newly appointed commander of the 9th Luftwaffe Parachute Division Lebelstar. The division was a phantasm dreamed up by the drunkards and madmen in the Chancellery, another gloriously named spearhead unit that would save the Reich, another ragtag band of old men, boys, the walking wounded and shell-shocked veterans who had somehow survived the carnage on the Eastern Front to die in this theatre of the absurd. When Hoffman shut his eyes in this place he sometimes glimpsed stark images from the plays he had seen in Paris before the war, existentialist dramas by Beckett and Brecht that had so fascinated and disturbed him, on the border between theatre and reality. It was as if he had been seeing a premonition of his own final act, here where the stage setting also seemed surreal, on another level of consciousness, yet awash with real blood and real anguish and horror.

He undid the leather flap of the holster on his waist, took out his Luger, ejected the magazine and checked that it was full, then pushed the magazine in again and cocked the pistol, shoving it back in the holster but leaving the flap open. He thought for a moment, then snapped the flap shut. The *Feldgendarmen* must see no hint of his intentions. He felt for the two extra magazines in the pouch on his belt, then straightened his jacket and peaked cap, passing his hand over the Luftwaffe badges on his tunic and the Knight's Cross at his neck. He prayed that he and the battery commander had got the timing right. All radio communication with the Chancellery had ceased the day before. There had been rumours that the Führer had killed himself, and then a Chancellery secretary who had fled across the Tiergarten had confirmed it. A Soviet red banner had been seen flying over the Reichstag, glimpsed in the light of a flare during the night, and the barrage of shells and rockets had diminished. There had clearly been some kind of ceasefire, but Hoffman knew it could not last. The Chancellery and Gestapo headquarters were defended by battle-hardened remnants of the SS-Nordland and SS-Charlemagne divisions, fascist sympathizers from occupied Europe who had volunteered for the force. It was the final ghastly irony, that the last-ditch defenders of

Germany should be foreigners fighting in the name of an Austrian psychopath because the army he had created to defend his adopted homeland was an army of ghosts. With daylight now, it could only be a matter of time before the Soviets realized that the SS would not surrender, and unleashed hell. As soon as that happened, any hope of surrendering the flak tower and saving the thousands of lives inside would surely be lost.

A drop of condensation splatted on the open diary in front of him. He quickly blotted it out with his sleeve, smearing the pencil writing of the final paragraph. He tore three blank sheets from the back of the book, folded them and put them with the pencil in his tunic pocket, then closed the book, resting his hand on the embossed gold swastika and eagle symbol on the front. He had written his diary in a foolscap army order book so that prying eyes might think he was drafting a plan of battle for his phantom division. Instead he had written down everything. *Everything*. It was an eyewitness account of the last weeks and days of the Reich, by one who had been close to the monsters who had created it. Hoffman had been a Luftwaffe ace, had chalked up enough missions to win the Knight's Cross with oak leaves and swords, but after being wounded and grounded he had become one of Hitler's strutting peacocks, a Nazi war hero. He had been promoted, showered with honours, feted. He had been inches from Hitler, from that chalk-like face, those eyes like a snake's, the foul breath. He had played with Goebbels' children, their names all beginning with H in honour of Hitler, their lives inextricably bound up with the fate of their Führer; he remembered the oldest girl, Heine, with her sad eyes, last seen in the Führerbunker when he had left it two days before. He had attended parties and celebrations, his face preserved for all time in the newsreels and propaganda photographs, waving and smiling as the Führer bestowed yet another award, inspected yet another doomed Hitler Youth regiment. And as the final months had passed, as the Red Army had closed in, it had become even more grotesque. Only ten days before, he had attended the final concert of the Berlin Philharmonic to hear the last act of Wagner's Ring Cycle so beloved of the Nazis, the *Götterdämmerung*. On the way out, uniformed boys of the Hitler Youth had offered them trays of cyanide tablets to keep ready for the last curtain in Hitler's own opera. Then Hoffman had been obliged to join the inner circle on a trip to the circus, and had watched the performers on horses go round and round, swirling like some vortex in his mind, amongst SS officers with plump fräuleins on their knees, laughing and crying, maudlin and self-pitying, the champagne flowing. And meanwhile the killing had gone on all round them: the *Feldgendarmen* stringing up deserters from lamp posts, summary executions of slave labourers in the streets, bodies left in pools of blood to join those killed by the Allied bombing and the relentless Soviet advance.

His own son. He steeled himself again. That was the only reason he had gone along with it all. *The only reason*. He knew what had happened to the families of those who had plotted against Hitler the year before. He had been on the Eastern Front then with his squadron, just trying to stay alive. But since being posted to Berlin and being sucked into the vipers' nest, he knew that the eyes of the Gestapo and their informers had followed him everywhere, reporting his every move.

Hitler the Führer loved his war heroes, but Hitler the man loathed them because he could never be one himself. Himmler was even more mercurial, the slipperiest of them all. It was a terrible truth, but every day of suffering in Berlin, every day in which thousands more died, was another day of hope for Hoffman's family. The longer the Soviets could be staved off, the more chance there was that his wife and son might escape. They lived near Elsholz, thirty kilometres south of Berlin. Hoffman could not go there because any attempt to leave the city would be met with instant retribution from the *Feldgendarmerie*. General Zhukov's Third Army was sweeping in from the east, the Americans from the west. Terrible stories were reaching Berlin of mass rape by Red Army soldiers. He remembered, on his way back from that awful night at the circus, helping a limbless veteran of Stalingrad back into his wheelchair in a bombed-out S-Bahn station. The soldier had raised a stump in an ironic Heil Hitler salute. *Don't bother with me*, he had said. *If the Ivans do to us only half of what we did to them, then what you see of me now, this half of a man, this is nothing*. There had been a chance, just a chance, that the Americans might get to Elsholz first, that the defence of Berlin might hold the Soviets off long enough for Hoffman's family to fall into Western hands. But now there were reports of the Russians having passed west beyond the town and meeting the Americans on the Elbe. He could only pray that his wife Heidi and son Hans had escaped, and meanwhile try to save as many lives here as he could while there was still time.

He looked at his watch. Three minutes to ten. He stood up and placed the order book containing his diary on top of the left-hand crate, the embossed Nazi eagle and swastika on the cover facing up. He would tell the *Feldgendarmen* outside the door that the order books on his desk contained top-secret plans for a breakout from Berlin, that they were on no account to let anyone in, and that he would be returning shortly with the flak-battery commander to discuss tactics. In truth he had no intention of returning, but he needed to leave the diary where it might be found by a Red Army intelligence officer. He knew the savage punishment meted out by the NKVD to Russian soldiers who damaged anything of intelligence value, so any discovery like that would be likely to fall into the right hands. There was another book lying on the crate, an open copy of Schliemann's *Troy* that had been there when he had arrived, evidently being read by the unpleasant Dr Unverzagt while he had guarded the crates. He moved the volume so that it partly concealed the diary. He noticed that the opened page showed drawings of ancient pottery with swastika decorations, and he remembered a tediously mystical lecture by Von Schoenberg, a student acquaintance of his at Heidelberg University and now one of Himmler's Ahnenerbe, about the swastika, claiming that it had been the symbol of the first Aryans, even of Atlantis. Hoffman curled his lip in disdain. *Atlantis*. He shut the book. He hoped the Soviets would see these artefacts for what they were, as treasures for all mankind, and that their place in history would be shorn of all the twisted fiction that had been used to justify the appalling crimes committed by Himmler and the SS.

There was a sudden commotion at the door. It swung open, and one of the *Feldgendarmen* clicked his heels. 'Herr Oberstleutnant. This man insists on seeing you. He tried earlier, but you were on the roof with the flak gunners. I've checked his papers. He's a member of the Nazi party.'

Hoffman strode irritably over. 'Who the devil is it?' Then he saw the unsavoury form of Dr Unverzagt trying to squeeze in, being held back by the other *Feldgendarm*. Hoffman waved his arm dismissively. 'I have no time for this man.'

The *Feldgendarm* nodded and pushed Unverzagt roughly back, but he shouted out: 'Herr Oberstleutnant. Listen to me. I have news of your family.'

Hoffman stared at him. Saying that was the easiest way to gain entrance. Everyone wanted news of their families. *But it might be true*. He gestured at the guard to release him. 'All right. Two minutes, no more.'

Unverzagt sprang forward, and then pushed the door nearly shut. He turned back and hurried over to Hoffman, speaking urgently. 'Herr Oberstleutnant. When was the last time you saw Reichsführer Himmler?'

Hoffman stared at him in contempt. He grabbed the man by the lapels and dragged him further in, then marched over and slammed the door. He took the man again and forced him towards his desk. 'You fool,' he snarled. 'Keep your voice down. Don't you know that Himmler is discredited? He tried to negotiate with the Americans, and Hitler found out. He's been branded a traitor. The *Feldgendarmen* will kill you just for mentioning his name.'

Unverzagt tried to push him away, and Hoffman held him tight for a moment before relenting. The man straightened his lapels, then pulled something out of his coat pocket, keeping his fist closed around it. 'The Reichsführer has always had your best interests at heart, Hoffman. Do you remember as a boy it was he who directed you to join the Luftwaffe? And he has always looked after your family. I am to tell you they are safe from the Russians, in Plön on the Baltic Sea. They are being guarded by the SS. If all goes to plan, you will be joining them soon.'

Hoffman stared at the man. 'What the devil are you talking about? How do you know this?'

'Five months ago, Himmler took you to visit SS headquarters at Wewelsburg Castle. He took you to the vault below the SS Generals' Room, and showed you something. Do you remember what it was?'

Hoffman kept staring. This was absurd, to dwell on Himmler's nonsense at a time like this. He remembered the visit well enough, a tedious tour through all the rooms named after mythical Aryan heroes, before the lecture about the swastika by the Ahnenerbe man. But he especially remembered what Himmler had shown him, in a secret vault deep inside the castle. He had been sworn to utter secrecy.

Unverzagt peered at him. 'Good. Your face betrays nothing. That is what the Reichsführer saw in you as a boy. Utter reliability. You have kept your word. Your loyalty will be rewarded.' He opened his hand, took Hoffman's and put something in it, a folded piece of paper. Hoffman opened it and looked, then closed his hand over it. It was the same symbol he had seen in the vault in the castle. *The reverse swastika*. He stared at Unverzagt.

'What do you want with me? Now of all times, for Christ's sake? Haven't you seen what's going on outside?'

Unverzagt remained unmoved. 'Five months ago, after you'd recovered from your wounds, the Reichsführer saved you from certain death on the Eastern Front by having you posted to Berlin. It was essential that you were in the very heart of the Reich, a war hero feted by the Führer. And then two days ago you were posted here, to the Zoo tower. There is something hidden here, something that will fulfil our destiny. Your role will soon be revealed to you. I am here to forewarn you. Remember your family, Herr Oberstleutnant. Remember little Hans. He awaits you.'

Unverzagt turned to leave. Hoffman remained rooted to the spot, his mind in a turmoil. The man strode to the door, then turned. 'Herr Oberstleutnant. I meant to check. You can still fly, after your wound?'

Hoffman stared at him, baffled. 'Fly? Of course.'

'Good. And you are an expert night navigator. You attended the training school last year. We saw to that. Until we meet again, Hoffman. For the new Reich. For the new Führer. *Sieg Heil.*'

Unverzagt opened the door and was gone, pulling it shut behind him, leaving Hoffman rooted to the spot. *What the hell was that all about?* Was it yet another desperate scheme, another deluded fantasy of salvation? He opened his hand again and saw the symbol on the piece of paper, the reverse swastika inside a red roundel. He shook his head. It was all nonsense. Himmler would surely be dead by now. Unverzagt was unhinged, had dreamed up this fantasy in the oxygen-starved bedlam below. Hoffman's visit to Wewelsburg would be well known among Ahnenerbe fanatics like Unverzagt, who had seen Himmler promise to induct him into the SS when the war was over. It had even made the front page of the SS newspaper. And Unverzagt would have known about

Himmler's special interest in him from all the hero propaganda feting his achievements as a Stuka ace, glorifying the wisdom of the Reichsführer in encouraging him to fly at an early age. Hoffman crumpled the paper into his pocket and put the encounter from his mind. There was enough madness in here already. He picked up his binoculars, slung them round his neck and then turned round one last time to look at the place where he had spent these last hours, on very probably his final day alive. In the corner was a marble bust, lying broken and forgotten among the flecks of paint that had fallen off the wall in the vibrations. It was Bismarck, the Iron Chancellor, the portrait bust that used to preside over the Troy exhibit in the Museum. Hoffman stared at the forlorn scene. What was it Bismarck had said? *War with Russia must be avoided at all costs*. On impulse, he came to attention and clicked his heels, then he turned and marched quickly towards the open door and the shrieking hell of the Soviet onslaught.

13

A few minutes after 10 a.m., Hoffman emerged on the roof inside the flak-battery command post, a circular concrete shelter like a truncated cone with walls that rose a metre or so above his height. He looked up, squinting at the overcast sky, and saw the dark pall of dust and soot that hung over the city. The sky seemed to reflect a red glow from the flames, and from the dust of millions of pulverized bricks that hung in the air like a mist of blood. Climbing up the stairs from the squalor and seething humanity below, Hoffman had thought of the medieval *axis mundi*, the ascent to heaven that seemed to be promised by the smudge of daylight he had seen at the top of the stairs; yet when he reached there, all he found was another vantage point over hell, as if he himself were fated to be among the orchestrators of this horror. He remembered swimming in the lakes of Bavaria as a boy, looking down and seeing the lens of sulphur that divided the living lake from the dead lake below, and never having the courage to dive through it. Here it was as if he were trapped beneath that opaque layer, cut off for ever from the light of the sun. *Beyond the sight of God*.

He felt his nostrils burn, and the grit of brick dust on his teeth. After the atrocious stench of the stairwell, he had yearned to take a breath of fresh air, but out here it was acrid, fume-laden, and caught in his throat. Yet the pall of dust had lessened with the ceasefire of the last few hours, and he could discern other smells too: a waft of cordite from the flak guns; wisps of black *markhorka* tobacco, brought for the flak gunners by the boys who stole out at night from the tower to loot Russian corpses, some never to return; and the honey-sweet smell of decomposing flesh, rising up everywhere from the rubble of the city. And there was another smell, not a Berlin smell but the farmyard smell of Russia, of thousands of horses dragging supply wagons for the Red Army that snaked into the city behind the advancing soldiers and tanks, coming from nearly every direction now. Two days ago, the remaining German perimeter had been a rough rectangle five by fifteen kilometres. Now it was little more than the Tiergarten and the strongholds on either side. He felt as if he were standing on a precarious mound of solid ground in a lake of lava. Soon they too would be swamped, islands in a sea of blood, and then submerged in the red tide like some ghastly modern-day parable of Atlantis.

He pushed past crouched helmeted figures to the only officer present, a Luftwaffe *Hauptmann* with aviator wings on his tunic like his own, another pilot in an air force that no longer had aircraft. The man wore a battered forage cap and radio headphones that were hooked into the fire control panel. Hoffman lifted one earphone, cupped his hand and bellowed into the man's ear. 'Where's the battery commander?'

The man looked up quickly, his face grey and unshaven, then gestured repeatedly with one arm. 'The ammunition elevator,' he shouted. 'Trying to restart the backup generator.'

Hoffman released the earphone and looked over at the massive iron cupola that protected the elevator shaft. He and the battery commander had banked on having the big guns in action to divert attention while they went below and carried out their plan to surrender the tower. He would give the man ten minutes. *No more.*

He climbed up to the rim of the command post and gazed around. The concrete exterior was pockmarked from Soviet shrapnel and shell fragments. The roof was about half the size of a football pitch, with circular bastions at each corner containing the twin 128mm flak guns, and beyond that an outer curtain with 37mm and quadruple 20mm guns. Some five hundred metres beyond the Zoo tower to the north-west, he could see the top of the L-Tower, another concrete monstrosity containing the giant Würtzburg radar that directed the fire of the guns against Allied bombers. Month after month they had come, week after week, relentlessly, American by day, British by night. Many times during his posting in Berlin he had seen the flak guns do their work, and watched American B-17s split in half and flutter down like giant silvery leaves, and the burning parachutes of British aircrew plummeting like flares in the night. But the last raid had been ten days ago, and that already seemed like another war. The barrels of the big guns had been lowered to provide counter-battery fire against the Soviet howitzers, and then to fire point-blank into the advancing infantry and tanks. Now they were at their lowest possible elevation, eighteen degrees below horizontal, poised to fire their last salvos before the Red Army stormed into the Zoo grounds below.

Hoffman shut his eyes for a moment and listened. It was the first time he had been up here and not been overwhelmed by the roar of Russian artillery and the shriek of Katyusha rockets, the ever-enclosing ring of fire that seemed to course round the city like a giant electrical current. He could hear voices on the gun platforms, hoarse with cordite, raised against their own deafness. He heard the rumble of falling masonry, like the sound of calving glaciers he had seen from his aircraft in the fjords of Norway. But he could tell that the ceasefire was beginning to unravel. He heard the harsh roar of tank engines in the distance, the sound of churning tracks. Somewhere the fighting had started up again; he heard the ragged rip of a German Spandau machine gun, a hollow echoing sound in a faraway street, then the rattle of Soviet sub-machine guns and the thud of grenades. The Russians had been using captured German Panzerfaust anti-tank weapons to blast their way through rooms, house by house, street by street. Beneath the storm of artillery and rocket fire this was still an infantryman's war, a war of sniping, grenades, man-pack flamethrowers, desperate knife fights in the darkness, the incessant sub-machine guns. No quarter was being given by either side. He could hardly imagine what was happening to the civilians still in their homes, those who had not sought refuge in the suffocating hell of the bunkers and the flak towers like this one.

He heard the drone of an aircraft, then opened his eyes and saw a solitary Soviet Il-2 Shturmovik dive-bomber bank and begin its dive directly towards him. He shaded his eyes, and watched with professional detachment. There would be no chance of the bombs damaging the concrete tower, but they could disable the guns and kill the crews. Already bombing and Soviet artillery had put most of the 37mm and 20mm guns on the outer gallery out of action. But it was a doomed attack. The pilot had needed to begin his dive from a higher altitude, yet that would have put him above the pall of smoke, unable to see his target. As it was, he would be unable to reach a steep enough angle to aim his bomb. Exactly on cue, the remaining 20mm quadruple gun on the platform erupted in a sharp crackle. The aircraft was shredded and then disintegrated, plummeting out of sight below the edge of the tower into the Tiergarten and exploding in a fireball, the metal fragments pattering harmlessly against the concrete walls below.

Hoffman recalled his own glory days as a Stuka dive-bomber ace during the Blitzkrieg five years before, when the whole world seemed to be falling to German force of arms. Then, he had thought little about the Nazis; he had been driven by a young man's exuberance and the small world of camaraderie and loyalty and honour. And now here he was, commander of the newly formed 9th Luftwaffe Parachute Division Lebelstar, the last-ditch defenders of the Reich. They were all here on the roof now, his division: the thirty-odd boys of the Hitler Youth and Luftwaffe auxiliary who still survived from the flak battery. As soon as the Soviets advanced beneath the minimum trajectory of the guns, his orders were to remuster these boys as elite paratroopers, somehow find weapons for them and lead them out to final glory in the scorched and blasted streets below. And he had been given no choice. The *Feldgendarmerie* would execute anyone who faltered, himself included. The Nazis did not even trust their own heroes.

A boy detached himself from the group in front of one of the big guns and came running towards him. He could be no more than twelve, and was wearing lederhosen shorts and an outsized helmet that wobbled as he ran. His face was tense, wax-like beneath a shock of blond hair, and smeared with filth and tears. Dried blood caked his neck below his ears where they had been bleeding. Hoffman had taught the boy to leave the chin strap unfastened on his helmet, to open his mouth and grimace to equalize the pressure in his Eustachian tubes, to lean forward to avoid the blast of the guns ripping his lungs, but there was nothing he could do to save the boy's hearing. The lad had latched on to him when Hoffman had arrived for the first time on the roof two days before. Maybe he reminded him of his father, probably dead like the fathers of most German children, remembered only by a photograph of a man in a uniform like his own. 'Herr Oberstleutnant,' the boy piped breathlessly, coming to a halt in front of him. '*Wann kommt der Russ? Wann kommt der Iwan?*'

It was a child's question of a father, asking the unanswerable. Hoffman knelt down in front of him. There were no *Feldgendarmen* up here on the gun platform; like most Nazi thugs they were frightened of it, of the reality of war. It was the one place where nobody was listening or watching. He tapped the boy's helmet. 'Can you hear me?'

'*Was?*' The boy screwed up his face. Hoffman raised his voice.

'When you know Ivan is coming, take off this helmet, right? You don't want to look like Hitler Youth.' He reached into his trouser pocket and took out a half-finished packet of cigarettes. 'These are American. Save them and offer them to Ivan, right? Then find an officer. You know how to recognize Russian officers? Show him the room where I've been working. Tell him there are important secrets there, in the order books. You understand me?'

The boy clutched the cigarettes, put them carefully in his pocket and looked at Hoffman, nodding. Hoffman felt a knot of anguish in his stomach. He remembered Goebbels' children, the girl with the sad eyes. He remembered the pilot in his squadron who had made a forced landing near a Ukrainian village, and had seen the SS-Einsatzgruppen at work. He had returned to the squadron shocked. 'Their children cry just like our children,' he had said. Hoffman put out his hand to touch the boy's face, then remembered watching Hitler doing the same only a few days before in front of a ragged line of Hitler Youth, the Führer's left arm shaking uncontrollably behind his back, his right hand stroking cheeks, tweaking ears. It had been repulsive. Hoffman let his hand drop to the boy's shoulder, and squeezed it. He nodded towards the gun. 'You'd better get back to your post. It won't be long now.'

He turned to look for the battery commander. Then he heard the boy yelling: 'Alert! Alert!' Hoffman spun back and saw the boy at the parapet, looking out. Others rushed to join him, and Hoffman followed. For the first time since coming up here, he gazed down at the ruins of the city looming out of the smoke, at the gutted shells of buildings with their upper windows open to the sky. East over the Tiergarten he saw only a shifting miasma of smoke, and he followed the boy's gaze down to the street to the south beyond the Zoo grounds, where they knew the Russians would come. About five hundred metres away he saw the lingering smoke of an explosion, and the dust of a collapsed building. They all watched, and waited. Then the man next to the boy jostled him and put a hand on his arm. 'Ivan's out there, you can count on it. But don't tempt him. Let's get back to the guns.'

They left the parapet, but Hoffman remained, looking down at the smouldering wasteland between the base of the tower and the beginning of the city block. In the nearest buildings lay the first line of German defenders: the odd surviving machine gun, a sniper he had seen go out camouflaged in black like a wraith. Between the buildings and the tower lay the ruins of the Berlin Zoo, pocked by shell craters filled with black and yellow scorch marks. Down there was the last line of defenders, boys and old men of the *Volkssturm* militia armed with the final wonder-weapon the Reich had thought fit to issue them: the *Volkshandgranate*, made from a charge of explosive embedded in a piece of concrete, useless against tanks and barely effective against men. The Zoo animals were still there too, in broken cages and blasted compounds: dead gorillas and elephants, shell-shocked baby baboons clinging to their mothers. He stared, watching a monkey outside its shattered cage, limping round and round, half-crazed. He could hear songbirds, and wondered if they were deafened to the sound of their own music. He remembered the flowers that day he had come here with his son. It had been late spring then, as it was now, and the rhododendrons should be coming out. He smelled that farmyard smell again, the dung from thousands of Russian horses. It conjured up an image he had seen in the room below in the book by Heinrich Schliemann on ancient Troy, a woodcut of the ruins before the excavation: a pastoral scene of grazing animals and shepherds among the tumbled walls. He wondered whether Berlin could become like that, or whether this place would be too poisoned and blighted by history ever to nurture life again.

Then he saw it. He whipped out his binoculars. *The boy had been right*. The ghostly shape of a Soviet T-34 tank poked through the rubble at the end of the street, probing forward. He saw flashes, exploding shells, lines of tracer bullets, the lick of a flamethrower. An engine screamed, and then he saw the tank dip and roll over the rubble, its turret traversing, seeking a target. He could see the padded black helmet of the tank commander. Behind it an American Studebaker truck lurched into view, disgorging troops. *An American truck*. His heart leapt, but then he remembered dive-bombing a merchant ship off Norway with lines of those trucks lashed down on its deck, destined for Russia. The soldiers fanned out on either side of the street, picking their way through the rubble. One appeared tottering along on a bicycle, with a Panzerfaust anti-tank rocket strapped to the front. Hoffman remembered the parade he had attended with the Führer a few days before, seeing off boys of the Hitler Youth as they rode into battle on those bicycles. It was hard to tell whether the Russian cyclist was deadened to the danger around him, or whether he was deliberately cycling to his nemesis like the German boy who had ridden the bicycle before him. Suddenly the cyclist flopped sideways, his head disintegrating in a spray of red from a sniper's bullet. There was a burst of sub-machine-gun fire and the sniper's rifle clattered down from an upstairs window into the street below. The falling bike set off the Panzerfaust, which screeched into the building opposite, exploding and bringing down the entire facade in a cascade of brick and dust. On the upper floor a bathroom was revealed, the porcelain bathtub hanging precariously from the open frontage with a shattered mirror behind, a jarring scene of domestic intimacy. The T-34 roared and squealed forward, the driver grinding the gears as he negotiated a route through the piles of masonry. He ran over the fallen cyclist, popping and squeezing the body like a toothpaste tube, leaving a bloody clot on one track that reappeared with each turn as the tank lunged forward. Another glorious death in battle, another wreathed photograph on a mother's mantelpiece. Hoffman watched the infantry come up behind, picking their way through the rubble. He heard the distinctive echoing rip of a German Spandau machine gun, and three of them fell. Then the tank gun traversed and cracked and a tottering pile of masonry disintegrated, silencing the Spandau. In minutes the Soviets would be under the elevation of the flak guns, and the tanks would be firing point-blank at the steel covers over the windows of the Zoo tower, trying to punch a hole large enough for a flamethrower to spurt fire into the thousands of people crammed in the darkness below. Unless they surrendered it soon, the tower would become a giant crematorium.

Then Hoffman heard another sound, nearby on the platform this time, a groan of machinery followed by a whirring and rattling noise. He looked over towards the ammunition elevator and saw the first 128mm shell emerge, then watched three boys struggle to carry it to the nearest gun. As a tactic against the Soviet advance, it was a futile gesture. The tanks would be under the guns' minimum elevation by the time they were ready to fire. But he and the battery commander had devised the plan to keep the *Feldgendarmen* convinced that they would fight to the end, and to provide a distraction. The gunners would fire ten rounds a minute until the ammunition was expended. The noise and vibration inside the tower would be horrendous.

He saw the battery commander crawl out from the shaft, streaked in oil, his head wreathed in a blood-stained bandage. The man immediately hunched down and set to with a wrench unscrewing the fuses as each new shell appeared, surrounded by crouched boys. Hoffman knew that the remaining ammunition for the big guns had been time-fused for high-altitude airburst, and the fuses would all need to be reset. It was of no consequence now, as it was the noise of the guns that would create the distraction. But Hoffman saw that the gun crew were in their own world, locked into their drill in this final act. The commander looked up for a moment, gazed around frantically, not seeing him, and then hunched over again. Hoffman had a sudden cold realization. *He was going to have to do this alone.*

Then he felt it, a strange brushing sensation, barely perceptible, an unsettling feeling that seemed to come from all directions at once. The soldiers who had been in battle called it the devil's breath, the wind caused by the blast and suck of thousands of exploding shells. He looked towards the

Reichstag, but the Tiergarten had disappeared in an eruption of dust and smoke. Soon the creeping barrage would reach the flak tower. He looked south, and saw the ripple of flame from the Soviet howitzers on the horizon, then the multiple fire-streaks of Katyusha rockets. In moments the sound would reach them, the pulverizing roar of artillery, the shriek of the rockets, sowing terror just as the siren in his own Stuka dive-bomber had once done.

What he had seen in the street outside was just a probing attack. Now all hell would be unleashed. He felt his chest tighten. The whole earth seemed to be shaking. He watched men and boys scurrying around him, seeking shelter from the onslaught to come, in a blur.

Another smell assailed his nostrils.

It was the smell of fear.

Hoffman ran back towards the entrance to the spiral staircase that led into the bowels of the tower. A cluster of shells burst in the grounds of the Zoo, sending shrapnel clattering like hail against the concrete below. From their new positions the Russian gunners were finding the range, aided now by forward artillery spotters in the ruined buildings in sight of the tower. Hoffman glanced at the flak gunners loading the breech of the nearest twin 128mm gun, its barrels aimed towards the street below. He prayed that they would have enough time to fire their salvo and give him the distraction he needed to get out with a white flag. He saw the boy in the lederhosen, helping to heave another shell towards the breech. *Let him survive*. The din suddenly became horrendous: the roar of tank engines, the rattle of tracks, the crack of tank gunfire, the rippling boom of howitzers, the screaming salvos of rockets, the noise echoing and rolling through the open doorway. He lurched inside and heaved the steel door shut, closing off the worst of it. The stench of seething humanity wafted up to him. He suddenly felt terribly claustrophobic. *He had to get out of this place.*

As he turned to go down the spiral stairs, he heard the clatter of someone running up from below. A helmeted face appeared under the one bare bulb still lit on the upper stairway, and stopped, breathless. 'Herr Oberstleutnant.' It was his orderly, an elderly *Volkssturm* wearing a faded First World War tunic. The man leaned forward, panting, holding his stomach, looking half-dead. 'You must come at once. To your room. Important visitors from the Reich Chancellery. A prisoner under escort.'

The Reich Chancellery. Hoffman stopped on the stairs. What the hell did they want? He clenched his teeth. 'Who is it?'

The soldier's skin was pasty, like porcelain, and there was a numbness in his eyes. 'Herr Oberstleutnant, I don't know. I really don't know. One of the *Feldgendarmen* grabbed me and sent me up to find you.'

'All right. How many?'

'Five, I think. Two SS guards, two senior-looking officers and the prisoner, bound and hooded. They came through the cable tunnel from the L-Tower. That's all I know.' The soldier's voice cracked, and he slumped against the wall.

Hoffman took a deep breath, and swallowed hard. His throat was still burning from the acrid air outside. 'All right. Go back to your duties. Don't give the *Feldgendarmen* any reason to pick on you. There's going to be a lot of killing soon. Get on.'

The soldier gave a faltering salute and stumbled back down the stairs. Hoffman followed him, clattering down as fast as he could. The stench was indescribable. He passed the entrance to the hospital and glimpsed bloodstained operating tables inside. Part of the hospital was an emergency *Sanitätsraum*, a maternity ward. The vibration of the guns had pushed women into early labour, as if life were frantically regenerating in the face of extinction. He had heard the screams of women giving birth in the night and the wail of a baby, so at odds with this place of death.

He thought about what his orderly had said. *In his room.* All he could think of was the crates with Schliemann's artefacts from Troy. In the last hours of the Reich, had they come to claim their remaining loot? *But with a prisoner?* He reached the second-floor landing. He could see the throng of civilians below, in the emergency lighting now provided by the backup generator. The stairwell funnelled the noise upwards, a sound like the engine room of a ship, humming and pulsating. Above it he heard the occasional shriek, then a snatched voice of reason as someone tried to bargain for space, for food. Two days ago he had watched families arrive in their best clothes, carrying cardboard suitcases with thermos flasks and sandwiches. Now they surged up the stairs like a nightmare image, pressing against the line of *Feldgendarmen* who held them back. This was the truth of Goebbels' *Volksgenossenschaft*, 'patriotic comradeship'. These were the ordinary people of Berlin, the women who had waited in vain for their soldier husbands to return, the children, the elderly who thought they had endured the worst of war a generation ago. Two well-dressed women suddenly disintegrated into a vicious fight over a scrap, snarling and scratching until one of the *Feldgendarmen* slammed his elbow into them and they fell back into the melee, screaming. Hoffman remembered a line from Brecht's *Threepenny Opera*. *First comes food, then morals*. Only for so many of these people, morality had been sucked out of them by the Nazis long ago.

He approached the door to his room. The two *Feldgendarmen* had gone, and had been replaced by two men wearing Waffen-SS camouflage smocks and forage caps and carrying Sturmgewehr-44 assault rifles. Their lapels carried the round *Sonnenrad* sun-disc symbol of the SS Nordland Division, the same symbol Hoffman had seen in the floor at Wewelsburg Castle. One of the men put up a hand, swathed in a bandage and missing a thumb, and Hoffman halted. He suddenly felt uneasy. Perhaps he had been wrong about the Schliemann treasure. *Maybe they were here for him*. Had he given them some excuse, failed in his duty somehow? He remembered what he had left on the crate. *His diary*. He had never imagined that anyone would return to that room before the Russians arrived. If a *Feldgendarm* or SS man still loyal to the Reich saw even one page of it, then it was all over for him. He felt a cold trickle of sweat run down his back. A voice barked inside, and the soldier missing the thumb beckoned him forward. At that moment a shudder rent the tower as one of the big flak guns fired. Hoffman knew that the worst vibration was a whiplash effect a second later, and he instinctively put his hands to his ears. As he did so, the soldier deftly undid his holster and took the Luger from him. Hoffman dropped his arms and walked into the room. His heart began to pound. *So this was it.*

He saw two men inside, wearing army greatcoats and officers' peaked caps, their faces obscured in the gloom. They wore the shoulder insignia of SS generals, *Obergruppenführer*, and they were streaked with mud. Then he saw a third man, the prisoner, shorter than the other two and wearing a civilian brown leather coat, a white hood over his head and his arms tied behind his back. The door shut behind Hoffman. The smaller man suddenly released his own hands without help and ripped off the hood, then walked towards Hoffman's makeshift desk, where the bare bulb hanging over it was lit. One of the generals gestured for Hoffman to follow. He clicked his heels, touched his Knight's Cross, pulled down his jacket lapels and straightened his cap, then walked over briskly and came to a halt, slamming his foot down and remaining at attention. He felt strangely calm. Why there had to be three of them he did not know. A single *Feldgendarm*, a single bullet, was all he had expected. At least he was not being guillotined in Gestapo headquarters, or strung up with piano wire like the Hitler plot conspirators the year before.

The smaller man threw off his greatcoat and smoothed back his oily hair, then turned round under the light and stared at him.

Hoffman froze. It was not possible. The man in front of him should by all rights have been dead. *It was Reichsführer Heinrich Himmler.*

14

Oberstleutnant Ernst Hoffman stood inside the entrance to the concrete room that had served as his office, the two Waffen-SS guards behind him and the shadowy figures of the two SS generals in greatcoats standing against the wall to the left. For a frightening moment he felt unable to breathe, as if the closed-down ventilation shafts had finally excluded all air from the flak tower, and the remainder had been sucked out by the pulverizing Soviet bombardment overhead. When he did take a breath, his nostrils filled with the same cloying smell that had sickened him in the Führerbunker under the Chancellery a few days before, the reek of wet wool, stale sweat, nicotine and alcohol, the hint of incipient decay that had made the bunker already seem like a tomb.

He stared at the man facing him in front of his desk. The man had been wearing an eye patch, now pulled off, and had shaved his moustache, but there was no doubting who he was. *What was he doing here?* Hoffman had been this close to Himmler many times over the last months of his posting in Berlin, and earlier when Himmler had taken an interest in his Luftwaffe career. The pasty complexion was there, the weak chin, the squirrelly jowls, the small, close-set eyes behind little round spectacles, looking at him with one eyebrow raised. Hoffman snapped to attention, clicked his heels and raised his right arm in the Nazi salute. 'Herr Reichsführer-SS. *Heil Hitler.*'

Himmler waved dismissively. 'You can dispense with the *Heil Hitler*. Adolf is dead.' His voice was ice-cold, precise. Under the civilian overcoat Hoffman could see that he was wearing the field grey of a Wehrmacht officer, not the usual SS black. Then Hoffman remembered that Hitler, in one of his final acts of madness, had appointed Himmler commander of Army Group Vistula. Himmler had seemed inordinately proud of his role, but had never held a field command before in his life. Everyone knew he had failed to be selected for front-line service in 1918, and it grated on him. Army Group Vistula had disintegrated weeks ago, but Hoffman knew there was a reason why Himmler was still wearing the uniform: three days earlier, Himmler had gone of his own volition over the Elbe to the advancing American army, to try to negotiate a ceasefire. An SS uniform would not have made him many friends there. His proposal that the Allies join with the remnant Wehrmacht to fight against the Russians had been rejected, but when Hitler found out about his attempt to parley he was incandescent and had him branded a traitor. Hoffman himself had been next to Hitler in the bunker and had seen the rage. Himmler had expected to be the next Führer, but instead Hitler had appointed Grand Admiral Dönitz. Himmler had disappeared, and was presumed dead. But now the man himself was standing here, very much alive. *And it was Hitler who was dead.*

Himmler waved again at Hoffman's raised arm, then offered his gloved right hand. Hoffman watched his gaze, remembering how it roved disarmingly over a person's countenance before fixing on one's eyes, penetratingly. He remained ramrod straight, but lowered his arm, taking the proffered hand. He felt the pudgy fingers, soft and clammy, and the limp shake. Himmler was still looking at him questioningly, one eyebrow cocked. In that instant, Hoffman knew he was being tested. *Of course. The Führer is dead. Long live the Führer.* He snapped his right arm back up. *'Mein Führer. Sieg Heil.'* Himmler gave him a lopsided, humourless smile, then took off his leather gloves and slapped them against his thigh. 'I have always been impressed by your loyalty, Hoffman. You and your family. Dear little Hans. Have you heard from your wife? These are testing times.'

'They are in Elsholz, *mein Führer.* At my wife's family home. The Russians are close.'

'Then I have excellent news for you. Two days ago, my men took them to Plön, near the Baltic coast. They are safe from the Russians.' He pulled a postcard with a seaside view out of his pocket and passed it to Hoffman, who glanced down at it. There were just a few lines, but it was enough. He recognized his wife's writing. They were by the sea. *Waiting for him.* He felt weak with relief. Dr Unverzagt had been telling the truth about that, at least. He stared at Himmler, not betraying a flicker of emotion, and clicked his heels again. 'I am most grateful.'

Himmler waved his hand, then pulled a dagger out of his belt, unsheathed it, and ran one finger over the flat of the blade, flinching as he touched the edge. It was an SS officer's dagger, black-handled and mirror-bright, with runes etched into the steel. Hoffman remained stock still. *So this was to be it.* Not a bullet, but a knife. He was surprised that Himmler had the stomach for it. Himmler stopped toying with the knife and looked at Hoffman. 'As I said, I have always been impressed by your loyalty. Not like those snivelling swine at Army Group Headquarters, always undermining me. Not like those sycophants in the Führerbunker. The only ones I have ever trusted are my beloved SS, and you, Hoffman. But now it is time to regenerate, to purify. The Nazi party is dead. The SS lives on. Kneel down.'

Hoffman held his breath. *Just get it over with.* He sank to both knees, still ramrod straight, staring past Himmler. He closed his eyes, trying to imagine his son, holding him sleeping against his shoulder, standing on the lake shore at his father's home in Bavaria, feeling the warmth of the infant's breath on his neck. He felt a tap on his shoulder, then opened his eyes and saw Himmler resheathing the knife and looking down at him. 'You know the SS oath?'

Hoffman swallowed hard. '*Meine Ehre Heisst Treue.* My honour is loyalty.'

'Arise, SS-Brigadeführer.'

Hoffman rose to his feet, stood to attention and clicked his heels. He felt physically sick. '*Mein Führer.* It is the greatest honour.'

Himmler put the dagger on the desk, slapped down his gloves beside it and then went round to Hoffman's chair. He sat down heavily and raised his legs on the desk, rattling the half-bottle of schnapps that Hoffman had left there. He took off the shoulder satchel he had been carrying and pulled out a swaddled package, putting it on the table beside the dagger. Hoffman followed every movement, his heart pounding, keeping his eyes from straying to the top of the crate where he had left his diary. *He must not see that.* Himmler took off his spectacles, blew on them and wiped them clean with a handkerchief, then replaced them and stared at Hoffman. 'I am a practical man, SS-Brigadeführer. I have absolutely no wish to go down with the rats in the sinking ship. The Americans have disappointed me. But they will do my bidding, when the time comes. Of that I can assure you.'

The light bulb above the desk trembled, and the dust in the air shimmered. There was a screeching groan, and then another. The electricity jolted off with each shuddering percussion, and the luminous paint on the ceiling flashed pastel blue as the bulb flickered on and off. Himmler dropped his feet back to the ground and leaned over, holding his ears and grimacing; the two SS generals in the shadows did the same, unused to the terrible noise. Hoffman clapped his hands to his ears. This would be it. *The final barrage.* The battery commander would be firing the south-facing flak guns simultaneously in salvos, for maximum noise effect inside the tower. There would be twenty, maybe twenty-five rounds. He and Hoffman had planned the barrage to give them cover, to allow them to get out unnoticed by the *Feldgendarmen* and surrender the tower to the Russians before the final onslaught, to save the thousands of civilians crammed inside. It had been a desperate scheme, but now it appeared a forlorn hope. There seemed no chance that Hoffman could escape from this room – and whatever scheme Himmler had for him – in time to reach the Russians and call for a ceasefire.

Hoffman's mind raced. *What was Himmler's game?* The man was as mercurial as the many hats he wore. Head of the Ahnenerbe, the Department of Cultural Heritage. Head of the SS and the Gestapo. All the Nazi arteries of hate seemed to lead to him. Even the Ahnenerbe was malign, a racist front. Before the war, Hoffman had thrilled as much as any schoolboy to the newsreel footage showing heroic German expeditions to Tibet and Iceland and the Andes, searching for lost Aryan civilizations. He had even applied to be a pilot on one of those expeditions, far too young but overcome by his passion to fly. Himmler had made a public spectacle of him, had called him to Berlin and paraded him as the perfect Nazi youth, willing to volunteer to serve the Fatherland even before he was of age. But then Himmler's scientists had shown him photographs and skull measurements of Tibetans and native Greenlanders. Hoffman had said nothing, but he had realized that the treasure they were seeking was not so alluring after all. It was only later that he understood that those measurements were another instrument of hate, part of the collection of data that supposedly gave proof of the physical superiority of the German people.

He had seen what Himmler's other hats meant too. A few months ago he had been invited to a party at Gestapo headquarters on Prinz-Albrechtstrasse, where he had been shown the manacles for hanging prisoners and the guillotine room. The victims were so-called political prisoners, anyone who displeased Himmler. Berliners who heard the screams at night called it the House of Horrors. And there was worse. As a university student in 1938, Hoffman had witnessed Kristallnacht, the smashing and burning of Jewish shops across Germany. Later, on a tour of factories as a Luftwaffe hero, he had seen Jewish slave labour at the V-1 and V-2 rocket sites. Everyone knew how the Jews were treated; you could see them in work gangs around Berlin, with their Star of David armbands. Then one afternoon six months ago, on one of his last missions as a Stuka pilot over the Eastern Front, Hoffman's aircraft had been leaking fuel and he had been forced to land in Poland near the town of Oświęcim, where they had flown over a vast camp with barracks and a railhead. The aircraft engine had nearly choked on a thick cloud of smoke that smelled like roasted meat. His gunner in the rear seat had glimpsed the scene below: crowds of people disembarking from a train, men, women, children, a ragged line leading to an underground entrance next to the source of the smoke. He had seen the Star of David armbands, and guards kicking and beating people. The Polish labourers in the field where they had landed called it *Todesmühle*, the death mill. When he came to Berlin for his new posting, Hoffman discovered that it was Reichsführer Heinrich Himmler, the man in front of him now, who had been the architect of that horror, something he referred to with his humourless grin as *die Endlösung*, the Final Solution – in his mind a logistical challenge that continued to preoccupy him even after Hitler had got bored with the Jewish question and had shut out everything except his dream of an art museum at Linz.

The tremors stopped. The guns had ceased firing, as if a monster had expended itself in a final frenzy. Hoffman could smell the freshly pulverized paint from the walls, and the reek of vomit and shit seeping in through the door from the people crammed in the stairwell below. Himmler took his hands from his ears, dusted himself off and raised his feet back on to the planks of the desk. He reached over and picked up the bottle of schnapps, uncapped it and took a long swig. He exhaled hard, put the bottle down and looked at Hoffman. Then he smiled again, crookedly. 'We are not a nation of partisans, are we, Herr SS-Brigadeführer?'

Hoffman did not know what to say. He clicked his heels. '*Mein Führer.*'

'No, we are not.' Himmler took another swig from the bottle, then slammed it down, smacking his lips. 'This new partisan army that's supposed to carry on the war in the forests. What did Adolf call it? *Werewolf.*' He sniggered. 'And this force you were posted here to command? The 9th Luftwaffe Parachute Division Lebelstar. A crack new division? The snotty little boys on the roof.' He cocked an ear theatrically, then stared penetratingly at Hoffman. 'And speaking of which, is that not the end of the shooting I hear? Was that not to be your cue, to remuster the crews from the flak guns and lead them into battle?'

Hoffman clicked his heels again. His heart was pounding. *This might be his chance.* '*Mein Führer.* I must go. My duty . . .'

'Your duty, SS-Brigadeführer, is to me,' Himmler snarled, slamming his hand on the plank. The bottle of schnapps tottered, then smashed on the floor.

Hoffman felt the blood drain from his face. '*Mein Führer.*

Those were to be my words exactly. I have sworn the SS oath.' He snapped his arm up in the Nazi salute. '*Sieg Heil!*'

Himmler suddenly relaxed, and waved again. 'Take your arm down. We don't need that nonsense in here, you and I.' He looked wistfully at the broken glass, then back up at Hoffman, leaning forward. 'Now, to business. What do you know about the *Wunderwaffe*?'

Hoffman stared past Himmler, unflinching. *So that was it.* Moments of apparent sense, moments when Himmler derided the last-ditch schemes of Hitler and his cronies, then back to the madness. The mythical *Wunderwaffe* was the biggest delusion of all, the wonder-weapon that was going to save the Reich. First, it was going to be unleashed on the day of President Roosevelt's death, as some kind of a holy sign. Then on Hitler's birthday, ten days ago. But of course nothing had happened. Hoffman cleared his throat. 'Reichsleiter Goebbels promised it. A secret weapon to be used at the chosen moment.'

Himmler waved his hand again. 'Goebbels. That little monster. I always loathed him.' He gave his disarming grin. 'His children are dead, you know, in the bunker. Goebbels' fallen angels. An injection of morphine, then a cyanide tablet forced into their mouths while they were asleep. Only I'm told they weren't all asleep. Not the oldest one, anyway.' He pushed his spectacles up his nose, then peered inquisitively at Hoffman. 'Well? What weapons?'

Hoffman remembered the older Goebbels girl. He swallowed hard. 'In the Luftwaffe, we knew about the rocket programmes, the V-1 and the V-2. A few months ago I toured the test site at Peenemünde with Reichsmarschall Göring.

There was talk of another rocket in secret production, a V-3.'

Himmler waved his hand and snorted contemptuously. 'Göring. That fat pig. He stole art from this storeroom for his chateau, you know. And the rocket factory is history now, bombed to oblivion by the English. Anyway, rockets are just vehicles, not weapons.'

Hoffman carefully calculated what he thought Himmler would want to hear, something he had become skilled at judging over the past few months around the Nazi inner circle in Berlin. 'The atomic programme. The research at the Kaiser Wilhelm Institute for Physics.'

Himmler's eyes glinted. 'Now *that's* a weapon. But the programme was never close to actuality. Not enough uranium.'

Hoffman watched the little eyes dart around his face, then fix squarely on him. He was playing Himmler's guessing game. 'Poison gas?'

Himmler gave a high-pitched laugh, and slapped the table. 'Good. The Spandau gas research facility. Sarin and Tabin nerve gas. But no. Those were *Verzweiflungswaffen*, weapons of despair. Lance Corporal Hitler had too many bad memories of the last war, when the gas our side released wafted back into our own trenches and blinded him. Anyway, gas is inefficient. You need lots of it, and lots of bombs and shells to disperse it.'

Hoffman stared at Himmler, his mind racing. He had heard other rumours. A few months ago, a former professor of his had invited him for dinner in Heidelberg. After too much schnapps, he had told Hoffman of his secret work for the Ahnenerbe, the Department of Cultural Heritage. He had said that the search for Aryan roots, for precursor civilizations – for Atlantis – was not all that it seemed. And it was not just the sordid business of collecting craniological measurements to support racist theory. There had been another purpose, equally sinister and top secret. They had scoured the world for ancient medicines, for ancient cures: among primitive peoples, in mummies, under polar ice, deep underwater. *But*, the man had drunkenly whispered, *it was not the cure they wanted. They wanted the disease.* Hoffman had not been the only one the man had spoken to after too much drink, and the Gestapo had got wind of his indiscretions. He had disappeared soon after into Himmler's House of Horrors. Hoffman pursed his lips and shook his head. It was time to allow Himmler his flourish. 'Nothing, *mein Führer*. I can't think.'

Himmler slapped the table, then drew himself forward on his elbows, his face gleaming. 'Well, I will let you in on a secret.' He opened his arms expansively. 'What went on in this room, here in the Zoo flak tower?'

Hoffman looked straight at him. 'It was a storage vault for the treasures of the Berlin museums, placed here in 1942 when the English terror-bombing began.' He glanced at the crate to Himmler's left, then instantly regretted it. Himmler's eye had followed his. *The man saw everything.* Himmler reached over and put his hand on the crate inches from the order book Hoffman had used as a diary. He rubbed a smear of dust, saw the dirt on his hand and then wiped his fingers on the cover of the order book. Hoffman could barely breathe. Himmler sat back, pulled out his handkerchief and wiped his hand again, then inspected his fingernails. He gave Hoffman an amused look.

'You think these crates contain some kind of *Wunderwaffe*? They are what they say they are. They contain Schliemann's treasure from Troy. I blackmailed that cretin Bormann into leaving these three here, on pain of telling Hitler that Bormann was actually stealing the rest for himself. Adolf dreamed that all of these treasures were going to his fantasy Führermuseum in Linz, that absurd architect's model he kept poring over in the bunker. Well, these three crates I kept for myself. I believe you have met Dr Unverzagt, who was watching over them when you arrived? I had hoped to return for them once the Americans had joined us, but now they will be taken by the Russians. It is of no moment. My best treasures await me elsewhere, in another secret bunker, all of my greatest artefacts from Wewelsburg as well as the best of those from Troy, the ones the public never saw. I even have a small art collection of my own, including my favourite Raphael. You see, I am a far more discerning collector than Göring or Bormann. These men were merely gangsters.' He jerked his head at the broken bust of Bismarck on the floor behind. 'The Iron Chancellor was a friend of Schliemann's, you know. Perhaps they talked of taking the world by storm, with the broken pieces of myth in these crates from Troy. You approve, Herr SS-Brigadeführer, of this talk of world domination?'

'*Mein Führer*.'

Himmler patted his pocket, took out a silver hip flask, shook it, and then grunted. One of the SS generals in the shadows behind Hoffman reached over with a flask of his own. Himmler unscrewed the lid, sniffed it, then offered it back to the man. 'You first, Herr Obergruppenführer.' The man clicked his heels and took the flask, and Hoffman heard the sound of trickling and swallowing. The man whipped out a handkerchief, wiped the flask and handed it back to Himmler, then stepped back into the shadows. Himmler swilled the flask around, then put it on the desk. 'Perhaps not,' he muttered, looking at the general and then eyeing Hoffman. 'And certainly not for you, Herr SS-Brigadeführer. For what is to come, you need a clear head.'

Himmler reached over for the swaddled package he had taken from his satchel. As he did so, Hoffman realized that something was different outside. The background vibration of exploding shells against the concrete of the gun platform had ceased. The Russian infantry must have taken the Zoo grounds, and would be too close for their heavy artillery to carry on targeting the bunker. Hoffman tensed. The flak tower was now in the eye of the storm; it could only be a matter of time before the Russian tanks began firing armour-piercing rounds point-blank at the steel window shutters, punching holes for the flamethrowers to shoot through. Hoffman saw that Himmler sensed the change too, that he knew their time was running out. He leaned forward, the crooked smile gone. 'Listen to me, Hoffman, and listen well. You said you knew about the Spandau gas research laboratories. Well, the Zoo tower was not just for the storage of treasures. There is another chamber, deep below the water reservoir. The reservoir walls act as a barrier to prevent what is inside from escaping, from being released into the atmosphere. You understand me?'

'*Mein Führer.*'

'My Ahnenerbe men searched the world for ancient diseases, for ones long thought dormant, diseases against which people today would have little resistance. They scoured the ancient literature. A particularly fastidious young researcher in Heidelberg eventually found an account of what we wanted: an extraordinarily toxic waterborne bacterium that may have killed Alexander the Great. Under the pretence of searching for a lost civilization under the ice, my explorers and scientists went to the most extreme fresh-water environments in the world, to Iceland and Greenland, seeking the deadliest strain of the bacterium they could find. Eventually they discovered it, at a place that only the most courageous of my divers could reach. We had already embarked on another quest, for a particular virus. This time we did not need to look so far back in history. It was the Spanish influenza virus that killed twenty million people at the end of the First World War. A virus that Hitler saw as divine vengeance against the world for inflicting such humiliation on the German people. *A virus that I saw as the tool of ultimate power*. For years my scientists thought it could never be recovered. They exhumed body after body across Germany. But the Blitzkrieg and the conquest of Europe greatly expanded the search area. Eventually, in the Père Lachaise cemetery in Paris, they found the well-preserved corpses of two influenza victims who had been buried in lead-lined coffins. They took them to a bunker laboratory deep in a forest in Upper Saxony, and they isolated the virus from the cadavers. I ordered a labour camp to be set up, disguised as a camp for forest workers. We brought in prisoners of all races, young men and women, strong, healthy, the backbone of any country. After many experiments with the virus, my scientists tested the most promising mutations on the prisoners. They added the bacterium to make it more potent. Gradually we improved it until all of the infected people died. Our work had produced a deadly weapon. A *Wunderwaffe*, yes?'

Hoffman felt physically sick. 'A *Wunderwaffe, mein Führer.*'

Himmler reached over and pulled the swaddled package on the table towards him, clunking it on the planks. It sounded heavy, metallic. He looked at Hoffman intently. 'My detractors think I am obsessed with the occult, with mystical symbols and rituals. They think it clouds my reason, but that is what I wished them to think. In reality I use it to cloak my intentions. I needed an artifice to shroud my wonder-weapon in mystique, to convince those who would follow me that the plan to use the weapon was in the Nazi cause. What better than the ancient symbolism I myself had nurtured, and had placed at the heart of Nazi ideology?' He waved his hand at the crates. 'Schliemann's greatest treasure was not found at Troy but at the Greek citadel of Mycenae, buried under the Mask of Agamemnon. It was a most astonishing discovery, and fell into my hands when we dug beneath Schliemann's house in Athens after we had conquered Greece in 1941, to follow a rumour that he had concealed treasures there. We found it wrapped with a note by Schliemann's wife Sophia about the discovery, placed there after his death. It was nothing less than the sacred palladion of the Trojans, brought back to Greece by the victorious Greek king Agamemnon. The Trojans thought the palladion had fallen from heaven, a divine gift to the founder of their city. In a sense they were right: it was a meteorite, probably brought to Troy millennia before from some distant place. Meteorites are found most easily on ice, and I convinced my followers that this was vindication of *Welteislehre* – the so-called world ice theory developed by my Ahnenerbe scholars, a mad fantasy – and that it was a sacred artefact from the supposed Ice Age precursor civilization that had led us to scour Iceland and Greenland for clues. At some time in prehistory the meteorite had been fashioned by human hands into the shape you will see, and then melded with gold: meteoritic iron on one side, gold on the other. I told my followers that it had been forged in Atlantis. It is the most ancient Aryan symbol, a swastika.'

Hoffman stared in amazement at the shape within the package, about fifteen centimetres across. Himmler held him in his gaze. 'With the iron surface facing down, it is a reverse swastika, a symbol of ancient Troy. You can see it decorating ancient potsherds from Troy illustrated in Schliemann's book. But there's more. When my scientists analysed the meteoritic iron, they found it had a unique magnetic signature. One of them came up with an ingenious idea. By holding the palladion with the iron facing down, it could be used as a key, one that could never be replicated. A magnetic mechanism aligned to the unique signature of the meteoritic iron could allow doors to be opened, doors to the secret vault that contained the *Wunderwaffe*.'

'The chamber beneath this tower?' Hoffman murmured.

'I embedded the palladion in the most secret core of SS ideology. It was concealed below the floor of my SS headquarters at Wewelsburg Castle, like a sacred reliquary. Every new SS general had to swear an oath on that spot. You yourself have been there, when I showed you the cover to the reliquary with the reverse swastika on top, the arms of the cross bending to the left instead of the right. But only a select few knew the significance of what lay concealed beneath – the palladion – and its use as a key. For those, I devised an activation signal called the Agamemnon Code. A simple message, an image of the reverse swastika inside a red roundel, would be sent to a few chosen followers when the time was right. It would signal the start of *my* plan. Not Adolf's plan, but my plan. A plan for a new Reich and a new Führer, but a Reich of global dimensions, one based far away from the squalor and mess of Nazi Germany.'

Hoffman suddenly remembered Dr Unverzagt. He reached into his tunic pocket, and pulled out the crumpled piece of paper the man had given him. He smoothed it out and held it up, showing the reverse swastika. 'You mean like this?'

Himmler nodded. 'Dr Unverzagt was one of the select few. I knew that Wewelsburg would be stripped bare by the Allies when they captured the castle, so I had the palladion removed to a secret location deep inside a salt mine in Poland. Then, with the advance of the Russians, it was taken to the bunker in the forest in Upper Saxony where the disease weapon had been perfected. The bacterium was kept there, and the virus in the secret storeroom below us now in the Zoo tower. Both could only be accessed using the palladion as a key. Twelve days ago, I persuaded Hitler to issue the command to destroy the infrastructure of Germany. My followers were ready, and the Agamemnon Code was activated. The palladion was brought to me. Most of my followers are now dead, those who believed I was merely a devoted acolyte of Adolf, those who were deluded into thinking that releasing the *Wunderwaffe* was to be a final act of loyalty to Hitler. They served their purpose, as obediently and loyally as I had apparently served

Adolf. Their elimination was also part of my plan. Only a select few survived, those who knew my true intentions and were loyal to me and my cause above all else. Unverzagt was the penultimate link in the chain. Now it passes to you.'

Hoffman stared at the package. *Was his own elimination part of that plan, too?* 'If I am the last link, why am I only finding out about this now?'

Himmler leaned back. 'It was essential that this plan appeared to most of my followers to be about loyalty to Hitler. That way I could attract the most fanatical Nazis, the most ruthless. It was a plan to enact once Hitler was dead. It would seem to Hitler's followers like Götterdämmerung, the final act of loyalty to the Third Reich. With impending annihilation, their loyalty could easily be switched to self-destruction. They believed that my intention was to release the disease weapon and inflict as much horror as possible on the world that had betrayed Hitler, and then to join Adolf in some kind of Valhalla with all the Aryan heroes and gods of the past.'

Hoffman stared at Himmler, barely able to believe what he had been hearing, the full truth of it only now hitting him. Himmler had always seemed so obsequious to Hitler, idolizing him. If he was telling the truth now, if this was not just some insane pipe dream, then it had all been a sham, all those years when Himmler had seemed like the bulwark of the Third Reich, the man whose administrative efficiency made up for the incompetence of Hitler and the others of his inner circle. Hoffman cleared his throat. 'But for you the wonder-weapon has another purpose?'

Himmler stared at him. 'The victors in this war, the English, the Americans, the Russians, those who delude themselves that they are the world powers to come, have their own *Wunderwaffe*, the atomic bomb. We know the Americans already have it, and I ensured that the key developments of our own atomic research programme at the Kaiser Wilhelm Institute were left there to be captured by the Russians. This means that the Americans and the Russians will be trapped in a stalemate. Neither side will be able to use the weapon against the other, knowing that to launch it would provoke a response that would destroy the aggressor as well. But my new weapon is different. When I reveal it to the Americans and the Russians, they will know that I am prepared to use it. They have discovered the death factories. They know that if I can do that to the Jews, then I am capable of anything. The Final Solution was not just about crackpot racial theory. That was a cover for me too. And the threat of destruction will be entirely one-sided. I will be safe, and they won't know where to hit back. I can hold the world to ransom. We will be safe. In our new Atlantis.'

Hoffman's throat was dry. How much of this was he to believe? Was it all a huge delusion, another Nazi fantasy of salvation? His mind raced back over the last few days, searching for anything that might corroborate Himmler's story. He remembered the orders he had received to report to the Zoo flak tower, issued from Gestapo headquarters. That had been unusual, but nobody disobeyed orders from the Gestapo, with instant executions going on all round. Hoffman had been desperate to escape from the Chancellery and the Führerbunker and had welcomed the orders without a second's hesitation. It had never occurred to him that the order might have come from Himmler himself, since by then

Himmler had been excommunicated and was on the run, possibly dead. But it made sense. If the Gestapo and the SS knew that Himmler was still alive after Hitler's death, their first loyalty would be to him, and they would obey any instruction he gave them. Himmler had created a nexus of power that had bound the strongest and most fanatical Nazis to him, knowing that that was what would matter in these final days. He had seen the fall of Berlin coming, and had planned for it. Hoffman had a sudden flashback to the Wagner concert a few days before. Behind all of Himmler's symbolism, all the mythology, the heroic illusion that Wagner so embodied for the Nazis, there was a malign purpose. Himmler had been playing them all along. *He had been orchestrating this since before the war*.

Hoffman thought hard. Himmler had set up the Ahnenerbe more than ten years before, when he had begun to create the fantasy SS order-castle at Wewelsburg. Hoffman was beginning to think the unthinkable. He remembered all the hats Himmler wore, his tentacles in every limb of the Nazi state, his fingerprint on all the worst crimes: a man who had the ear of Hitler, who could feed the delusions, who could stoke up Hitler's insane interventions in all aspects of the war, dooming the Reich to collapse and orchestrating the slide into defeat. He recalled what he had seen that day from his aircraft over Poland, the death camp at Auschwitz. Was this what that had really been all about? Had the most vile crime against humanity been part of the scheme of one man to usurp Nazi power, to elevate himself to the status of a god? *All the death and suffering*. The mass of humanity extinguished by this monstrosity seemed incomprehensible in its scale. He could only think of the children in the Führerbunker, of the boy in the outsized helmet on the rooftop, his ears bleeding, doomed for ever to hear the guns of this place. Who had been the true Führer? Had they really all been dancing to Himmler's tune?

He looked into the cold eyes opposite. Were they the eyes of a madman? *Or were they the eyes of a ruthlessly calculating gangster, a megalomaniac whose time had come?*

'Do you have a torch?' Himmler demanded.

Hoffman snapped back to the present. He had to keep focused. He patted his tunic pocket, and nodded. 'Essential in the tower when the generator fails.'

'Listen well. From here you will go to the entrance of the ammunition elevator. My two Waffen-SS guards will accompany you. You will take the spiral staircase down to the magazine. From there, follow the tunnel to the underground water reservoir, then the walkway round to the far wall. You will see a swastika symbol impressed into the wall, every metre. A *reverse* swastika.' He put his hand on the swaddled object in front of him. 'Go to the fifteenth swastika to the left from the entrance. You will use the palladion to open the door behind it, keeping the iron side of the palladion inwards. The door lock is magnetic and will spring open. Go down the shaft, and follow the tunnel that leads under the reservoir. There you will see another door with the same symbol. Use the key again. Inside you will find a lead box, and inside that a metal cylinder like a cigar case that contains a phial. Do not unscrew the cylinder. Seal it in your tunic pocket. You are with me?'

'*Mein Führer.*'

'If you lose count and try any other than the fifteenth

symbol, the chamber will self-destruct. The Zoo tower will collapse inwards. A hundred thousand tons of concrete will fall on you. Do you understand?'

'Completely.'

'Go back up the shaft to the walkway around the reservoir. The guards will have been waiting for you there, and they will leave you and return to tell me of your success. Count four doors to the right from the shaft, and you will find another door with the swastika, leading to your escape tunnel. On opening that door with the palladion, you will have thirty seconds to close it behind you. Explosive charges around the reservoir will detonate, flooding the chamber beneath it and sealing off all the entrances. You understand?'

Hoffman nodded, his face set grimly. It seemed another absurd farce, symbols and secret passageways like Wewelsburg Castle, but he had no choice. His family's salvation was at the end of that escape tunnel. Himmler eyed him closely, his face set in the quizzical smile, then continued: 'We planned for this contingency – for an enemy onslaught – when the complex beneath the Zoo tower was built, and it is essential now that we activate the self-destruct charges, because the Russians are using the city sewer system to come up behind our lines. But my engineers also secretly laid massive charges below the foundations that will destroy the Zoo tower entirely. That is the job of the two generals behind you. Their families are here in the tower. I arranged that, so they could be reunited. Now their task is to destroy the tower before the Russians move in, to erase all evidence of what went on beneath the reservoir. They too are now SS knights. Herren SS-Obergruppenführer?'

'*Mein Führer.*' The two men spoke in ragged unison, gruffly, and Hoffman heard their heels click. He felt a cold trickle of sweat down his back. *Destroy the tower.* Thirty thousand civilians were cowering inside. It was not the Russians the people of Berlin should have feared the most, but their own leaders. He saw images of the circus again, the insane spectacle he had been forced to attend after the Wagner concert, flashing and swirling before his eyes, confusing him. He was dizzy, reeling. He must try to stay in control, for the sake of his family, if they were truly still alive. *There was still a chance.*

Himmler looked at him. 'The tunnel from the reservoir exits beneath Gestapo headquarters on Prinz-Albrechtstrasse. Use the palladion again as a key to get out. Close the door, and thirty seconds after that the tunnel will self-destruct.' Himmler glanced at his watch. 'Waiting outside the tunnel precisely thirty-five minutes from now will be two Gestapo officers who will be your security guards. The Gestapo headquarters building is defended by remnants of the SS-Charlemagne and SS-Nordland divisions, who will fight to the death. You understand me?'

'Completely.'

'You will arrive there after dark. There is an improvised landing strip on the street, kept clear by the Waffen-SS. A Fieseler Storch aircraft is waiting under cover. You can still fly, Herr SS-Brigadeführer?'

'Naturally.'

'Of course you can.' Himmler cracked the crooked smile again. 'That is why I chose you for this mission. You are one of our best pilots. Do you remember coming to me when you were a boy, wanting to fly for the Ahnenerbe? I was most impressed. *Most impressed*. You were the perfect age, the perfect material. And who do you think arranged for you to be posted six months ago to Berlin, to be feted, to be part of the inner circle where I could deploy you to this tower when the time was right? You were a hero of the Reich, a man with the perfect credentials, the perfect wife and family. Do you remember that it was I who introduced you to Heidi? I have looked after you in every way. I needed you here once I knew the end was near.'

Hoffman swallowed hard. It was true. *He had been played all along*. And maybe Himmler had been right. Hoffman had been a fearless pilot, but maybe he had been too compliant. His passion for flying had clouded his ability to question the purpose of the war. Perhaps that was what Himmler saw in him, and nurtured. And his beautiful blonde wife, had that been arranged too? He banished the thought from his mind. He forced himself to smile, shaking his head as if in dawning realization, in wonder at Himmler's scheme. '*Mein Führer*. It is a great honour.'

Himmler waved his hand dismissively. 'The Storch has fuel and maps to get you to Plön by the Baltic Sea. You will fly low out of Berlin, down the streets. The Soviet gunners will be taken by surprise, as they believe the Luftwaffe is finished. You are an expert night navigator. Do you remember when you were ordered from your squadron to attend night navigation school? Odd for a Stuka pilot, didn't you think? After landing at Plön, you will be taken to see your family for half an hour, and then to a secret U-boat base. When the enemy finds out that Heinrich Himmler and his most loyal officers have escaped, they will think we intend to carry on some pretence of Adolf's thousand-year Reich.' He curled his lip contemptuously. 'The thousand-year Reich? It was always going to be a mess with Adolf in charge. I knew him twenty-five years ago when he was an obscure agitator. I *created* him. Good at rabble-rousing, but not much else. Perfect for my purposes.'

Hoffman had a terrible realization. What was going on now, the fall of Berlin, the horror in the Zoo tower, all of this was part of the theatre, too. The Nazi machinery had not been brought to its knees through incompetence and madness. *It had been part of a plan.* He stared at Himmler. 'Where shall I go?'

'You will keep the cylinder with the phial and the palladion with you. When the U-boat arrives at its secret destination, you will be shown your quarters. There will be a reverse swastika in the wall. Use the palladion again. Put the cylinder inside, and close the door. Your task will be complete. Then your family will be sent for from Germany and will come to you themselves by submarine. There is too much risk to put them in a U-boat now, with you. The sea lanes are still under enemy attack, and your wife and child will be safer where they are until the time is right. I have little Hans' best interests at heart.'

A cold shiver went through Hoffman. 'And you?'

'Once the two Waffen-SS guards have returned to me here from escorting you below, I will leave by the tunnel to the L-Tower and then make my way across the Elbe at night. I must visit Grand-Admiral Dönitz. Hitler was persuaded in my absence to appoint Dönitz his successor. That was not in my plan. It is intolerable. *Intolerable*. Dönitz must be removed.

Then I must go in disguise to the bunker near Bremen where something remains that I must retrieve, something my SS follower who was dispatched there two weeks ago has failed to deliver to me. After that I will return to Plön. Once there is a radio signal to show that you have arrived, I will leave to follow you out in the last U-boat. I will personally accompany Heidi and Hans. *Personally*. That is my assurance. Do you understand?'

Hoffman clicked his heels. '*Mein Führer*.' It seemed a fantasy plan. If Himmler attempted to go in his absurd disguise to Upper Saxony, he would be behind enemy lines and would be captured. As for his family, Hoffman thought he understood all too well. This much he had learned over the last months in the Chancellery and the Führerbunker, in the heart of the Nazi empire: the web of lies, of deceit and counter-deceit, a world where nobody was trusted. It was the price for extinguishing morality. How could you trust your minions to be loyal, when you had taken away their ability to judge right from wrong? Hoffman knew exactly how he was being played: the guards had taken away his Luger, and would now accompany him down to the water reservoir to the point of no return. He was to follow a one-way tunnel, with Gestapo waiting for him at the other end. *Then his family*. Protected, or held hostage? He remembered the two generals standing behind him, both wearing the field-grey uniforms of the Wehrmacht. They were as much SS as he was, newly created fantasy warriors. Their families had been brought to this dungeon not out of any act of charity, but to provide the same leverage. They had no choice but to follow Himmler's instructions. Their only reward would be the chance to create their own end, but that would be enough to keep them compliant. Everyone knew what the Russians did to the families of senior officers.

There was a huge screech outside the door, the sound of a Russian rocket that must have impacted on the gun platform above. All Hoffman could do now was think of his family. Carrying out Himmler's plan was the only chance he had to see them again. He took a deep breath of the putrid air, and turned to go. A sudden banging rattled the door, and it swung open. A boy's voice rose above the noise, shrill and panic-stricken. *'Herr Oberstleutnant! Alarm! Alarm! Der Iwan kommt! Der Russ kommt!'* The boy with the lederhosen stood between the two SS men, panting, his face smudged with cordite and his clothing dishevelled. For a moment everything seemed paralysed, as if time had stopped. *The Russians were coming.* The boy looked at Hoffman, then wrenched off his outsized helmet, tossed it down and ran back towards the mass of people on the stairway, disappearing from view.

'Go!' the voice behind him ordered. 'I will leave by the other tunnel. *Schnell!'* Himmler thrust the swaddled package into the satchel, and Hoffman slung it over his shoulder. It was incredibly heavy. *Gold and meteoritic iron.* He tried to remember what he had been told, how he was to use it. As he passed the two generals, he caught the eye of the one nearest to him. They were locked into Himmler's plan as much as he was. The general's eyes were grey, devoid of hope, the eyes of a man who knew his last act would be to kill his own family to save them from the Soviets. But Hoffman hoped he saw something else, a humanity, something that Himmler would not even be able to recognise. When it came to it, when the two officers sat with pistols to their heads in front of the detonator switch, they might not do it. The people in the tower might be spared. *The little boy might not die.*

He reached the door. The rooftop entrance to the gun platform above the spiral staircase had been left open, and he felt the pressure waves of explosions pulsing down the stairwell. The Katyusha rockets were flying directly overhead now, shrieking like Valkyries. This was real-life Götterdämmerung, the battle at the end of the world. Only it was not a battle fought between gods, and no heavenly hall awaited the heroes. The new breed of gods who had created this horror were dead or cowering in underground places, or planning new schemes of apotheosis like the monster in this room with him now.

The two SS guards loomed out of the dust and fell in beside him. Then the voice spoke again. '*Halt.*' Hoffman felt his stomach lurch. The diary. *Had Himmler found it?* Perhaps he would die in this place after all. He braced himself and turned around. Himmler was walking towards him, the SS dagger in his hand, still sheathed. He fumbled with it, nearly dropping it, then offered Hoffman the hilt. Hoffman took it, feeling the clammy sweat on the grip, then stood to attention and clicked his heels. Himmler took something out of his pocket and pressed it into Hoffman's other palm. Hoffman looked down and saw a silver ring with the *Totenkopf* design, the death's-head insignia of the SS. Around the sides of the ring were three roundels with runic signs. Two of them he vaguely recognized from the symbols he had been shown at Wewelsburg Castle, but the third was unfamiliar, a curious construction of parallel and right-angle lines like two garden rakes set front to front. Himmler watched him staring at it, then closed Hoffman's palm around the ring. 'That symbol is an ancient rune my Ahnenerbe explorers discovered in the place that is now your final destination. I have made it the symbol of my new order. This ring is for you to give to Heidi. It is my token of assurance to her. Keep it safely.' He reached up and adjusted Hoffman's Knight's Cross, patting him. Hoffman could smell his breath, just as he had smelled Hitler's when the cross had been awarded. The crooked smile was on Himmler's face again, his eyes roaming until they fixed on Hoffman's. 'That dagger is now your sacred symbol. Show it to others in the SS, and they will know you have my authority. And Heidi will have my greatest symbol of respect and honour. In your task ahead, think always of your family. We will be the new *Übermenschen*, the new supermen, yes? The new gods of Atlantis.'

Hoffman clicked his heels and turned away. His world had closed in, as if the noose tightening around Berlin were tightening around him as well. All that flashed before his eyes was the panic-stricken boy in the dishevelled lederhosen, as if that were the last image of light he had seen, imprinted on his retina. The jarring of the explosions made him see repeated images of the boy's face, lining the edge of his vision, and then ahead of him a swirling image of the reverse swastika, drawing him into the underworld. He opened his eyes and breathed hard, thinking of what he had written in his diary. That was history, a terrible history of crime and horror. But what he knew now, the future that lay ahead if Himmler's plan were to be carried out, was incalculably worse. He remembered the sheets of paper he had torn off and put in his pocket, the pencil. Somehow he must find a way of writing a message for posterity, in case the truth died with him and the deadly weapon remained intact. If he was unable to thwart Himmler, someone else might.

He thrust the SS knife into his pocket, unsheathing it and grasping the exposed part of the blade as hard as he could, savagely, feeling the blood from his fingers ooze out. A rage coursed through him, the rage and adrenalin he had once felt as he held the stick in his Stuka dive-bomber, hurtling towards the target, the siren screaming. He knew why his family would not be joining him until he had completed Himmler's task. His wife and boy were being held to ransom. But Himmler had forgotten what he did, what he was good at, how he had survived five years of war. He remembered Himmler's pudgy hands fumbling with the knife. These people had created the worst killing machine in history. But for them the killing was remote, abstract. It was other people who did their dirty work for them, people like those boys on the roof, like the countless dead soldiers outside, like the thugs of the SS and Gestapo, people like Hoffman. That was Himmler's biggest weakness. For him the SS knife was a symbol, not a weapon. He had lost sight of another aspect of humanity.

What it was that made men kill.

PART 3

15

Wewelsburg Castle, Germany

J ack swung his legs out of the car and stood in the car park,
stretching his arms and savouring the cool morning air.
Even though he had not gone inside the Nazi bunker in the
forest the day before, he still felt as if some of that horror
were clinging to him, filling his lungs as it had filled the lungs
of the first Allied soldiers who had entered the death camp
beside the bunker almost seventy years before. He took
another deep breath, then watched as Maurice Hiebermeyer
clambered out of the car on the driver's side, adjusting his
trousers around his ample waist and pushing his little round
glasses up his nose, then picking up a shoulder bag and
coming round to stand beside him. For Maurice, the bunker
experience had been far worse, not only for the sheer horror
of what he had seen but also because of his German

background, and Jack knew that his intense focus on planning their visit today had been a way of pushing away an experience that had unsettled him, something that Jack himself had found difficult to watch.

Together the two men stared up at the great bulk of the castle in front of them, its off-white masonry stark against the blue sky. It looked unreal, as if it had just been completed, too good to be true. Jack had to remind himself that he was not in England, where so many castles were ruins; in Germany, castles like this had been continuously occupied through to modern times. He caught sight of the name at the entrance to the car park: *Wewelsburg*. This castle was a special case, reinvented in the twentieth century as the bastion of a new knightly order, an odious fantasy in one man's mind and the centrepiece of his dream of world domination.

'The castle's early medieval originally,' Hiebermeyer said. 'When Heinrich Himmler bought Wewelsburg in 1934, he set about transforming it into his fantasy SS order-castle. From 1939, the slave labour used in the reconstruction came from a concentration camp set up nearby at Niederhagen, eventually including Soviet prisoners of war as well as Jews. Over a thousand of them were worked to death. *A thousand*. It was everywhere, you know, everywhere in Nazi Germany, the taint of racism and slave labour. Since being in that bunker, I can't look at anything from that period without feeling physically sick. I can't believe that I never felt that before. I think the whole of Germany must have been in a state of shock after the war, for years afterwards, even my generation.' He looked down, distraught for a moment, and then took a deep breath and shook himself, clearing his throat and pointing to the walls. 'The most dramatic transformation of the castle was where we're meeting my aunt Heidi, in the so-called Obergruppenführersaal, the SS Generals' Room in the North Tower. It's a kind of perverse realization of King Arthur's Camelot, where Himmler's top SS generals would meet as if they were latter-day Knights of the Round Table.'

'Have you been here before?' Jack said.

'Once, when I was a child.' Hiebermeyer glanced at his watch, then leaned back against the car. 'We've got twenty minutes until I said we would meet her. I wanted to fill you in on a few things before we go into the castle. You and I have known each other since we were boys, and we know pretty well everything in each other's minds, but this is a chapter I've kept mostly to myself. We could go to the café?'

'Here is good.'

'Okay. Probably best not to be overheard. Do you remember at boarding school in England when I did a presentation on the Nazis and archaeology? A pretty edgy subject for a German boy in those days, but my parents' estate was in Westphalia, near here, and I was determined to get to the bottom of it all.'

'As I recall, the main excitement was a story you'd unearthed about a German expedition to Egypt to uncover a fabulous treasure of the pharaoh Akhenaten. Something you didn't tell the class about in your presentation, but you did tell me in secret later that day.'

'Still a big one on our to-do list, very big,' Hiebermeyer said, the old glint in his eyes back for a moment. 'But it wasn't just about following up treasure stories. I also wanted to distil the true archaeology from the nonsense. Himmler was influenced by a mystic named Karl Maria Wiligut, who convinced him that Westphalia would be the site of an apocalyptic battle between East and West, one in which the West would triumph and the River Rhine would run red with blood. At the time, people made the mistake of dismissing Himmler's fantasies as harmless nonsense, even some fellow Nazis. But like his anti-Semitism, all his obsessions had a horrible fallout in real life. It was Himmler who pushed Hitler to launch Operation Barbarossa, the invasion of Russia in 1941, and there's no doubt he would have incited Hitler by regaling him with the story of that mythical showdown between East and West.'

'And yet when it came to the Rhine running red with blood, it was the Western Allies who were the enemy, and this time the Germans were doomed to defeat.'

Hiebermeyer pursed his lips. 'Yet even that showdown may have been preordained by Himmler, and I don't mean in mythology. The more I studied him, the more it seemed as if he were willing the Reich to self-destruction. He was Hitler's right-hand man, in many ways the brains behind the Nazi ideology. It was he who engineered the Holocaust, with ruthless efficiency and attention to detail. He was capable of the kind of cold-headed and practical decision-making that mostly eluded Hitler. Yet it was Himmler who pushed Hitler to make some of his more catastrophic decisions, above all the invasion of Russia. That single decision doomed the Third Reich. I began to look again at Himmler's obsession with the occult, with all the absurd symbolism and ritual, and to me it seemed more and more like a smokescreen. It was almost as if he had wanted the higher echelons of the Nazi party to treat him as something of a joke, in order to keep them from poisoning Hitler against him and to retain the ear of the Führer, to make sure he was there to influence the most important decision-making. If he'd exposed too much of his rational side, others in the party might have warned Hitler that he was a threat, a possible Führer-in-waiting.'

'These are some pretty radical ideas for a boy archaeologist,' Jack said.

Hiebermeyer paused. 'I felt a need to tackle my own past, my family's, that of Germany. For me, it was not just a matter of acknowledgement, but of questioning.' He gestured up at the castle again. 'This place seemed to represent the dichotomy in my mind about Himmler. On the one hand, Wewelsburg is a Nazi fairy tale, a kind of perverse Disneyland. From that viewpoint, it's easy to walk in there and dismiss all the occult symbolism as absurd. On the other hand, it was the stronghold of an empire Himmler had carved out for himself, the ideological headquarters of the SS and the focus of the Ahnenerbe, the Department of Cultural Heritage. In 1941, Himmler even declared that Wewelsburg would become the centre of the Third Reich. That might seem little more than a grandiose statement of his ambitions for his cult, but it could also be read at face value. When he said it, some must have known his mind, a hard core of followers, perhaps a secret cadre within the SS. His pronouncement may even have signalled the beginning of the process he had been building towards since acquiring this place years before the war even began. It came in 1941, just at the start of Operation Barbarossa, the beginning of the countdown to apocalypse.'

Jack turned to Hiebermeyer. 'Are you suggesting that Himmler engineered that? And that he was setting up a rival Reich?'

Hiebermeyer paused. 'A kind of shadow Reich. But not here, no longer at Wewelsburg. That was part of the smokescreen too. He would have known perfectly well that the castle would not survive the fall of Hitler, that it would be taken by the Allies. And the idea in those final days of April 1945, when he tried to negotiate with the Americans – that Himmler really saw the Third Reich as viable, with himself at the helm, fighting alongside the Western Allies against the Russians – has always seemed to me to be at odds with the man's cunning intelligence. Nor do I believe that he was fuelled by the fantasy of some kind of miracle deliverance that sustained the remaining Nazis in Berlin in those final dark days. I began to think that he had another scheme, and that he had only been trying to buy time, perhaps for a plan of escape to some other secret base that required a few days more to pull off, with the hours suddenly running short as the Red Army closed in.'

'And by April 1945, Wewelsburg was already in American hands.'

Hiebermeyer nodded. 'But Camelot's a movable feast. With so much focus on the ideology and mystique, Himmler could persuade his followers that the bricks and mortar had become less important. A new order-castle could be built elsewhere. Gangsters always have more than one hideaway. I began to think that his vision for a future Wewelsburg lay beyond Germany, beyond Europe. But there I left it. When we were at school, in the 1970s, there was still a lot of speculation about top Nazis who might have escaped to places like Argentina and Brazil, men who for decades may have con-templated a resurgent Reich. There were dozens of novels and investigative books and films. For me to have speculated about Himmler in that way would just have added to the slush pile on some literary agent's floor.'

'Especially as Himmler had committed suicide in British custody in May 1945,' Jack said.

Hiebermeyer nodded. 'Something didn't go quite to plan for him in those final few days after Hitler's own suicide, when Himmler was on the run. He'd been at Grand Admiral Dönitz's headquarters at Plön, close to the last surviving U-boat pens, and I can't help feeling there was a connection. There have always been rumours about U-boats taking fleeing Nazis away.'

'And that's why you were so interested in those Ahnenerbe expeditions? Because you thought Himmler was really searching for a new Camelot?'

'I came to believe that the expeditions weren't just about finding evidence for Aryan roots, for anything that could be hijacked and slotted into the Nazi foundation myth. They were about shoring up the future. Specifically, about shoring up *Himmler's* future. But this was not just about refounding Camelot. This was about something more grandiose, more audacious. Remember, this was a man who brazenly stated that Wewelsburg was to be the centre of the world. Wherever he was going, even if it involved no bricks and mortar, even if the archaeology he so yearned for was elusive, made up, he would preside over his new citadel of power, the one that had driven him to send out expeditions searching for evidence of the greatest lost civilization. Not Camelot, but *Atlantis*. Atlantis refounded.' Hiebermeyer nodded at the edifice in front of them. 'Because I believed that Himmler's fantasies overlaid a ruthless practicality, I felt that he was looking for more than just a bolthole. There had to be some basis for continuing power, something that would allow him to pursue his dream of world domination. I began to think about the wonder-weapons in production at the end of the war. The German atomic research programme seems unlikely; by April 1945, Himmler would have known about the Manhattan Project – the Allied effort to produce the first atomic bomb – and realized that the threat of a single nuclear bomb, even if the Germans had one ready, would not have been enough to bring the world to its knees. Gas or chemical weapons would never have been practical, requiring aircraft or missiles or artillery for delivery. That left one possibility: a biological weapon.'

Jack stared at Hiebermeyer. 'Good God. *The bunker.* You think that wasn't about some apocalyptic scheme of Hitler's to take the world with him, but a plan for post-war global threat by Himmler.'

'It fits the bill exactly. The Spanish flu virus would be the perfect weapon. A single phial would have been enough, a threat to release it in one large city. And it seems consistent with what we can make out of the secretive nature of the experiments at the bunker, the SS involvement, the Agamemnon Code, which seems to have activated a chain of agents. I believe that Himmler had been planning to take the virus with him to his secret destination, or to have an agent do it for him in advance, and that was what he had been trying to arrange in those final days.'

'Your aunt Heidi,' Jack murmured. 'Wasn't she a scientist?'

Hiebermeyer nodded. 'A toxicologist. She'd been a

biochemistry student when the Nazis came to power, and then worked as a medical researcher in a hospital in Berlin until her son Hans was born. I know that she gave herself up to the British near Plön, where she was hiding with Hans. She was evidently seen as a good catch, and was given a succession of research positions in England, where she remained until retiring back to Germany in the 1970s.'

'Her son was the one who joined the Baader–Meinhof gang?'

'He died in an explosion in 1972. He'd been a brilliant student, but had been seduced by the anarchists. Aunt Heidi once told me she saw it as part of the legacy of the Nazis, the damage wrought on the next generation. I don't think she's ever got over it, especially after losing her husband too, in the war.'

'The Stuka pilot? I remember you talking about him.'

Hiebermeyer nodded. 'Ernst Hoffman. One of the top tank-busters of the war. Knight's Grand Cross with oak leaves and swords. He was grounded after being wounded on the Russian front, and was posted as some kind of attaché in Berlin. Aunt Heidi said he disappeared like so many others in the final Soviet onslaught, presumed killed.'

'So why does Heidi want us to meet here now?'

Hiebermeyer paused. 'I'm not sure. But there was a connection with Himmler, something that dogged Ernst right to the end. Heidi told me that as a boy, he'd seen a newsreel of an Ahnenerbe expedition to Tibet showing biplanes flying over the Himalayas, and had written to Himmler to volunteer as a pilot. After that, Himmler took an undue interest in his Luftwaffe exploits, and arranged his final posting to Berlin, where Ernst was feted as a war hero. Several years before that, it was Himmler who had organized the party where Ernst had first met Heidi. Himmler brought his favourites to Wewelsburg, and maybe Ernst and Heidi came with him. There must be something here she wants us to see.' He looked at his watch, and stood up. 'It's a quarter to eleven. We'd better be on time.'

Fifteen minutes later Jack and Hiebermeyer stood at the entrance to the Obergruppenführersaal, the SS Generals' Hall, on the ground floor of the north tower of the castle. It was a stark room, devoid of furniture or wall hangings, focusing the eye entirely on the architecture and the pattern in the floor. Surrounding the open central space of the chamber were twelve columns joined by a groin vault, and between them lay deeply recessed apses with tall windows. The daylight coming through the windows illuminated the symbol in the centre of the floor, a green marble *Sonnenrad* sunwheel with a central axis of gold. Jack knew that this had been the epicentre of Himmler's vision for Wewelsburg, the place where he had summoned his twelve top SS generals for ideological preparation before Operation Barbarossa in 1941. He heard a low electric hum, and a wheelchair appeared from one of the window niches. Sitting in it was an elegant woman wearing a flowery dress, her white hair done in the fashion of the 1930s. She had a striking face, with high cheekbones and startlingly blue eyes. She waved at Hiebermeyer, who bounded over and kissed her forehead. 'Heidi,' he said, holding her hand. '*Meine liebe Tante.*'

Her bright eyes caught Jack's and he quickly proffered his hand. 'Frau Dr Hoffman. Pleased to meet you at last.'

'Call me Heidi,' she said in beautifully precise English, with the clipped accent of the 1930s. 'You must be Jack Howard. It is such a pleasure to meet you. Maurice used to tell me about you when he visited during his school holidays, but by then I'd moved back to Germany and he never did bring you along. I was delighted when Maurice phoned to tell me you would be joining us. Ever since reading your Atlantis book, I've wanted to bring you here to show you some symbols. My son Hans sketched them once, but I can't find his drawings now.' She took a tissue out of her sleeve and dabbed one eye. Jack saw that her hands were shaking. He glanced across at Hiebermeyer. So that was it. *Some symbols.* The place was filled with symbols, every kind of device the Nazis had come across, including at least three different runic sequences that Jack could see. Some were genuine transcriptions of medieval runes; others clearly were made up. There were bound to be a few that looked like those they had discovered five years ago in Atlantis. For a moment Jack wondered if he was about to be sucked into the world of fringe archaeology, of so-called evidence collated by Himmler's Ahnenerbe, picked from disparate sources and then arranged together in an apparently convincing whole. For all of the reality of their discovery in the Black Sea, he knew there would always be those who preferred to inhabit this parallel world, where the dream of Atlantis would remain just beyond reach.

'Tante Heidi,' Hiebermeyer said, glancing again at Jack. 'When did you come here before? When Hans was a boy?'

She put away her tissue. 'Once, when he was a high-school student, to try to interest him in a mystery. But of course I had been here before, when I first came to this chamber and the vault below and saw what I am going to show you now. Have you told Dr Howard about Ernst?'

'He knows as much as I know.'

She took a deep breath, shuddering slightly, then composed herself. 'Himmler brought us here on a celebratory tour after Ernst had been awarded the oak leaves and swords cluster to his Knight's Cross. We were the perfect image of the Nazi couple, the war hero and his blonde Aryan wife, heavily pregnant. Only it was a charade, of course. We were taken first to this chamber, where Ernst was anointed an honorary knight. I thought Himmler was about to induct him into the SS, which would have been the worst horror for Ernst. Fortunately, Himmler said it was more important for the time being that he remain a shining star of the Luftwaffe.'

'You always told me he only thought of the men in his squadron, Aunt Heidi,' Hiebermeyer said quietly. 'That was where his loyalty lay, and to you and Hans.'

Her eyes filled with tears again, and she wiped them. 'It seems just like yesterday. I feel as if I could walk out of this wheelchair into the sun of the courtyard, see little Hans and hold Ernst by the hand. They were days of happiness, but it was a time of horror. In truth I cannot go back to them, even in my mind's eye. When I shut my eyes, I only see again the horrors that I myself witnessed.'

She shuddered again, then held her hands tight on the armrests of the chair. 'Now, we must go down the stairs, to the vault below.' She raised herself with a walking stick that had been leaning on her wheelchair. The two men quickly took an arm each, and walked alongside her as she moved slowly to the spiral staircase, where Hiebermeyer led, with Jack taking up the rear. In a few minutes they had reached the bottom. They were in a gloomy beehive-shaped chamber, about eight metres high, positioned directly below the SS Generals' Room and dug into the bedrock. Heidi pointed up to the vault with her stick. 'There's a swastika in the apex, directly below the *Sonnenrad* sun symbol in the floor above,' she said. 'The vault's based on the shape of a Mycenaean Greek tomb, the so-called Treasury of Atreus at the ancient site of Mycenae. Himmler was obsessed with warrior kings of the ancient past. This vault is really a shrine to Agamemnon, the king of the Greeks who attacked Troy, the hero of another war between West and East.' She brought down her cane and tapped on a marble slab in the centre of the floor. 'If you look under this, you'll see why.'

She sat down abruptly on a wooden bench beside the wall. Jack stared at the floor, but saw nothing in the closely fitted marble slabs to suggest an opening. Hiebermeyer knelt down and put his hand on the slab she had tapped. 'How do you know anything's here, Aunt Heidi?'

'Because Himmler showed it to me. Ernst regarded all of Himmler's archaeology as occult, and found a ready excuse that day to avoid the tour by volunteering to fly Nazi officials who accompanied us over the site of the castle to see Himmler's grandiose construction scheme from the air. Himmler brought me down here alone. I never told Ernst what I saw; he would have scoffed at it. Himmler was very proud of this chamber. It was meant to be a kind of holy of holies, and a burial vault for the ashes of the greatest SS heroes. His top SS officers were meant to come and swear allegiance over the object buried below. But only a select few knew what it was.'

'Is it still here?'

'You can see where it rested.' She tapped her stick against the wall behind her, then tapped it again, as if trying to find the right spot. The second tap produced a hollow sound, and where Hiebermeyer had been looking, an octagonal slab of marble about the size of a large dinner plate rose a few inches out of the floor. 'There,' she said. 'I'm probably the only one left who knows how to do that. Even the curators of this place don't know this is here. Go on, Maurice, pull it out.'

Hiebermeyer got down on all fours, grasping the block by two recessed handles on either side. He lifted it up and set it down beside the hole. Jack took out a Mini Maglite and knelt beside him. About six inches below was a ring of symbols, surrounding a hollow shape cut into the rock. Jack peered closely at the shape, panning his torch over it, then looked at Hiebermeyer. 'Is that what I think it is?'

Hiebermeyer was staring at it. 'Incredible.'

Jack's mind raced. *A reverse swastika*. It was the same as the shape in the bunker laboratory door. And it was the shape he had seen six months before in the strongbox he and Costas had retrieved from deep inside the mine in Poland, the shape of an object that Saumerre had so coveted but which had remained elusive.

'It was for the ancient Trojan palladion,' Heidi said. 'At first I thought the palladion must be another fake, but I came to believe it was genuine. We all knew the swastika was an ancient shape, and had been found decorating pottery at Troy. Himmler told me that Heinrich Schliemann had discovered the palladion in the Tomb of Agamemnon at Mycenae, where it had been looted from a temple at Troy. It was the most sacred Trojan object, dating back thousands of years before the fall of Troy, supposedly a gift from the sky god. It was meteoritic on one side, gold on the other. It's gone now, though I don't know where. But I brought you here to see the symbols around the edge of the hollow.'

Jack peered more closely. There were two circular rings of symbols, the first one close to the lip of the hole, the second inside and below the first ring, obscured in shadow. The symbols on the upper ring were similar to the ones they had seen in the hall above. 'They're runes,' he murmured. 'Eight of them altogether. Some look like the Futhark, the Scandinavian runes of the Middle Ages. But there are other symbols too, presumably Nazi additions. I can see two swastikas.'

Heidi pointed with her stick. 'They're the creation of Karl Maria Wiligut, Himmler's occult guru. He retained some of the original Scandinavian runes, but added some with no historical precedent as runes but based on other ancient symbols. As well as the swastikas, you can see those two symbols of a crossed ring, derived from the Phoenician symbol tēth.'

Hiebermeyer looked at Heidi. 'These SS runes have Roman letter equivalents, don't they?'

She nodded. 'Entirely made up by Wiligut, but applied consistently. The tēth symbol means T, and the *Hakenkreuz*, the swastika, means A. And you can see the *Sig* rune for the letter S, familiar enough from the SS insignia. The other three symbols are the *Heilszeichen* rune for L, the *Odal* rune for N and the *Leben* rune for I.'

Jack stared again, panning his torch from symbol to symbol, then running over it again. 'Good God,' he said under his breath. 'They spell out ATLANTIS.'

'Now look at the second ring of symbols,' she said.

Jack panned his torch deeper into the hole and stared, his heart pounding. 'It's incredible,' he whispered.

'What is it?' Hiebermeyer said.

Jack sat back, his mind racing. 'The symbols Costas' ROV photographed two days ago on that cave wall in Atlantis, the ones that Katya is working on interpreting.' He took out his iPhone, pressed a few keys and passed it to Hiebermeyer, who stared at the image on the screen and then squatted down, looking at the rock-cut symbols in the marble and then at the screen again. 'There are twenty-six symbols on your screen. Each one of the eight symbols here in the rock is represented. They're the same.'

'You recognize them?'

Hiebermeyer nodded. 'It's the Stone Age code.' He looked at Heidi. 'These symbols are found on cave paintings of the Upper Palaeolithic, most extensively in the famous caves in France and Spain. What does seem incredible is that they are virtually identical across the world.' He showed her the screen, pointing. 'The zigzag lines, the clusters of dots, the parallel lines are all found in rock art in North and South America, Europe, South Africa, Australia. Some scholars have tried to argue that these are just common jottings that the artists could have invented independently, but that doesn't wash with me.'

'You think these symbols could have spread around the world from one origin?' she murmured.

Hiebermeyer nodded emphatically. 'We know people moved huge distances in the Ice Age: across the Bering Strait and to South America at least twenty thousand years ago, and from Asia to Australia at least thirty thousand years before that. Armchair scholars who dispute the idea look at maps and see apparently insurmountable barriers in the seas and deserts and mountain ranges, whereas those like Jack who've tried to retrace the routes realize that the sea especially is often an aid rather than a hindrance to long-distance travel.'

'What's the date range of the symbols?' she asked.

'Towards the end of the last Ice Age, from about twenty-five thousand to twelve thousand years ago. But they could have survived as relic symbols after the Ice Age, maybe in rituals.'

'At least until 6000 BC,' Jack said quietly, getting down on his knees and shining his Maglite at the far side of the recess. He took his iPhone back from Hiebermeyer, stared at it and then shone the torch again. 'Well I'll be damned.'

He straightened up and smiled broadly. Hiebermeyer pushed up his little round glasses and peered back. 'I've seen that look before.'

'I've just seen one I recognize above all others. It's astonishing.'

Hiebermeyer followed his gaze. The torch lit up a symbol like a garden rake, a single slash with four lines coming off it at right angles. 'Is this what I think it is?'

Jack scrolled down his screen. 'It's symbol number twenty-three in the Stone Age alphabet, what they call "pectiform", from the Latin for comb-shaped, with short lines extending off a single line. According to Katya's email to me summarizing the code, it's quite rare, only occurring at five per cent of the cave sites. But it first occurs in the oldest groups, twenty-five thousand years ago.' He tapped the screen again, and showed it to Heidi. 'That's why I'm so excited.'

The screen showed the cover of Jack's monograph publication on Atlantis, based on their discovery of the site five years before. In the centre was the symbol they had first seen on the papyrus that Hiebermeyer had discovered in the Egyptian desert, the account by the ancient Greek traveller Solon of his visit to the Egyptian high priest who had told him the story of Atlantis. It was the symbol that Jack and Costas had found on the golden disc from the Bronze Age shipwreck, a disc they realized had been created in Atlantis more than five thousand years earlier, before the citadel had been drowned by the rising waters of the Black Sea. Heidi peered at it, then at Jack. 'The symbol here is a mirror image of the Stone Age symbol. It's as if that pectiform symbol had been flipped over.'

Jack nodded. 'You won't believe it, but my colleague Costas and I saw this very symbol underwater at Atlantis during our dive, on a stone pillar at the entrance to a tunnel into the site. We call it the Atlantis symbol. We believe it was shaped like that in the form of two wings, and was meant to represent an eagle or a vulture, a sacred bird. And it also served as a map, like a labyrinth. Five years ago, we were able to follow the shape of the symbol in the tunnels and galleries in the rock of the volcano that formed the summit of the citadel, until we reached the holy of holies.'

'The place you and Costas revisited a few days ago,' Hiebermeyer said.

Jack nodded. 'Unfortunately the volcano decided to heat up just as we were about to enter the chamber. But we did manage to photograph a section of the wall containing these other symbols, clearly much older. I believe that this older Stone Age code and the newer Atlantis script were the preserve of priests and shamans, rather than a widespread writing system. That these two scripts should exist side by side fits in with some extraordinary ideas we've been developing about the dawn of civilization. On the one hand, the Atlanteans would have retained something of the rituals and beliefs of their Ice Age ancestors, particularly shamanistic rituals involving animals and the hunt. That's what we see in the Palaeolithic cave art, where the symbols first appear. On the other hand, early farmers were developing new belief systems. The old animal gods of the spirit world were being eclipsed by anthropomorphic gods, created when people were beginning to see that they could determine their own destiny. The new script, its sacred meaning, may have been tied up with that. The period when Atlantis was destroyed may have been a time of tension and even bloody conflict between the two belief systems, between shamans of the old ways and priests of the new. When we went back to Atlantis, I wanted to find out who those new gods were.'

Hiebermeyer pointed to the symbols in the floor. 'And now the big mystery. How on earth did these Stone Age symbols get here?'

Jack paused. 'I've just been thinking about that. The Palaeolithic cave art of France and the Pyrenees, at famous sites such as Lascaux, was known by the 1930s. Given the Ahnenerbe obsession with runes and symbols, it makes sense that they would have cast their net that wide. They would have known about the great antiquity of the caves, and might have associated the symbols with the fantasy of Aryan origins. It would have been fitting to reproduce those symbols in this secret place, this Nazi holy of holies, really a kind of sacred cave too.'

Heidi looked at him. 'You're right. I myself knew the scholar who had been to the Lascaux cave, a secretive Ahnenerbe expedition that took place after the occupation of France in 1940. He penetrated further into the caves than anyone has done since, and found many paintings with animal art and these symbols. Back at Wewelsburg, the SS ideologues assembled the symbols as evidence not just of Aryan ancestors, but of Atlantis. Their theory was that the survivors of Atlantis huddled in the caves, where they sought refuge after the flood. That day here with Ernst we attended an indoctrination lecture on Atlantis, given by an acquaintance of Ernst's from university days who insisted that he come along. It was a clever lecture, not occult nonsense, and I remembered enough from my schooling in the classics to know that the lecturer was talking sensibly about Plato. But it was there that I first saw the symbols, the same ones I was to see that afternoon down here with Himmler. The lecturer showed us some slides taken by the primitive underwater cameras of the time revealing symbols incised on what seemed to be a cavern wall. He said it was the most astonishing discovery ever made by the Ahnenerbe, in conditions of great danger to the divers.'

'Divers,' Jack exclaimed. 'Where was it?'

'The location was not revealed. He showed a picture of an underwater habitat that had been secretly developed in the

U-boat base at Lorient, an early version of the ones Captain Cousteau and his divers used in the 1960s and 1970s. It was very rudimentary by comparison, like two bathyspheres joined together. He said the divers used it as a base for their explorations, but I doubted it. I thought the habitat was too small for that, and afterwards wondered if it had been some kind of storage facility. I remember seeing fish, tropical fish. I took up scuba-diving myself in the 1950s, and often went to the Caribbean and the Red Sea. It could have been one of those places, or somewhere else in the tropics. Remember, the Ahnenerbe got everywhere, especially in the late 1930s, leading up to the war.'

Jack squatted down, and peered at Heidi. 'When you were down here with Himmler, did you actually see the palladion?'

'Only briefly. He treated it like the Holy Grail. Another man came down to lift it from that hollow and show it to us, an unpleasant Nazi named Dr Unverzagt, who was its custodian. I saw it for long enough to notice that it had symbols around the edge. There was no doubt in my mind that they were genuine, as old as the time when the gold was melded to the meteorite and the metal was forged into the swastika shape, far back in prehistory. The symbols on the palladion were exactly the same as the symbols that Himmler had carved into the marble in front of you.'

'Including that early Atlantis symbol?' Hiebermeyer asked.

'I remember it vividly on the edge of the palladion. There was no other symbol quite like it.'

Jack looked at Hiebermeyer. 'We've got some brainstorming to do.'

'You start.'

'The palladion, the most sacred symbol of ancient Troy, was taken by Agamemnon to Mycenae, where it was buried in the Royal Grave Circle and then discovered by Heinrich Schliemann. He hid it away under his house in Athens, where it was discovered by Himmler's Ahnenerbe men and brought here.'

'Right,' Hiebermeyer replied. 'The palladion was meteoritic in origin, exactly in accordance with the ancient Trojan legend that it had been the gift of the sky god. Meteorites are most easily found on ice, suggesting that the original artefact was in the hands of the ancestors of the Trojans long before the time of the recorded citadel, perhaps as far back as the end of the Ice Age, when the glaciers were close to northern Greece and the Black Sea. Some time between then and Bronze Age Troy, the meteorite was fashioned into the swastika shape and melded with gold, when it had those symbols added.'

'Symbols of the Ice Age.'

'Symbols identical to those found at Atlantis, the first great civilization after the Ice Age, whose inhabitants fled with their belongings after the glacial meltwaters finally flooded the Black Sea basin in the sixth millennium BC.'

'And their first landfall to the west would have been the Dardanelles, and the site of Troy.'

Hiebermeyer slapped his thigh. 'Troy was founded by the Atlanteans.'

'The palladion came from Atlantis.'

'Bingo,' Hiebermeyer said triumphantly.

'The only question is, how could Himmler's people possibly have associated it with Atlantis?' Jack murmured.

'I think it goes back to what I was telling you before we met up with Heidi. The Ahnenerbe collected a lot of real-life artefacts, some of them extraordinary treasures like the palladion, but then assembled them into a story according to their own mythology. Yet by accident, or sometimes by design – because there were occasional genuine scholars involved – some of that held a shadow of the truth. Behind the Aryan obsession lay a reality that we ourselves are uncovering, the spread of early Neolithic culture in prehistory, the advance of agriculture and Indo-European language, something we now know goes back to the diaspora of Atlanteans from the Black Sea. And behind the Nazi idea of a worldwide precursor civilization lies the truth of a people we know did profoundly influence the rise of civilization elsewhere. I'm certain that Himmler could have had no evidence that the palladion came from Atlantis or the meaning of that pectiform symbol, but sealing this sacred artefact in a hole surrounded by the word Atlantis in fake Nazi runes is exactly what we should expect.'

'And in their search for Atlantis, the Ahnenerbe chanced on a place where someone who could only have come from Atlantis inscribed those symbols into a cavern wall, underwater and somewhere in the tropics,' Jack murmured. 'With the symbols being identical to those inscribed on the palladion, it must have convinced them that the place those divers had found held huge significance. And they may have been right.'

He turned to Heidi. 'Is there anything more you can tell us about the palladion? Anything you remember from when you saw it?'

She looked pensive, and then clasped her stick. 'It had peculiar magnetic properties. The meteoritic iron was strangely affected by changes in the earth's magnetic field, becoming dramatically heavier at certain places. For Himmler, this seemed to add to the mystique. The marble hollow in the floor has a magnet embedded in it, and when it was activated, only the palladion could unlock it. Himmler enjoyed the fact that the palladion was stuck there like Excalibur embedded in the rock, another Arthurian fantasy. It apparently had a unique magnetic signature.'

Jack stared at Hiebermeyer. He remembered the shape in the bunker door. *The palladion was a key.* He looked back at Heidi. 'Anything else?'

She paused, and then looked Jack full in the face. Her eyes were moist again, and she suddenly seemed very old. 'I need to get out of here now. I need to leave this grim place, and feel the sun on my face.'

'Tante Heidi,' Hiebermeyer said, concern in his voice. 'Let's get you back to your wheelchair immediately, and we'll go out into the courtyard.'

She rose unsteadily, then put a hand on Hiebermeyer's, staying him. She looked at Jack again. 'There is something else,' she whispered. 'Something I've never told anyone, not even my son. I know where you've seen the shape of that reverse swastika before.'

'Tante Heidi?' Hiebermeyer said.

'You've seen it in the bunker in the forest.'

Jack stared at her. 'How do you know about that?'

'In the door of that horrible death chamber. I was there too, in the autumn of 1944. You know that I was a toxicologist. I was one of the scientists who worked there. That's my terrible secret. When you called and told me about the discovery of a lost art cache in a bunker beneath the NATO base, Maurice,

I knew what was also there and that you would find it. That's really why I called you here now. I had to tell you what I knew, a truth I had hoped would remain buried in that bunker and die with me. I will tell you everything now. But first I need the sunlight.'

16

Jack leaned back in his chair below the castle wall, reeling at what he had just heard. Over the past twenty minutes, Frau Hoffman had told them everything she knew about Himmler's secret project to develop a deadly biological weapon. They had learned how two victims of the 1918 Spanish flu epidemic had been exhumed from Père Lachaise cemetery in Paris and secretly transported to the bunker in the forest, where Heidi herself had been part of the team who dissected the bodies and isolated the virus. They had learned how another lethal microbe had been sought, a waterborne bacterium hinted at in the ancient sources that Himmler's scholars thought had been the cause of Alexander the Great's death in the third century BC. From the late 1930s, Ahnenerbe expeditions had scoured the world looking for it, eventually finding a place where the conditions were right for its growth and returning to the laboratory with a sample. The two weapons had been kept apart, the virus and the bacterium, ready to be used as a threat against the world in a scheme by Himmler that far exceeded in horror any secret wonder-weapon the Nazis were previously known to have contemplated.

Jack in turn had told Heidi everything they knew about Saumerre and his scheme: about how Saumerre's grandfather had been in the concentration camp next to the bunker and had come to know of the secret research being carried out there; and how he and his son and grandson had pursued the truth of it as they built up their criminal empire, the prospect of a secret Nazi weapon being the greatest prize they could offer to the terrorist clients whose cause Saumerre himself supported. Jack had begun to understand more clearly the link with Atlantis, how the search for a lost Aryan civilization had been used by the Ahnenerbe to shroud the truth of what they were really after; and how an underwater archaeological discovery somewhere in the tropics had provided the perfect place for a hideaway that allowed Himmler to continue the ruse, a place that Jack felt certain was the landfall for the western exodus from Atlantis that he had hoped to find. It was now vital that they discovered every clue they could to its whereabouts, with each moment that passed risking Saumerre losing his patience and deciding to sell to the highest bidder the phial Auxelle had stolen for him from the bunker.

Hiebermeyer walked across the terrace with a glass of water for Heidi, who sipped it gratefully. He turned to Jack and spoke quietly to him. 'I've just had a call from Major Penn. He was keen to help, so this morning he went ahead and contacted my friend in the Berlin underground group and asked him for the measurements of the impressed reverse swastika symbol in that corridor under the Zoo flak tower. Apparently it's exactly like the one we saw in the bunker, but whatever's beyond it in the corridor is flooded and crushed beneath tons of rubble. And there's been another development. Auxelle's been found murdered in an abandoned warehouse in Berlin.'

'The phial?'

'Penn was contacted before the scene had been tampered with. Auxelle had been stripped naked and garrotted. There was no phial.'

'That doesn't surprise me. He'd served his purpose for Saumerre. From now on, your aunt has a full-time escort until this is over.'

'You think Saumerre knows about her?'

'He and his family have been on this trail for years. We have to assume they know about everyone still alive with any possible connection to Himmler's schemes.'

Hiebermeyer pursed his lips, then resumed his seat on the other side of Heidi. Jack leaned towards her. 'A crucial question,' he asked. 'Which phial was it that Auxelle took from the bunker?'

'The bacterium. The Alexander bacterium.'

'So that's what Saumerre has now,' Jack murmured. 'And the *virus* was stored in the chamber under the flak tower. That's the missing ingredient, what Saumerre assumes must have gone to Himmler's secret lair.'

Hiebermeyer looked down, trying to say something. Jack had seen how distraught he had been after Heidi revealed that she had been in the bunker. He seemed to marshal his strength, and looked up again. 'Tante Heidi,' he said quietly. 'Yesterday, inside that bunker, I saw something terrible, too awful for words. I saw the remains of the corpses on the gurneys that you must have worked on. But there were other bodies, young people, that looked as if they'd been dissected alive. They'd been left there to die in agony. I have to know . . .'

'*Nein, nein, nein*,' she said, raising her arms as if to cover her face, then closing her eyes tight for a moment and shaking her head vehemently. 'I had nothing to do with that. *Nothing*. But I knew it was going to happen. I knew that once the scientists had isolated the virus, they would want to experiment with it, to mutate it and try ever more potent forms. I knew they had wanted to use healthy young adults born after the 1918 epidemic, people whose bodies had not built up the resistance of those who'd lived through the outbreak. And the Alexander bacterium was a completely unknown quantity: it needed to be tested. As soon as they started to expand the concentration camp next door, originally a camp for Russian prisoners, I knew what it was for and that I had to get out. They thought I could become like the SS female auxiliaries who ran the camp. I was desperate. My salvation came in the call for women to join the Lebensborn.'

'You were part of that? The Nazi eugenics programme?' Hiebermeyer exclaimed, aghast.

'It was a year before I met Ernst. None of us were forced into it, but some of us, like me, were there as an escape from worse situations. And I was the ideal physical specimen: blonde, blue-eyed, healthy, the perfect mother-to-be. We called the place the cattle farm. Truckloads of SS men would be driven up to visit us, every day. It was supposed to be a baby factory, but to them and to us it was a whorehouse.'

'*Mein Gott*,' Hiebermeyer whispered. 'I never knew anything about this.'

'How did you find out about Himmler's plan?' Jack said. 'I know you saw what was going on in the laboratory, but you've told us more than Himmler's men would surely have revealed to a junior technician.'

'Being a junior technician, a woman, and then volunteering for the Lebensborn programme probably saved my life,' she replied. 'The scientists seemed to disappear at regular intervals and be replaced. I think people were liquidated as soon as they'd done their task, and the turnover ensured that only a few knew the full picture. But remember my new job in the cattle farm. We mainly served the SS, whose ranks would have provided Himmler with the fanatical followers he could trust. In the bedroom, men will talk.'

'Who was he?'

Heidi gripped her stick, and hesitated. 'After four months, I had failed to get pregnant. That was the usual time limit, and I was terrified of being sent back to the laboratory. But there was one escape route. The brighter girls like me who failed to conceive could become part of the Lebensborn group used to repatriate children of Germanic background from eastern Europe, to make them into good little Nazis. For repatriate, read kidnap. I worked in the temporary hostels in Poland and was never present at the snatchings, but involvement in that awful episode was my crime against humanity. It was why, for as long as I was physically able after the war, I spent half the year working in a children's hospice in Poland near the

Auschwitz camp. It made me feel worse about what I had done, not better, but at least I was helping children and not causing them dreadful unhappiness any more.' She seemed to slump forward, and Hiebermeyer handed her the glass of water again.

'Tante Heidi, this is too much. You must rest.'

She waved him away, and straightened up. 'Let me get it over with. In answer to Jack's question, his name doesn't matter. He was Hungarian, a volunteer for the Waffen-SS who had risen through the ranks to become an officer, a hardened veteran of fighting the Canadians in Italy and then the Russians. He was one of the core of real soldiers that formed Himmler's innermost circle. When I was sent back to the cattle farm in Germany after working in Poland, I was given a new lease of life there as a medical assistant because of my background. But even those of us who weren't being used to make babies were still expected to perform. The best arrangement was to find a man who would frighten others away, and stick with him. My Hungarian visited me for five months, until Himmler spotted me on one of his many visits and thought I would be a suitable partner for Ernst. One night when we heard the terror bombers overhead on yet another attack on Berlin, my Hungarian said it didn't matter if we lost the war because Himmler had a secret weapon that would see the world cower in front of him. Before the war he'd even been with the Ahnenerbe on expeditions as a student, and later helped to acquire samples of one of the deadly components of the weapon. He told me that now he had the most important job: to go to the bunker in the forest – the same one where I had worked – when Himmler gave the signal and retrieve the weapon, then take it to Berlin. He told me about the Agamemnon Code, the secret signal that would be passed among the chosen few when the time was right. He told me how the palladion had a special purpose as a key to unlock the chambers with the phials. He told me everything I've told you.'

Jack remembered the image Hiebermeyer had described of the body of the SS man entangled with Major Mayne in the entrance to the bunker laboratory. If that was Heidi's Hungarian, if Mayne had died preventing him from getting inside the laboratory and retrieving the phial, then he truly had prevented the terrible catastrophe that would have ensued had the biological weapon somehow been deployed. Jack remembered Hugh Frazer, Mayne's friend who just recently passed away, and it sent a judder of emotion through him. He wished he'd been able to tell Hugh that Mayne had not died a meaningless death. He took a deep breath, and turned to Heidi. 'So then you met Ernst. And you must have quickly become pregnant.'

'It wasn't quite like that,' she whispered. 'I thought I couldn't conceive. Even so I took precautions, but then it happened.'

Hiebermeyer stared at her. 'When was this?'

'March 1944. I know what you are going to ask. I conceived Hans three weeks before Himmler introduced me to Ernst at a party. I knew the meeting had been arranged by Himmler because he wanted Ernst to have a good Aryan wife, and I looked the part perfectly. It was a match made for the newsreels. I jumped at it. I truly fell in love with Ernst, but it was also my escape from the Lebensborn. I realized about a week later that I was pregnant. I had to make a decision. The timing was close enough to pass the child off as ours.'

'Did Ernst know about your involvement with the Lebensborn programme?'

'He thought I was one of the care workers, the nannies. Himmler even encouraged him to visit me, so that the cameramen who followed Ernst everywhere could capture images of the war hero with the little blond children, the next generation of Nazis. Ernst told me he loved to see me with the orphans, that I was a natural mother. He was very tender with them, but he always looked troubled. The German people were never told that many of the so-called Lebensborn children were snatched from Polish parents; they were told that those children were orphans of German parents living in Poland, innocents caught up in war when the Poles had foolishly resisted the Nazi invasion in 1939. But Ernst had been there, during his first deployment as a Stuka pilot, and he knew what had happened to so many of those Polish parents, taken away at night and executed as the Nazis tried to exterminate the entire Polish professional class. We in Germany all knew what was going on in that war, you know. For some it was just small snippets in day-to-day life: seeing Jewish work parties, watching Jewish families disappear from your neighbourhood, working in factories alongside slave labour, or – if you were a soldier – watching the SS-Einsatzgruppen at work and seeing the bodies of women and old people hanging in every village. You didn't have to know about Treblinka or Sobibor or Belsen to be aware of the evil that was going on. Don't let any German who lived through those years tell you otherwise.'

Hiebermeyer sat down heavily on the chair opposite Heidi. 'Did you tell Hans?'

'Not for years. I left it too late, probably.' She was weeping, and took out a tissue to wipe her eyes. 'Ernst was dark-haired and brown-eyed, and Hans grew up blond-haired and blue-eyed. I could pass that off to him as my legacy, but as the years went by, he looked nothing like Ernst. Because of Ernst's fame as a pilot, Hans became obsessed with him as a teenager and even learned to fly because he felt it must be in his genes. But then as a university student, he watched one of the old newsreels showing Ernst being feted followed by one showing a Lebensborn farm, with blonde young women surrounded by happy blond orphans. The film was shot about six months before Ernst and I met. Hans recognized me in the group.'

'And that's when you told him?'

Heidi nodded, sniffing. 'He learned that he was the blond, blue-eyed son of a Hungarian thug who had volunteered to join the SS. It devastated him. Few of the Lebensborn children who discovered the truth lived happy lives. It put Hans on a path of self-destruction, to the anarchists and then the Baader–Meinhof terrorists. He was finally shot by the police in a stand-off. He had been given the chance to surrender, but I knew it would never happen, that in his mind there was no life ahead for him. I watched it all on TV, as if I was watching one of those newsreels from the war.' She bowed her head. 'Do you know the Wilfred Owen poem, "Strange Meeting"? It was unfinished when he was killed in action in 1918. He wrote of escaping from battle down some profound dull tunnel, but then realizing it had only taken him to hell. Often I feel as if the war has never ended for me, as if I'm on an ice sheet on a lake trying to escape from the broken ice of the past, but every step I take just breaks more. I only hope that what I've been able to tell you now will bring resolution to one awful legacy.'

Hiebermeyer gripped her hand. His face was drawn with emotion, and his voice was hoarse. 'I remember Hans from when I was a boy. He used to lift me on his shoulders, and I remember his thick blond hair, feeling very safe as he carried me along the lake shore to where we went fishing. I wish I'd known. I could have told him it was all right.'

Heidi put her hand on Hiebermeyer's head, and bowed her own, saying nothing for a moment. Then she looked up to Jack. 'The last time I saw Ernst was just before dawn on the second of May 1945. I was in a farmhouse outside Plön, near the Baltic coast. Two nights previously a Gestapo team had taken Hans and me from our house in a village south of Berlin, just as it was about to be overrun by the Russians. I had no idea what was going on. Gestapo coming in the night was usually bad news, but I was grateful. I thought there was no chance that I would have survived the Red Army. But then while Hans was still asleep that night at Plön, Ernst arrived with an escort of two SS men, having just flown in from Berlin. We only had twenty minutes alone together. I told the SS this might be our last chance for a while. I knew how to talk to these men, remember. I took them out of Ernst's earshot while he was looking at Hans asleep and said that if they returned later, I would see that they were not disappointed. When we got into the bedroom, all Ernst did was talk. He told me he'd come from the Zoo flak tower, and had been visited by Himmler. To my horror, I realized that he had become part of Himmler's plan. I also realized that Hans and I were being used as a bargaining chip. Ernst told me he had secretly written a diary of everything he knew, all the secrets and subterfuge of those awful final months in Berlin, and that he had left it with some crates of artefacts in the Zoo tower for the KGB to discover. He was carrying a satchel with something heavy in it. I didn't ask what it was, but he said he also had something he'd retrieved from a secret place under the Zoo tower. I knew instantly what it was, because that was where the refined product of our research in the laboratory was to be stored. I now knew that it was a weapon that Himmler had secretly created and planned for his own purpose. Ultimately, only a single sample had been saved, all others having been destroyed deliberately to ensure that Himmler had complete control.'

'The Spanish flu virus,' Jack said quietly.

She nodded. 'Ernst showed me the small metal tube. He said a U-boat was waiting, one of the latest types that could go stealthily for weeks without refuelling. At the U-boat's destination, he was to unlock a chamber and place the phial inside; once he had done that, word would be radioed back and Hans and I would follow in another U-boat, accompanied by Himmler himself.'

'But you knew that plan was all a charade,' Jack said softly.

'Ernst held my hand. He said he would do everything in his power to send that phial to the deepest depths of the ocean. He said he knew there would be men in the submarine watching his every move, whose task was probably to eliminate him once the delivery had been made. But he said he'd spent hours in a Type-21 U-boat during a promotional visit to a shipyard, and had been fascinated by the machinery. That was

Ernst for you. He could ignore all the horror around him as long as he had a good machine to play with. He said he'd worked out how to fire a torpedo, and he'd realized on the flight from Berlin how he could eject the phial from a torpedo tube. He said he would find a way of sealing himself in the torpedo room and doing it, even if it meant no chance of escape for him.'

'Do you believe he did it?'

Heidi swallowed hard, suddenly looking very frail. 'I knew I'd never see him again. Part of me wanted that. If he'd found out the truth about Hans, about me, it would have destroyed him. You must remember, with the advance of the Red Army, we all thought we were going to die. But even if I were to live, I wanted that happiness we had experienced in the few days of his leave during our brief time as man and wife to still be there, to be sealed in the past where I could go when I shut my eyes. I only wish I had been right about that. I yearn to see it again, but I can't.'

'You will, Tante Heidi,' Hiebermeyer said, holding her hand. 'You will.'

She turned to Jack. 'In answer to your question, yes. With all my heart I believe he would have done it. I have never doubted that the virus was destroyed, somewhere at the bottom of the ocean.'

'We don't want Saumerre knowing that,' Jack murmured. 'Our plan depends on him thinking that what his man Auxelle took from the bunker was a lesser toxic agent, far exceeded by the virus. If he thinks the virus is destroyed, he might be tempted to use what he has, the Alexander bacterium. That would be bad enough.'

'What do we do now?' Hiebermeyer said.

'Two things.' Heidi firmly put Hiebermeyer's hand away and straightened herself up, drying her eyes. 'I am going to organize you.'

'That sounds like the Tante Heidi I remember,' Hiebermeyer said.

'First,' she said, 'you need to find out where the U-boat was heading. All I know for certain is that it was the place where Himmler's men discovered those symbols, the underwater cavern I saw in that slideshow at Wewelsburg. Here's the only clue I can give you. The Ahnenerbe man who gave that lecture on Atlantis, Ernst's old student acquaintance? He's still alive.'

'How do you know?' Jack said.

'As I get older and so many of us die, historians more often come to me for interviews about my experiences in Nazi Germany. And there are always treasure-hunters who think they're on the trail of Nazi loot. One researcher came to my home recently, a few weeks ago. He said he'd found a surviving Ahnenerbe man in Canada who knew I was alive because I'd been interviewed for a TV programme he'd seen, and he'd advised the researcher to find me.'

Jack cast Hiebermeyer a concerned glance, then looked back at Heidi. 'What did he want?'

'Really he seemed to want me to talk much as I have to you. To reveal something he thought I knew, about Himmler and his plan. Once I knew who the Ahnenerbe man was, that didn't surprise me.'

'But you didn't tell the researcher anything.'

'Of course not. All I told him was that I'd been a willing sex worker in the Lebensborn. That really I'd just been a prostitute. I'm quite capable of putting that act on again, you know. That shut him up.'

'So who was the Ahnenerbe man?'

She paused. 'Ernst knew him from Heidelberg University before the war. He was much more of a scholar than Ernst, quite aloof. I got to know him because several times I had . . .' she paused, 'accommodated him at the Lebensborn farm. He was not at all the right Aryan type, tall and thin and Prussian, but Himmler often sent favourites down to us for entertainment, really using us as little more than a whorehouse. As I said, you always find out things in the bedroom that shouldn't be said. He told me he had denounced to the Gestapo his and Ernst's old professor, a reluctant Ahnenerbe recruit who had become a drunk and talked too much. Later, after he saw me in the audience of his lecture at Wewelsburg with Ernst, he forced me to visit him in secret for sex, saying he would tell Ernst the truth about me otherwise. A true Prussian gentleman. I'd been fascinated by that slide showing the underwater cavern and asked him where it was, but he himself had not been on the expedition and he hadn't been told. But if anyone has clues, it's him. His name was von Schoenberg.'

Jack looked stunned. 'Von Schoenberg? *Professor* von Schoenberg? The classical scholar?'

'You know of him?'

Jack turned to Hiebermeyer. 'While we were students at Cambridge, he came on sabbatical to work with James Dillen. Do you remember we went together to his seminar on Phoenician exploration in the Atlantic?'

'*Mein Gott.* Yes. I argued with him that it wasn't the

Phoenicians, it was the Egyptians who first circumnavigated Africa.'

'It's an extraordinary coincidence,' Jack said. 'Dillen called me and said he returned from Troy to a barrage of emails and phone messages from Schoenberg saying he had something of great importance he wanted to tell. Dillen said that in the past, Schoenberg had always been trying to pin him down on matters of great importance, usually some tiny contentious detail in a translation. But the odd thing this time was that he specifically wanted to see me.'

'Maybe not so odd after all,' Hiebermeyer said. 'If we know about him, Saumerre might too and could have got to him first, somehow persuaded him to draw you in and reveal what you know.'

Jack clicked on his iPhone, checking his directory. 'Dillen's sent me his address in British Columbia.' He turned to Heidi. 'Your second thing?'

She grasped her stick and leaned forward, speaking in a low voice. 'I know how to create a vaccine against the bacterium, which will make it far less dangerous as a potential weapon. We scientists knew that the bacterium would never be as deadly a threat as the virus.'

Jack gasped. 'Go on.'

'That was my job just before I left the laboratory to join the Lebensborn. They were all worried about themselves, the scientists and their SS handlers, about getting infected. They couldn't find a treatment for the flu virus, but they set me to work on the bacterium. I'd been a top biochemistry student before the war, you know, and had spent a postgraduate year at Oxford. That's where I acquired my English. After the war for many years in England I carried out research for the Ministry of Defence, where my speciality was antidotes for biological weapons they thought the Russians might use. I never revealed anything about the Alexander bacterium, because I just wanted to forget all about that bunker and I was fearful that leading anyone to it would result in contamination and expose the world to a deadly plague. But I carefully recorded all of my research data so that I could resume the work some time in the future if necessary. There was only one component missing.'

'Go on,' Jack said.

'The Alexander bacterium. One would need a fresh sample to prove that the vaccine works, and as far as I know only the one sample was saved by Himmler's people.'

Jack thought hard. 'Could you still do it now? Could you perfect it?'

'I still have very close colleagues working in high security government labs who would relish the task. I would gladly tell them all I know. My science became my life after the war, and it's still what keeps me going. And in answer to your next question, yes. I know where they found the bacterium. Schoenberg knows too, because he was there, part of the Ahnenerbe team who were supposedly looking for Atlantis but in reality were scouring the world for the bacterium mentioned in the ancient sources. They needed icy-cold freshwater places, where the water runs over limestone. They found it in Iceland.'

'*Iceland*,' Jack exclaimed. 'Do you know exactly where?'

She reached into her pocket and handed him a slip of paper. 'This is what my Hungarian told me. He was very proud of being a trained diver and had been on that expedition. It was very dangerous for them, with their primitive equipment.'

Jack paused. There was one thing he needed to know, to be sure that all of this was true. 'Your Hungarian,' he said slowly. 'When he woke up the next morning after telling you everything, he must have berated himself. He would have sworn secrecy to Himmler. If you'd told anyone else and he'd been fingered, that would have been the end for him. He was getting nothing out of you after you'd met Ernst. Why didn't he concoct some reason to have you dealt with by the Gestapo?'

Heidi gave Jack an unfathomable look. 'Because I kept seeing him. I knew that if I didn't, I was doomed. All the time I was with Ernst, the Hungarian was still my lover. I saw him while Ernst was on the Russian front, and while he was in Berlin. The Hungarian knew that Hans was his son. The last time I saw him was in that house at Plön on the second of May 1945, only a few hours before Ernst arrived on his way to the U-boat. I never saw either man again. Within days, weeks at the most, both were dead.'

Jack glanced at the paper, reading the details, then carefully folded it and put it in his pocket.

'Okay.' He stood up 'I have to ring Costas. And set up a flight to British Columbia. But before that, Maurice, I need you to ring your friend Major Penn. Heidi's innocent act with that researcher may have put Saumerre off for the time being, but after Auxelle's death, I suspect that everyone who knows anything about this will be eliminated as soon as they cease to be useful. I know Penn was desperate to do something after his sergeant was murdered, and I got the impression that he was frustrated not to be the one to take care of Auxelle. But providing round-the-clock protection for Frau Hoffman is as important as it gets.'

'I'm sure he'll be happy to oblige.' Hiebermeyer took out his phone, then stood up, suddenly looking tired. 'I'm going to take Tante Heidi home,' he said. 'Then I've got a pregnant wife to attend. Hope you don't mind.'

Jack put a hand on his friend's shoulder. 'You know what I think.'

'Aysha,' Heidi said, suddenly beaming. 'I can't wait to meet her.'

'Sevety-two hours,' Jack said, looking at Hiebermeyer. 'Then we'll be planning that expedition to find Akhenaten's treasure in Egypt.'

'Promise?'

Jack looked at his friend's face, remembering what he had gone through in the bunker, something he had volunteered to do in Jack's place. 'You can count on it. But meanwhile, the clock's ticking. I need to visit Professor Schoenberg. And I need to think about diving again.'

17

Near Tofino, Vancouver Island, British Columbia

The de Havilland Canada DHC-2 Beaver banked and swept low over the treetops, the roar of its single Pratt & Whitney 350 h.p. propeller engine intensifying as they dropped below the level of the surrounding hills. Jack was in the co-pilot's seat, having just relinquished the controls to the woman beside him, a Canadian bush pilot who had considerably more experience than he did at landing on the edge of the Pacific Ocean. He pressed the microphone on his headset. 'Thanks for that. I haven't flown a Beaver since I got my pilot's licence when I was at school in Canada.'

'Best plane ever made,' she replied, flashing him a smile. 'Built in 1946, and still going strong. Out here, the people living in these remote bays wouldn't be able to function without us. The last road along this coast ended twenty kilometres back.'

The aircraft levelled out for its approach. To the right, beyond the forest, Jack could see the distant peaks of the Coast Mountains of mainland British Columbia, and to the west the glistening expanse of the Pacific. It had been an exhilarating half-hour flight north from the fishing port of Tofino, complete with the spectacular sight of humpback whales breaching on their migration towards the waters off Alaska. Jack turned to Costas, who was sitting in the back gripping the pilot's seat, looking like a wartime pilot in his headset and aviator sunglasses. 'You good?' he said.

'Better now that you're not flying. I always hated roller coasters.'

'It's called tactical flying.'

'It's called being rusty.'

Jack gestured at a book with a swastika on the cover that Costas had been reading, and a pad where he had been jotting down notes. 'You missed the whales.'

'I was boning up on this guy we're visiting. What he and his colleagues in the Nazi Ahnenerbe were up to in the late 1930s. It makes for pretty unsavoury reading.'

The pilot interrupted them. 'We're landing now. Brace yourselves.'

Jack sat back, checked his seat-belt harness and watched as the floats beneath the aircraft skimmed the water and then sent up a sheen of spray, completely obscuring the view. A tremendous vibration shook the plane, as if they were in a car with a tyre blowout, and then the aircraft slowed and settled in the water, rocking on the ocean swell. He could see a wooden jetty sticking out of the rocky shore ahead, leading to a floating dock with a Zodiac inflatable boat tied up alongside. The pilot throttled down and manoeuvred the aircraft close to the dock, then switched the engine off, opened the hatch and jumped out, swiftly uncoiling the ropes that were lying ready and tying them to each end of the starboard float. She gestured for Jack and Costas to follow, and they both unbuckled themselves and jumped on to the dock. Costas made a beeline for a wooden deckchair at the end, splaying himself out and closing his eyes. 'I'd really like to soak in the rays for a while.'

'Don't be duped by the weather,' the woman said. 'This place is shrouded in sea mist and rain for a lot of the year.'

'Sounds as if that'd suit the guy we're visiting.'

She shrugged. 'We get a lot of recluses out here. We don't ask questions.' She pointed at the Zodiac. 'You guys good with that? I guess so. It's gassed up. His house is about two kilometres up the sound on this side. I usually deliver supplies for him every two weeks. Keep at least a hundred metres offshore to avoid the rocks, and then you'll see the beach and a little jetty where you can pull up.'

'How much time do we have?' Jack asked.

She looked at the sky, and then at the sea. 'The wind'll pick up by early afternoon. I want to be out of here by noon. If you plan to leave his place at eleven a.m., that gives you an hour and a half from now. Is that okay?'

'You're the boss,' Jack said. 'I've got the radio. Call if you need us earlier.'

She nodded, let her hair loose from under her cap and sat down on the deckchair where Costas had been slumped.

'My turn. This is the first sun we've had for a week.'

Jack jumped into the inflatable, squeezed the fuel pump on the 40 h.p. Mariner outboard and pulled the starter cord. It coughed to life, and he sat down beside it with his hand on the tiller. Costas untied the painter and leapt in, and then Jack put the engine into gear and swung out past the dock and into the centre of the channel, slowly opening the throttle. Costas slid back halfway down the opposite pontoon and raised his voice above the engine. 'So you've never been here before?'

'I came to Vancouver Island on holiday as a kid, but never this far out. I had no idea that Schoenberg lived here until Dillen told me. I knew he'd been a university professor in Ontario and then retired out west twenty-odd years ago, after his wife died. He must be in his early nineties now. His name was *von* Schoenberg, originally. His family was Prussian, fairly aristocratic. There were plenty of Nazis among the old Prussian elite, but many of them were contemptuous of Hitler and his cronies. My guess is he ditched the von when he was captured by the Russians.'

'He was a prisoner of war in Russia?'

'In the Gulag, in Siberia. He was one of the last batch to be released.'

'I've just been reading that most of the surviving German prisoners not released by 1949 were judged by the Russians to be war criminals, and weren't let go until after Stalin died in 1953.'

'Dillen said Schoenberg tried to pass himself off as an ordinary Wehrmacht soldier, but he thinks the Soviets must have suspected him. Discovering he was one of Himmler's select followers in the Ahnenerbe would have been enough to brand him a criminal. He would have been lucky to escape execution.'

'So Dillen knows him from way back?'

Jack nodded, swinging the boat to port to avoid a patch of kelp. 'Schoenberg came to Cambridge on sabbatical just before his retirement, and they worked together on a translation of ancient Greek inscriptions from Athens. Schoenberg had been a classical scholar before the war, and eventually finished his doctorate in Canada. He was in Cambridge when I was a graduate student, and I attended a seminar he gave on the early Greek geographers, his speciality. We talked afterwards, and he was fascinated by my diving expeditions. He said his greatest exhilaration had been an expedition he undertook to Iceland as a young man to search for archaeological sites. I think that talking to me took him back to the heyday of his youth in the late 1930s.'

'That expedition was with Himmler's Ahnenerbe, the Nazi Department of Cultural Heritage. Already the Jews in Germany were being persecuted and the language of racism was everywhere. It would hardly have been a carefree jaunt.'

'Schoenberg told Dillen that his involvement in the Ahnenerbe was purely scholarly, and that he joined the Nazi party only because refusal was impossible.'

'Didn't a lot of ex-Nazis come to Canada?'

'Quite a few former prisoners of war were allowed to come here after they were released by the Soviets in the late forties and early fifties. Plenty of them made new lives for themselves and the last thing they wanted was to hark back to the war. But there were some, including former SS, who remained diehard Nazis. Unlike released prisoners who went back to Germany – who saw the devastation and then the years of reconstruction, who themselves were part of the creation of the new Germany – some of those who went abroad after their release still lived in a fantasy world and refused to accept what had happened. I knew former German soldiers in Canada who would still openly celebrate Hitler's birthday.'

'Schoenberg?'

Jack paused. 'It's hard to imagine how anyone who let slip that their greatest exhilaration was during their time working for Himmler could not be nostalgic, whatever they may say about being coerced. You've just been reading about the real purpose of the Ahnenerbe: to provide Himmler with so-called evidence for racial superiority that he then used to justify the Final Solution. When you see that old man today, remember the pictures of the concentration camp at Belsen, and those terrible images Maurice saw in the forest bunker. That's what the Ahnenerbe was really all about. But we have to try to keep our cool. We're here because he wants to tell us something. We have to encourage him to talk, not to clam up.'

'He'll presumably expect some questions about his Nazi past,' Costas said. 'I've got some fresh in my mind from that book. It would be odd if we didn't ask him something. That might raise his suspicions.'

Jack nodded. 'Just don't lay it on too thick.'

'You could show annoyance with me for doing it. Might help to get you into his confidence, to open him up.'

Jack nodded. 'Whatever he says in response to queries about his Nazi past we have to take with a pinch of salt. But I doubt whether we'll need to tease the truth of his convictions out of him. Those will come anyway, little words here and there, more openly if he thinks he's in like-minded company. He's very old and has been living as a recluse for more than twenty years, probably inhabiting that world of his past more and more in his mind. Anyway, I want to play him on something else. We have to find a way of bringing up the Brotherhood of the Tiger. I've expected Shang Yong to be on my tail ever since we took out most of his business assets two years ago, and the Brotherhood is just the kind of outfit Saumerre would contract after his disappointment with the Russian hitmen last year. Ben told me he thought he'd seen the tiger tattoo on a man in the airport concourse at JFK when he arrived there with Rebecca from Istanbul.'

'You suspect Schoenberg is involved with Saumerre?' Costas said.

'It's just a hunch. Frau Hoffman knew about him, and knew he was still alive. If they are the last survivors of those who may have been close to Himmler's scheme, then we have to remember that Saumerre – and before that his father and his grandfather – have been on this trail for years. If we know about Schoenberg's background and where he lives, then Saumerre almost certainly will too.'

'You think Saumerre may have got to him and offered some kind of deal?'

Jack throttled down and let the engine idle for a moment, marshalling his thoughts. 'This is what I think. I think the fantasy world of the Nazis, all that nonsense at Wewelsburg Castle, disguised a terrible truth of ego and poisonous ambition in Heinrich Himmler. But I think that fantasy world was so embedded in the young men and women whose minds were warped by the Ahnenerbe that it will still be there in those few who survive today. Schoenberg may well have something genuinely exciting to tell us, as Dillen himself firmly believed, something about Atlantis that still burns within him because of the fervour for finding an Aryan proto-civilization that was kindled in his soul during his formative years. He could hardly have avoided being influenced by the Ahnenerbe, not only by the ideology but also by the com-pulsive, almost manic excitement that surrounded it, an infectious enthusiasm it would be hard for a young man to deny. For him, re-stoking that enthusiasm might be important now because he's an old man harking back to his youth, and that's something we can exploit. But there's another, darker possibility: that the fantasy for a select few was also to be part of a terrifying vortex of escape and rebirth that Himmler had contructed for himself, one that required men like Ernst Hoffman to bring it to fruition.'

'And you think Schoenberg may be one of those.'

'I don't know. He may just be a retired scholar with a past that was beyond his control. But if I'm right and Saumerre has got to him, then we have to be doubly cautious, because he could be playing us too.'

'How do you mean?'

'We're looking for the site of Atlantis reborn, right? The place where the survivors of the exodus inscribed those symbols we know from Atlantis in the Black Sea, symbols that Himmler's Ahnenerbe archaeologists who discovered the new Atlantis copied in that secret chamber in Wewelsburg that Frau Hoffman showed to Maurice and me. We know from her that the new Atlantis was where Himmler decided to build his secret hideaway, the destination for the U-boat dispatched with Hoffman and his deadly cargo in the final days of the war. We know that he shrouded the place with the mystique of Atlantis, which had for so long been the obsession of the Ahnenerbe, a mystique that may continue to motivate a man like Schoenberg. We're on this trail now with such urgency because of the deadly virus that may have been successfully delivered by the U-boat to this new Atlantis, a virus Saumerre desperately wants to get his hands on. A man like Schoenberg could be caught in between, ignorant of the deadly biological weapon and Himmler's true purpose, but passionately believing in the association of the place with the dream of revealing the Aryan roots of civilization that he now wants to see fulfilled before he dies.'

'So you think Saumerre could have made a deal with him.'

'I think Saumerre may have told him to give us all the information he has. Remember, Saumerre *wants* us to find this place. He has his contracted thugs, the Chinese gangsters of Shang Yong, but he doesn't have the resources or the expertise to follow the archaeological trail we're now on. He's watching and waiting for us to get there. As soon as he knows enough to allow him to organize the logistics needed to get his men in place with the right equipment, he's going to have a go again at kidnapping Rebecca so that he can blackmail me into revealing the location. It's why I asked Mikhail to get Rebecca out of school to his place in the Adirondacks. I'm not going to let that happen again.'

'You'd give away the location if it came to it?'

Jack gave him a steely look. 'I have a plan.'

'Okay. Just keep me in the loop.' Costas looked out, shading his eyes, and pointed ahead. 'That must be it now.'

Jack saw a narrow strip of beach on the shoreline to the right, and the eaves of a low wooden house in the forest behind. He turned the boat towards the beach, throttled down and stood up, one hand on the tiller and the other holding the painter line to steady himself. He steered into a small cove beside a spine of rock jutting into the bay, and then brought the boat against a small floating dock. He sat down, flipped the gear lever to neutral and threw the painter line to Costas, who leapt out and secured it to a wooden post. After switching off the engine, Jack climbed out, and together they made their way along a rickety boardwalk towards the beach.

He clicked on his cell phone and paused to read two urgent text messages, one from Lanowski and one from Katya. He called Costas back. 'Incredible stuff. It really takes us forward. You remember Lanowski's Plato code, the idea that Plato and Solon before him embedded Pythagorean messages in their texts? Well, take a look at this. He's found a code in Solon's text, the Atlantis papyrus that Maurice and Aysha discovered in the desert five years ago.'

Costas peered at the message. 'He says it's a simple geometric code, easy enough to understand if you play chess in three dimensions. Typical Lanowski. For easy, read impossible. Sounds like he's found a soulmate in Solon.'

Jack scrolled down. 'Lanowski translates the ancient Greek as *The priestess prophesied that the new Atlantis would be founded over the western ocean, where the palladion becomes heavy again and where the two mountains form a saddle and two peaks like the horns of a bull*.'

'That's what Lanowski thinks Solon was told by the high priest at Saïs, but that he instructed Solon not to write it down because it was sacred.'

Jack nodded. 'It's fantastic. Remember the weight of meteoritic iron along the North Anatolian Fault, at Atlantis, and the shape of the volcano? It may simply be saying that the new Atlantis will be founded at a site very similar to the old, but if that's what the fleeing Atlanteans were looking out for, so should we.'

'You've got something from Katya too? Not personal?'

Jack shook his head. 'Read it. She's worked on those Stone Age symbols on the cave wall at Atlantis. She's convinced they're syllabic, and two proper names. It seems incredible, but the nearest equivalents among known early names she can come up with are Uta-napishtim and Gilgamesh.'

'Not really so incredible though, is it, Jack? They've been staring at us from the Epic of Gilgamesh all along.'

'And now we know they're embedded in the reality of the Neolithic, in Atlantis,' Jack said, shaking his head slowly. 'Maybe that's who we should be trying to see, real men, not mythical demigods, when we imagine a voyage west to that place where the palladion was heavier and the mountain had twin peaks.'

Costas jerked his head up to the treeline. 'We'd better get moving if we're going to use our time well.'

Above the berm of seaweed at the high-tide mark were huge bleached logs that had been washed in by winter storms, jumbled on the beach like a line of natural sculpture. They clambered over them and made their way up a wooden stairway towards the house. They could see an old man with a stick waiting for them, wearing a bandanna neck scarf and a straw hat. Jack raised his arm, and the man waved back, then beckoned for them to follow him as he turned towards the open screen door of the veranda.

18

Ten minutes later, Jack and Costas were sitting in wicker chairs around a low glass-topped table piled high with books and papers, with steaming mugs of coffee in front of them. Schoenberg had taken his hat off to reveal a full head of white hair, neatly swept back. He was a tall man, lean-limbed, with fine features, and moved with an easy confidence. It was hard to reconcile the genial image with the world the man had grown up in and his role in it, and for a fleeting moment Jack thought that maybe he had been wrong, that the man should be judged for what he had become and what he had made of his life. He looked at the brown leather document case that Schoenberg had placed on the table between them. They had exchanged niceties and news of Dillen's latest work, but Jack had remembered that Schoenberg was not one for small talk.

'I've been hoping for this moment for many years, to share

what I know with the right person,' Schoenberg said, his German accent still marked despite more than half a lifetime in Canada.

'James Dillen said it was most important that I come to visit you now. I'm fascinated to hear what you have for us.'

'You are, I know, very familiar with the *Periplus Maris Erythraei*.'

Jack stared at him, then nodded. 'The *Periplus of the Erythraean Sea*. A Roman merchant's guide to the Red Sea and Indian Ocean, written in Greek in Egypt. One of the most extraordinary ancient texts on seafaring and maritime exploration to survive. Two years ago, we discovered a Roman shipwreck in the Red Sea with a huge trove of gold bullion destined for India, the best corroboration yet of the ancient trade across the Indian Ocean described in the *Periplus*.'

'I followed the excavation on your website. It was a marvellous discovery. Then you know something of the Heidelberg Codex?'

'*Codex Palatinus Graecus* 398, containing the *Periplus*? A compilation of copied ancient texts on geography and exploration put together in about the tenth century, probably in a monastery in the Byzantine East. My colleagues Maria de Montijo and Jeremy Haverstock travelled with me to Heidelberg University to examine it. They've done a complete palaeographic analysis of the text of the *Periplus*, and Dillen has been working on a new translation.'

'Ah. He didn't say. We've been out of touch since my retirement.'

'I expect he wanted to tell you first about the new passages of Homer, *The Fall of Troy*. They came from the ancient library we discovered three years ago in Herculaneum. That's been the huge excitement of the last year, in conjunction with the excavation at Troy, which has even produced a wall painting of a bard called Homeros.'

Schoenberg nodded, his eyes rapt. 'A remarkable find. *Remarkable*.Your work is so much what I envisaged all those years ago, when there were those of us in the Ahnenerbe, the genuine scholars, not the charlatans and the frauds, who saw our future had we won the war just as you must have first envisaged your own institute.'

Costas narrowed his eyes, and Jack said nothing for a moment, watching Schoenberg, then took a sip of coffee. 'Back to the *Periplus*. While Costas and I were excavating the shipwreck, Maurice Hiebermeyer and his team dug up a Roman merchant's house at the Red Sea port site of Myos Hormos. They found fragments of inscribed potsherds that seemed to be a first draft of the *Periplus*, containing digressions that were excised from the final version, the one copied by the monk who compiled the *Codex Palatinus Graecus*. One of the digressions mentioned Roman legionaries who escaped from Parthian imprisonment and went east through the mountains of central Asia towards China. Following that lead put us on the trail of a group of Romans who thought they'd found their own El Dorado, who had heard about the fabled riches of the First Emperor Shihuangdi's tomb in China. They never made it that far, but settled on the distant reaches of the Silk Road, where their descendants still live today.'

'Fascinating,' Schoenberg said. 'Blond-haired, blue-eyed? We heard these rumours in the 1930s. Himmler wanted to find descendants of the Aryan master race who might still exist in pockets of racial purity in isolated places around the world, as well as in Germany.'

'The trail got us in a little bit of trouble, as usual,' Costas grumbled. 'Marxist guerrillas in the Indian jungle, then the cross hairs of a sniper in Afghanistan. We came up against some pretty sinister modern-day opponents.'

Jack glanced at Costas, then looked back at Schoenberg. 'They were a Chinese secret society. For more than two thousand years they had been on the trail of a fabulous jewel they thought had been stolen by one of the custodians of the First Emperor's tomb. The search for the jewel became enshrined in their mythology, the basis for a warrior cult. The society today is a fully modern criminal cartel steeped in the drugs and arms trades, with its headquarters somewhere in the Taklamakan Desert. But finding the jewel remained their paramount obsession. They thought one of the Romans had taken it from the fleeing tomb custodian two thousand years ago, and that we knew where it was. They're called the Brotherhood of the Tiger, and the one who undertakes the quest to find the jewel is the Tiger Warrior. Have you heard of them?'

Schoenberg looked taken aback, then pointedly shook his head. 'I'm just a scholar.' He smiled, then curled his lip. 'But you have nothing to fear. When I was still an undergraduate at Heidelberg in 1938, I was specially selected above dozens of others to join an Ahnenerbe expedition to Tibet. We of course encountered many Mongoloids there, including agents of China sent to keep an eye on us. You were in no danger. They are an inherently weak race.'

Jack sat back. 'All I know is that I personally shot the

latter-day Tiger Warrior in a remote valley in Afghanistan. As far as I know his bones still lie there along with the dream of the jewel. Our information led to the Brotherhood's activities outside China being shut down, and all they are now is a gang of guns for hire. Their leader Shang Yong would like to see me dead, but any threat he poses will evaporate in about a week's time, when Chinese internal security finally takes out his headquarters in the Taklamakan. Any promise Shang Yong might make to his clients now is as hollow as the place in his fantasy world for that jewel. One thing, though, that his men are very good at is assassination. Once he realizes he is under threat, I have no doubt he will send out his remaining thugs to kill his clients to cover his tracks.'

Schoenberg looked uncertain for a moment, then waved his hand dismissively as if ignoring what Jack had just said. 'You two, James Dillen, your palaeographers, your divers. A team effort. That's what I love about your projects. They remind me of the best of our research in the 1930s, bringing together the clues that led us on fabulous expeditions to Tibet, to the Andes, to Iceland. It was an exciting time.'

'All in the cause of Nazism,' Costas murmured. 'Searching for evidence of racial superiority.'

Schoenberg gave him a cold look. 'Not all of us were ardent Nazis. And we had no choice. Either we worked for the Ahnenerbe, or Himmler put us on the blacklist of dissidents who ended up in Dachau. I personally found the anthropological research distasteful, but measuring skulls and photographing racial types seemed harmless. It was only later that we realized how much this was fortifying Himmler's views. None of us had any idea then where it would lead. And for us as young men, searching for a lost Aryan civilization, for Atlantis, was a huge adventure. Surely we were not the only nation to use archaeology to search for our roots.'

'You were the only one to use archaeology to help justify the extermination of an entire people.'

Jack gave Costas a warning look, seeing Schoenberg watching him. 'Atlantis. That's what we're here to talk about, isn't it?'

Schoenberg nodded, his lips pursed, then turned to Jack. 'I am not an apologist for Nazi extremism, but I want to tell you how it was. We were not all madmen and psychopaths.'

Jack looked at him impassively. 'James Dillen holds your classical scholarship in high regard.'

'I was a sane man trapped in a lunatic asylum. Wewelsburg Castle was the asylum, and I did all I could to avoid spending time there. The expeditions were my escape, and we always found new reasons to go, to justify ever more fantastic projects. The moment I stepped away from the castle, I could look forward to the fresh air of the mountains, the sea, the ice, the thrill of new horizons to explore.'

'Atlantis was one of those projects?' Jack asked.

Schoenberg paused. 'There were many schemes. You have heard of "world ice theory", *Welteislehre*, yes? We were supposed to believe that our Nordic ancestors grew strong in a world of ice and snow; ice is the cosmological heritage of Nordic man. For a time, I had to teach this nonsense at the SS ideology school at Wewelsburg.'

Costas cleared his throat. 'Did you teach them that world ice theory was promoted by the Nazis as the antithesis of the theory of relativity, which was seen as abhorrent because Einstein was Jewish?'

Schoenberg waved his hand. 'More nonsense. More fantasy.'

'The type of fantasy that helped to tip Himmler towards the Final Solution.'

Jack narrowed his eyes at Costas. '*Atlantis*. Carry on, Professor.'

Schoenberg paused. 'Atlantis was another of the schemes. Himmler was under the spell of a man named Karl Maria Wiligut, who claimed to be the last in a line of ancient sages who told of lost cities and vanished civilizations.'

Costas glanced at the notebook he had taken from his pocket. '*Wiligut*. That rings a bell. Hard name to forget. Here we are. Karl Maria Wiligut also taught that the ancestral enemies of the German people were the Jews. Founder of an anti-Semitic league. Head of the Department for Pre- and Early History within the Race and Settlement Office. Funny name for a scholarly institution, don't you think?'

Schoenberg opened his arms and sat back. 'Is this to be an interrogation?' he said, looking at Jack.

Costas stared at him, then closed his notebook and put it in his pocket. 'Do carry on, please.'

Schoenberg paused, then leaned forward again. 'In the mind of Himmler, Atlantis was the ancient foundation civilization, the original Aryan homeland. It existed in the Age of Ice, and evidence for it was to be found in Iceland, in Greenland, under Antarctica, high in the glaciers of the Alps and the Andes and the Himalayas, where people might live who were genetically untainted descendants of the original Atlanteans. But those of us who were genuine scholars knew better.

When your IMU team discovered the Neolithic citadel in the Black Sea, I felt an extraordinary vindication. If Plato's Atlantis was based on reality, we knew it could not have been in some remote location but must have been a vanished civilization of the Old World, right in the heartland of the first civilizations. The revelations of the Bronze Age, of the Minoans and Mycenaeans, of Troy, showed how much had been lost to history, and we assumed that Atlantis would be another civilization like that, waiting to be rediscovered by some latter-day Schliemann. But I also believed that a precocious early civilization would have spread its wings. My private quest was not to find Atlantis, but to find Atlantis reborn. We guessed that the most famous Bronze Age civilizations, the Egyptians, the Mesopotamians, the Minoans, might owe their extraordinary achievements to some precursor civilization, to refugees from Atlantis. But where else might the Atlanteans have gone?'

Jack leaned forward. 'Did you find clues in the Heidelberg Codex?'

Schoenberg's eyes lit up with fervour. 'When the order came from Himmler to scour the ancient sources in the search for Atlantis, Heidelberg was the first place I went. I'd been just about to start research for my doctorate at the university when I was fingered for the Ahnenerbe. My subject had been another periplus, the ancient *Periplus of Hanno*, one of the other texts bound up in *Codex Palatinus Graecus* 398 with the *Periplus of the Erythraean Sea*.'

Costas looked at Jack 'Were these original texts?'

Jack shook his head. 'Tenth-century AD copies. Until Hiebermeyer's discovery of those pottery fragments with the

Erythraean Sea text, the Heidelberg Codex represented the earliest surviving versions of the geographical works it contains. The monk who transcribed them may well have copied from exemplars dating from antiquity, though probably even those were not the originals.'

'That's the key to what I'm about to tell you,' Schoenberg said. 'Even the most careful monks could lose concentration and introduce errors, and of course they copied any existing errors in the versions they were transcribing. Sometimes if they recognized errors they tried to rectify them, yet they often failed to grasp the original meaning and in so doing made it worse. The biggest problems are with texts that have also gone through translations. With those, the more knowledgeable monks sometimes added their own comments in the margins, where they felt they might fix a questionable translation or clarify a passage. Where they include reference to other ancient sources to make their point, this can reveal the existence of other works now lost.'

'So what's your point?' Jack asked.

'Do you remember which text comes next in the Heidelberg Codex after the *Periplus Maris Erythraei*?'

Jack cast his mind back to the day he had spent with Maria and Jeremy at Heidelberg. 'It's your speciality, the *Periplus of Hanno the Carthaginian*, the extraordinary account of Hanno's voyage in the sixth century BC down the west coast of Africa. Folio pages 55v to 58v, if I remember correctly. I can vividly recall the excellent seminar you gave on it at Cambridge when we first met. The *Periplus of Hanno* really illustrates your point about transcription problems. It was originally inscribed on bronze tablets on a pillar in Carthage, and then was translated into Greek. We glanced at it when we were examining the codex but didn't have time to study it in detail.'

'Nor did I, to begin with,' Schoenberg said, beaming. 'My study of the codex for my doctoral research was interrupted when I was recruited into the Ahnenerbe. It was only when they sent me back to the library to look for clues to Atlantis that I had the chance. And even if you *had* read it, you wouldn't have seen what I saw.'

'Go on,' Jack said.

Schoenberg picked up the leather document case in front of him and opened it, taking out a brown envelope. He held it for a moment, then looked at Jack. 'You must understand me. I've kept the contents of this envelope secret since the war. In April 1945, when the Russians were closing in, I was forced into the *Volkssturm* militia for the defence of Berlin. My unit defended the western part of the Tiergarten below the Zoo flak tower. I was one of the lucky few who were captured. I say lucky now, but we didn't think so at the time. We were taken to a prisoner-of-war camp in Siberia. Most of my comrades who weren't summarily executed or worked to death died of disease or starvation. When I was finally released in 1954, I went to Germany to retrieve this case from where I had hidden it and then took advantage of the lifting of immigration restrictions on former Nazis by the Canadian government to emigrate. They needed manual labour, and for several years I worked as a lumberjack. Then I was able to resume my studies, to complete my doctorate and embark on an academic career. I married, had children and now have great-grandchildren. The past was behind me. I had no wish to reveal anything while my children were still growing up that might expose what I had been and what I had done.'

'Why now?' Jack asked.

'Because I am old, and sitting here looking over the ocean, imagining ancient explorers and seafarers, I dwell often in the past in Heidelberg, when I was so excited to be in that library. I took out this document a few days ago and smelled the old vellum of the codex. It brought it all back to me. That's when I called my old friend James Dillen. I could not die without revealing this to someone. And there is a specific reason why I wanted it to be you.'

'Let's see it,' Costas said, leaning forward on his elbows.

Schoenberg took a deep breath, then reached in and pulled out two sheets from the envelope, placing them on top of the table. The upper sheet was an A4-sized black-and-white photograph of an old manuscript. 'This is an image of folio 23v of *Codex Palatinus Graecus* 398,' he said. 'You can see that the monk wrote the main text in minuscules – that is, lower-case letters – but put marginal headings in uncials, upper-case letters. That's how we can date it: Byzantine scribes only started writing Greek in minuscules around the ninth century AD, and this codex is one of the earliest examples. I'm showing you this page as an example because you can see where he has put comments and corrections in the left-hand column. Now look at this.' He lifted the photograph, revealing an old sheet of vellum, yellowed around the edges and crinkled at the bottom. 'This is an actual page from the codex, an insert before the first page containing the text of the *Periplus of Hanno*. The earlier translators of the codex in the nineteenth century failed to mention it. It's pretty obvious why.'

'Because it's blank,' Costas said.

'So it seems. It was inserted as a blotter, to prevent poorer-quality ink from spreading on the back of the preceding sheet. When I first saw this in 1942, I remembered similar blank pages inserted for that purpose in other codices. On a whim I raised the page and shone a torch through the vellum. I could see a faint imprint in reverse of the main text on the following page, and a clearer imprint from the monk's marginal notes where that part of the page had been compressed close to the binding when the book was closed. You can't see it with the naked eye, but with the light you can make out most of the text. It matched exactly the text on the following page, a mirror image, except in one place. Some time after the blank page had been inserted, one of the marginal notes on the following page had been erased: scraped away or painted over with a solution that dissolved the ink. The note only survived in ghostly reverse on the back of the blank sheet.'

'What was the subject of the text of the *Periplus of Hanno* beside the note?' Jack asked.

'It was the first sentences of the *Periplus*, where the text describes Hanno sailing past the Pillars of Hercules with fifty large ships and thirty thousand settlers. The erased note is opposite the line where Hanno talks about cities of the "Libyo-Phoenicians". He lists city names that occur nowhere else and can't be precisely identified, though several of them probably correspond to the known Phoenician outposts of Lixus and Mogador on the Moroccan coast facing the Atlantic. There's a clue in that note to which one of those cities he's referring to.'

'I've been there,' Jack murmured. 'My undergraduate study

tour, examining evidence for Phoenician exploration along the coast of west Africa. The archaeology of the very early period is pretty elusive, difficult to pin down. Go on.'

Schoenberg picked up a Mini Maglite, held the vellum vertically and shone the light through it. Jack gasped as he saw the faint imprint of letters. Schoenberg moved the torch and shone it on one side at the bottom. Jack could clearly see letters in Greek, lower-case letters with the words separated, like modern cursive script. 'I've transcribed it,' Schoenberg murmured, 'but you should be able to make out the original Greek. It's quite clear.'

Jack stared into the halo of light coming through the vellum, then reached out and held a corner to keep it still. He realized that he was looking at the obverse side, seeing the text the correct way round, rather than the mirror imprint on the reverse. He counted twenty-one words in the note, in three lines. Costas took out his notepad and pencil, and stared. 'Holy cow,' he exclaimed. 'Do you see what I see?'

Schoenberg peered at Costas. 'Of course. Your name, Kazantzakis. You read Greek too.'

Jack stared at the writing. *That word*. His heart was pounding, but he tried to stay focused. Costas wrote it down, keeping the lower-case script of the Greek minuscules: Ἀτλαντίς. He held the notepaper up so Jack could see it. *Atlantis*. Jack's mind flashed back to five years before, to the fragment of papyrus that Maurice Hiebermeyer had found in the mummy necropolis in Egypt, the words that had set in motion their quest for the lost city. That papyrus had been an original text of the early sixth century BC, written by the Greek traveller Solon after his visit to the high priest in the Egyptian temple at Saïs, the account that led Plato almost two centuries later to write about the legend of Atlantis in the book that became the basis for all modern speculation. Jack stared at the word, trying to remain analytical. This was a marginal note written by an unknown monk in the tenth century AD. Many monks in the Byzantine world would have known of Plato, and could have read the Atlantis story in his *Critias* and *Timaeus*. He thought of other ways the monk could have known that word. 'The Greek word Atlantis, that exact spelling, first appears in the *Histories* of Herodotus in the fifth century BC. But for him it meant Atlas, and was his name for the Western Ocean, Atlantis Thalassa, the Sea of Atlas. That's the first time in history that the ocean is called the Atlantic, and the monk could simply have been using the word Atlantis in that sense.'

'That's what I thought at first,' Schoenberg said. 'But despite its appearance so early in Herodotus, the more common Greek and Roman name for the Atlantic was simply Ocean. Pliny the Elder in his *Natural History* in the first century AD calls it that, Oceanus. The ancients of course knew about the Red Sea and the Indian Ocean, the Maris Erythraei of the other periplus, but to them there was only one Ocean, the huge expanse to the west beyond the Pillars of Hercules.'

Costas had been peering closely at the vellum. Now he sat back up, clearing his throat. 'What if all the scholars got it wrong? What if Herodotus too had heard the legend of Atlantis passed down from Solon, or at least part of it? What if Atlantis Thalassa really does mean the Sea of Atlantis, not the Sea of Atlas?'

Jack stared at him. 'Because we know Atlantis was in the Black Sea. We found it.'

Costas shook his head. 'No. I don't mean the *original* Atlantis. I mean Atlantis refounded.'

'The new Atlantis,' Schoenberg said triumphantly. 'My conclusion precisely. Now you see why I was so excited.'

Jack leaned over and peered closely, letting his eyes adjust to the faint smudges left by the ink. He took the notepad from Costas and wrote down each letter of the Greek: Απο έδωο Νωέ κάι Αλκάέιος άπο Ατλάντίς έπλέυσάν τη δύση βρήκέ μίά νέά πολή Ἡεπίγράφη έίνάί στο στυλάοβάτη έχ Ρλινη. Then he sat up and read it aloud.

Schoenberg looked at him intently. 'As well as the word Atlantis, there are three proper names. The first two, Noé and Alkaios, are individuals. Alkaios was a common enough Greek name, the original name of Heracles before he became a demigod and took his mother Hera's name. When I saw that, I wasn't surprised, as the deeds of Heracles would have been in the mind of anyone thinking about those western extremities of the known world visited by Hanno. It was there that Heracles supposedly took the Golden Apples from the garden of the Hesperides, the "Ladies of the West". But it was the first of those two names, Noé, that really intrigued me. The accent shows that it should be read with the last letter emphasized, as "ah".'

'Noah,' Costas said.

Jack looked at him, stunned. Noah. *It was not possible.*

Schoenberg nodded. 'Noah of course is a name familiar from the Hebrew Old Testament, though it probably has a much older Indo-European origin.'

Costas turned to Jack. 'Do you remember five years ago at Atlantis joking that we'd also found the basis for the story of

Noah's Ark? You speculated that an organized exodus from Atlantis as the flood waters rose would have included breeding pairs of livestock, even the giant aurochs that they bred for sacrifice.'

Jack stared at the notebook. 'I don't think I was joking. This is extraordinary.' He slowly translated the first sentence: '*From here, Noah and Alkaios from Atlantis set sail to the west, to found a new city.*'

Schoenberg pointed at the vellum. 'The word you've translated as "city", *polu*, the Greek word *polis*, can mean "city-state" or "state". The word *apo*, "from", before the word Atlantis, is unambiguous, as is the word *nea*, "new", before the word for city. They were going from Atlantis, to found a new city. When I saw that in 1942, I believed that the only rational explanation was that the Atlantis myth harked back to the fall of Minoan Crete in the Aegean Sea towards the end of the Bronze Age in the second millennium BC. Geographically this note seemed to make sense, that these two men, Noah and Alkaios, were refugees sailing west from the Aegean through the Mediterranean out into the Atlantic Ocean, to seek lands for a new city. In classical antiquity that would have been a familiar concept, with many Greek cities in the western Mediterranean being founded as colonies of their mother city. But now, with your discovery of a *Neolithic* Atlantis, I revise my theory. The direction of travel remains the same, from the Mediterranean to the west, but it is vastly older than I could have imagined then, as old as the sixth millennium BC.'

'That is, if this comment isn't just a bit of fantasy made up by a medieval monk,' Costas said.

'It's unlikely that a monk would make up anything involving a Biblical name, as that might have been seen as heresy,' Schoenberg replied. 'And the next line in the note clinches it.'

Jack took a deep breath, and read what he had written on the notepad: *Alkaios returned, and set up an inscription in unknown writing on the pillar. Ex Pliny.*

'Your translation is most interesting,' Schoenberg murmured. 'I translated stulobate, stylobate, as "plaque" or "stela", a stone panel. But pillar is possible, a stone pillar.'

'I must have been thinking of the Pillars of Hercules, but actually it does make sense,' Jack replied. 'Portuguese explorers in the fifteenth century placed stone pillars, *padrões*, where they made landfall, to stake claim to new land. We know that Hanno the Carthaginian left an account of his voyage on bronze plaques attached to a pillar in Carthage, and I've always imagined that one day someone will find a pillar marking his progress down the coast of west Africa.'

'Remember what you saw three days ago at Atlantis, Jack?' Costas said.

'Three days ago?' Schoenberg exclaimed. 'You have been to Atlantis again?' He leaned forward, peering at Jack eagerly.

Jack nodded. 'You're giving us your treasure, so I'll give you ours. Absolute secrecy, yes?'

'Of course. *Of course.*'

'Costas and I were able to carry out a dive on the site under the guise of a geological assessment. The fault line's active again and we ended up diving into a live volcano.'

'A live volcano.' Schoenberg leaned back, slapping his knee. '*A live volcano.* I never heard of such a thing. Marvellous. If only I could have told this to our divers in the Ahnenerbe.

But they never had the equipment you have. I believe it was the oxygen rebreathers. They were always going too deep. We lost three of them on our expedition to Iceland. I was there, waiting for them, but they never came up.'

Jack glanced at Costas, then back at Schoenberg. 'We found an extraordinary temple with carved pillars. We're sure it dates from the earliest Neolithic, eleven thousand years ago or more. My point is, these people were perfectly capable of erecting stone pillars, and indeed had a tradition of it.'

'So if this note is based on fact, we're looking for an inscribed stone,' Costas said.

'Somewhere on the coast of west Africa,' Jack murmured.

'That narrows it down.'

Schoenberg took the sheet of vellum and held it up to the ceiling light, peering at it closely. 'There's more. Those final words, *Ex Pliny*, are a shorthand to show that the source of the story is Pliny's *Natural History*. As you can imagine, I immediately found a copy of Pliny in the Heidelberg library and went to Book 5, Chapter 1, the text that deals with west Africa and the limit of Roman knowledge. There's the usual Pliny ragbag of facts and myths, including an account of the Hercules myth and the expedition of Hanno. He mentions the Roman emperor Claudius, his war against a local ruler in Mauretania and his founding of Roman colonies at Lixus and Traducta Julia, both probably corresponding to the old Punic outposts in that list in the *Periplus of Hanno*. But there was absolutely nothing in the surviving edition of Pliny to corroborate this note. If the monk had seen a reference to Atlantis, it must have been in some lost text. It was a dead end for me, as without verification

I could take it no further. I put it away for decades. Until three years ago.'

Jack looked at Schoenberg shrewdly. 'You hoped for a lost version of Pliny's *Natural History*, containing its own marginalia.'

Schoenberg gave a slight smile, and nodded. 'One found three years ago by Jack Howard and his team in the Villa of the Papyri at Herculaneum in Italy. As I said, I've been a keen follower of your discoveries.'

'Good old Claudius,' Costas said. 'I knew you'd mentioned him for a reason.'

'Claudius had a special interest in Mauretania,' Schoenberg replied. 'Poor lame Claudius was desperate for military glory, to shore up his claim to the empire. It was the main reason he invaded Britain in AD 43. In the secret retirement you discovered he had enjoyed in Herculaneum after faking his death, he probably dwelt greatly on his place in history. In his library you found that copy of Pliny's *Natural History* with the marginal note about Claudius' meeting as a young man with Jesus of Nazareth, added to the scroll by Pliny when he appears to have spent time with his friend Claudius in those fateful final days before Vesuvius erupted. If Pliny was adding material to his text like that – told to him by Claudius – then he might also have added what Claudius knew about west Africa. Claudius had probably amassed huge amounts of information in his years working as a historian before he was reluctantly made emperor. He would have had a special interest in west Africa through his own imperial involvement in Mauretania, and particularly as the author of a history of Carthage, which would have given him considerable knowledge of Phoenician exploration along that coast. He seems to have been a magpie, much like Pliny, interested in fascinating snippets of information that others had ignored.'

'If you were interested, why wait until now to contact us?' Jack said. 'Why not three years ago, when we revealed the discovery of the library and the copy of Pliny?'

'Because I've been following progress on your website. By the beginning of last month, I knew your palaeography team in Naples had reached the end of Book 4 of Claudius' copy of the *Natural History*, so they should currently be unrolling and photographing the first paragraphs of Book 5.'

'Okay,' Jack said, looking at his watch. 'We have to meet our plane for the flight back. I'll put in a phone call to Naples. If that comment about Atlantis is in Claudius' copy, then we can surmise that it was in another copy made by Pliny in those final days, perhaps one that escaped destruction in his villa in Stabiae or that he dispatched to Rome, a copy that was seen by that tenth-century monk. Whatever the case, if our team have found the same marginal note, it would corroborate the note in the codex and take us one huge step closer on our quest.'

Schoenberg eyed Jack shrewdly. 'Where do you think it would be leading you?'

'For anyone leaving Lixus or Mogador and intending to go west, the current takes a very predictable southern and western swing from Cape Juby towards the Caribbean.'

'Can you be more precise?'

Jack pursed his lips. 'My money's on the north Caribbean, a landfall somewhere between Puerto Rico and Florida. We have another possible lead to explore, one that will become more real if that Pliny reference can be corroborated.'

'Can I help?' Schoenberg said.

'No later than tomorrow, I hope. I'll be in touch.'

'I can tell you more about the Ahnenerbe. Some of the trails we were on that really did seem to go places, and were thwarted only by the war. We could work together.'

'I'll hold you to that. Tomorrow.'

Costas got up. 'One question. Why did you remove that page from the codex? Did you want to keep this secret, for the eyes of the Ahnenerbe only? Were you planning an expedition to find that pillar?'

Schoenberg shook his head. 'It was that name, Noah. I had seen first-hand Hitler's rage against the Jews. I had been intimate with the Nazis; I had smelled the sweat on Hitler when he was excited, seen the glint in his eyes. Already there were book-burnings, the destruction of Jewish art. The *Codex Palatinus Graecus* was my passion, my life's work, and I intended to return to it after the war. I was not the only Ahnenerbe researcher sent to the Heidelberg library; others were there to keep an eye on me. Nazi Germany was a police state, and the mentality of suspicion and counter-suspicion seeped into every corner of life. The men Himmler recruited as spies were sticklers for detail, men like himself, and would leave no stone unturned if they felt they had to check up on me. I was terrified that one of them would find this page and see that word. Anything to do with Jewish history was to be expunged. When I saw that the note had been erased by some later hand from the original text, I imagined a monk doing that because he might have been alarmed that the codex contained heretical materials, something about Noah that might contradict the Bible, but that he felt the same way that

I did about the need to preserve the book. He removed the note, but didn't see the imprint on the blank insert. If Himmler's spies had followed me and seen it, there could only have been one outcome. The whole codex would have been destroyed.'

'And now the time has come to reunite the page with the codex,' Jack said.

'That is my intention. If you are successful, this apparently blank page with the word Atlantis may become the greatest single treasure of the Heidelberg library.'

Jack thought for a moment. They had got what they wanted, and there was nothing now to be lost. He needed to know for sure. 'You said you were intimate with the Nazi inner circle. Did you know Oberst Ernst Hoffman?'

Schoenberg went pale, then quickly regained his composure. 'Hoffman? I knew of him, of course. He was a Luftwaffe ace, one of Hitler's favourites. Perhaps I met him in Berlin. I don't remember.'

'You met him at Wewelsburg, to be precise. He was one of Himmler's favourites too. Himmler nurtured his interest in flying.'

Schoenberg looked discomfited. 'Perhaps. Many officers passed through the Wewelsburg indoctrination school. I can hardly be expected to remember all of them. And Himmler had plenty of favourites.'

'Indeed,' Jack said coldly. 'Actually, you knew Hoffman before that. You were students together in Heidelberg before the war.'

Schoenberg raised his hands. 'Am I being interrogated again? It was a big university. Perhaps I knew of him. But he was no scholar. He was only interested in flying.'

'You had a professor who taught you both Greek. You excelled at it and Hoffman didn't, but he and the professor became fast friends. The professor was forced into the Ahnenerbe, but hated it and let drink get the better of him, then spoke too much. He was last seen being led away screaming to Goebbels' chamber of horrors in Gestapo headquarters in Berlin. Word was he was fingered by a former student of his who coveted his senior position in the Ahnenerbe hierarchy and miraculously moved into that office the next day.'

'Who do you mean? How do you know this?'

'Because before coming here we had a very interesting visit to Wewelsburg Castle with an expert guide. Frau Heidi Hoffman, to be precise.'

Schoenberg swallowed hard, reached for his stick to get up and then sank back again into his chair. 'Frau Hoffman. Yes. She has talked to you about the Ahnenerbe?'

'She has told us a great deal.'

Schoenberg rose again slightly on his stick, and for a moment his face was contorted in contempt. 'You should be very careful what you believe. This woman is not to be trusted. Did you know she worked for the Lebensborn? She even volunteered herself to be impregnated by SS men. The Lebensborn programme was designed to create a new generation of the master race. Peasants fornicating with peasants. Do you know they even went to Poland to snatch children just because they were blond and blue-eyed? Being blond and blue-eyed is not enough to make you Aryan. They were *Poles*, for God's sake. And that woman is a whore.'

Jack nodded at Costas, then got up and followed him to the door. He stopped and looked back. 'When you scoured the ancient texts, when the Ahnenerbe went to the glaciers, to the icecaps, you weren't just looking for Atlantis, were you? There was something else. Something Reichsführer Himmler wanted. Something terrifying, from the distant past. Something that could be made into a wonder-weapon.'

Schoenberg stared at him, then narrowed his eyes. 'I am a scholar, Jack. You know that. The Reichsführer may have had other dreams, but they were not mine. These wild theories died on the funeral pyre of the Reich in 1945.'

'Thank you for telling us what you know. We'll be in touch.'

Jack led Costas through the door and closed it. They crossed the veranda and clattered down the wooden steps to the beach, then began to walk towards the jetty and the inflatable boat. The tide was coming in, pushing foaming sheets of water almost to their feet, backed by rolling Pacific breakers that made a muffled roar. It was time to get back to the aircraft before the wind and the water rose any more. Costas hurried up alongside Jack. 'That was pushing it. Asking about Frau Hoffman and Himmler.'

'I wanted him to be on edge. I want him to know that we know.'

'It was revealing that he called Himmler Reichsführer, a little respectfully I thought, after you did.'

'That was intentional on my part.'

'He was there in Iceland.'

Jack nodded. 'He was there, though I'm not convinced he knew the real purpose. Anyone Himmler let in on his scheme was probably doomed to be liquidated. I don't believe

Saumerre will have told him the truth either. My guess is that Schoenberg doesn't know a lot more than he's told us. He evidently was not one of the Ahnenerbe men who discovered the ancient site in the Caribbean, though he must have known it was an area where they'd been searching for Atlantis. Once Himmler had decided to use the site for his own purpose, those men were probably all removed from the equation early on. If Schoenberg knew the location, we wouldn't be here now, and the world would be a much more dangerous place.'

'There's a lot of contradiction in Schoenberg,' Costas said, jerking his head back towards the house. 'A scholar who tears a page out of an ancient manuscript to prevent it being destroyed by the Nazis. A senior Ahnenerbe man who was under the spell of Himmler, yet was perfectly aware that most of the stuff was nonsense and that many of his fellow Ahnenerbe men were beneath contempt. A Prussian aristocrat who is scornful of Nazi thugs, and of peasants. A family man fearful of his children finding out about his past. A racist who despises Poles and Chinese. And if we're to believe Frau Hoffman, a man capable of shopping his old professor to the Gestapo.'

'I believe Frau Hoffman.' Jack clicked on his phone, put it to his ear and made a call. He hung back for a few moments behind Costas, and then caught up. 'I was speaking to Ben. Frau Hoffman needs beefed-up protection. The first thing Schoenberg is going to do is call Saumerre and tell him we've been talking to her. We need her alive to be able to work on that antidote to the bacterium, and I'm sure Major Penn and his men will be more than happy to have some of our IMU security team along as well.'

'You buy Schoenberg's story about the manuscript, what we've just seen?'

Jack nodded. 'I've spent enough time with Maria and Jeremy looking at old vellum to know the real thing when I see it, and the imprint of the text was authentic. It's not that I'm worried about. Schoenberg was playing us. He wants us to take this to its conclusion, to use all our skills to find whatever lies at the end of this trail.'

'That word, Jack. The word we've just seen in the ancient text.'

Jack took a deep breath and stopped walking, putting his hands on his hips and staring out to sea. He turned to Costas. '*Atlantis.*'

Costas slapped him on the back. 'Pretty amazing. I thought that word was history for us, but here it is shining again like a big red neon light.'

'It's explosive,' Jack said, his voice tight with emotion. 'Absolutely explosive. If we can prove they went west, find where they went, then it looks as if we might be on the way to bending history again, as big a bend as you can imagine.'

'Noah and Alkaios, Uta-napishtim and Gilgamesh? You think these are the same two men?'

'I'm convinced of it. We already know from Katya's interpretation of those symbols on the cave wall at Atlantis that Noah was Uta-napishtim, and Enlil was Gilgamesh: the shorter names were like nicknames, the longer ones more formal shaman names. But Alkaios makes complete sense to me as another name for Enlil-Gilgamesh. Alkaios was the hero of the West, the early version of Heracles. If Enlil-Gilgamesh returned from his huge ocean voyage, leaving

Noah-Uta-napishtim in his new Atlantis, he may have acquired mythical stature among those people of the north African coast – the "Ladies of the West" as Pliny calls them, maybe at Lixus itself – who may have equated him with their ancient god Alkaios. Over time he became Heracles, and it would have been natural for Pliny to use this familiar name for a god-hero already associated with the gateway to the Western Ocean, the Pillars of Hercules.'

They reached the boat, and Costas untied the stern line and jumped in. Jack gestured at his phone again and climbed the rocky spur to get better reception. A few minutes later he pocketed the phone, and bunched his fist. 'Yes.' He clambered back down, untied the painter and hopped in beside Costas, resuming his position in the stern beside the engine. 'Two very quick phone calls clinched it.'

'Spill it.'

'The first one to Maria, who's in Naples. She saw that marginal note in Claudius' manuscript of Pliny's *Natural History* yesterday morning, but assumed it was probably a reference to the Atlantis story in Plato. She was looking at the infrared spectrographic images of the first part of Book 5 as I called her, and she was able to read out the note. It was exactly the same as on Schoenberg's sheet. *Exactly the same*. That confirms it. It wasn't made up by a medieval monk. It was copied from Pliny.'

'And?'

Jack grinned. 'The second call was to Dillen. He was back in his office in Cambridge, having closed the excavation at Troy yesterday. It was something that's been niggling me ever since we saw those Stone Age symbols at Atlantis. I knew I'd seen something like them before, and I don't mean the symbols on Palaeolithic cave paintings, but somewhere unexpected, the reason why it didn't click for me straight away. You remember I said that when I was a student I did a study tour of Phoenician sites in west Africa? When Schoenberg mentioned Lixus, I suddenly remembered. At the top of the acropolis I found a large hole, probably where masonry had been dug out centuries ago from the Roman site for reuse. At the bottom was a much older stone, worn, apparently toppled sideways, with barely discernible symbols on it that I assumed were early Phoenician. I asked Dillen to dig out my study tour report from his shelves and take a look at my photograph. He said there were only three very worn symbols visible, but that they looked like a crescent, a V and three slashes. Those were the first three symbols from the Atlantis cave that Katya interpreted as the name Gilgamesh.'

Costas looked incredulous. 'The pillar mentioned by Pliny? You mean you found it more than twenty-five years ago?'

Jack grinned again. 'Sometimes things stare you in the face for a long time. You just have to know what you're looking at.'

'That makes it real for me,' Costas said. 'An ancient exodus west across the Atlantic from Lixus following the current would very probably land you in the Caribbean.'

Jack nodded. 'When we were on *Seaquest II* in the Black Sea after our dive into the volcano, do you remember I brought up Thor Heyerdahl and his Ra expeditions? I guessed that an exodus west from Atlantis and the Mediterranean would have gone south with the current towards Cape Juby just as Heyerdahl did, and then west across the open ocean. I knew after talking to Frau Hoffman that Himmler's men must have chanced on the site of the Atlantean landfall in the Caribbean, and that was where he must have decided to establish his secret hideaway. So I phoned Rebecca's foster-father Mikhail and asked him to look into any evidence for unusual German activity in the Caribbean before the war, as well as any U-boat sightings in May and June 1945. I told him to liaise with Lanowski to correlate anything he found with geological evidence for a likely underwater site. Mikhail's a military historian, and I knew from spending time with him last year that he'd recently written a book on the strategic significance of the Caribbean at the outset of the Cold War. A moment ago, when I spoke to Ben, he was on Mikhail's farm in the Adirondack Mountains in upstate New York, where he took Rebecca this morning for safety. Ben passed the phone to Mikhail, who'd just received a package of material from the US National Archives. I could sense his excitement. He thinks it's exactly what we want.'

'Any details?'

'It involves one of the last combat missions against the Nazis. Three weeks *after* the German surrender. It sounds like something out of the annals of the Bermuda Triangle, but it's much more real and much more horrifying than that. Mikhail's still working through the file, but he's going to tell me the full story when I get there.'

'We're going to the Adirondacks?'

'*I'm* going to the Adirondacks.' Jack picked up the phone again, then paused. 'The Embraer's all fuelled up at Tofino and it's going to fly us to Syracuse in upstate New York, where I'm going to rent a car and drive into the mountains. I should arrive at Mikhail's place before dawn tomorrow morning. You're going on from Syracuse to *Seaquest II* off Bermuda. I need you in the operations room to kick up a brainstorm with your new best buddy Lanowski. As soon as we can pinpoint a location for the Nazi hideaway in the Caribbean, we need everything we can get on the geology and oceanography, and the predicted weather conditions over the next forty-eight hours. That's the time frame we're looking at. The Embraer's going to return from Bermuda to Syracuse and I'll aim to join you with Rebecca on *Seaquest II* tomorrow evening, after Mikhail's told me what he's found out. Then all eyes south to the Caribbean.'

Costas jerked his head back to the bungalow above the beach. They could just make out Schoenberg's straw hat in the window, and a cell phone clamped to his ear. 'You gave that one away. You told him that's where we were heading.'

'We're all playing each other. Saumerre will be playing Schoenberg just as Himmler once played his Ahnenerbe cronies, convincing them that the archaeology was the main prize, letting only a chosen few know his true intent and then disposing of them when they'd served their purpose. Schoenberg's telling him that as soon as I've followed the lead I told him about, I'll get back to him to reveal where we're heading. He believes I'll do that because he offered me more information about the Ahnenerbe, about other treasures waiting to be discovered. Part of Schoenberg, the scholar and adventurer, just won't believe I'd pass up on a chance like that, that somehow he and I will go off together on fantastic voyages of discovery. Another part of him, the Nazi, believes that what he revealed to us in that rant about Frau Hoffman will come as a terrible shock and persuade us that everything she said about Himmler and his plan was a pack of lies. Schoenberg would like to think that we're after the archaeology, not the deadly weapon that Saumerre wants. Remember what we saw at Wewelsburg Castle. That place poisoned everyone who came in contact with it, whether real scholars like Schoenberg or the academic failures and thugs who formed the core of the Ahnenerbe, the spies and sycophants whom Schoenberg despised. For Schoenberg, sitting there overlooking the sea dreaming of unresolved quests, the fantasy is reborn in his mind after all these decades, something that we've used to get information out of him, just as Saumerre has too.'

'So you really intend to tell him the probable location?'

'As soon as Mikhail tells me, and just before I board the plane to Bermuda. That way I'm in control. I want to push this to a confrontation. Saumerre may become impatient and events may move faster than we predicted. Ben's convinced that Shang Yong's hitmen will know about the farm and will have assumed that's where Ben went with Rebecca when she left school this morning in Manhattan, where they've been shadowing her.'

Costas looked at his watch. 'Better get going. Our pilot will be waiting.'

Jack pulled the starter cord and the Mariner coughed to life. He stared for a moment back at the figure in the bungalow, now with the phone down, watching them. 'Part of me would still like to think that he's just another victim of that war.'

Costas shook his head. 'Remember what you told me when we went to see him. What it was really all about, the

Ahnenerbe. Racist theory that resulted in the corpses and the living dead in the concentration camps, and on those gurneys in that bunker. Those were the victims.'

Jack nodded. He gunned the engine, driving the boat out into the channel, then throttled back for a moment and gave Costas a steely look. 'Forty-eight hours to endgame.'

'Roger that.'

19

Above the Bahamas, 3 June 1945

Squadron Leader Peter White gripped the control wheel of the B-24 Liberator and straightened his back, straining against the harness and feeling the blood return to places in his legs that had been pressed against the unfamiliar seat for more than three hours now. It was his first long-haul flight in the Liberator, and he was not yet attuned to the nuances and idiosyncrasies that made an aircraft seem like an extension of the pilot's being. For more than eighteen months before the Nazi surrender he had flown a Lancaster bomber, the four-engine warhorse of the British air offensive over occupied Europe. The Lancaster was an instrument of death and destruction, but he had grown to love his aircraft, to trust in its ability to return him again and again through the flak and the night fighters while other bombers were falling out of the sky around him. His crew believed that it was he who had the luck, he who would see them through when two thirds of their fellow-crews did not make it. They called him Uncle, because he was an old man of twenty-nine; he knew they revered him. Their faith was so strong that he had volunteered for another tour to skipper the men who were only partway through theirs. But for him there was nobody to elevate to god-like status, nothing except the machine. The relationship of a bomber pilot to his aircraft was impossible to explain to anyone who had not endured night after night flying to the seat of Satan himself, to the place where the simmering evil below seemed only to be stoked by the rain of bombs, where airmen who were about to die saw hell not as a nightmarish final vision but as the reality below them as they plummeted towards the raging firestorms they themselves had helped to create.

White leaned forward to peer over the instrument panel at the shimmering expanse of the Caribbean Sea some three thousand feet below. He had loved his Lancaster, but he had not yet learned to love the Liberator. It was not just the poor forward visibility from the flight deck that was the problem. When he had arrived at the Operational Conversion Unit in the Bahamas two weeks ago, his instructor had called the Liberator a cantankerous beast, lumbering and draughty, heavy on the controls. White had learned the ropes quickly enough doing circuits around the base at Nassau, but this flight was his first experience of wrestling with the controls over a long mission. The aircraft was a bugger to trim, and he was constantly having to horse it around to keep it on a straight line. And the din when he lifted his earphones was indescribable. The Liberator was fat-bellied by comparison with the Lancaster and the B-17 Flying Fortress, and the open ports for the waist-guns meant that the fuselage was like a musical soundbox that magnified the noise of the engines and the propellers and the slipstream as it roared by, reverberating through the aircraft. He was glad they were flying at low level and not at ten thousand feet or more as they had done over Europe, where the cold in the B-24 would have been horrendous. But as each hour had passed this morning, he had grudgingly begun to see the sense of her. She was like a charging bull, bellowing and roaring through the sky, reeking and pawing the air. He realized it was the first time he had thought of the aircraft as *she*. That was always a good sign. And he could see why they had been made to fly the Liberator before converting to the upgraded version, the B-32 Defender, the purpose of their flight scheduled for tomorrow across the United States to the US base on the island of Guam in the Pacific. The B-32 was by all accounts a thing of luxury, with a pressurized cabin. But by training on the B-24, they would never forget the beast within, one they would soon be riding into the whirlwind of another war.

'Skipper, we're two minutes from a course change.' A clipboard with a nautical chart appeared from behind, and White took it from the navigator, Flight Lieutenant Alan Cook, an Australian, who crouched down beside him and pointed at the ruled lines in red pencil across the map. 'We're just coming up to the northern tip of the island of San Salvador,' Cook said. 'From there we turn to compass bearing thirty-five degrees and drop to five hundred feet above sea level to begin our run in. At a speed of two hundred and twenty knots, dead reckoning puts us over our target in just under fifteen minutes.'

White stared at the clipboard, reminding himself of the features he had memorized during the mission briefing at Nassau, then handed it back. He increased the volume of the intercom microphone to try to exclude as much of the din as possible. 'Bomb-aimer, did you hear that?'

'Righto, Skip,' a New Zealand drawl responded. 'Eyes peeled ahead.'

White glanced at the co-pilot, who had been looking at him expectantly, and nodded at him. 'Altering course now.' He turned the wheel smoothly, pushing the control column forward and pressing the left rudder pedal. As the aircraft banked to port, he looked out and saw the northern tip of the island, and ahead of that the turquoise waters of the reefs that covered the outer banks of the Bahamas. He checked the mixture controls for each of the four engines to make sure they were on auto-rich, then levelled out at a compass bearing of thirty-five degress and pitched the plane forward into a shallow dive. He pulled the throttle levers back to reduce the airspeed, then let go of the levers and blew on his nose to equalize the pressure in his ears as they dropped in altitude. At eight hundred feet he began to level off, edging the throttle levers forward until the airspeed stabilized at two hundred and thirty knots at an altitude of five hundred feet. He trimmed the aircraft until she was slightly nose-heavy, then scanned the instruments: oil pressure, fuel pressure, oil temperature, cylinder head temperature, all good. He glanced again at the co-pilot. 'Right. I'm taking a breather. She's yours for five minutes.'

Flight Lieutenant Bill Parker nodded. 'Taking over the controls now.'

White slowly let his feet up from the pedals, feeling the boards stay in place where the co-pilot had his own pedals in position, and then let go of the control column. He shifted his legs around, getting the circulation going again, and stretched his arms as far as they could go against the glass panes of the cockpit above him. He breathed in deeply a few times. He desperately needed a cigarette. Smoking was not allowed in RAF bombers, and the Liberator in particular always smelled strongly of fumes; there were horror stories of US crews lighting up and their B-24s igniting in a fireball. The craving usually kicked in about twenty minutes into an operation, and was why he had never taken the Benzedrine tablet that was given to them with their last meal before a sortie over Europe; the craving kept him alert until they were over enemy territory and the adrenalin and fear took over.

There was no fear now, but he was still on edge. It seemed odd, five weeks after the death of Hitler, being in an aircraft that was all bombed up on its final run in to a target, albeit a decommissioned minesweeper that had been anchored for depth-charge and strafing practice off the north coast of the Bahamas. For him, the end of the war had been a disconcerting experience altogether, nothing like his father's memory of the moment of the 1918 Armistice, that instant when the guns stopped firing and there was a sudden shocking end to it all. They had flown their last bombing operation six weeks earlier, in April, as the lead pathfinder aircraft in a five-hundred-bomber raid destined for Bremen that had been diverted to destroy an area of forest infiltrated by remnant German troops near the concentration camp of Bergen-Belsen. Their final op two days after that had been dropping relief supplies to a medical unit trying to help survivors of the camp. It should have felt good, a mission bringing succour rather than destruction, but it had not. Earlier in the war, White had stayed with his sister at Stechford in Birmingham during a devastating German raid. The experience had steeled him, had taught him about total war. It meant he knew exactly the effect of the bombs that he rained down night after night on the cities of Germany. He had become an instrument of destruction, the reason why the humanitarian mission was so jarring. And seeing the smouldering fires of the concentration camp had shown him what they had failed to prevent in six long years of war, an obscenity that could only haunt those whose bombs could have fallen years before on the camps and the railheads and perhaps thwarted the worst crime in history.

At the back of every serviceman's mind in Europe that summer had been the continuing war against Japan, and it had come as a relief when his crew and three others from his pathfinder group were selected for secret operations in the Pacific. That final op flying relief supplies had filled him with a terrible apprehension about his life after the war, a future he had never allowed himself to contemplate; even the few snatched days of leave with his wife and child in their little cottage had been about the present, not the future, and the sheer happiness he had experienced then had been contingent on the war itself protecting him from reflecting on what he had become and what he had done.

On the night of VE Day, a senior US Air Force intelligence officer had arrived at their base in Lincolnshire and shown them the latest newsreels from the Far East. They had seen footage of the jungle war being fought by the British and Indian armies in Burma and the Australians in New Guinea, and the horrendous island battles of the Americans leading up to the assault of Okinawa. They had seen kamikaze attacks on US and British ships in the Pacific. The Germans had fought with savage professionalism, but not like that. The officer had warned that as the Allies reached the Japanese mainland it would become a war of attrition. He said the pathfinder crews had been chosen for their expertise at precision targeting, but also because they had all dropped the 'Tallboy' and 'Grand Slam' bombs, the huge 12,000- and 22,000-pound bombs that had been used to destroy the U-boat pens and fortified sites across Germany. He told them that the US had developed a new breed of battlefield weapon, bombs to be dropped behind the front line that could vaporize all life within a half-mile radius, far more powerful even than the Grand Slam. That was to be their new role, killing soldiers rather than civilians, destroying command and supply lines rather than cities. They and their US Air Force counterparts would be in action with the new battlefield bombs by the end of August, and would help to end the war against Japan before it sapped the lives of troops from Europe who were already being remustered to fight in the Far East.

White remembered the last time they had dropped a Tallboy, looking down at the inferno, watching the flash of the explosion and the ripple of the shock wave as it pulsed out through the flames. It had been the night of their last raid against Berlin, before they had left it to the Russians to finish the job. That was another reason why VE Day seemed like a hollow victory. They all knew that Heinrich Himmler had tried to negotiate with the Americans for the remnant Wehrmacht and SS to join the Western Allies against the Russians. There was the prospect of a war ahead that would make the final chapter of the struggle against Japan seem nothing more than a mopping-up operation. At Bomber Command HQ he had seen strategic planning maps drawn up with half the world in red, as if a tide of blood were seeping into the nooks and crannies of the borders of Europe and Asia, ready to drip through and burst the barriers. Already the death of Hitler seemed like a historical sideshow, a footnote on a stage that had expanded to encompass the entire world, where the forces of war set in motion by the last six years had taken on a momentum of their own, creating the prospect and the weapons of true apocalypse.

He banished the thought from his mind and settled back into his seat, concentrating on alleviating the discomfort of the next four hours as they hit their target and then flew back to Nassau. He looked at his coffee flask, and then at the piss tube beside his seat, remembering the last time he had used it and the howls of outrage from the waist gunner, who had been sunning himself in the open gunport and received a faceful in the slipstream. It was another small design glitch of the Liberator. He was pleased to have his old crew still with him, all except the tail gunner, who had been demobbed on compassionate grounds after his wife had been killed in one of the final V-2 rocket attacks on London. The US intelligence officer had said that the crew were to stay together for conversion training to the B-24 so that they would be most effective together in the new aircraft. The only problem was that the Lancaster had a crew of seven and the Liberator ten, so taking into account the absent rear gunner, there were four new faces: the co-pilot, the two waist gunners and the rear gunner, all of them experienced pathfinder crew. He had warmed to the rear gunner, Flight Sergeant Brown, when they had first met on the tarmac in Nassau and he had seen the ribbon and rosette of the Distinguished Flying Medal and bar above the silver pathfinder badge on Brown's tunic. He was a cheeky chap, an English emigrant to Canada who had joined the RCAF three years ago, and the only one of them who had flown in Liberators before, in 1943, during a tour with Coastal Command. It was always good to have a cheerful rear gunner, given his chances of survival if the plane went down. The old Liberator hands called the pilot's seat a coffin, from the shape of its armour-plated sides and back, leaving only the legs unprotected from below; but if anyone was in a coffin it was the rear gunner. The British Boulton Paul turret had no opening to allow him to bail out, and his only chance was to disengage himself from his harness and crawl back through the fuselage, a difficult enough task even while the plane was on the ground. The fire from a burning engine could wrap around the fuselage and cook the rear gunner alive. White had watched many times on raids over Europe as turrets had broken free from disintegrating bombers and fallen ten thousand feet or more, the gunners trapped inside. He had sworn that if he were ever to order his crew to bail out, he would remain on board and go down with the aircraft if he were unable to get the rear gunner out. It was a small pact with fate, and it meant that he always felt a particular affinity with the rear gunner. He clipped on his mask and spoke through the intercom. 'How's Tail-end Charlie?'

The intercom crackled through his ear muffs. 'That's Charles to you, skipper.'

White grinned to himself. 'Seen anything interesting?'

'Only those blue holes in the reef, hundreds of them.'

'Anyone know anything about them?' White asked.

'Some of them are incredibly deep,' Brown replied. 'I had a week at Nassau before you lot arrived, and the station commander discovered I was a keen fisherman. He flew me out in a Catalina to a huge blue hole on Andros Island, where we landed on the sea and hauled in enough fish for all the messes on the base that night. The local Bahamians are terrified of the blue holes. They say fishermen and children who go too near them are sucked in. They think they contain monsters, and they say that seeing a whirlpool is a sign of a hurricane on the way. The station commander was some kind of geologist in Civvy Street and thinks it might be based on truth: a kind of vortex effect in the water when the tide comes in, maybe exacerbated by a rising onshore wind that makes the swell build up the water over a hole. When we dropped in altitude a few moments ago, I saw a hole with a white swirl in the centre, and I think that's what he was on about.'

'All right,' White said. 'But if it turns out to be a monster, let us know. A little excitement wouldn't go amiss.' He leaned left and stared at the sea behind the aircraft, searching for the hole Brown had spotted but seeing only a turquoise bank of reefs extending into the blue depths, the beginning of the open Atlantic to the north of the Bahamas. He remembered that last sortie over Berlin, looking down and seeing a different kind of vortex. Instead of dropping marker flares with the other pathfinders, they had dropped 'window', thousands of thin aluminium strips that spoofed the German radar. As the huge searchlights played across the night sky, he had watched the silver strips swirling round and round, not falling but rising up around them, as if they were in the eye of a hurricane. A fully laden Lancaster ahead of them had exploded, and they had dropped hundreds of feet into the vacuum created by the fireball, a terrifying freefall through the swirling vortex of silver. They had been directly over one of the huge flak towers, a fortress like a medieval castle next to the site of the Berlin Zoo. The debriefing officer told him that the tower housed tens of thousands of Berliners seeking refuge from the bombing and the coming Russian onslaught. Perhaps what he had seen was the rising heat of confined humanity escaping upwards from the roof of the tower. It was the one image from those nights over Berlin that was seared on his retinas, and he saw it when he closed his eyes now. It had been like medieval paintings he had seen of the *axis mundi*, a link between heaven and earth and the underworld, a vortex that seemed not like an escape route for souls to heaven but a swirling funnel that had nearly sucked him down to hell.

He felt a nudge on his arm, and turned to see the co-pilot looking at him. 'Five minutes are up, sir. Do you want me to take her in for the attack?'

White straightened in his seat, then put his feet back on his pedals and his hands on the control wheel. He suddenly felt bone tired, and shook himself, scanning the instrument panel. 'I have to log this one as pilot, to keep our US Air Force handlers happy that we're not just treating this as some kind of lark.'

'Righto, skipper. On your mark.'

'She's mine.' White took over, immediately feeling the aircraft bucking against him, giving leeway to the controls until he could feel his way into the soul of the beast. He glanced right and saw Parker's hand reach up to the fast-feathering switches above the windscreen, waiting to see that the pilot was in control of the aircraft before making any adjustments to the propellers. The trim came out perfectly this time, slightly nose-heavy, but the plane yawed a few degrees to starboard and Parker pushed up the switches to feather the propellers on the port side. 'A north-easterly wind is picking up,' he said to White. 'We're low enough now to be affected by the surface wind, and you can see it ruffling the sea.' The aircraft came back to level, and the compass wobbled around the thirty-degree mark. White played with the throttles, listening above the din for the harmonious sound of all four engines in sync, while Parker tapped the propeller pitch levers to maintain the same rpm. White glanced at him. *He was good*. He knew Parker had done nearly two tours as flight engineer on a Lancaster, and had that special knack of reading a pilot and his relationship with his aircraft. He felt a surge of confidence. Whatever lay ahead of them, in the Pacific and beyond, he knew he could meld the new men into his crew. Their survival was what counted, in this confined, ear-splitting beast where they lived only in the present, where all that mattered was the sheer fact of being alive.

The navigator tapped him on the shoulder. 'Five minutes to target, skipper.'

'Right. Dropping to two hundred feet.'

He felt his pulse quicken. He nosed the aircraft down,

coming level again a minute later. It was rougher now, more turbulent over the denser air, like driving across cobbles, as if they were riding the waves themselves. He felt the tail shake that could indicate imminent stall, but he knew it was just buffeting as the slipstream at low altitude corkscrewed around the tail planes. Most of the crew had no proper seats or safety harnesses, another of the less endearing features of the Liberator. A sudden impact could be fatal to any of them. He peered out of the port window at the whitecaps, now alarmingly close, and then glanced up at the long narrow wing. That was the one thing about the Liberator that really frightened him. They were sound, reliable machines, with greater range than the Lancaster or Flying Fortress, and had been quickly adopted by RAF Coastal Command as long-range anti-submarine planes. But they were not amphibious like the other mainstays of Coastal Command, the Catalina and the Sunderland, and they had very poor ditching characteristics: high wings, a big tub belly, and a nose that collapsed on impact if the pilot failed to trim the aircraft so that the tail was down, not always possible in the circumstances of an emergency landing. He gripped the control wheel hard. They could not ditch, and at this altitude they could not bail out. He focused hard, reminding himself. *This was a training mission. Nobody was shooting at them. They would be all right.*

The bomb-aimer's voice crackled on the intercom. 'Should I open bomb-bay doors, skip?'

'Roger that. Open bomb-bay doors.' He heard the hydraulics as the doors swung open, then felt more buffeting as the open doors increased the drag. The din inside the fuselage was even more pulverizing. They were carrying three two-thousand-pound depth charges, shaped like oil drums. The charges were normally used against deeply submerged submarines, but these ones were pressure-fused to blow at a depth of only thirty feet and represented a revolution in thinking about anti-ship warfare. The bombs and torpedoes that had been the standard anti-ship weapons of the war impacted against the armour-plated sides and superstructure of ships, whereas depth charges might be dropped to explode beneath the vulnerable lower hull. The bomb-aimer had trained with 617 Squadron, using the bouncing bombs that had been deployed on the famous dambuster raid, and they were going to try the same technique against the target, with the charges spinning anticlockwise so that when they hit the side of the hull, the traction of the spin would carry them under the keel to explode. That was the theory, anyway. It had never been tried before on a ship. Privately White thought that it was a game devised to keep an experienced crew amused before they went on to the real business in the Pacific in the days to come.

Parker reached over to the top of the instrument panel between them and tapped the compass housing. 'The gyro's gone on the blink.'

White remembered what the briefing officer had told them, and then tapped the housing himself. 'It must be the magnetic disturbance near the fault line north of San Salvador that they talked about. At least it shows we're in the right place.' He squinted at the sun, noting its position between the metal frames of the cockpit window. 'We're going to have to fly by dead reckoning. Everyone, eyes peeled for the target now. It should be coming up in a few minutes. Bomb-aimer, take position. Gunners, cock weapons. After we've dropped our charges, I'm going to come round so you can have some target practice on whatever's left of that minesweeper.'

'Have some fun, you mean, sir,' Brown's voice crackled in.

'Whatever you say, Charles.' White smiled wryly to himself, then took a deep breath. Without the compass, he felt like an ancient mariner on an unknown ocean, as if the beast he was riding were on some unseen current in the air that would take them inexorably to their destination. Instinctively he looked for the only talisman he had ever carried, a little metal butterfly pendant he had been given by his eight-year-old daughter on leave after his first tour. He had told her how on a daylight raid his aircraft had risen above the clouds into the brilliant sunshine, and how the clouds had seemed as white as angels' wings, as if he were being conveyed directly to heaven without death. What he did not tell her was how the clouds were peppered with the burst of flak, how other aircraft were falling burning all round him, and how the Tallboys they dropped through the orange and red skymarkers to the unseen target below had shaken and rippled those white clouds with their blast, sending up black clouds that curled and billowed through the white as if the fires of hell had broken through to heaven itself. His wife had said they would pray every night for those angels to cleave a path ahead of him through the bullets and the shrapnel so that he would return safely to them. After that last mission, he had gone back to his aircraft to retrieve the butterfly, but on the way he had seen the new pilot, a fresh-faced boy who could not have been more than nineteen, who would be flying into the reach of death even in those final days and would need all the luck he could get. As he passed him, the boy had smiled, saying nothing but waving him a breezy salute, and in that moment, White felt as if he had transferred all that was within him to the future. He had left the butterfly pinned to the instrument panel of his Lancaster, the only place that seemed right for it. Now he looked below the gyro compass to where he was so used to seeing it, and remembered his final night of leave two weeks ago, when he had left his wife and daughter asleep in their cottage before the long flight to Nassau. The butterfly had kept him safe. But soon he would need a new talisman, for a new war.

Another voice crackled on the intercom. It was the forward gunner, crouched behind the twin fifty-calibre Browning machine guns in the nose turret above the bomb-aimer. 'Skipper, you're not going to like this. There's a submarine dead ahead, just surfaced. It's about a mile away, just before that lighter patch of sea that must be the edge of the reef. It seems to be heading west, directly into the reef. There must be a passage through.'

White groaned. *Christ*. There were supposed to be no vessels in the live-fire zone. The last thing they wanted was a sub commander reporting them for rattling his boat. He straightened up for a better view over the protuberant nose turret, and then pressed the rudder pedal so that the aircraft yawed slightly to port. He squinted hard at the horizon, seeing only the whitecaps, remembering the forward gunner's exceptional eyesight. Then he saw the sub, about five degrees to starboard, a dark sliver on the water below the horizon. Their target vessel was still not visible, presumably just out of sight beyond. *What was a sub doing here?* The zone designation had only been put in place two weeks ago, and it was just possible that a sub returning from a long patrol might have failed to pick up the warning. But it didn't make sense. The war in the Atlantic had been over for weeks, and there had been no need for subs to remain submerged and out of radio contact. He would be over it in less than a minute. He had to make a snap decision. They would abort until the sub was well away, and come round again. Rather than let the sub commander report him first, he would radio the sighting back to Nassau now. He pressed the intercom against his face to try to exclude the throbbing of the engines. 'Can anyone make out the type?'

Parker loosened his harness and raised himself up from the co-pilot's seat, gazing through a pair of binoculars. 'Well, it's not a Type VII U-boat. The conning tower's too big.'

'We're not going to be seeing U-boats, Bill. The war's over,' White said.

'Sorry, skip. I did my first ops in Coastal Command; that's what the word submarine means to me. I think this one must be American.'

'All right. Navigator and wireless operator, I want a position fix and I want it radioed through to Nassau now. We'll send a follow-up message when we see the sub's recognition code as we fly over it. There'll be hell to pay, but we'll let the station commander sort that out with the US Navy.'

The wireless operator came on. 'I can't get through, sir. Electromagnetic interference. Must be the same problem that's affecting the compass.'

White groaned again. 'All right. Navigator, what's your estimate for the position of the sub?'

The navigator rattled off the co-ordinates, and White repeated them under his breath, keeping them running through his head. He could see the conning tower of the submarine clearly now, and the wake where it had surfaced from deep water and was now slowing over a shallow section of reef.

'It's one of those blue holes, skipper,' the forward gunner said.

'What do you mean?'

'I mean the sub's heading towards one of those blue holes in the reef, about two subs' lengths ahead of it. You can see the dark patch in the water now. It's a really big one, about twice the distance across of the sub.'

White stared at the scene. *What the hell was going on?*

The co-pilot still had his binoculars trained ahead. 'There's something not right here. That's *not* an American sub. My last bombing op was over the U-boat pens at Valentin on the Baltic, so I think I know what I'm looking at. Now that I can see the conning tower, there's no question about it. That's a German Type XXI U-boat.'

A U-boat. White's mind raced. He knew that much of the surviving U-boat fleet had been destroyed in the bombing, or scuttled by their crews after the surrender. But the Type XXI was more advanced than any Allied submarine, and there would have been a scramble by the Allies to capture intact vessels. It could be one of those, recommissioned as an American or British boat. *If only they could make radio contact.* But there were other possibilities. There had been rumours of U-boats in the final days of the war sneaking away from Baltic and Norwegian ports carrying high-ranking Nazis and their loot to secret destinations in Latin America. Or this could be a maverick captain, a fanatical Nazi who had refused to accept the surrender and was still fighting the war on his own terms. White felt a chill down his spine. It was too late to pull away, to keep out of range. They were committed now.

'Sir!' the forward gunner yelled. 'They're manning guns!'

White froze. He stared at the sub, now less than a thousand metres ahead. He tried to remember the Type XXI specs. There would be two turrets on the conning tower with twin 2cm flak guns. This sub also had a forward deck mounting, probably the standard 10.5cm gun. A single hit from that could blow the Liberator apart. And there would be machine guns, MG-42s, mounted on the conning tower railing. He squinted against the sun. The barrels of the deck gun and the turrets on the conning tower should have been clearly visible, but were not. In an instant he realized why. *They were aimed directly at them*. He saw flashes like a Morse code signalling lamp, and then red streaks of tracer that zipped past the cockpit.

'Sir! They're shooting!'

They would be over the sub in seconds. He could take evasive action, try to corkscrew away, or he could go in for the attack.

'Open fire!' he yelled. 'Bomb-aimer, on my mark!'

'Drop to one hundred and fifty feet!' the bomb-aimer yelled.

The twin Brownings in the nose turret opened up in a deafening cacophony as the plane plummeted, sending tracer rounds hosing towards the submarine in a great undulating wave. The plane lurched sideways, and he heard the ripping and drumming sounds of bullets from the submarine impacting somewhere on the port wing. He fought to bring the aircraft back to level, using the forward gunner's tracer rounds like guiding lights to keep the plane on target. He saw where the Brownings had found their mark, splattering against the hull casing of the submarine and then into figures around the deck gun, who crumpled and were blown backwards into the sea. *Three hundred yards now*.

'Steady, skip, steady,' the bomb-aimer said. 'Bombs gone!'

The plane lurched upwards three times as the depth charges dropped at one-second intervals, spinning away to hit the sea and bounce towards the submarine. White wrestled to maintain pitch as the centre of gravity in the aircraft went haywire. Seconds later they were over the submarine, and the tail gunner opened up with his quadruple Brownings. White struggled to keep the aircraft from pitching and yawing, regaining the nose-heavy pitch but failing to stop the sideways slippage. *Something was badly wrong*. Then he remembered the ripping sounds from the wing. He glanced to port, and at that moment a succession of three enormous concussions pulsed through the aircraft, forcing him to look back to the controls. 'Bull's-eye, skipper!' the rear gunner yelled. 'She's still firing her deck gun, but the third charge blew off the bow and she's going down into that blue hole. I could swear she fired a torpedo. The other two charges detonated against the side of the hole, and it's collapsing around the sub.'

White barely registered what he had heard. With the Brownings silent, he could hear the engines properly now, a discordant vibration that throbbed and grated in his ears, echoing off the water. He looked to confirm what he had seen a moment ago. The port wing beyond the outer engine was shredded and the propeller was a mess, windmilling and breaking up. The engine was on fire. He knew what that terrible noise was. Other pilots who had survived bailing out from a stricken bomber had tried to describe it to him.

It was the aircraft's death rattle.

He quickly shut down the engine and pressed the fire extinguisher, but it was still burning. He gunned the inner port engine to compensate and banked the aircraft with the dead engine high, but the plane began to slew round. The sea was terrifyingly close now, the whitecaps less than a hundred feet below. They were losing altitude, and there was nothing he could do about it. He dared not open the throttles of the other engines to try to climb, as that would only increase the yaw and they would end up cartwheeling into the sea. He had no choice but to ditch. He switched off the turbo superchargers and throttled down the other three engines. He looked at the airspeed. A hundred and thirty knots. That much was good: safe landing speed. At the last moment he would heave on the control column to pull the front of the aircraft upwards, trimming it backwards to avoid the fragile nose and cockpit impacting with the sea and disintegrating.

'The port wing fuel tank is on fire!' It was the rear gunner, screaming. White watched a large round from the submarine's deck gun fly by, nearly spent at this range and clearly visible. Then he turned and saw the huge eruption of black smoke and flame now spewing out of the port outer engine cowling. With sickening certainty he knew that it must be licking round the rear fuselage, engulfing the tail. He remembered his vow to do everything he could to save the rear gunner. If he pitched the plane backwards into the sea, he might douse the turret in time. *There was still a chance.* He needed as much weight as possible aft. 'Prepare for ditching!' he yelled. 'Everyone clear the nose, move aft!' He remembered what the training officer at Nassau had told him about ditching in the sea, to repeat the co-ordinates on the intercom so that crew who survived could use the radio in the life rafts to relay their position. He switched the intercom to emergency call. He had been repeating the numbers under his breath since the navigator had told him, and now he did so loudly, insistently, over and over again: *242446 north, 742799 west. 242446 north, 742799 west.*

Suddenly he felt a violent hammer blow, saw a red flash and then heard nothing at all, just a ringing in his ears. He looked to the right. The co-pilot was still strapped in his seat, but there was a mangled mess where his head and upper body had been. A gaping hole in the side of the cockpit extended below. White looked down, only able to move in slow motion, as if time itself had slowed down. The waves flashed by beneath the co-pilot's feet. He reached out his hand slowly to touch the flecks of foam, to feel the warmth of the sea. He would go swimming when they got back, would strip off his battledress and life jacket and swim down, far into the depths, exuberant at having survived. He knew now he could let go, at last. *The war was over.*

He stared down in front of his own seat, and saw his legs hanging over the open hole, ragged bloody stumps with shattered white bone sticking out. He pursed his lips. It was another design glitch of the Liberator. It needed armour plating under the pedals. He would talk to them about that too when he got back.

He felt himself falling forward. The plane was pitching

down. He would need to do something about that, pretty damn soon. His head felt terribly heavy now, but he looked up and saw the place below the compass where he had kept the little metal butterfly in his Lancaster. He saw the butterfly again, and he smiled. His angels would look after him. He would be safe.

Then blackness.

20

The Adirondack Mountains, New York State, present day

Jack switched the headlamps of the rented SUV to high beam as he turned off the paved road into the gravel lane that led to the farm. He had driven out of Syracuse airport in upstate New York a little over two hours before, having flown there overnight from Vancouver with Costas in the IMU Embraer. The aircraft had gone on from Syracuse to Bermuda to take Costas to *Seaquest II*, which had made maximum speed from the Mediterranean and was approaching the island ready to sail south towards the Caribbean. It was scheduled to return to Syracuse for Jack later that day, and meanwhile all of Jack's attention was on the text message Mikhail had sent him the evening before about his research into U-boat sightings in the Caribbean in the weeks following the Nazi surrender in

May 1945. Everything they had found out so far, from Frau Hoffman, from the Ahnenerbe man Schoenberg in British Columbia, had pointed them to the Caribbean, to a place where Himmler's men had apparently built a secret installation at the site of an extraordinary landfall dating to more than seven thousand years before. But that still left thousands of square miles of ocean to explore, with numerous uncharted islets and reefs. Jack hoped against hope that Mikhail would provide a lead, something that would allow them to pinpoint a location. All the time Saumerre's men would be closing in, watching and waiting, their patience wearing thin. Jack knew that the gamble he had taken to keep Saumerre from ordering his men to attack would only succeed if he and Costas arrived at the site very soon. What he found out here today from Mikhail might prove decisive.

He stopped the vehicle at the top of the lane and switched off the engine, then opened the door and stepped out to enjoy a moment of silence. The first light of dawn revealed wisps of mist that hung between the dense line of cedars on either side of the lane. The forest extended off in all directions, rising up the foothills of the Adirondacks, which formed dark ridges on either side. He remembered the preternatural quiet of this place, more than twenty miles from the nearest town and separated from other farms by dense tracts of forest. Somewhere in the distance he heard the yipping and howling of a pack of eastern coyotes, an eerie sound that sent a shiver up his spine. During the week he had spent here six months ago, he had hiked with Mikhail and Petra all over the surrounding Adirondack hills, the three of them struggling to keep up with Rebecca. He took a deep breath, savouring the chill morning air. *Rebecca*. She was here too, with Jeremy. She knew he was coming, but he had hoped to arrive before she was up. He got back into the SUV and switched on the engine, looking through the tunnel of light created by the headlamps down the lane. The house lay in a clearing more than a quarter of a mile ahead, surrounded by irregular fields hacked out of the forest by pioneer settlers more than two centuries before, when this had been Iroquois territory.

He edged the vehicle forward, hearing the tyres crunch on the gravel. After about two hundred metres he passed over a small creek with swampy ponds on either side, and saw the dark shadow of the barn ahead. Any hope of a quiet arrival was shattered by the raucous barking of the pair of German shepherds that Mikhail kept in a fenced compound beside the house; then a cluster of motion-sensor halogen lights lit him up. He accelerated to the end of the lane between the barn and the house and switched off the engine, taking his fleece and getting out just as a figure appeared out of the gloom holding a rifle muzzle-down, like a soldier. Jack extended his hand. 'Mikhail. Good to see you.'

'Jack.' Mikhail took his hand from the rifle grip and shook Jack's, smiling warmly at him. He was about Jack's age, a few inches shorter, with cropped grey hair, a Russian whose features were more Viking than Slavic, and he spoke English with a slight accent.

Jack pointed at the rifle, a British Lee–Enfield .303 that he knew Mikhail used for deer hunting. 'Have you had any trouble?'

Mikhail shook his head. 'Nothing yet. But we treat every arrival as suspicious. Your security chief Ben Kershaw and the

British secret service guy, John, have both been here for the past two nights, ever since Rebecca and Jeremy arrived. One of them is always on the perimeter near the road. John does the day shift, Ben the night. Ben was probably within sniffing distance of you at the head of the lane, but I know he wouldn't reveal himself even to you.'

'When he was in the SAS in the 1980s, that's what they got good at,' Jack said. 'Squatting in hedgerows in South Armagh in Northern Ireland for hours and days on end, waiting for IRA terrorists.'

'Jeremy's making breakfast. I expect you'll need some. I've got some really exciting stuff to show you, Jack. It could be just what you want.' They walked past the dogs, both quiet now, and then up the path to the house, where Mikhail opened the screen door and ushered Jack in, closing it and locking the main door behind them. They went through a room that had once been the pioneer log cabin and then into a spacious modern extension, up a wide staircase to a large open-concept pentagonal room that served as a living area as well as Mikhail's study. On every side above bookcases were wide windows that gave an unimpeded view over the farm up to the edge of the field clearings, now visible in the light of dawn. Mikhail walked a few steps down to a sunken sitting area in the centre of the room, with easy chairs surrounding a rustic table made from sections of hardwood trunk. He opened the bolt of the rifle, extracted the round that had been in the chamber and pressed it back into the magazine, then closed the bolt over the rounds, placing the rifle on the table beside several other guns. He and Jack sat down opposite each other as another figure appeared up the stairway. Jeremy looked half asleep, with dishevelled hair, and he wore a sweater and jeans that looked as if they had just been thrown on, but he was carrying a tray of coffee mugs and croissants.

'Grub's up,' he said, putting the tray on the table and grinning at Jack. 'Isn't that what your old seadog grandfather used to say?'

Jack took a coffee and smiled. 'Hello, Jeremy. Is Rebecca awake?'

'I'll knock on her door if you want.'

'No,' Jack said. 'It's only just dawn, and she is still a teenager.'

Jeremy grinned again. 'As you keep reminding me. She can't wait to see you.'

'Let's see what Mikhail has to say first.' Jack leaned forward, took a gulp of coffee and put the mug down on the table. He pointed to where the Lee–Enfield lay beside three other weapons, a Ruger 10/22 semi-automatic rifle, a Beretta side-by-side 12-gauge shotgun and a revolver, alongside a cardboard box filled with ammunition. 'That's quite an arsenal.'

'Ben and John are both carrying Glocks,' Mikhail said. 'These are just my farm guns, for hunting and personal defence. I know how good you are with the Lee–Enfield, from shooting with you here last year, but I've only just sighted it in for new ammunition I've reloaded myself so I'll take that. If the need arises, Rebecca has the shotgun and Jeremy the Ruger.'

Jack looked questioningly at Jeremy. 'Have you done much shooting?'

'I grew up in rural Vermont, where just about every boy I knew had a 10/22. You just have to know the limitations of the .22, even the hyper-velocity rounds. For anything bigger than a squirrel, that means less than fifty yards and always a head shot. But with the right shot placement, that rifle could kill a man instantly.'

There was a rustle from a corner of the room and Rebecca appeared bleary-eyed around a door, her long dark hair hanging over an oversized T-shirt. She gave a small wave, then shut the door again. Jeremy turned back to Jack. 'I know what you're asking. I haven't pulled a gun on a man before, but I'll do what it takes. We've got assets to protect.'

Jack reached over and picked up the revolver, a heavy break-top Webley. 'So it looks as if this is mine.'

'It's an old British service revolver,' Mikhail said. 'A lot of Webleys were sold as surplus into the States in the fifties and sixties. It's a man-stopper, .455 calibre, designed to put down fanatical tribesmen on the Afghan frontier. It's my home defence weapon.'

Jack spun the cylinder, then cupped his hands around the grip and aimed the pistol. 'Scott Macalister has one of these, and I've practised with it from the ship.' He pressed the lever on the receiver with his right thumb and broke the pistol open, pivoting the barrel and cylinder forward and letting the ejector snap out and fall back again. He reached over to the cardboard box and took out a container of .455 ammunition, opened it and loaded six cartridges into the cylinder, leaving the pistol broken open and laying it back on the table. 'If Saumerre's men do try to attack, what's the drill?'

Mikhail sprang up from his chair and went up to the window on the opposite side of the house from the barn, gesturing for Jack and Jeremy to follow. Jack mounted the stairs and stood beside him, looking over the lush green winter wheat that carpeted the field towards the pine and maple trees bordering the forest beyond. Mikhail opened the mosquito screen on the window, took a compact laser rangefinder from the ledge below and peered through it, finding a target and holding the rangefinder steady with both hands while he pressed the activator on the top. 'That large dead pine at the end of the field is three hundred and twelve metres away,' he murmured. 'That's the furthest line-of-sight distance in any direction from the house.' He took down the rangefinder and pointed to a large aerial photograph of the farm pinned to the wall beside the window, showing the three main fields extending off from the buildings like fingers penetrating the forest. 'It's all near enough for me to shoot using the battle sights on the Lee–Enfield without any need for range adjustment.' He looked back, scanning the far edge of the field for a moment, and then pulled shut the mosquito screen. 'It's been done before,' he said, looking at Jack. 'During the war of 1812, the place withstood a combined British and Iroquois attack. The farmer and his boys only had flintlock longrifles, but it did the trick.'

'Should one of us be standing lookout?' Jeremy said.

Mikhail shook his head. 'No need until we're certain there's a threat. Best to rest and keep alert. At the moment Ben is the first line of defence, and the dogs provide an early-warning system. I built the pen so they have a full run around the house. They're very territorial and want to attack anything that intrudes on this place. They'll let us know.'

Jack gestured at a spotting scope on a tripod beside the window. 'It looks as if you designed this room as a defensive outpost.'

Mikhail gave a wry smile. 'I'm a pretty serious birder. Rebecca's probably told you all about it. I used to drag her along to all kinds of places to spend hours sitting beside some swamp at migration time. When we bought this farm, the house was derelict and I had this room built as part of an extension, custom-designed as an observatory.'

'And a place to write your books. I envy you that.'

Mikhail paused. 'There's another reason for the design of this room, the open-plan concept with the continuous window. Even when I'm absorbed in writing, I'm not comfortable in a room where I'm not aware of my surroundings. I can't sleep unless the windows are open. It's a small legacy of war.'

Jeremy eyed him cautiously. 'You were in Afghanistan during the Soviet war, weren't you? Before you defected? Rebecca told me, but I know you don't like it spread about. Plenty of people here haven't forgotten the Cold War and still think of the Russians as the enemy.'

Mikhail walked over and opened the top drawer of a small wooden chest beside the sofa. He took out two badges and tossed them on the sheepskin carpet on the floor in front of them. One was a hammer-and-sickle design within a star surrounded by golden sheaves of wheat; the other was a red-enamel pentagonal star containing a white-metal image of a Soviet soldier holding a rifle. He looked at them ruefully. 'The Order of the Red Banner and the Order of the Red Star. They dished those out to everyone who fought in the battle for Hill 3234, to the men who survived and the families of the men who died. I was an intelligence officer attached to the 345th Independent Guards Airborne Regiment. We were ordered to occupy a nameless ridge 3,234 metres high overlooking the road from Gardez to Khost near the Pakistan frontier. It was the night of the seventh of January 1988. A single reduced company of thirty-seven men fought off waves of attacks by hundreds of mujahideen all night long. By the time we were relieved, we'd suffered thirty-four casualties.'

'And you survived unscathed?' Jeremy asked.

Mikhail pulled up his left sleeve, revealing an ugly scar under his bicep. 'You may have noticed that I can't really use all the fingers of my left hand. The mujahideen who shot me was using an old British service rifle, a Lee–Enfield. Somehow having one of those rifles here and being in control of it helps me to deal with the pain. He came right up to our perimeter and I killed him with a grenade.'

'That's one less Taliban today,' Jeremy murmured.

'Maybe. But if we hadn't invaded Afghanistan in 1979, there'd have been no mujahideen and then maybe no Taliban and no al-Qaeda. The only thing I can be sure of is that I fought in the last campaign of the Cold War and that our defeat brought about what I so desperately wanted, the collapse of the Soviet Union. Just like Korea and Vietnam and numerous other proxy conflicts between communism and the West, fighting mujahideen on the Afghan frontier served as a pressure-relief valve that kept the prospect of nuclear annihilation at bay. That's the way I see it as a historian, though as a soldier you only see yourself and your mates. Without the breakdown in the Soviet security system that was precipitated by the Afghan War, Petra and I might never have defected and I wouldn't be a professor of history in the United States today.'

'And Rebecca wouldn't have had such marvellous foster-parents,' Jack said.

Mikhail walked around and peered out of the window facing the driveway. 'The difference between here and Hill 3234 is that we held a mountain ridge with three-hundred-and-sixty-degree visibility down into the surrounding valleys. What nearly finished us was the sheer force of mujahideen numbers, as well as the rocky terrain that allowed them easy concealment as they came up the slopes, and the limitations of our weapons and ammunition supply. What mainly concerns me here are the two places where the forest comes within seventy metres of the house. But let's leave that to Ben and the dogs. I want to show you what I found in the archive, Jack.'

'Good. The Embraer's returning to Syracuse for me this afternoon.'

They walked down the steps and sat around the table. Mikhail picked up a large manila envelope from beside the guns and slid out a sheaf of papers that looked like scanned documents. He peered at Jack, his eyes alight with excitement. 'You asked me for two things. First, to try to get the inside story on the discovery of those crates of Schliemann's treasures in Moscow in the 1980s, the artefacts from Troy taken by the Russians in 1945 from Berlin. My contact in Moscow is looking into it, and it's very promising. She says the curator who found the crates also discovered a package of documents with it, German military order books that the Russian soldiers who seized them must have shoved into one of the crates and then forgotten. She thinks they still exist in the museum store, and she's on the trail.'

'Hoffman's diary,' Jack murmured. 'Frau Hoffman told us he'd mentioned it to her during their brief final encounter before he embarked on the U-boat, that he'd left it with the crates in the Zoo tower for the Soviet intelligence people to find. He told her it contained everything he knew about the final months of the Third Reich.'

'That could be explosive,' Jeremy said.

'As soon as we're done here and Rebecca's safely in your hands, I'm on a plane to Moscow,' Mikhail said. 'This kind of thing comes to a historian once in a lifetime.'

'And the second thing?' Jack said. 'The reason why I'm here?'

Mikhail leaned forward. 'You asked me to look for any reports of U-boat sightings in the Caribbean after the German surrender on the eighth of May 1945, for anything unexplained or odd. At first I was sceptical. The Caribbean was a major area of operations for long-range U-boats in 1942 and 1943, with many merchantmen torpedoed and at least a dozen subs sunk in the area by Allied aircraft and ships. But the last recorded attacks on Allied shipping in the Caribbean were in July 1944, and the last known U-boat patrol there ended the following month. Most reports of sightings after that can be put down to jittery coastguards, seeing dark shapes on the sea at night. But it's true there has always been a big question mark over the final weeks of the war. There are some who believe that U-boats secretly sailed through the Caribbean on the way to Costa Rica and Brazil and other south American destinations, taking fleeing Nazis and their plunder.'

'A voyage like that could have extended well beyond the eighth of May,' Jack said. 'A U-boat could have set off from the Baltic just before the surrender and then taken a circuitous voyage across the Atlantic to avoid detection.'

'Right,' Mikhail replied. 'Two Type IX U-boats, U-530 and U-977, refused Grand Admiral Dönitz's order and didn't surrender until the tenth of July and the seventeenth of August respectively, both in Argentina. But as for U-boats in the Caribbean, that's only ever been speculation. By yesterday afternoon I thought I'd reached a dead end. But then I remembered something from research I did in the US National Archives in Washington almost twenty years ago, soon after my defection. In Moscow I'd been a student of military history and then a defence analyst before being called up for service in Afghanistan. After my debriefing at Langley, I worked for several years as a researcher for the CIA historical division. They allowed me access to classified material in order to bring a Soviet intelligence perspective on periods of Cold War arms build-up that still remained poorly understood. As you know, Jack, my speciality has become the shift of Allied and Soviet strategic planning from the defeat of Nazi Germany to the Cold War stand-off, particularly during those crucial first months after the Nazi defeat. My interest really began when my CIA handlers asked me to file a report on the earliest Soviet plans for tactical nuclear bombing, for the use of atomic bombs as battlefield weapons. They let me look at classified files relating to comparable US plans, and that's when I came across this account. I still have security clearance and was able to order a scan of the contents and have it couriered to me yesterday evening. The access records show that from the date when the file was boxed away in August 1945, nobody else has ever looked at it. I'd remembered it because it was so unusual, and also because it was the eyewitness report of an experienced combat aviator who would have known what he was looking at.'

'Go on,' Jack said, leaning forward.

Mikhail took an A4 black-and-white photograph from the file and slid it over the table. 'You recognize that?' Jack stared, then nodded. The picture showed a large-bellied four-engine aircraft in wartime British Royal Air Force camouflage, white underneath and on the fuselage sides, and khaki and olive green above, with a large RAF roundel on the centre of the fuselage and the red identification letters MA below the cockpit. In front of the letters was the image of a scantily clad woman and a roaring red dragon, and the words 'Dragon Lady'.

'It's a B-24 Liberator,' he said. 'Somewhere in the tropics, judging by the palm trees beyond the tarmac. That's the RAF Coastal Command camouflage scheme, isn't it? Was this a submarine hunter?'

'It's a Liberator of 111 Operational Training Unit, based at Nassau in the Bahamas and used to train new aircrew on four-engine bombers. A lot of the aircrew were Canadians of the RCAF, as well as British and Commonwealth RAF men who had done their initial training in Canada. The Liberator had a longer range than the other main four-engine bombers used in the European war, and many of the crews were destined for the Far East to take part in operations against the Japanese.'

'You mean about the time when the Americans were gearing up to drop the first atomic bomb.'

Mikhail nodded. 'That's what I was researching when I came across the records box with that picture. The box was peculiar because it contained papers and logbooks relating to 111 OTU in May and June 1945, material that would normally be found in England with the squadron operations records in the UK National Archives, or under restricted access along with other Second World War material still held by the Ministry of Defence. Its location in the US archives in Washington only made sense when I began reading the files and realized that they related to a secret training scheme co-ordinated by the US and were intimately tied up with the events of early August 1945, with the atomic bomb programme.'

Jack peered at the photograph. 'My father was an RAF Lancaster pilot in the final months of the war. He told me I owed my existence to a silver butterfly that had kept him and his crew alive. It was a pendant left in the aircraft by the previous pilot, who'd brought his crew through two tours. My father kept the butterfly and had it in his hand when he died as an old man. That's virtually all I know about his wartime experiences, as he never spoke of them. He said he was one of the lucky ones who was able to live for the future. I think that pendant had something to do with it. But he did talk a lot about his beloved Lancaster, so I grew up knowing a bit about planes. I was right, wasn't I? This Liberator may have flown with a training unit, but she's armed and equipped for operational flying.'

Mikhail nodded. 'This is B-24D, serial number FK-856. You were right about Coastal Command. She'd been a Royal Canadian Air Force U-boat hunter based in Newfoundland, but with the Battle of the Atlantic winding down by early 1945, she was one of a number sent to operational training units. You can see she still has the chin fairing that houses the air-to-surface-vessel radar, and the airfoil winglets below the cockpit that carried eight five-inch rockets. Both of those features were removed when she went to 111 OTU, but the bomb-bay adaptation to carry depth charges was retained.'

'What about the crew?'

'That was what really piqued my interest. When I looked at the crew lists, I saw something odd. The usual operational conversion crews were men straight out of flight school. But the final crew to fly this Liberator was very different.' Mikhail picked up the scanned sheets and flipped through them. 'An inordinate amount of attention was paid to their selection, with secret reports from their squadron and station commanders as well as detailed intelligence assessments on each man. They were all highly experienced aircrew from the same elite RAF pathfinder group, the bombers that had flown ahead in the raids on Nazi Europe and marked the targets. Every member of the crew of FK-856 had flown at least a full tour of thirty missions over Europe, several of them a lot more; all four of the NCO gunners had Distinguished Flying Medals, the officers had Distinguished Flying Crosses and the pilot had the Distinguished Service Order as well. With the war in Europe over, many Lancaster crews were being remustered as part of "Tiger Force", the plan to send RAF and Commonwealth squadrons to bomb Japan, and I could only think that this crew had been selected for special duties to get them to the Far East as soon as possible and were being converted to fly anti-submarine operations in the Pacific. But then I found the top-secret memo that explained it all. They were being given flight time on the Liberator before being sent to a secret destination in the Pacific to be upgraded to the Liberator's successor, the B-32 "super-bomber". They were being groomed to be the first generation of bomber crews to drop tactical nuclear weapons on the battlefield, something Allied commanders envisaged had the Hiroshima and Nagasaki bombs failed to persuade the Japanese to surrender.'

'But then the war against Japan did end, and the programme was scrapped,' Jeremy said.

Mikhail nodded, then pursed his lips. 'Too late for these men, though. They may well count as the last combat casualties of the war against the Nazis.'

'Explain,' Jack said.

Mikhail picked out one sheet with a yellow marker stuck to it. 'It was the morning of the third of June 1945. The crew had only been in Nassau for two weeks, having previously been involved in the airdrop of relief supplies to the emergency hospital units dealing with survivors of the Belsen concentration camp. One of their last bombing missions had been over Berlin, an attempt to use the "Tallboy" twelve-thousand-pound bomb to break the flak-tower defences. It was their expertise with those bombs that caught the eye of the US intelligence officers scouting for pathfinder crews suitable for conversion to nuclear bombing. The bomber crews were very tightly knit, and the pathfinders were the best of the best. The psychological reports show that these were not the kind of men who desperately counted down the last missions to the end of their tour, traumatized by what they had seen and done and by the constant fear. We often forget that some men relished it. The men in this crew seem to have been pleased to be selected to go out to the Far East ahead of Tiger Force, eager to get back into action again. These were precisely the kind of men the intelligence officers would have been looking for.'

'So that day they were on a training mission?' Jack asked.

Mikhail nodded, then took out a photocopied map with ruled lines on it. 'It was their last operation in an intensive week. They were due to take their Liberator across the United States to the island of Guam in the Pacific the next day. They were fully armed as if they were on an anti-submarine patrol, with three depth charges in the bomb bay and the machine guns in the turrets fully belted up. The depth charges were an experimental type designed to bounce on the surface of the sea, hit their target and roll under it to explode, like the famous dambuster bombs. Their mission was to fly three hundred and fifty nautical miles east of Nassau to a designated live-fire zone just north of the central Bahamas chain, find a decommissioned minesweeper that had been anchored as a target and expend all their ammunition on it before returning in a clockwise route to Nassau. Their last radio contact shows that they made it to the live-fire zone, a rectangular area of about fifty square miles extending north from the island of San Salvador. Intermittently, there's severe electromagnetic disturbance at this location, on the edge of the abyssal plain where the Bahamas shelf extends over the Atlantic plate, an extension of the Puerto Rico Fault Line that's still poorly understood. It's the kind of thing that would get Bermuda Triangle fantasists all excited, but an oceanographer colleague of mine at Columbia University thinks it might be a localized upsurge of the magma that affects the geomagnetic field, an anomaly that might also disrupt compasses.'

'I've heard that before,' Jack murmured, thinking hard. 'About the North Anatolian Fault off Turkey, at the site of Atlantis. It makes some meteoritic materials seem heavier.'

'That reference on the pillar at Lixus,' Jeremy interjected. '"Where the palladion becomes heavier."'

Jack nodded, leaning over and staring at the map. 'I take it there was no more contact.'

'None whatsoever. Over the next few days hurricane conditions prevented search-and-rescue flights, and by the time the weather had cleared, the Nassau station commander deemed that there was little chance the crew had survived. They found the anchored minesweeper completely untouched, so assumed the Liberator must have gone down before reaching it, on a flight path that was meant to take them on a compass bearing of thirty degrees from the northern tip of San Salvador out to sea towards a coral ridge where the minesweeper was anchored. The aircraft was meant to attack at very low level, and the base commander's log concludes that she may have clipped the waves in the rising wind and gone into the sea intact, accounting for the absence of floating debris. That was pretty unusual for the Liberator, which tended to break up on ditching, but the pilot, Squadron Leader White, was exceptionally skilled. The case was closed, but was briefly reopened nearly three weeks later, when a horrifying discovery was made almost three hundred nautical miles south-east of their target off the far end of the Bahamas chain.'

He pulled out another photograph and passed it to Jack, who took it and stared. 'Jesus,' he said quietly. 'I've seen harrowing pictures of survivors of wartime sinkings who'd endured weeks at sea in lifeboats, but this is one of the worst.' He stared for a moment longer, and then passed it to Jeremy. It was a low-level aerial photo of a one-man inflatable boat Jack recognized from the survival equipment his father had once shown him in the RAF museum at Hendon. The pontoons were smudged and criss-crossed with markings. Inside was a man, apparently naked, beneath a scrappy awning that seemed to have been rigged using his battledress and life jacket. He was in a foetal position, but his face protruded under one side of the awning, blackened and horribly ulcerated.

'Surely he can't have been alive,' Jeremy said.

'He was, just,' Mikhail replied. 'He was so dehydrated that his eyeballs had shrunk into his head. After his emergency rations ran out, he'd survived by fishing, making his first catch using pieces of his own flesh as bait. He'd been trying to drink his own blood. That's what those markings on the pontoons are, like finger painting, all kinds of numbers and slashes that must have been his way of marking the days. The Catalina aircraft that spotted him managed to land on the sea and pick him up, and he was taken back to Nassau. By then, 111 OTU unit had departed and everything was winding down. In the hospital he was debriefed by the last remaining US intelligence officer on the base, an inexperienced man who had been sent out to take the records of the secret programme back to Washington for classified storage. His report from that day is in the file. The rescued airman had no chance of recovery and died that night, but during brief periods of lucidity he told the story that caught my eye when I unearthed that box in the archives almost fifty years later.'

'Go on,' Jack said.

'His name was Flight Sergeant Brown. He was the rear gunner of Liberator FK-856. You won't find his name or those of any of the other crew on the Commonwealth War Graves Commission website, as officially they were lost in a peacetime training accident. He was English but had emigrated to Canada to make a new life on the prairies. His parents had been killed in the Blitz and he had no other recorded family. He was twenty-six when he died. From the debriefing, it's clear that the pilot was talking to the crew right up to the plane's final moments, fighting to keep it level as it dropped towards the sea. The Boulton Paul rear turret on the RAF Liberators was a deathtrap at high altitude if a plane went down, but it often came away on impact in a forced landing, and that's probably what saved him. He said there was a fire, but the pilot managed to ditch the plane nose-up, dousing the rear turret with seawater before the flames reached him and causing the turret to break away. The Liberator's poor ditching characteristics were mainly a result of the lightly built bomb-bay doors, which tended to collapse on impact, causing the fuselage to fill up quickly and sink. He said that when he recovered consciousness the aircraft had disappeared and the pilot and other crew were nowhere to be seen. At that location the plane could well have gone down beyond the abyssal wall, where the ocean is more than a mile deep, and by the time the surviving crew had struggled out of their harnesses it may have been too deep for any hope of escape.'

'So a fire caused the crash?' Jeremy asked.

'He claimed they were shot down.'

'*Shot down?*' Jeremy said in disbelief. 'Nearly a month after the war had ended? No way.'

'That's what the intelligence officer thought. Flight Sergeant Brown was delirious, in and out of consciousness, and I think the officer recorded what I'm about to tell you only as a matter of getting something into the debriefing report before closing the file. Brown kept repeating that they had depth-charged a U-boat over a blue hole, but had been shot down. The officer noted in pencil on the side that he'd checked Brown's personnel record and seen that before joining the pathfinders he had done a tour with Coastal Command and had a similar experience, flying rear gunner in a Liberator in 1943 that depth-charged a U-boat off Newfoundland but was hit by machine-gun fire and forced to ditch. The officer evidently thought that the 1943 ditching was a traumatic experience that came out in Brown's delirium. Even the blue-hole story was dismissed out of hand. Blue holes are a striking feature of the Bahamas from the air, and the officer noted that from his position of boredom cramped in the rear turret for hours on end, Brown may have become fixated on them.'

'You mean the sinkholes where so many cave divers die?' Jeremy said.

Jack nodded. 'The Bahamas land mass is a limestone plateau, and during the last Ice Age the sea level was over a hundred metres lower than it is today. Rainwater percolated through the limestone and created huge cavern systems that became submerged as the sea rose after the end of the Ice Age. Where the roofs of the caverns have collapsed, they appear as deep blue holes in the reefs, or as depressions where the limestone fragments from the ceiling have collapsed and filled up the caverns.'

Jeremy turned to Mikhail. 'But when you read the file, you believed Brown's story?'

Mikhail paused. 'I've been to war, and I know about post-traumatic flashbacks. The streets and hospitals of Russia are strewn with veterans of the Afghan war who've never been able to deal with it. The trauma, the flashback, is rarely generalized or conflated. It isn't a mishmash of memories. It tends to be one specific event, remembered in exacting detail.'

'You're saying that Brown's account wasn't a product of delirium.'

'I'm saying that if he was traumatized by his U-boat experience with Coastal Command in 1943, he wouldn't have seen a blue hole in the flashback. He would have remembered everything from that event in 1943, but not added other memories. And anyway, the trauma idea doesn't ring true. The intelligence officer was assuming what we might assume, that experiences such as that 1943 ditching must have been traumatic. But that's just wrong. Flying night raids over Germany was about the most terrifying thing a man could do in that war, yet Brown and his fellow crew had done it over and over again, and volunteered for more. There was a reason they were selected for the nuclear programme. They were the toughest of the tough. Some people just don't get traumatized.'

Jack peered at the map. 'If he really was describing one specific blue hole, the trouble is there are hundreds of them in the Bahamas over several thousand square miles. All we have to go on is the last reported position of the aircraft over that sector north of the island of San Salvador.'

'I looked into this with my oceanographer friend,' Mikhail said. 'At the co-ordinates of the target minesweeper noted in the file, the Liberator would have been beyond the land-mass plateau of the Bahamas and probably over the abyssal plain, beyond the huge underwater cliffs that run up from the Puerto Rico Fault along the Atlantic side of the Bahamas towards the coast of Florida. The plain is at least a mile deep and you won't find blue holes there. But there's one crucial feature we noticed. Off San Salvador there's an undersea ridge that extends about twenty-five nautical miles north-east, rising up from the abyssal plain. The detailed bathymetry was unknown in 1945, but I wondered whether there might be sections of reef shallow enough to have been upstanding land mass in the Ice Age, enough for rainwater erosion to have formed caverns that might have become blue holes as the sea level rose. We just don't know enough about the sea and reef at that point. That whole sector was a weapons test range, designated in April 1945 and in the event seeing little use. After the war it became part of the Atlantic Test and Evaluation range for anti-submarine weapons, continuing to be an exclusion zone even after the decision had been made to use another sector of undersea trench closer to Nassau for most testing. The San Salvador ridge extends beyond the twelve-nautical-mile Bahamas territorial limit, but the weapons test zone remains in force beyond the end of the ridge and we couldn't find any record of exploration or diving there. So it's possible that there *is* a shallow reef and a blue hole that has never been properly charted.'

Jack reached over and picked up the photograph showing the raft with the airman's body slumped inside. He looked closely at the dark smears on the pontoons and the mass of marks the man had made with his own blood. He could just make out a sequence of numbers, possibly repeated several times, but the image needed to be magnified and sharpened for there to be any hope of reading it. He stared, his mind racing. Something was niggling him, something his father had told him when they had seen the survival equipment at the museum at Hendon, about how pilots were trained to think of what information the crew who escaped from a ditched aircraft might need to call in a rescue. *He needed to get this image to Lanowski.*

At that moment Mikhail's two-way radio crackled and he spoke into it briefly, then got up. 'Okay. That was Ben. There's a propane tanker truck beginning to back down the lane. This was scheduled. Ben's going to remain concealed, and will stay at the top of the lane until he's relieved by John. I need to go out and make sure the path's clear for the men to drag the hose to the propane tank. It's hidden under a cedar growth beyond the barn.'

'I'll come with you,' Jeremy said, getting up and stretching. 'I need some fresh air. I'll see if Rebecca's out of the shower yet.'

'Can I use the internet and a scanner?' Jack asked.

Mikhail pointed to a monitor on a desk in an alcove. 'Be my guest. It can be a little slow out here. There's Skype if you need it.'

Mikhail and Jeremy left the room together, and Jack went over to the desk and sat down. He opened up the IMU home page and quickly logged on, then accessed his email account and clicked on the Skype. He checked his watch. *Seaquest II* was in a different time zone, one hour ahead of Bermuda, and he guessed that by now Lanowski and Costas would have their heads down over the computers in the operations room. He picked up the landline phone and dialled IMU Head-quarters in Cornwall. The phone was answered immediately. 'Hello, this is Jack Howard. Please patch me through to *Seaquest II*. Get me a secure line. This is a priority call.'

21

Seconds later, the line crackled as the satellite link connected Jack to the officer of the watch on *Seaquest II*, and then he was through to the operations room. A slightly annoyed voice answered. 'Lanowski here.'

'This is Jack. Switch on your Skype.'

'Jack!' The voice lightened up. 'I was just in the process of terraforming the Caribbean during the Ice Age.' A face materialized on Jack's screen, the familiar lank fringe and little round glasses staring somewhere just below the webcam, presumably at another screen. Lanowski looked up and peered closely into the camera. 'The computer isn't up to it, as usual. But I refuse to dumb down and give it simplified data. Computer programs are only as big as the brains that create them. Costas tells me I need to make my own, and he's right. But meanwhile here's the score. We've just been looking at the Bahamas outer ridge abyssal plain. Interesting layering of megaturbitides along the fault line, with magma extrusions rising alarmingly high into the plate divide. Drop anything down there and it would sink through about a mile of silt and then into the molten core of the earth. I've got James Macleod and the geology team at IMU very interested in doing a sub-bottom probe survey.'

'Is Costas with you now?'

An unshaven face appeared from one side of the screen. 'I'm with you, Jack.'

'Okay. Keep all that geomorphology data up and running. I've got a possible lead from Mikhail.' He quickly ran through the story of the Liberator attack and the airman's account. As he talked, Lanowski emailed through a link that flashed on his screen. Jack clicked on it, opening up a detailed topographical and bathymetric map of the Bahamas islands. 'Okay,' he said. 'I can visualize the flight route east from Nassau to the sector of sea north of the island of San Salvador.'

'That's beside the fault line we've been looking at, about dead centre on the map,' Lanowski said.

Jack zoomed in on the island. 'Yesterday I called James Macleod and asked him to trawl through our database for anything that might hint at undersea research in the Caribbean in the late 1930s, anything odd. I need to know if he found anything on the Bahamas.'

'We're on to it already. He's been liaising with us this morning,' Lanowski said. 'Let me give him a call now. This might take a few minutes. Stay online.'

Costas' face reappeared on the screen. 'How's tricks?'

'Mikhail's got this place locked down,' Jack replied. 'Ben

and the MI6 guy are doing perimeter security. They know Saumerre's men have been shadowing Rebecca since she arrived in New York from Turkey two days ago. The farm is about as remote as you can get in the Adirondacks, but Mikhail's not taking any chances.'

'I found out something interesting,' Costas said. 'The MI6 file on Saumerre passed to our security people shows that he's a diver. He trained at Cambridge when he was a student and qualified with the British Sub-Aqua Club. If he thinks this place in the Caribbean is going to give him his biggest prize, he might want to get involved personally this time and not just leave it to his henchmen.'

'They'll all be divers too. You remember his previous men, the Russians we encountered in the mineshaft in Poland last year?'

'I remember how incompetent they were as divers, and how none of them got out alive.'

'This time might not be so easy. Saumerre will have learned his lesson with the Russians. Shang Yong and the Brotherhood of the Tiger only employ the elite.'

'You're sure it's them?'

'Ben saw a man he was convinced was trailing Rebecca in New York. His description of the tattoo on the man's wrist, the distinctive grimacing tiger, clinches it. We've seen that tattoo before, in Afghanistan two years ago, remember? And I trust Ben's appraisal of the people he thinks we're up against. He says they're good, very good, skilled operators in an urban environment like Manhattan, where he thinks they stalked Rebecca while she was at school over the last two days. Mikhail's calculation is that a group of Chinese gangsters are going to be less familiar with the forests of the Adirondacks, and that he'd have the upper hand out here.'

'How is Rebecca?'

'Not really woken up yet.'

'Jeremy looking after her?'

Jack gave a wry smile. 'After the course in small arms that Katya seems to have given her in Kyrgyzstan, I think Rebecca can look after herself.'

Costas moved aside and Lanowski reappeared, pushing his hanging fringe behind one ear and staring closely at the camera, his eyes gleaming. 'Jack. Are you there?'

'I'm waiting.'

'Bingo,' Lanowski exclaimed triumphantly. 'Bingo. Macleod has worked through all the records he could find for the British Virgin Islands and the Bahamas. Because the Bahamas are British territory, a lot of the older archival material is readily accessible in England. He's got security clearance to view material that's still classified. Take a look at this.' His face disappeared and a scanned document appeared on the screen, with the Government of the Bahamas logo along the top and a few brief paragraphs of faded typescript below, slashed across with thick lines in red pencil; below that was the text of another letter, in bolder Gothic typescript. 'The upper text is a record duplicate of a letter signed by the military commander of the Bahamas garrison on the third of February 1938, nineteen months before the war started. Below it I've pasted in the text of the letter to which it's a response, from the master of a German-registered cargo vessel. The military commander is acknowledging notice that the master intends to spend two weeks offshore along the north-eastern bank of the Bahamas. The master's letter is a courtesy notice to explain that the vessel contains a scientific team studying the fault line between the Atlantic and the Caribbean. This was before plate tectonics were fully understood, so it's plausible research. The master states that their expedition was a follow-up to a visit two years before, in the summer of 1936, when a German oceanographic group experimenting with diving equipment and underwater photography had spent several weeks in the same area of reefs beyond the territorial limits of the Bahamas, but had also made their presence known as a courtesy to the authorities.'

'Good God,' Jack exclaimed. 'That could only be the Ahnenerbe expedition that Frau Hoffman talked about. For oceanography, read archaeology. They were hunting for signs of Atlantis in the Bahamas, and they were the ones who found the place with the ancient symbols. Two years later, Himmler sends a team back. This is it, Jacob. We're on target.'

Lanowski nodded. 'There's more. The master explains that he's written the letter to be forwarded to the Governor General of the Bahamas in order to ensure that the purely scientific nature of their work is understood and that their presence does not atract Royal Navy attention. That's exciting enough for us, Jack. But there's the clincher in the final little paragraph. They intend to stop at two places and lower seismic measuring equipment. In those days that meant fairly primitive heavyweight gear, probably in bulbous pressure capsules like the early bathyspheres developed after the war. Costas told me you said Frau Hoffman mentioned an underwater habitat secretly developed in the U-boat base at

Lorient. That could be what we're looking for, Jack. And check out the location noted by the German master. It's not precise, surely deliberately so, a sector of about two hundred square miles of ocean, but the latitude and longitude co-ordinates encompass that undersea spur north of the island of San Salvador.'

Jack stared, his heart pounding. It seemed inconceivable, but the location of Himmler's lair might have been embedded in official British records all along. Rather than attempting to be secretive, something that would have been virtually impossible with a ship of the size needed to transport the undersea habitat, Himmler's men had brazenly publicized their mission and relied on the British weakness for gentle-manly behaviour to ensure that their courtesy notice was taken at face value, meaning that the Nazi team would not be bothered while they established the site where Himmler intended to hide away the worst weapon of mass destruction the world had ever known.

Costas' voice came from offscreen. 'That ridge would have been the perfect location. It's right on the edge of the abyssal plain, so U-boats could have crossed the Atlantic and come up to it submerged, only having to surface for a few hundred metres to cross the reef edge before dropping down into a blue hole large enough to take a submarine. And remember what Frau Hoffman told you she saw in that wartime photograph, Jack. An underwater habitat like that would not have been meant for continuous use, but could have been a refuge established for a time in the future when Himmler intended his plan to come to fruition. He would never risk U-boats going to it during wartime, when Allied patrols might spot them. But two U-boats were to arrive after the Nazi surrender, the first one with Oberst Hoffman and his precious cargo, and the second one carrying Himmler himself. In the event, we know the boat carrying Himmler never set off from the Baltic, but the one with Hoffman certainly did.'

'And that's the U-boat sighted on the third of June 1945, when Liberator FK-856 just happened to be passing by,' Lanowski murmured.

'What's the red mark across the text on that document?' Jack asked. 'I can see a date stamped on it: the twenty-seventh of November 1940.'

'That's an ugly twist in the tale,' Lanowski said. 'Before looking at the 1930s material, Macleod's researchers began by examining wartime records, to see if there was any indication of secret U-boat bases that might have been established in the Caribbean in the lead-up to the war. British naval intelligence were on the case by late 1939, when U-boats had begun to sink merchant ships in the Atlantic. One particularly assiduous intelligence officer discovered these letters in the military commanders' files in November 1940 and passed them on to the Governor of the Bahamas, requesting that a minesweeper and motor gun boat be sent to check out the ridge where that German ship had been in 1938. His fear was that mines might have been laid, but there was also the possibility of secret U-boat replenishment bases being established in the Caribbean before the war. Apparently the Governor angrily vetoed the request, saying that it was a waste of war resources. The intelligence officer noted in a sheet attached to those letters that the Governor often spoke openly to his staff about how he believed it was just a matter of time before the British

Government struck a deal with Hitler, and how they would join forces against the Jews and the Slavs.'

'Good God,' Jack exclaimed. '*Of course.* That was the Duke of Windsor, wasn't it, the former King Edward VIII? He'd made no secret of his Nazi sympathies in the 1930s and was even photographed reviewing SS troops on a visit to Germany. To get him out of the way in 1940, Churchill had him appointed Governor of the Bahamas.'

Lanowski nodded. 'I'm sure Himmler would have considered the Duke far too dim-witted to include in his plans, but it would have been a matter of some convenience to have a Nazi sympathizer as governor of the area where his hideaway happened to be located, a position the Duke held until early 1945, when the U-boat war was effectively over in the Caribbean. The Duke himself may never have known that by vetoing that search he was aiding the efforts of Himmler, but anyone who sympathized with that regime was conniving in evil.'

Jack tapped his fingers on the desk. 'So what we now believe is that the U-boat that took Oberst Ernst Hoffman from the Baltic in the last days of the war very probably was the one attacked by the Liberator, just as the sub reached its destination. What we now need to find out is whether Hoffman was still on board, and whether he had that deadly phial with him. And we need to find the exact location of that blue hole.'

'Is there anything else from the debriefing documentation on that airman?' Lanowski asked. 'Any maps, photos?'

'Only this.' Jack clicked the mouse to send the scanned photo of the airman in the raft. 'This is Flight Sergeant Brown, the sole survivor of the Liberator crash. The markings on the pontoon, the slashes and the line of numbers below his head, were made with his own blood.' He saw Lanowski peer intently at the screen for a few moments, then work the keys and turn away before looking back at him.

'I'm trying to sharpen it up,' Lanowski said. 'I want to see what he's written.'

Jack stared at the photo as it repixellated, seeing the numbers clearly now: *242446, 742799*, repeated exactly below. He suddenly remembered his flight in the RAF Tornado three days before, something Paul Llewelyn had told him once about wartime Coastal Command training. *That was what he remembered from the visit with his father to the RAF museum.* When aircraft were about to ditch into the sea, the pilots were trained to give a position fix over the intercom to ensure that the crew knew their co-ordinates and could relay them from their rafts if they survived and the pilot and navigator did not. The pilot would repeat the co-ordinates, over and over again. Jack's heart suddenly began to pound. *Of course.* 'Jacob, run that line of numbers as geographical co-ordinates.'

'I'm there already, Jack. Translate that into degrees, minutes and seconds, and you have a point almost due north-east of San Salvador Island, about thirteen and a half nautical miles offshore. It's bang on that ridge, just before it drops off into the abyss.'

Jack tensed with excitement. 'Mikhail says there's no detailed bathymetry available because this was a military exclusion zone, but can you get a satellite view? What we're looking for might be visible from the air.'

'I've got Landsat imagery streaming online now. Click on the link I've just sent.' Jack stared, waiting for it to appear. He looked up for a moment from the monitor and saw the dawn sky through the windows. The dogs suddenly barked and he heard a steady beeping sound, evidently the propane tanker reversing down the lane towards the house. Mikhail appeared up the stairs, quickly made his way to the table and picked up the Lee–Enfield and a box of .303 cartridges. 'The licence plate of the truck checks out,' he said. 'It looks like the usual two guys in the cab. Jeremy's going to meet them and keep an eye on things. Rebecca seems to be turning her shower into a sauna. Any luck?'

Jack gave him a thumbs-up sign. 'Touch wood. We might well be on to something.'

'Okay. I'm off to do my usual morning recce around the treeline. I'll be less than half an hour.'

An icon flashed on the screen and Jack clicked on it, opening up a Landsat view of a sector of sea. The focus co-ordinates were the same numbers the airman had written on the pontoon of the boat. He clicked the mouse to zoom in on a line of white on the sea, evidently breakers over the edge of a reef, with deep azure waters to the right and lighter blue to the left. The target co-ordinates lay on the reef, at a spot indistinguishable in colour from the surrounding water. He zoomed in closer and saw a ripple on the surface, and realized that a wind was obscuring the view he would have had in calm conditions through the shallows to the bed of the reef. He looked at the webcam. 'Jacob, can we do anything about that wind?'

'I'm searching for an archive photo in calmer seas. Okay, here we go.'

After a short delay, the image transformed. The line of

breakers disappeared, and the distinction in colour between the reef and the deep water became more sharply delineated. 'That drop-off must be awesome,' Jack murmured. 'A mile straight down into the abyss.' He stared at the target co-ordinates, about five hundred metres into the reef from the abyss wall. Dark and light patches showed undulations in the reef depth. He estimated the underwater visibility at perhaps thirty metres, with the darker patches showing sea floor at about that depth or greater and the lighter areas no more than ten or fifteen metres deep. The arrow showing the target co-ordinates lay over a slightly darker circular patch perhaps two hundred metres across between two very light areas two or three times that size. He clicked to maximum zoom, looking down at the sea as if he were three hundred feet overhead, about the altitude from which the Liberator gunners might have seen it during an attack run. He tried to contain his disappointment. He remembered years before flying a helicopter over blue holes when the first *Seaquest* had sailed to the Caribbean. The holes were absolutely distinctive, deep blue circular patches in the reef, indigo against the aquamarine of the surrounding shallows. 'I don't think that dark patch is clear enough to be a blue hole.'

'Wrong,' Lanowski replied.

'What?'

'Wrong.' Lanowski's face appeared on the screen, flushed with excitement and shaking. 'Wrong, wrong, *wrong*.'

Jack saw Costas' hand clamp down on Lanowski's arm. 'Okay, Jacob,' he said. 'Slow down. Explain.'

Lanowski tried to raise his arm, and seemed to shudder. His voice was hoarse with excitement. 'Blue holes are collapsed caverns, right? Caverns have roofs. A lot of blue holes have rims remaining that overhang the edge of the hole, and those can collapse too. What happens when a U-boat dives into a blue hole followed by three depth charges totalling, what, two tons of high explosive? Bang.' He chuckled, shaking his head. 'And I mean *bang*. The U-boat sinks. The rim of the blue hole collapses. What we're looking at here is not what Squadron Leader White or Flight Sergeant Brown saw as the Liberator went in for the attack. What we're looking at is the blue hole after the equivalent of a small earthquake, its appearance after the Liberator had done its work.'

Jack stared at the satellite picture. The depression in the reef was uniformly round, distinct from the irregular mottled patches indicating undulations in the reef depth around it. 'I have to say it, Jacob, you're a genius,' he murmured.

'I know,' Lanowski replied, chuckling and shaking his head. '*I know.*'

Jack paused, thinking hard. 'If we're right, then this is also where the Ahnenerbe archaeologists in 1936 discovered the Atlantis symbols we saw in Wewelsburg Castle. Jacob, can you use that terraform programme to give me a picture of the reef at this spot seven and a half thousand years ago?'

'You mean at the time of the Black Sea flood?'

'I mean the time when a shaman of Atlantis fleeing the flood might have made his way into the Mediterranean and across the Atlantic, and then found a landfall in the Caribbean.'

'Okay.' Jack heard the rapid tapping of keys. 'We have a tree-ring date of 5545 BC on those freshly felled logs you found in the timber yard at Atlantis five years ago,' Lanowski said. 'Let me feed that date into the program.' He paused.

'Today there's nothing in the entire Bahamas chain higher than sixty metres above sea level. That's why I was interested in those abyssal megaturbitides, the layers of silt. Not only have you got sea-level rise since the Ice Age, you've also got massive erosion of surface land mass, especially in an area that's often hit by hurricanes. I think Macleod's probes would find thick layers of coral debris at the bottom of those cliffs.' He paused again, and Jack watched him scan the screen below the camera. 'Okay,' he continued. 'I'm looking at the eustatic sea-level curve since the last glacial maximum. We've got an average of about one hundred metres' rise in sea level from Meltwater Pulse 1A, about fourteen thousand years ago. 5545 BC falls just before the trigger event that happened about seven thousand years ago, a final big melt that brought the sea level close to its present state. Since 5545 BC we're looking at around a thirty-metre rise. Add the effects of erosion, maybe another twenty to thirty metres in places, and you've got land at this point rising fifty or sixty metres high, with peaks as high as a hundred metres.'

'Not exactly the mountain the fleeing priests were looking for,' Costas murmured.

'No,' Jack said. 'But imagine looking at a coastline in a storm with no way to gauge scale. A modest elevation could seem like a mountain. And remember, the only description we have is from the man who returned, the one Pliny recorded from the pillar at Lixus as Alkaios, who we know was Enlil-Gilgamesh. He himself may only have seen the shoreline in the distance, perhaps deterred from going closer by a storm, or perhaps because he had only ever intended to accompany Noah-Uta-napishtim to the point where the prophesied destination was visible: where he knew Noah would go on and disappear from history, but where he, Enlil-Gilgamesh, would carry out his secret plan all along of turning back to make a triumphant return to Lixus as a hero and a god.'

'Remember the only topographical hint we have, Jacob, from that encoded message you found in the Plato text,' Costas said.

Jack felt himself tense. *This was the real clincher.* 'Twin peaks, Jacob,' he said quietly. 'We're looking for twin peaks, just like the appearance of the volcano behind Atlantis in the Black Sea.'

Lanowski tapped the keys again. 'All I have to go on is those undulations in depth you can see in the reef surrounding that hole,' he said. 'But allowing for a bit of imagination, it could have looked like this.'

His face disappeared, and Jack's screen transformed into a CGI rendition of a coastline behind a pulsating line of surf. He held his breath when he saw the dark silhouette of the land mass behind. It showed a jagged ridge line, but in the centre was a saddle flanked by two conical hills. It looked just like the image of Atlantis before the flood. '*Yes,*' he said, bunching his fist. 'That's it. We need to move fast.'

Costas' face reappeared on the screen. 'There's a problem, Jack. A hurricane's coming.'

Jack closed his eyes. *A hurricane.* 'How far off?'

'Macalister's been in touch with the US National Hurricane Center. The eye is about three hundred and fifty nautical miles north-east of San Salvador, and it's tracking directly towards the central Bahamas chain, exactly where we don't want it to go.'

'Time frame?'

'Touchdown for the leading edge of the hurricane at that reef in about thirty hours.'

Jack looked at his watch. 'That's 1500 hours tomorrow. I can be out of here in an hour. I'll take Rebecca and Jeremy with me. The Embraer should be waiting for us at Syracuse by the time we get there. That puts us in Bermuda and then on *Seaquest II* by mid-evening. How far south does Macalister reckon we'd have to sail to be within helicopter range of the island?'

Costas leaned over and showed Jack a torn-off sheet of computer printout. 'The best scenario puts *Seaquest II* about two hundred and eighty nautical miles north of San Salvador and a hundred miles west of the leading edge of the volcano at about 0900 tomorrow morning, after spending the night steaming south from Bermuda at maximum speed. That puts San Salvador within range of the Lynx using long-range fuel tanks, with the payload limited to two of us and basic diving equipment. It would be a close-run thing, but we could be dropped on the reef, do the dive, be winched up to the helicopter and then be flown out beyond the leading edge of the hurricane as it tracks west, to reach *Seaquest II*'s position of safety to the north. If the storm comes on more quickly, the Lynx could drop us, return to the ship and stand off while the storm rolled over us, and then return to pick us up afterwards. It would be a risk for us, but if we were able to get under the collapsed material we think is clogging up the blue hole, we might be protected from the worst of the hurricane.'

'What about permission to dive in the weapons test range?' Jack said.

'We might have to wing it. We don't want to excite interest, and we haven't got time to go through official channels. It hasn't been used for that since the flight of Liberator FK-856 in 1945. And don't think permission to dive is the issue that would be troubling Macalister, Jack. I think the issue will be that hurricane, and the possibility of *Seaquest II* becoming another statistic in the Bermuda Triangle.'

Jack remembered their dive at Atlantis three days before, under the noses of the international monitoring team and into a live volcano, with *Seaquest II* well within the danger zone. He had sworn he would never put Macalister through anything like that again. *Seaquest II* would have to stay outside the predicted path of the hurricane. It would all be down to the helicopter. 'We'd need a pilot with a hell of a lot of nerve,' he murmured. 'He'd be seeing the leading edge of the hurricane on the horizon ahead of him. He'd have to go against all his instincts and fly directly towards it, then after dropping us make the decision himself whether to wait for us. I'd never ask it of one of our regular crew.'

'What about your old RAF friend Paul? I thought he was at a bit of a loose end now. Didn't you say he was a qualified helicopter pilot too?'

Jack thought hard. *It might work*. He nodded. 'Okay. Stay online. I'll use my cell phone to try to contact him.' Three days before, after leaving Jack at the old NATO base beside the Nazi bunker in Germany, Paul had flown his Tornado to RAF Lyneham in England before taking leave ahead of his new posting at the Ministry of Defence. Jack prayed that he would have been unable to wrench himself away from aircraft for his final few days as an operational pilot and would still be at Lyneham. The second IMU Embraer was at its base in Cornwall at the Royal Naval Air Station at Culdrose, and could be at Lyneham in a matter of a few hours to pick Paul up and fly him out over the Atlantic.

Jack dialled, and a voice answered almost immediately. 'Paul? This is Jack. You remember our parting words on the tarmac in Germany? I've got a job that might interest you.' He quickly ran through a plan that would get Paul to Bermuda and out to *Seaquest II* overnight, in time to familiarize himself with the custom specs of the IMU Lynx and take off before dawn with Jack and Costas and their diving equipment for the Bahamas. Paul instantly agreed, and Jack gave him the IMU number to liaise with the Embraer pilot. Then he clicked off his phone and sat still for a moment, hearing only the morning chorus of the birds outside the windows. He stared at the aerial photo of the reef on the screen, trying to see in his mind's eye down into the collapsed blue hole and imagining what might lie there. He spoke again into the webcam. 'Okay, guys. Paul thinks we can do it.'

'On a wing and a prayer, Jack,' Lanowski said, slightly awkwardly.

'Where have I heard that before?' Costas said.

'It's what Paul used to say about our student expeditions when I first knew him, when we seemed to survive on minimal equipment and lots of duct tape.'

'Sounds like we might be going back there again, Jack. With the Lynx stretching the envelope, it's just going to be whatever equipment we can carry on our backs.'

Jack opened the directory on his cell phone. 'I need to put in a call to the Bahamas.'

'Anyone we know?' Costas said.

'The office of the Prime Minister. He was a student contemporary of mine at Cambridge.'

'The old boys' network?'

'Something like that. I don't want anyone near that site before we dive, but I want to arrange for backup from the Royal Bahamas Defence Force. If all goes well and we find what we want to find, the site will need round-the-clock surveillance while we get in a full IMU excavation team to reveal everything that might lie within that blue hole. I'll see if the Prime Minister can have his people call through directly to Captain Macalister. Meanwhile, the next you'll hear from me will be from the tarmac in Bermuda. Thank James Macleod at IMU for me. Excellent work, Jacob.'

'I've just remembered something,' Costas said. 'Wasn't San Salvador where Christopher Columbus first made landfall in the Americas?'

Jack paused. He had barely allowed himself to think about the archaeology. Since leaving Atlantis three days before, the extraordinary seven-thousand-year-old trail they were on had been overshadowed by the present-day danger. For a moment he focused his mind back on that sunken chamber they had found inside the volcano at Atlantis, on the fantastic vision it had given him of events at the very dawn of civilization. They were following perhaps the greatest ancient voyage of discovery ever made, not some hazy exodus lost in time but the voyage of one man who had become enshrined in the foundation myths of the Western world. Yet what they had found in that chamber in Atlantis, what they might find ahead of them now, would reveal a truth about the past that could rock those foundations to the core. Jack felt the familiar surge of excitement coursing through him. He looked intently at Costas. 'Not just Christopher Columbus. We might find that he was pipped to the post seven thousand years before. If we're lucky.'

'A wing and a prayer, Jack,' Costas said, grinning.

'If that hurricane allows us. Over and out.' Jack reached over and switched off the Skype. For a few moments he sat in silence, trying to clear his mind and relax. As soon as Mikhail returned, he would get Rebecca and Jeremy to collect their things and drive them to Syracuse airport. He suddenly needed to see Rebecca. The dark cloud that had hung over him since her kidnapping last year suddenly seemed finite, and for the first time he felt there was a chance they might see it disappear completely. He took a deep breath, and steeled himself. *If the next twenty-four hours panned out as he had gambled.* One horror would be taken out of the equation if they could recover the bacterium sample from Saumerre. As for the other, the Spanish influenza virus, they would only know whether that too survived, whether Hoffman had carried out the mission Himmler had given him, once they had dived into that hole. And with Saumerre's people watching their every move, there was no time to waste. They could not risk Saumerre discovering their destination and getting there first.

He was no longer hearing the reversing sound of the propane truck; it had been replaced by the low roar of an auxiliary engine powering the pump. He leaned back and stretched, realizing how dog-tired he was, then reached down and drained the tepid coffee from his mug. He got up and climbed the steps towards Rebecca's door, then glanced through the window towards the barn and saw the yellow top of the propane tanker parked beside his SUV. He walked towards one of Mikhail's spotting scopes and peered out. Two men in dark overalls were talking to Jeremy at the rear of the truck, pulling the hose from its reel. He heard the screen door to the house slam and saw Rebecca walk up the path towards the truck wearing a fleece, her hair glistening from the shower. One of the men rolled up his sleeves and knelt down to reach under the truck. Jack took the caps off the spotting scope and trained it on the edge of the woods beyond the barn, remembering Mikhail's concern about the proximity of the treeline. There was another problem in the morning mist: the likelihood that anyone in camouflage moving stealthily would be nearly invisible. He spotted a pair of deer, following their bobbing white tails until they disappeared beyond the trees. He moved the scope back towards the propane truck, and focused on the man who had stood back up and was rolling down his sleeves. Jack zoomed in, amazed at the quality of the optics. Suddenly he froze.

The man had a tattoo.

Jack took his hands off the scope to stop it wobbling, and stared. The man turned his wrist away to do up his sleeve. Then he turned it back, and Jack caught another glimpse. There was no doubt about it. He had seen that before, two years ago in the mountains of Afghanistan, through the scope of a Lee–Enfield rifle.

It was the tattoo of a tiger.

Jack turned and began to run.

22

'Freeze. Down on the ground. *Now!*'

Jack snarled the words as he aimed the Webley at the head of the nearer man, shifting his aim quickly to the other one and then back again, the hammer cocked and both hands tightly on the grip. Out of the corner of his eye he saw Rebecca and Jeremy, still standing where they had been talking to the men while Jack had crept up from behind the truck. He kept the pistol trained but glanced at Jeremy. 'Get back to the house, now,' he said. Jeremy and Rebecca stumbled and then ran. A figure in black appeared with a Glock pistol, the MI6 man John who was helping to provide protection for Rebecca. The two men from the truck remained immobile where they had been reeling out the propane hose. A voice called out from behind. 'I'm here, Jack.' He glanced over and saw Mikhail, his Lee–Enfield cocked and levelled.

Jack snarled again at the two men. '*Down.* Hands on your

heads.' They both slowly dropped to their knees on the gravel, their hands raised. John came up behind them and expertly kicked both in the small of the back so they fell forward on the ground, gasping. He holstered his Glock, took out two plastic wrist ties and in seconds had the two men handcuffed. Jack saw it again, the smudged tattoo of the tiger on one man's wrist, identical to the tattoo he had seen on Shang Yong's man two years previously in Afghanistan. John body-searched both men and removed a small arsenal of handguns and knives from their overalls, and several cell phones. He unholstered his Glock and trained it again, glancing at Jack. 'Ben and I only had one plan of action should this happen. He scouted out a ravine a few miles away where body disposal won't be a problem. Do you want to question them first?'

Jack knelt down beside the nearer man, seeing his Chinese features for the first time. He thrust the Webley into the nape of the man's neck, and leaned down so close he could smell the man's breath. 'If you make the slightest move,' he said quietly, 'this .455 slug is going to empty your head of everything inside it.'

John approached from behind. 'Let me do this, Jack.'

Jack put up his free hand to halt John, his other keeping the Webley pressed against the man's neck. He had just seen these men inches from Rebecca. It had been his worst nightmare, and it had nearly happened again. He felt a rage well up inside him, the same rage he had felt six months ago after Rebecca's kidnapping, when he had hacked one of her assailants to death in the mineshaft in Poland. With the hammer cocked, it would take the slightest nudge of the trigger to fire the pistol. He would be protecting Rebecca again. But then the rational side of him took over, the side that had planned what to do from the moment he had spotted that tattoo from the house. He was in control of this situation, and he must continue to be in control if they were to reach the endgame he had planned.

He spoke up so the other man could hear too. 'Listen to me, and listen well. Two of our security men are going to put you in your truck and drive you out of here. They are going to release you, return your cell phones and give you back your truck. You will tell your master that I know the location he wants in the Caribbean. I will give you a piece of paper with the precise co-ordinates. My team are on their way there now. Listen very closely. You will tell him that we know the prize he wants is in that place. We are willing to let him have it if we have the Nazi gold we know is there too. We both go away happy. But we also want the phial he already has, from the bunker. I will meet Saumerre at the site at 1500 hours tomorrow afternoon. Do you understand me?'

The man said nothing. Jack pressed the pistol hard against his neck. He felt the temptation again, stronger than ever. 'Do you understand me?' he snarled.

'Fifteen hundred hours tomorrow afternoon,' the man mumbled into the ground. 'The co-ordinates you will give us. He gets the prize. You want the gold. Bring the phial from the bunker or nothing happens.'

Jack kept the Webley pressed in hard, took a deep breath and then released it. He saw that Mikhail remained stock-still, his rifle still trained. He stood up, and nodded at John. 'They're all yours.' He turned to the house, seeing Jeremy outside the door holding the Ruger and Rebecca with the shotgun. 'Okay, you two. Get your things together. We're out of here in ten minutes.'

Fourteen hours later, Jack sat strapped in the rear compartment of the Lynx helicopter, charting their progress on the digital flight map as they neared the Bahamas chain. Out of the door window on the port side, he could see the leading edge of the hurricane, an ominous billowing darkness forked with lightning, a creeping malevolence that seemed immobile at this distance yet which Jack knew was a whirling maelstrom of wind. Paul had kept doggedly on course, having calculated their fuel consumption and the helicopter's turnaround schedule with military precision. They would be on site in eight minutes now, would have four minutes to egress and then Paul would be able to return to *Seaquest II* having used almost exactly his fuel capacity, relying on the headwind in front of the hurricane to give him the edge he needed to get back. The storm would pass south of *Seaquest II* while they were diving, clearing off west by the time they expected to be back on the surface using their waterproof radio to call Paul back to pick them up. That was, if their luck held out. And if they survived the showdown that lay ahead.

Jack had taken a huge gamble. He and Costas had given away enough to Schoenberg the day before to allow Saumerre to prepare himself for operations in the Caribbean. He had given the co-ordinates to the two men on the farm assuming that Saumerre would not be able to get to the site any faster than he could. The biggest gamble had been the bargain he had proposed. Saumerre knew that Jack had enough to discredit him, that Jack would never meet him without having a contingency to expose him if anything went wrong. If he could convince Saumerre that they could maintain a stand-off, as they had done for the past six months, then the agreement to share the spoils might work. The Nazi gold was no more than an educated guess. If Himmler had dispatched a U-boat on its final mission to take the deadly weapon to his hideaway, the chances were he would have filled the boat with the loot that top Nazis like him were hoarding at the end of the war. Gold was the favoured commodity. Himmler would have needed to buy himself a future if his plan to ransom the world with the threat of the biological weapon failed. He was too shrewd an operator not to have had a backup plan. Jack had no idea whether the virus phial was actually at the site, but he desperately hoped that Frau Hoffman had been right in her instinct that Ernst would have managed to destroy it. He remembered the account of the Liberator bomber, the rear-gunner's insistence that they had hit the U-boat as it entered the blue hole. Even if Ernst had not already found a way of ditching the virus, the attack might have destroyed the submarine and prevented him from taking it into the underwater habitat that Heidi said had been installed at this site before the war.

And getting Saumerre to bring the other phial, the Alexander bacterium, was another gamble. Yet Saumerre would have known that the bacterium was not a proven killer in modern times, that the virus was far more terrifying. He was a wily operator, an intellectual, a politician, very probably a fundamentalist sympathizer, but above all a gangster at the head of a criminal empire. For people like that, the bargain Jack had offered would strike a chord that would make him forget who Jack was, forget that profit and greed were not the only motivations for engaging in a deadly duel like this. He had to believe that Jack – like most of those he dealt with – had been seduced by the lure of gold.

Jack shut his eyes tight for a moment. Somewhere in that blue hole, in a cavern that would have been accessible to Ahnenerbe divers, were the ancient symbols that Heidi had seen in the slide show at Wewelsburg Castle in 1944. Finding those – finding just one symbol that proved the truth of the exodus from Atlantis – would be worth all the gold in the world to him.

Paul's voice crackled over the intercom. 'Apologies for the reception. We've got some kind of radio interference, maybe a localized electromagnetic phenomenon. There's activity on site. The radar's just showing a boat speeding away in the direction of San Salvador Island.'

'Anything from the drone?'

'It's had to turn back because of the weather. But Lanowski's just sent a message. It's what you want to hear, Jack. The drone showed a boat bang over the blue hole, with two divers getting in the water before it sped off.'

Jack tensed. 'Good. If there's any sign of it returning, Macalister has a hotline to the head of the Royal Bahamas Defence Force to order an intercept. I don't want it done yet in case the boat captain has some way of contacting Saumerre and he realizes what we're doing. But if needs be, you can say we suspect it's a drug-runner.'

That much had gone according to plan. The MQ-1 Predator drone had been an inspirational idea of Lanowski's, and a masterpiece of string-pulling involving Macalister, their MI6 contact, Ben and finally Mikhail, who had gone straight to his CIA handlers at Langley and explained enough of the situation with Saumerre and the potential terrorist threat to have a drone launched from a secret US installation in Florida, with the imagery streamed via the airbase to Lanowski's computer in the operations room on board *Seaquest II*.

'Okay,' Paul said. 'Target in sight now. T minus two minutes.'

'Roger that,' Jack said. He made a diver's okay sign at Costas, who was sitting beside him with his helmet visor already down, his e-suit covered by the tattered remains of the trusty old boilersuit he had somehow found time to patch and sew together after parts of it had melted during their volcano dive in the Black Sea four days previously. Costas patted his pockets, checking them, and Jack saw the grapple gun they had used in the volcano poking out of one side and attached by a metal carabiner to a hook under his arm. Jack snapped down his own helmet, made sure the rebreather system was operating and quickly scanned the digital computer readout inside his helmet. He listened to his breathing, keeping it cool, measured. He remembered what Paul had said. With their helmets now on and no intercom link to the pilot, the signal would be three sharp bangs on the metal bulkhead behind the pilot's seat. Crude, but effective. He glanced at Costas again, visually checking his gear, and saw Costas doing the same for him. He reached up and grasped the sliding door handle, and then whispered the words he always said before a dive: *Lucky Jack*.

The helicopter pitched slightly to the rear and he felt it descend, seeing only a shroud of spray from the rotorwash out of the window. Then he heard three bangs. He looked at Costas, pointing his thumb down, and Costas did the same. They opened the sliding doors simultaneously, into a maelstrom of noise and water. Jack swung his legs out, contacted the skid with his fins, crouched down and rolled forward, holding his helmet with one hand and his backpack with the other as he somersaulted into the sea. He dropped a few feet underwater and then rose to the surface again, patting his head with one hand to show Paul that he was safe. He saw Costas do the same, his yellow helmet just visible in the sheets of spray against the looming blackness of the storm coming in from the east. Jack pressed his buoyancy compensator exhaust to expel air and then he was underwater, the tumult of the surface gone, feeling the instant sense of calm he always did at the beginning of a dive. Costas came alongside him, and they exchanged okay signals again and a thumbs-down. *This was it.*

Below them lay a massive jumble of rock and coral, fragments as large as houses that Jack knew must have been blown off the side walls of the blue hole by the explosions of the three depth charges dropped by the Liberator in 1945. In the centre was an opening, a gap between the rocks about ten metres in circumference, ten metres or so below the surface. They dropped through it, and were immediately confronted by an astonishing sight.

Wedged into the hole beneath the rocks was the rusted hulk of a submarine, clearly identifiable from its conning tower as a German Type XXI U-boat. It was angled down at about forty-five degrees, and they could see in the gloom below that the bow had been sheared off. As they swam slowly down the hull, they became aware of extensive evidence of damage from gunfire, with holes peppering the outer casing and the gun turrets; the forward deck gun was still loaded with a round in the breech and the barrel was angled high off to starboard. Costas stopped just before the bow section and put his hand on the casing, raising a puff of rust. 'This confirms the airman's story,' he said into his intercom. 'This U-boat was sprayed with machine-gun rounds, fifty-calibre, and then the bow was blown off by one of those depth charges that also collapsed the blue hole all around it.'

'Remember Heidi telling us that Ernst had mentioned the torpedo tubes?' Jack said. 'If we're going to find any evidence of whether or not he carried out his plan, it's going to be there.'

They swam down into the twisted wreckage, immediately recognizing the forward tubes. Costas swam closer, and then backed out. 'Bingo,' he said. 'The forward left tube's been fired, and hasn't been sealed shut. It must have happened just before the Liberator attack, even during it. Hoffman cut it fine.'

'God only knows what was going on in those final moments in this boat. I only hope he had the satisfaction of knowing he'd succeeded before the end came. My guess is he would have been holed up in here, with no chance.'

'Jack, take a look below you. You're not going to believe it.'

Jack swam back about a metre and stared into the silt. He looked again, astonished. An object lay there, half inside a rotting leather satchel, something that seemed to have preoccupied them for as long as he could remember now, the object that had caused Rebecca's kidnapping. It was a golden swastika, the reverse side up, the other side a slightly rusty iron colour. *The palladion*. He quickly reached down, pushed it into the satchel and picked it up, then strapped it to the front of his e-suit. It was incredibly heavy for its size. 'Okay,' he said. 'Hoffman must have been given this by Himmler as the key to get into a chamber to store the virus phial. We can use it as a bargaining chip with Saumerre.'

'Where are they?' Costas said. 'The two divers the drone spotted?'

'In the habitat. Up above us, to the left of the U-boat's bow.' Costas followed his gaze. Perched against the only intact side of the blue-hole wall was a construction that looked like an early space-lab satellite, like two bathyspheres joined together, the whole structure secured on metal stilts on a rocky ledge.

'This is what that German ship in 1938 must have been doing, placing this installation on the spot where the Ahnenerbe divers had made their discovery two years previously,' Jack said. 'The symbols Heidi said they found must have added to the mystique, allowing Himmler to sell this place as the new Atlantis, though what really mattered to him and his scheme was that they happened to have discovered a place perfectly suited to his needs: far outside territorial waters, on the edge of the reef drop-off accessible to U-boats, and suitable for putting in a secure storage facility like this.'

'Hardly a centre of operations for Himmler after the war, though,' Costas said. 'Each of those spheres has barely enough room for a couple of people inside.'

'It had one purpose only,' Jack said. 'It was to store the biological weapon. Himmler himself must have had other plans for his own base, in South America perhaps. What's clear is that the story he told Hoffman and Heidi about their future was a lie, as it doubtless was to others of his followers he used to get his plan in motion. Nobody was ever going to live here, safe from the pandemic raging on land. This was no Wewelsburg reborn.'

'Just as it was no Atlantis reborn, by the look of it,' Costas said. 'So what's the plan?'

'We play the game I've set up for as long as it takes Saumerre to relax and believe me. As soon as I have the bacterium phial from him, we make a move. If we can crack the valves on his diving tanks, we can empty them to prevent him from getting out, but fill the habitat with enough air for him to survive until the US Navy team we have on hold arrive to pick him up.'

'I thought this was personal business for you, Jack.'

'With the level of his terrorist connections, the US is the best bet for keeping him under lock and key permanently.'

'I can think of a better place for him.' Costas was staring at the silted floor of the bows, where space below the deck level of the U-boat was visible. 'Jack, there's something else here you should see. The palladion wasn't the only gold on this boat. You were right.'

Jack followed Costas' gaze. He dropped down and wafted some silt away. 'Well I'll be damned,' he murmured. The sea floor was carpeted with gold bars, hundreds of them, spilling out of the U-boat where it had been blown open. Saumerre clearly had not seen the palladion when he dived down here just before them, but he must have seen this. Jack looked at Costas. 'Okay. Let's move.'

★ ★ ★

Five minutes later, they stood dripping inside the first sphere of the habitat. The tanks that Saumerre and the other diver had been wearing were on the floor beside the entry hatch, and had clearly been partly emptied into the spheres to create a breathable atmosphere. The interior was spartan, like the inside of a recompression chamber, with only a table in the centre of the room and a metal bed on either side of it, but nothing to suggest that people had ever spent time inside. Jack and Costas took off their fins but kept the rest of their gear on, only raising their visors. A voice spoke from the second sphere. 'Dr Howard. We meet at last.'

Jack ducked through the hatch into the second sphere, followed by Costas. Saumerre was sitting at the bench in the centre, wearing a wetsuit, his black hair slicked back; the other man was standing beside him. Jack had seen images of Saumerre many times in the media, his face familiar from his public front as a European Union politician, but this was the first time he had seen him in the flesh. Beyond them he saw something that made his heart pound. It was a small metal container against the wall, like a safe, with the reverse swastika depression in the front. It was closed. *So far, so good.* He stared at Saumerre, saying nothing.

'To business,' Saumerre said. 'Do you have the palladion?'

'Give me the bacterium, and I will give you the palladion.'

'I don't believe you have it.'

Jack pointed at the leather satchel strapped to his waist.

Saumerre hesitated. 'You don't know any better than I do whether the virus phial is in there or not, do you?'

Jack looked at him impassively, and said nothing.

Saumerre narrowed his eyes. 'Why would you be allowing me to have this virus?'

'Because I believe there's no chance you'll use it. You're an educated and civilized man. You'll be like Himmler, keeping it as a bargaining chip for the future. Spreading the word in the underworld that you have a Nazi wonder-weapon will make you a hugely powerful man. As for me, every archaeologist who sees enough of it eventually succumbs to gold. With that amount, I can ditch the whole tiresome scientific business and set myself up as a treasure-hunter. Others of my team will come along with me.' He jerked his head towards Costas, who smirked. 'And be very rich men.'

Saumerre looked cautiously at Jack for a moment, and then a smile crept over his face. 'So. The famous Dr Howard has seen the dark side, and he likes it.'

'Leave us the gold, and you take the virus. But I want the bacterium. I can play your game, too. You know it's far less deadly. It's never been tried. And there's an antidote.'

'Not possible. Nobody has worked on this since the war.'

'Professor Dr Heidi Hoffman has.'

'Ah, yes. Of course. Your confidante.' Saumerre hesitated again, then held out his hand. 'The palladion?'

Jack reached down and unwrapped the leather satchel he had retrieved from the U-boat. The leather was strong enough to hold together, tough cowhide, but had perished on the surface and came away in his hands. He wiped them on his e-suit and took out the golden swastika inside. Saumerre gasped, and the other man's eyes were riveted on it. Jack held it with one hand, his arm muscles straining with the weight, and held out his other hand, waiting. Saumerre unzipped the pocket of his buoyancy compensator, took out a waterproof box and opened it, revealing a cylinder inside the size of a large pen. Jack quickly checked it, seeing the marks Heidi had told him to look for and the sealing cover, still intact. Saumerre closed the box and handed it to Jack, who let him take the palladion and immediately slipped the box into his leg pocket. Saumerre turned and slotted the palladion into the depression on the metal safe, where it fitted perfectly. A lock clicked, the door opened slightly and the palladion was partly ejected from the hollow. Saumerre took it and placed it on the table, then turned back to the safe.

Jack glanced at Costas, looking at the grapple-gun handle just visible in his boilersuit. Costas nodded almost imperceptibly.

Jack held his breath. If the virus was in there, they were set for a deadly standoff in which there could be no winners. If it was empty, then he and Costas could seize the moment and gain the upper hand. He thought of Hoffman, of the U-boat outside with the fired torpedo tube, of Heidi's absolute faith that Ernst would have done the right thing.

Saumerre opened the door to the safe.

It was empty.

Costas whipped out the grapple gun and held it to Saumerre's neck. Jack picked up the palladion and thrust it at the other man, who buckled under the weight, falling on his knees and allowing Jack to slam his fist into his temple and knock him out. He picked up the palladion, grabbed the satchel and retreated through the hatch to the first sphere. Costas followed, keeping his gun trained on Saumerre, who seemed too stunned to move. 'Visor down,' Jack yelled, closing his own visor and waiting until Costas had done the same before unscrewing the regulators from the two tanks and cracking the valves open, thankful that their closed helmets dulled the noise of two-thousand-odd p.s.i. of compressed air escaping in such a confined space. After about twenty seconds the noise abated and the tanks emptied. Jack unhooked the hose from his own backpack and vented it for good measure, so that there was enough air in the chamber to ensure that Saumerre survived for at least a couple of hours. He hooked the hose back into his helmet, strapped the package with the palladion to his chest, and looked at Costas. 'Let's get out of here.'

They donned their fins and dropped one after the other through the entry hatch at the base of the sphere, then swam off over the U-boat. Jack checked his air pressure. He had vented half of his supply, but there was little risk with the surface only fifteen metres above them and Costas beside him with virtually full tanks in case of emergency. They stopped together beneath the crack between the rocks that led to the surface. 'Good to go?' Costas asked.

Jack looked around. There was one thing he had not seen. There had been no ancient symbols, no artefacts. He knew they would come back here after Saumerre was removed, would scour the place, but he still wanted to know now. He had spotted only one opening leading off the main chamber, about ten metres deeper beyond the bow section of the U-boat, a tunnel in the wall. He pointed. 'I'd like to have a quick look down there.'

'It's too deep for the Ahnenerbe divers, probably almost thirty metres,' Costas said. 'We have to remember that the

Nazi divers only had pure oxygen and that becomes toxic below ten metres depth. If you're looking for the place where they might have found those symbols, that can't be it.'

'It could lead into a shallower cavern. And if you look at the wall directly ahead of us above that tunnel, there's a place where I think there was a fissure connecting with this chamber, at about fifteen metres. It looks as if it was blocked by the explosions. That depth would have just about been possible with primitive oxygen rebreathers.'

'How's your air supply?'

'Not a lot of margin, but if you stay close by, we'll be fine.'

'It'll be an overhead environment in there, Jack. We haven't got a safety line or spare tanks.'

'No more than twenty metres in, I promise.'

Costas paused for a moment, floating still. 'Okay. Your call.' They dropped down and were soon at the tunnel entrance, a jagged hole about three metres wide and five metres long. They swam through into another chamber, the size of a small church, the walls rising high above them on every side. Jack ascended until his depth gauge read fifteen metres. Costas swam off to one side, looking hard at the cave walls, searching for anything man-made. 'I'm remembering Lanowski's CGI model of this place about 5500 BC. Where we are now would have been inside one of the hills he thought lay on either side of the cavern that became the blue hole. We'd have been maybe ten metres above sea level at this point. I'm just thinking of a guy in a boat arriving here after a trip across the Atlantic, exhausted, famished, thinking he'd seen the promised twin-peaked volcano but then realizing it was an illusion, yet still needing shelter. The cavern below us would have been a subterranean cave beside the sea, perfect for pulling a boat into during a storm. Where we are, higher up, could have been a separate cavern, almost like a mezzanine. You can imagine him finding a way up the rock and holing up here.'

'And slowly going mad,' Jack said.

'Maybe not so slowly,' Costas replied. 'If it was hurricane season, he could have collected rainwater from the rock pools on the surface, and anyone who'd survived an Atlantic crossing on an open boat like that must have been a reasonably adept fisherman. But once the rains stopped, that would have been it. He would have had to move on. I don't see him building a new Atlantis here.'

Jack stared at the walls, remembering Heidi's description of the underwater cave in the primitive photograph she had seen, and knowing himself what he was looking for. Suddenly he spotted something close to the base of the ledge of the upper cavern, and swam towards it. As he got close to the wall, his heart began to pound. 'Bingo,' he said.

Costas swam towards him, Together they stared at a line of five carved symbols, eroded and obscured by marine growth. 'Look at that,' Jack exclaimed. 'Those first three symbols: the pectiform symbol, the half-moon and the cluster of dots. That's what Katya identified from the Stone Age code as the shaman name for Noah, Uta-Napishtim. It's identical to the name Little Joey saw on the cave wall in Atlantis, except here I don't see the symbols for Enlil-Gilgamesh. After Noah's name, there's the Atlantis symbol. And finally there's the half-moon with dots over it, the symbol Katya interprets as meaning "west".'

'It's like a carving on one of those castle dungeon walls in England. "I was here."'

'Dungeon is probably about right,' Jack said. 'But I think it says more than that. I think it says Noah-Uta-napishtim was here, from Atlantis, or going to Atlantis, to the west. It's fantastic. It's exactly what I wanted to find. It confirms one of the greatest voyages of discovery in prehistory, the fact that travellers from the most ancient civilization of the Old World went across the Atlantic more than seven thousand years ago. And I know where he was heading. I know where the new Atlantis lies.'

'Jack, we have to move. Now.'

Jack felt a tug on his legs, but Costas was now several arms' lengths away, moving rapidly across the cavern but somehow without finning. Jack suddenly realized what had happened. *The tide had turned.* He saw Costas drop down to the tunnel and begin to fin hard, making slow progress against the current that was suddenly racing through the lower part of the chamber from the blue hole into the bowels of the reef beyond. Jack realized that he was being propelled around the upper part of the chamber in an eddy created by the current, but he found it impossible to follow it to the point where Costas had managed to get down to the tunnel. He saw that Costas had disappeared, but his voice crackled on the intercom. 'Jack. I'm through. There's no way you can follow me now. The current must have increased by three knots in the last minute. It's like a vortex in here, a twister that's sucking the water down. But I've got a line I'm going to feed back into the hole for you to grab. I should be able to pull you through.'

Jack let the eddy take him to a rocky outcrop protruding above the current, now clearly visible as a turbulent stream in the water. He held the rock with one hand and reached into the current with the other, feeling his hand almost rip away. Then he saw Costas' line snake through, a dark streak below him with a small orange buoy the size of a tennis ball at the end. It waved around violently, but it was at least three metres below the top of the current and there was no way he could reach it. He heard Costas again. 'I always keep a buoy attached to float the line. It should come up to you.'

'That's a negative,' Jack said. 'The current's too strong.'

'I don't have anything more buoyant on me.'

'How long is this current going to last?'

The intercom crackled, the interference worse now. 'A long time, Jack. It's a spring tide at the moment, and it's a high one. It's like a bathtub emptying, and you're somewhere down the sinkhole.'

'You mean hours.'

There was no reply for a moment, then Costas came on clearly. 'How's your air?'

Jack glanced at his readout, and suddenly tensed. Five hundred p.s.i. He only had a few minutes left. 'Bad,' he said. 'It was my call. I had to find the archaeology. I guess I'm paying the price.'

'I'm coming in for you.'

'Oh no you're not.'

'I'm going to find something to tie the line to out here, then tie myself off at the other end and work my way down the line through that tunnel. I should have the strength to kick out of the current long enough to grab you, and the line should be strong enough to allow both of us to use it to make our way back against the current. I'm probably going out of radio range, Jack. The interference is really bad out here. I'm going to find part of the submarine wreckage to tie on to. Hang in there.'

Jack pushed off and floated back up into the upper part of the chamber. There was no point struggling against the current. He tried to relax, to slow his breathing, to conserve his remaining air. He tried to keep calm. It was always like this in diving. Things happened quickly. One moment everything is fine, euphoric, but you take a little risk along the way, and before you know it everything has gone very badly wrong, in an instant. He was in his element underwater, but he knew it was utterly unforgiving. In a cave, one poor decision, one gamble gone wrong, and that was it. His gamble with his air had been based on Costas being beside him in case he had to buddy-breathe. But then something had happened that he should have factored into the equation. They had even talked about the current on the way down. He put it down to experience, for the next time they dived in this place.

He looked at the rock, seeing the symbols again: the Atlantis symbol that had come to mean so much in his career. The eddy had pushed him into a place of stillness in the water, like the eye of a storm, and he used his breathing to acquire perfect neutral buoyancy. He had always loved doing that, the feeling he got when he knew he had achieved total equilibrium, a sensation of utter oneness with his environment that was far better than any altered-consciousness experience he could imagine. He forgot for a moment where he was, what was happening, and just revelled in being where he had always wanted to be, underwater. Each breath, each slight exhalation was precious now, because he knew what was coming next, the greatest fear of all divers. He tested his breathing, trying a deeper breath. It was tightening. He was running out of air. He tried not to panic, to breathe like someone trapped in a prison cell, banging against the walls; he had to keep measured and calm until the final moment. *He did not want to die.* He felt his fingers and legs begin to tingle. He remembered something, and delved into a pocket on his leg, pulling out a small writing board with a plastic sheet and a pencil. He quickly pulled out his knife, cutting a piece off the sheet, and wrote on it, feeling his air going, realizing that his vision was tunnelling. He dropped the board and tucked the note into the sleeve of his suit, where it would be found. He began gagging and retching. His neck felt as if it were about to explode. He wanted to get his helmet off, to drown rather than suffocate, but he could no longer raise his arms. He began to sink, dropping down towards the current.

Suddenly something hit him hard, and there was a flood of air in his helmet. He breathed in, great gulping breaths, feeling his head reel, his body instantly coming back to life again. Costas was holding him tight, tying the line that was looped around his own shoulders to Jack's waist, keeping it free from the backup air hose that he had plugged from his backpack into Jack's helmet. He stared into Jack's visor. 'You okay?'

'That was a bit tight.'

'Okay. Let's get out of here.' Costas led up the line, his bulk providing a buffer against the current that Jack was grateful to follow, keeping close behind so that the air hose was not stretched. Inch by inch they pulled themselves back through the tunnel and towards the wrecked deck gun on the U-boat where Costas had tied the line. Ten minutes after leaving the cavern they were free of the current, which wavered in the water like a giant twister about five metres in front of the U-boat's bow. Jack began to relax, following Costas as he made his way up the casing of the submarine towards the conning tower. 'Okay. This is what I wanted to find.' Costas took out a small crowbar from his kit and set to work on a low metal cover about the size of a small bed. It came away easily, revealing a folded inflatable boat that had clearly been sealed in an airtight space, looking in remarkably good condition as Costas shook it out. He fumbled around beneath it, found what he wanted and leaned back. 'Heads up,' he said. He pulled a cord and the boat suddenly began to inflate, then billowed up and rocketed towards the surface some twenty metres above. 'Thought we may as well enjoy some comfort while we wait for Paul,' Costas said.

They began to ascend towards the irregular gap in the rocks that led to the surface, steering clear of the lethal whirlpool that whipped through the opening on one side. Jack looked up, seeing sunlight streaming through. Whatever had happened to the hurricane, it must have bypassed them. A dark shape came across the hole, about ten metres from them and five metres higher. Jack stared. It was impossible. 'Costas, we've got company.'

Coming towards them were two divers, Saumerre and the other man. They were both wearing primitive Nazi oxygen rebreathers. 'Shit,' Costas said. 'They must have found those inside the habitat. I didn't think to look.' Jack looked at his depth gauge. They were still eighteen metres deep, almost twice the safe depth for pure oxygen diving. The second diver seemed sluggish, trailing behind Saumerre, almost certainly showing the effects of oxygen poisoning. But he was carrying a vicious-looking knife, and they were closing in. Jack looked at Costas.

'The guy behind is suffering. Let's take him out first.'

Costas removed his grapple gun from its holster and loaded a round. They were less than eight metres away now, easily within range. He aimed quickly and fired, but the metal grapple shot just to the right of the man's legs and carried on for another few metres before dropping down, pulling the grapple line with it and catching the man's fin. He twisted round, trying to free himself, but only entangling his leg more, pulling Costas towards him. Costas fumbled to disengage the line from the carabiner, where it was hooked to his e-suit. Jack watched as the line with the grapple dangling below began to twist round and round into the whirlpool. To his horror he realized that it was pulling the man and Costas towards the vortex as well. He pulled out his knife and grabbed Costas, who had realized what was happening and was desperately trying to fin towards the rock wall. Jack finned hard against the pull of the line, then severed it with one swipe of his knife. They both rocketed forward out of the vortex. The man was already limp in the water, unconscious from oxygen poisoning, and Jack watched him plummet with horrifying speed down the whirlpool, disappearing through the tunnel to a place from which there could be no return.

When he looked up again, he realized that Saumerre had swum through the hole and was now over the reef heading out into the open ocean. It seemed a hopeless enterprise, but there was always the possibility that Saumerre's boat had not been apprehended and would return to pick him up. Jack and Costas were too encumbered with gear to catch up. Jack made a snap decision. They were only about eight metres deep now, so he could easily surface. The dive had been shallow enough to mean that they had not exceeded their no-stop decompression time, so they shouldn't have to worry about the bends. He took several deep breaths, then unlocked the quick release on his backpack and his helmet, pulling the unit off and pushing it away, then reaching down to where he kept an emergency mask in a pocket on his leg, quickly putting it on and clearing it. Costas look at him in alarm, but Jack did a quick okay sign and pointed towards the rapidly receding form of Saumerre. He powered after him, the palladion acting as a useful weight in the absence of his backpack.

He was out beyond the edge of the reef wall over the abyss, and reached Saumerre just as his chest began to tighten. His plan was to push Saumerre bodily down below the ten-metre safety threshold for the oxygen rebreather, then to leave him as he became unconscious. He was on Saumerre before the other man had realized what was happening, pushing down on his shoulders and powering down with his fins. Saumerre reacted instantly and with surprising strength, twisting round and grasping Jack's arms. His grip was like a vice. Jack remembered what he was carrying. He let go of Saumerre, reached into the satchel and pulled out the palladion, the gold and dull metal swastika, feeling its weight, seeing for the first time the Atlantis symbol impressed in the edge. Saumerre saw it too, and froze.

Jack held it out to him.

For an instant, Saumerre's hands remained gripped on Jack's arm. Then he let go, and grabbed the palladion, his eyes lighting up. He knew it now served no more purpose, that there were no secret chambers to unlock, but it had been a prize he had sought all his life, from the time his grandfather must have told him what he had seen in that awful bunker outside the concentration camp almost seventy years ago. He was enraptured by it. Jack watched him sink down, oblivious to its weight, staring at it. He must have reached fifteen metres, then twenty, and below him there was nothing but a sheer drop of a mile or more into blackness. Too late he realized his mistake. He let go of the palladion, and grasped his head in agony, tearing at the rebreather. Then he went limp. The palladion had caught in the webbing on his chest, and Jack watched it as Saumerre fell, his body face up and slowly spinning until all Jack could see was the golden shape of the swastika spinning round and round, shrouded in a swirl of tiny bubbles, until it disappeared into blackness.

Jack's lungs were screaming for air. A regulator was thrust into his face. He grabbed it and put it in his mouth, sucking hard, looking at Costas. The sun was shining brilliantly on the surface, and they could see the dark shape of the inflatable from the U-boat bobbing above them. Slowly they began to ascend together. Just before breaking surface, Jack looked down again, half expecting to see that shape somewhere below him, but there was nothing but darkness.

It was over.

Epilogue

'Jack, correct me if I'm wrong, but are you and I sailing off into the sunset together?'

Jack peered at Costas, then at the boat they were in, and then at the miles of empty ocean surrounding them, barely visible in the blinding sunlight. They were wedged opposite each other with hardly any space to move, but the old German inflatable seemed as strong as the day it had been packed on board the U-boat more than sixty-five years before, its CO_2 bottle still pressurized enough to fill the pontoons. Jack had stripped down the upper half of his wetsuit to his T-shirt, but Costas was still wearing his tattered off-grey boiler suit bearing the scars and patches from their encounter with molten lava in another ocean a few days previously. Jack was holding the waterproof two-way radio that Costas had taken from a special pocket in his boiler suit that miraculously remained watertight. After surfacing and struggling into the boat, they had immediately sent out a VHF call to Paul, who was on his way back from *Seaquest II* in the Lynx and due to arrive in a matter of minutes.

Costas reached into the waist of his boiler suit and pulled out a compressed bag. He unzipped it and extracted something that looked like a wedge of unleavened bread, with something colourful oozing out of the sides. He sniffed it, grunted, and took a bite. He looked at Jack as he munched away, then swallowed. 'Not bad,' he said, wiping his mouth. 'Tuna and cucumber. Want one?'

'You brought sandwiches. *Sandwiches*.'

Costas raised his arms. 'So what?'

'As if we were going on a picnic?'

Costas gestured with his sandwich at his boiler suit, speaking with his mouth full. 'Empty pocket otherwise. May as well fill them.'

Jack grinned, shaking his head, then reached into his own leg pocket and took out a small plastic water bottle, uncapping it and draining it completely. He took out another one from the other side, then leaned back, squinting at the sun and closing his eyes, enjoying the heat. He felt something hit his hand, opened his eyes and saw a baseball cap, then saw that Costas was wearing one as well.

'Sun hats. One for me too. You blow me away.'

'Be prepared. That's my motto.' Costas reached into another pocket and pulled out his old aviator sunglasses, putting them on at a skewed angle and looking at Jack, who was trying not to smile. Costas raised his arms again. 'What?'

'Got anything else in there?'

'You want to know?' Costas took a huge bite of his sandwich, and then began patting his boiler suit. The radio came to life, and Jack spoke into it for a few minutes. He put his hand over the receiver and spoke to Costas. 'I'm just talking to Macalister on *Seaquest II*. There's been an interesting development. Reuters is reporting a cruise missile strike in the heart of the Taklamakan Desert. Ben has been in touch with our MI6 contact, and they reckon the target was Shang Yong's headquarters. MI6 have been expecting a crackdown on his operations by China, but not so soon. The evidence is pointing to an offshore US strike, and that can only have come about through intelligence on a high-category terrorist threat. Ben reckons they must have been closely monitoring Saumerre, and that Shang Yong has paid the price for agreeing to work for him.'

'Rebecca will be happy,' Costas said, munching. 'That really closes the lid on the bad guys.'

Jack nodded. He felt the box in his suit pocket containing the phial he had persuaded Saumerre to give him. Once that was deposited in a secure containment facility and destroyed, the lid would truly be closed. He put the radio back to his ear and spoke for a few more minutes. Then he put it down and laughed out loud, the first time he had done that in months. He grinned at Costas. 'You remember a promise you made to a new friend a few days ago?'

'Huh?'

'You're going to need a tuxedo.'

'You've lost me.'

'Lanowski's getting married.'

Costas dropped his sandwich. 'You're kidding me.'

'Nope.' Jack offered him the radio. 'Speak to Macalister if

you want. It's the biggest news since we found Atlantis.'

Costas waved away the radio. 'You mean they actually met?'

'Yesterday, in Bermuda. It was love at first sight.'

'I can't believe I offered to be his best man. And that he accepted.'

'You're his new best buddy. You were the one who took him on that submersible ride over Atlantis.'

'Yes, but . . .' Costas pointed at the mess of tuna and cucumber on his boiler suit. 'Me? In a tuxedo?'

'Apparently they want the wedding to be in the submersible. It was that picture you took of him at the controls, the one he posted of himself on the dating website. That was what really did it for her. She's crazy about him. But Macalister has a plan. As well as a PhD, she's a *Vogue* model. We can sell the photo rights. It'll be the eccentric celebrity wedding of the year. And you'll be smack bang in the middle of it.'

'My God,' Costas moaned, putting his hands to his face. 'If only I hadn't opened my big mouth.'

Jack pulled his hat down to cover his eyes, then lay back on the pontoon. 'If you need any help with the best-man speech, just let me know. I did it for Maurice and Aysha.'

Looking dejected, Costas attempted to recover the debris of his sandwich from his lap, stuffing a piece of bread and tuna into his mouth. Then he pointed up, gesturing, and Jack tipped back his hat and shaded his eyes. He could see the speck of a helicopter, getting bigger as it approached, the noise reverberating off the sea. A minute later it swept low past them, then turned around and came in to hover a few hundred feet away, only about twenty feet above the waves. Jack saw Paul wave from the cockpit, and he waved back. The side door slid open and a female wetsuited figure jumped out, falling like an arrow with ankles folded and arms held tight, disappearing with barely a splash into the rotorwash below the Lynx. Moments later the diver's head appeared and a hand was raised giving the okay sign, then a mesh bag containing fins and a mask was dropped alongside. As the helicopter slowly turned to port and tilted forward, accelerating away over the waves, the diver put on the mask and fins and swam quickly towards them, dropping down underwater about twenty feet away and powering up the side of the boat until she was half inside, leaning on her elbows on the pontoon. She pulled off her mask and shook her long dark hair, tied up in a ponytail. 'Hi, Dad. Uncle Costas.'

'Rebecca.' Jack smiled broadly. 'I thought you might drop in.'

'Jeremy's in the helicopter,' she said breathlessly. 'Paul's gone off for a perimeter sweep, just to make sure there aren't any more bad guys lurking around.'

'I don't think he's got anything to worry about,' Costas said, looking at the empty pocket in his boiler suit where the grapple gun had been. 'We're well and truly alone.'

'What did you find?'

Jack took a swig from his water bottle. 'It was fantastic. Symbols carved on a cave wall. I want you to see it with your own eyes. As soon as *Seaquest II* is on station this afternoon, we'll go in there again. Just the three of us.'

'And Jeremy,' Rebecca said. 'Costas qualified him in the sea off Troy a week ago.'

'Okay.' Jack smiled. 'And Jeremy.'

'Nice one with the palladion, by the way, Jack,' Costas said, fishing for another sandwich. 'Never did like that thing. Too many bad associations. And I like the idea that we've put something real at the bottom of the Bermuda Triangle. Maybe it'll keep the pirates away from this place.'

'You found it?' Rebecca said. 'Where is it?'

Jack paused. 'It got, um, entangled. With Saumerre. They're somewhere down below us. About five thousand feet deep in the abyss. They probably haven't even hit the bottom yet.'

'And then there's one of Lanowski's megaturbitides,' Costas said. 'About another thousand feet of silt.'

'And then boiling-hot magma,' Jack added.

'So Saumerre really is gone?' Rebecca said quietly.

Jack reached out and put his hand on hers. 'It's finished.'

She looked away, closing her eyes, then looked back at him, blinking away the salt. 'I didn't want to say anything. But ever since I was kidnapped last year, it's been really difficult. Knowing he was still out there, not knowing whether it was going to happen again.'

'It's all taken care of.'

'Have a sandwich,' Costas said, his mouth full, offering her the bag. 'They're a bit flattened, kind of like toasted sandwiches without being toasted, if you see what I mean, a little soggy but surprisingly good.'

Rebecca smiled, wiping her eyes, then peered into the bag. 'A kind of underwater picnic. Really cool idea, Costas, one of your best. Thanks. Maybe later.'

Jack lay back again. 'There's a phrase from the Epic of Gilgamesh. "The dream was marvellous, but the terror was great. We must treasure the dream, whatever the terror." I feel like that now: as if those few symbols on that cavern wall were like the shining light at the end of the tunnel, like the star of heaven that once fell on those people far back in prehistory and became their guiding light, as if the dream of this discovery has drawn us through the terror and we're at the other end.'

'Do you remember the Walter de la Mare poem, about the silence surging softly backwards?' Costas said. 'I know what you mean. It's as if that great clamour from the past has gone, the cries of the shamans trapped in that chamber in Atlantis, the awful feeling Maurice had as he entered the bunker. He told me on the phone about his aunt Heidi, how she said for her it was as if the Nazi period had never ended, as if the tide of those terrible years had always seemed to sweep ahead of her.'

'Maybe now it's begun to turn,' Rebecca said quietly.

'So, Jack,' Costas said, finding something in the bag that might once have been a banana. 'What are we going to do with all that gold?'

'*Gold?*' Rebecca exclaimed

'Tons of it. In the U-boat.'

'*U-boat?*'

'Yep. There's one of those down there too.'

Jack looked at Costas. 'You remember last year we took Hugh Frazer to that home outside Auschwitz where they looked after elderly survivors of the concentration camp? We saw the old lady with the harp, the girl Hugh had seen in the camp near Belsen all those years before. There are very few of those survivors left now. But Frau Hoffman said she'd worked as a volunteer at a children's hospice near that place. I was thinking what a U-boat full of gold could do for a place like that. Nothing about atonement or restitution, nothing about the fact that a lot of that gold probably came from Jews and Poles, but simply to help bring happiness where there has been so little.'

'Great plan,' said Rebecca. 'Can I be the one to talk to Frau Hoffman about it?'

'I'm sure she'd love to talk to you,' Jack said.

'And about us. This quest. Where we go from here,' Costas said. 'You said when you saw those symbols in the cavern that you recognized the one that Katya thought meant "west". That means into the Caribbean islands and towards the mainland, to Mexico. Are we following Noah-Uta-napishtim?'

Jack looked into the sea. He could see far down, two hundred feet or more, and could just make out the top of the reef wall that rose up almost a mile from the abyss. He half expected to see some dark form beneath them, some lurking malevolence of the underworld come to punish them for discarding the palladion, but instead all he saw were thin trails of bubbles rising from far down in the abyss. He shifted slightly and saw his own reflection in the water, no details, just the silhouette of a man framed by the sun staring down. It seemed a timeless image. He remembered the voyage of Noah and Gilgamesh. For the first time it seemed real, not myth, like watching Second World War footage in colour. Noah had been here, in a boat not much larger than this one, smelling the sea breeze, trailing his fingers in the sea, looking down at the bubbles and the phosphorescence. Somewhere near here, Noah the shaman had gone on, and Gilgamesh the hero, the man who would be a god, had turned back.

Jack remembered the carnage and human sacrifice they had

seen in the inner sanctum at Atlantis. That too had been real, as real as the horror of the Nazi bunker. He turned to Costas. 'Do you remember, four years ago when we dived in the sacred cenotes of the Yucatán in Mexico, going to the site of Chichen Itza and seeing the appalling evidence of human sacrifice? You yourself said it was a society where something had gone terribly wrong, that had not developed normally, as if someone had come from over the sea and imposed a distorted memory of Egyptian and Near Eastern civilization. You said the Maya were like a cult brainwashed by a madman.'

'You mean the madness of Noah-Uta-napishtim,' Costas murmured.

'Perhaps Noah was on his own voyage into insanity, pushed towards it by what he had seen and done in that chamber of horrors in Atlantis, then by the sun and starvation and exhaustion as he came to this place, and then by the desperation that drove him to leave and sail ever further west until he hit the mainland and met people who lived as he knew his ancestors had done, a way he admired. He taught them what he knew from Atlantis, how to build pyramids and how to sacrifice, something that came to an awful head thousands of years later in the orgy of bloodletting by the Maya and the Aztecs.'

'Not a place we want to go,' Rebecca said.

Jack shook his head. 'I think we turn back, just as Gilgamesh did. We go back to the world where men became gods, and where it was a short step from those faceless pillars of the Neolithic temples to the tyrannical god-kings of the Middle East and the worst megalomaniacs of our time, to Hitler and Himmler and the other monsters of Nazism. But that's our legacy, and we know from what has happened today that we can transcend it. If we carry on west and follow Noah-Utanapishtim to his heart of darkness, I'm not sure if there is any happy ending. There's nothing for us there, no treasure at the end of the trail, just a horrifying vision of what human beings are capable of inflicting on each other.'

'We've seen enough of that in the past few days,' Costas muttered.

'So what's next?' Rebecca said.

Jack was dog-tired, but he felt that familiar adrenalin surging through him. 'We were speaking of Maurice Hiebermeyer. I owe him.'

'Egypt?'

Jack grinned. 'He and I have been planning it for years. It's so big, we've never quite wanted to go for it, both of us waiting until the time was right.'

'That statue with the inscription Maurice found at Troy?'

'That was the clue he needed. If I tell you this could be bigger than the discovery of the tomb of Tutankhamun, far bigger, you'll see where I'm coming from. It's about Akhenaten, Tutankhamun's father, the most mysterious and terrifying of the pharaohs, about where he came from and where he went. About what happened to his treasure. About finding his tomb.'

'Any diving?' Costas mumbled, now half asleep.

'Like you wouldn't believe. The most astonishing find has been made in the Red Sea.'

'No more deadly toxins? Doomsday weapons?'

'I swear.'

'Erupting volcanoes?'

'The dive site is beside a beach, one of those ones with parasols and reclining chairs and a little bar at the back serving cocktails.'

Costas tipped his hat up and squinted at Jack. 'You're kidding.'

'Nope.'

He leaned back again, sighing contentedly. 'For the first time ever, you think of me.'

'Only after you do your duty at Lanowski's wedding.'

Costas groaned and pulled his hat back over his face. Jack smiled at Rebecca, who raised her eyes and shook her head. He remembered the message he had written to her on the scrap of plastic when he thought he was going to die in the cavern below. He reached down to his buoyancy compensator pocket, felt for it, then discreetly took it out and dangled his hand over the pontoon, releasing the scrap into the sea and letting the waves wash through his fingers. The message would be there for her for ever, in the sea, Jack's spirit world, though the words would be erased by sun and water and would only ever be known to him. He felt a dawning happiness, as if that act had been the final release he had needed to throw off the burden that had weighed on him since Rebecca had been drawn into the nightmare of kidnapping and violence that had dogged their quest.

He lifted his hand from the water and shielded his eyes, looking up. The sound of the helicopter became louder, increasing to a roar as it took up position overhead. The downdraught kicked up a spray of water around the boat that sparkled as the sun shone through it, and for a moment it was as if they were in a vortex, one that would lift them to ever more fabulous places. Jack was suddenly coursing with excitement. He shaded his eyes and looked up, seeing Jeremy's helmeted figure leaning out of the door. Costas reached up and caught the winch line, then looked at Jack and Rebecca, making a whirling motion with his free hand and pointing up. 'Good to go?' he yelled.

Rebecca draped her arm over Jack's shoulders. Jack beamed at Costas, then tilted his head towards Rebecca, waiting. She turned and looked at him expectantly. Then she understood. She shook her head again, grinning, and they both shouted together.

'Good to go.'

Background
to the novel

When my first novel *Atlantis* was published in 2005, it was against a backdrop of extraordinary real-life discoveries that were transforming our view of the rise of civilization. A century ago, most scholars would have put that formative period at the beginning of the Bronze Age, some five thousand years ago; now we know that many of the key developments – the first towns, with walls, towers and even temples – had appeared more than five thousand years before that, soon after the end of the Ice Age. Cambridge University, where I completed my PhD in archaeology in 1991, had long been a centre of expertise in this era, and by the time I left my academic teaching career ten years later to write full-time, it was clear that the Neolithic period was where the most exciting breakthroughs were being made in understanding the past. Not only were amazing new sites being excavated – mainly in modern Turkey, on the Anatolian plateau – but archaeologists were thinking in daring new ways, using finds to question long-held assumptions about the transformation from hunter-gatherer to agricultural societies. Most excitingly, they had begun to address the belief systems of our distant ancestors, to try to get inside their minds, something long thought beyond the scope of archaeology but where the new finds were shedding dazzling light. Was this a time of conflict, as the old beliefs of the hunter-gatherers were replaced by the new? Was it the birthplace of the gods? Much remains uncertain, but this sea change in archaeological thinking provides the backdrop to *The Gods of Atlantis*.

Atlantis revisited

My novel *Atlantis* was based on the premise that the sunken city, uniquely known from the fifth century BC Greek philosopher Plato's dialogues *Timaeus* and *Critias*, was not Plato's fictional creation but was truly derived – as he claims – from an account by the early sixth century BC Greek traveller Solon, who had heard it from an Egyptian priest in the temple at Saïs in the Nile delta. The Egyptian priests had an unbroken tradition of knowledge extending far back into prehistory, and my novel began with the fictional discovery of a papyrus containing Solon's original account of his visit to the temple. However, instead of basing the story in the Bronze Age, on the second-millennium BC eruption of the Aegean volcano of Thera and its effect on Minoan civilization – as do many archaeologists who take Plato's story at face value – my Atlantis dated thousands of years earlier, a distant memory of a devastating flood and a lost city at the dawn of civilization, not in the Aegean, but in the Black Sea to the north-east. This placed Atlantis in the Neolithic – the 'New Stone Age' – at the time when agriculture was first developed, a period dating from soon after the end of the Ice Age about twelve thousand years ago until the widespread adoption of copper technology from about the fifth millennium BC.

My inspiration derived from remarkable evidence published during the 1990s that the Black Sea may have been cut off during the last Ice Age from the Aegean by a land bridge across the Bosporus Strait, and that the Black Sea remained at its Ice Age level – a hundred metres or more below the present shoreline – until the global sea level rise caused the waters of the Aegean to breach the land bridge and flood the Black Sea basin. During the Ice Age, the glaciers themselves had not reached as far south as the Black Sea, but the great melt had a global effect on coastal settlement. The possibility that the Black Sea flood did not occur until the sixth millennium BC, more than three millennia after the beginning of the Neolithic, meant that the flood could have inundated early farming communities that may now lie underwater off the northern shore of Turkey. Evidence for the fecundity of this region suggests that it should be included within the 'fertile crescent' where agriculture first developed, stretching from present-day Israel up through Anatolian Turkey and down into the Zagros mountains of Iran.

The idea that there could have been a city with monumental structures was inspired by real-life evidence from the early

Neolithic: Jericho, in present-day Palestine, had city walls and a tower as early as the ninth millennium BC, and at Çatalhöyük in Anatolia, the excavations in the 1960s revealed a substantial town of the eighth millennium BC. Çatalhöyük even produced a famous wall painting that may show a town on the slopes of a double-peaked volcano, an image that appears in *The Gods of Atlantis*. I was also inspired by a theory that associated the spread of farming with the spread of Indo-European language, which had been sourced by many scholars to the Black Sea region about the seventh millennium BC. I could therefore imagine groups of early farmers fleeing the flood, some going overland to Mesopotamia and the Levant and Egypt, others by boat into the Aegean and further west – taking their animals with them, as we know happened in the Neolithic and may be remembered in the Old Testament account of Noah – and spreading agriculture, a common language and new technology far across Asia and Europe, and perhaps beyond.

The Neolithic revolution

The phrase 'Neolithic revolution' was coined in the 1950s by the prehistorian Gordon Childe to describe the dramatic changes that took place in the Near East after the Ice Age. As recently as 1980, when I first studied archaeology as an undergraduate, the Neolithic was still being approached in his terms, as a time when the invention of agriculture led to the first towns. This approach – in which economic rationale was the driving force behind change – and the rapidity of the 'revolution' seemed to be borne out by the evidence of Jericho and Çatalhöyük, towns that dated very soon after the first evidence for agriculture. But this picture has been turned on its head by new discoveries in eastern Turkey. It is less clear now that hunter-gatherers would have seen the advantages of agriculture in a region where foraging may have provided an easier livelihood; other factors were at play. The most extraordinary new finds are religious sites – temples, for want of a better word – that may have preceded the first towns and agriculture, yet whose construction required a level of labour organization that would have made these other developments – the construction of towns and monuments – possible. New religious ideas may therefore have been a driving force behind the rise of civilization. This stunning idea makes this period one of the most exciting in current archaeology. What has emerged is not only a new kind of Neolithic revolution, but also a revolution in the way we approach the past.

The site above all that has led to this revolution in ideas is in southern Turkey, at Göbekli Tepe, where excavations began in the 1990s and are still ongoing. In my novel *Atlantis*, Jack sees a Stonehenge-like structure in Atlantis that hints at the religious ideas that fleeing priests may have taken with them far to the west. At Göbekli Tepe, the archaeological reality behind this image is spectacularly revealed in an oval structure containing a circle of monolithic stones, carved in a way that suggests they may have been anthropomorphic. Extraordinarily, this 'temple' may date to 9500 BC, older even than Jericho. Another site in Turkey containing monolithic pillars has been discovered at Nevali Çori, and a third temple is at Çayönü. The finds from these sites discussed in this novel are all actual discoveries. The Çayönü site is now submerged by the waters of the Ataturk dam, suggestive of sites similar to these that may have been submerged along the Black Sea coast by another flood more than seven thousand years ago.

The birth of the gods

These 'temple' sites of the early Neolithic may represent a new form of religion, and the Neolithic revolution may above all have been a revolution in belief systems and the part they played in the rise of civilization. In order to understand what this new religion might have replaced, archaeologists have looked back to the rock paintings that first appear in caves in Europe about thirty-five thousand years ago. These caves, the basis for the fictional rock paintings in my novel, may have been portals into a spirit world, with spirit animals such as the bull – the aurochs – being used by shamans or seers as a way of transporting themselves into the supernatural, to a place where they could contact the dead. The famous female figurines of this period, with their exaggerated breasts and buttocks, may have been fertility symbols – good-luck charms – rather than 'gods'; the much later mother goddesses of the Bronze Age may hark back to a clay figurine of this type found at Çatalhöyük, but if she was a 'god', it may have been as a transmogrification from the fertility symbol rather than evidence for a Palaeolithic – Old Stone Age – goddess cult. Good luck with fertility, good luck with the hunt – represented perhaps by the spirit animals of the caves – and a way of dealing with death may have been the building blocks of the first coherent belief system, one which did not involve gods or acts of worship as we would understand them today.

Some of the clearest evidence for this older belief system

may be where it survived into the early Neolithic in private domestic contexts, visible for the first time in the earliest houses. Renewed excavations at Çatalhöyük since the 1980s have focused attention on the symbolism of art and artefacts within houses, including the bull's-horn 'bucrania' that have become an iconic image of the site. Houses may have taken on some of the significance of caves in the Palaeolithic, with bulls 'coming through' the walls in the same way that animals appear in cave paintings, suggesting that man-made walls had taken over from rock as a portal into the spirit world.

The Neolithic evidence has drawn in archaeologists of earlier prehistory who have long pondered the significance of cave art, and have come to believe that Palaeolithic religion may have involved practices similar to those of the shaman or 'seer' in hunter-gatherer societies recorded by anthropologists. Using techniques such as repetitive chanting and sensory deprivation – as well as hallucinogenic drugs – shamans could achieve a trance-like state comparable to that of worshippers during intensive acts of devotion to a god. The similarity of these experiences has led scientists to suggest that they have a common neuropsychological basis, that they are 'hard-wired' into the brain as the sensations of altered consciousness. Common sensations include being in a vortex or a tunnel, floating in water, and visions of an upper and a lower world, the basis for the tiered cosmology of heaven, earth and hell common to many religions. Just as devout believers can 'see' divinity all round them, so those who believe in a spirit realm can partly inhabit that world in their day-to-day lives; belief alone may be enough to propel them into a state of altered consciousness. This is what archaeologists mean when they talk of getting inside the prehistoric mind: trying to see the world in a way that is unfamiliar to many today who are not believers in the supernatural. In a prehistoric world where there may have been less fear of being 'out of control', the pleasure of surrendering to hallucinogenic experiences was also a factor. The strength of early religion – the draw to its participants – may have been these altered-consciousness experiences in which the voyage in the mind was more important than the destination, in a belief system that did not revolve around the worship of gods or reward for devotion with a favoured place in the afterlife.

How and why this type of belief system may have changed into the new religion seen at Göbekli Tepe, with its temple-like structures, is a matter for speculation. Earlier religious experience may have been inclusive, with access to the spirit world open to everyone, as reflected in its survival in the houses at Çatalhöyük; rather than being fixed to particular sites, religious practice may have been 'portable', involving sacred stones such as meteorites hinted at in the earliest foundation myths of the Bronze Age, noted below. The establishment of fixed sites for ritual may have come about during periods when the glaciers had receded and people were able to remain in one area for generations, particularly at the time of the first cave art in southern Europe and then after the end of the last Ice Age. That period, after about 10,000 BC, gave the ecological stability for long-term settlement that allowed the process to go further than it ever had before. Fixed places of ritual may have become increasingly *exclusive*, the preserve of shamans or priests empowered by their sway over increasingly large groups of hunter-gatherers who had begun to live in semi-permanent settlements. A new breed of priests may have been the first to exert authority over communities larger than kinship groups, and may have been behind the first communal endeavour in the building of 'temples' and then the organization of towns, agriculture and animal husbandry that were needed both to sustain the religious sites and to maintain and control population in one place.

The new religion

As people moved from 'wild' to 'civilized', as 'man made himself' – in another memorable phrase of Gordon Childe – we may see the first glimmerings of anthropomorphic gods. Ancestors who had been sought in the spirit world became ancestors who were venerated, and permanent sites of ritual meant that specific ancestors could be remembered in association with a particular place. The altered consciousness of the voyage to the spirit world was transferred to piety and worship, so that the religious experience remained similar even if the belief had changed. In looking at the crucial step from venerating ancestors to the creation of named gods, it is impossible not to see deliberate human agency at work, driven by the psychology of power and control. The faceless pillars of Göbekli Tepe and Nevali Çori may represent the very threshold of the gods, not the result of a gradual process but an act of creation by a group of ambitious priests.

Veneration can quickly change to awe and fear, and the tiered cosmology of the old spirit world transmutes into heaven and hell – where people are trapped between fear of hell and a need to fulfil the requirements of reaching heaven.

These changes were reflected in dramatically evolving lifestyles, from the unpredictability and excitement of the hunter-gatherer to the tedium and toil of the agriculturalist, where the new priesthood could present the promise of a better afterlife as a goal. It was these priests whose descendants would be the first kings, and it was they who were responsible for the birth of modern religion; the first acts of worship may in truth have been the first acts of obeisance to a new class of priest-kings. To paraphrase Gordon Childe, man not only made himself; he also made his gods.

The move from the natural world to a man-made world may also be seen on a much grander scale in a shift from sacred caves and mountains to burial mounds and pyramids. Whereas the 'old' religion may have carried on into the Neolithic in the private context of houses – much as older rituals were to do in later periods, for example in the continuance of pagan worship in Christian times – the new religion was focused on monumental sites such as Göbekli Tepe, which took over the function of caves and mountains as the focus for communal religious activity. The manipulation of belief by a new breed of priests may be the beginning of the tension between centralized, state-controlled religion and private belief and ritual, something I explored with early Christianity in my novel *The Last Gospel*. Throughout history this tension has been the cause of bloody persecution and conflict, and the possibility that this can be traced back to a violent dislocation at the dawn of civilization is suggested by the disturbing nature of the rituals revealed in the archaeological evidence, another part of the extraordinary revelation of the 'new' Neolithic.

Altered-consciousness visions

A common altered-consciousness experience is of travelling through a tunnel or vortex; the interpretation of this vision as a 'portal' into the spirit world may be seen in the swirling spirals of Neolithic rock art, and in the circular shape of prehistoric monuments ranging from Göbekli Tepe and Stonehenge to the huge concentric earthworks of prehistoric Britain. The strange swirling shape seen by Jack on one of the monoliths in Atlantis is inspired by a carving on a stone inside the Neolithic passage tomb at Knowth, Ireland, dating from the fourth millennium BC, believed by some to represent a face and by others to be a chance arrangement of circular and semicircular motifs. Although Knowth and the other 'Megalithic' sites of western Europe date four or five millennia after the earliest Neolithic sites of the Near East, they may represent societies at a comparable stage of development with similar belief systems, including rituals based on altered-consciousness experiences and the use of rocks and underground places as portals into the spirit world.

Human sacrifice

The stone basins in the inner sanctum of Atlantis in this novel were inspired by several beautifully decorated basins from the Irish passage tomb at Knowth, where they have been interpreted as receptacles for cremated remains or as water basins that may have been windows into the spirit world. At the Anatolian site of Çayönü, a stone basin was found with possible traces of human blood on its rim, the inspiration for Jack's idea that the basins may have been filled not with water, but with human blood. Another structure at Çayönü known as the 'House of the Dead' contained a flat stone with residues of human blood, as well as aurochs and sheep blood; and yet another building held a slab decorated with a carving of a human head, also with traces of human blood. Beneath the House of the Dead were no fewer than sixty-six human skulls and bones from four hundred additional people. A disproportionately large number of the skulls were from young adults, male and female, suggesting that they may have been selected for killing. The possibility that human sacrifice was widespread is suggested by finds at Çatalhöyük, where infants were found buried under the thresholds and in the walls of houses, and at Jericho, where several infant skulls were found with vertebrae still in place, showing that the heads had been cut from intact bodies rather than taken from skeletons. At Çayönü, one of the most telling finds was a long flint knife with traces of human blood on the blade, suggesting that the obsidian blades found in cached deposits in houses at Çatalhöyük – long thought to have some symbolic meaning – may well have served this chilling function.

Whether sacrifice was an invention of the new religion or an inheritance from the old is unclear. The religion of the hunter-gatherers may have involved shamans or 'seers' transporting themselves into the spirit world, using sacred animals – for example, bulls – as vehicles to aid their journey. The inception of the Neolithic may have seen a step from imagination to reality, from the dream animals portrayed in the cave paintings to real animals sacrificed so that the moment of their death opened the portal. It has even been suggested that the first large-scale animal husbandry may have been to provide bulls for sacrifice. The shift from caves to open-air sites for communal ritual may have been associated with developing rituals of excarnation, where human bodies were exposed to be eaten by birds, a possibility suggested by depictions of vultures with body parts in a carving at Göbekli Tepe and a wall painting at Çatalhöyük. The step from this to human sacrifice may have been associated with the emergence of the new priestly elite who could use it to instil awe and fear and exert control. The idea of sacrifice as an 'offering' may have come about as religious practice shifted from the spirit travel of the shaman to the worship of gods closely associated with that new elite. If this interpretation is correct, then the early Neolithic 'Garden of Eden' may have been not only a place of revelation and creativity, but also one of bloodshed and terror.

These extraordinary and disturbing discoveries bring to mind later traditions of child sacrifice in the Near East, from the Biblical story of Abraham and Isaac to the Phoenicians and their western Mediterranean successors, the Carthaginians; elsewhere in the world, human sacrifice also occurred at places – including submerged caves and sinkholes, as well as man-made altars and pyramids – that may have been seen as access points to the spirit world, for example among the Aztec and Maya and their predecessors in Mesoamerica. The importance of blood and dismemberment is also seen elsewhere, for example among the Moche of Peru. A similarity between European megalithic tombs and the interior layout of Mesoamerican pyramids has also been suggested, including passageways with horizontal and vertical axes that may have given access to the underworld as well as to a spirit realm overhead; these structures may be seen as successors to natural caves used in the same way during the Palaeolithic. The idea of an *'axis mundi'*, a special place where the supernatural world can be reached, is common to many religions. Whether or not these cross-cultural similarities should be seen in terms of lines drawn on a map, of the diffusion of people and ideas, will always be a focus of fascinating debate; what does seem likely is that the receptivity of distant peoples to new religious ideas, rituals and structures – for example, pyramids – may have been increased by common neuropsychological experiences and visions that might have allowed these ideas to be absorbed rather than rejected.

Epics and scripts

As well as pulling in the evidence of much earlier prehistory, the new finds from the Neolithic have caused scholars to look afresh at the foundation myths of the ancient Near Eastern civilizations to see whether they might hark back to a formative period soon after the end of the Ice Age. The Epic of Gilgamesh, probably first written down in Old Babylonian in the third millennium BC, is best known for its flood story, which parallels the Old Testament account and may derive from a memory of sea-level rise after the last Ice Age – perhaps even a Black Sea flood that inundated Neolithic settlements in the sixth millennium BC. If that is the case, it strengthens the idea that the central theme of the epic, the struggle and then friendship between the 'wild' Enkidu and the 'civilized' Gilgamesh, may reflect the period of transition between hunter-gatherers and settled ways of life in the early Neolithic. The epic is told largely as a dream narrative, suggesting the importance of dreams and their interpretation in a world where altered-consciousness experiences gave access to the spirits, and later the first 'gods', whose inchoate form is suggested by a reference elsewhere in Babylonian myth to the faceless 'Annu' coming from a mountain in the north, perhaps in the region of Anatolia or the Black Sea coast.

Another fascinating aspect of the Epic of Gilgamesh is the repeated reference to 'sacred stones', suggestive of the importance of stones in the archaeology of early Neolithic religion, and particularly the extraordinary account of the meteorite recounted here in Chapter 6: one so heavy that it could barely be lifted, bringing to mind the ancient Greek myth that the Trojan palladion was originally a thunderbolt sent down by Zeus, very probably referring to a meteorite. Meteorites in recent history have most readily been found on the polar icecaps, suggesting that these ancient stories may even recall discoveries made by hunter-gatherer ancestors – before the end of the Ice Age – of objects whose sacred significance was remembered into the Neolithic and the first period when the epics were being written down.

In my novel *Atlantis* I suggested that the symbols on the real-life Phaistos disc, a mysterious object found near the second-millennium BC palace of that name in Crete, may have been a lost Neolithic script of Anatolia. One of those symbols, the 'Atlantis symbol' seen by Jack and Costas as they dive through the lava tunnel, is on the banner of my website. While an early Anatolian origin for the Phaistos symbols remains possible, no writing system as we would understand it has yet been found pre-dating the early cuneiform of the clay tablets on which myths such as the Epic of Gilgamesh were first inscribed. However, as with so much else that is being overturned by the new discoveries from the Neolithic, we may need to reject the long-held assumption that writing developed in response to the need for record-keeping in the early cities, and instead look to the religious organization and belief systems that may have been behind such developments. The 'Stone Age code' in this novel is based on an actual assessment of symbols that are found repetitively and in groups in cave paintings of the Palaeolithic dating as far back as thirty-five thousand years ago. These and similar symbols could have been mnemonics, and together may have formed a narrative of myth or ritual; in that sense they may be regarded as a writing system. These new ways of thinking may allow us to see symbolic and narrative significance in artefacts that have already been excavated, even in the shape and association of stones. The extraordinary nature of the finds so far made at the Neolithic sites suggests that future excavations may reveal more certain evidence of this type than has yet been found.

Prehistoric voyages of the mind

In order to reach Uta-napishtim – the Babylonian Noah – in his mountain fastness, Gilgamesh undergoes a sea voyage that would have taken a lesser man 'a month and fifteen days', a span equivalent to a voyage from Mesopotamia to the tip of India or from the Strait of Gibraltar across the Atlantic. Voyages of this nature were well within the capabilities of people in the early Neolithic. Yet our understanding of the period has been plagued by the misconception that people were terrified of the open ocean, and that long-distance voyages only became common with the needs of colonization, trade and warfare after the first civilizations had developed. In fact, the fear of the open sea, fear of the unknown, that remains so strongly embedded in our psyche today may be traced back to this formative period in the early Neolithic, when people moved inland, when the resources of the sea became less important, and when control by the new elite involved keeping people in one place and restraining them from exploration. In the preceding period – the Mesolithic – people had lived near the sea and ranged widely, and hunter-gatherers of the Palaeolithic travelled thousands of miles over land and sea. People first crossed the ocean to Australia some fifty thousand years ago, and by fifteen thousand years ago people had travelled huge distances by sea along the west coast of the Americas from the Bering Strait.

To those early travellers the ocean was not a barrier but a conduit, the most important conclusion reached by the adventurer Thor Heyerdahl after completing his 'Ra' expeditions in 1970 using reed boats. He was referring to his experience on the Atlantic Ocean, where in the right place – sailing south from Gibraltar – it is difficult *not* to be swept westwards across the ocean, a voyage that would have been well within the technology of early Neolithic seafarers using reed, skin or wooden boats. Yet there is another aspect to early seafaring that new research on Neolithic religion brings to the fore. A sea voyage was the final journey in the dream world of Gilgamesh, his ultimate adventure; and watery visions, of water being an access point to the underworld and of floating in an endless ocean, are common altered-consciousness experiences. Among people who were sensitized to these experiences, a voyage such as one across the Atlantic could be perceived at a level of consciousness unfamiliar to those of us who have not been driven to hallucination – as many are when pushed to their limits at sea – or to interpret those visions within a system of ritual and belief that gave structure to the experience. I have tried to bring something of this across in the Prologue. To these early seafarers, reality may have merged with the spirit world; the sea voyage became a voyage of the mind. For those still steeped in the old religion – the religion of spirit journeys – ocean voyages may not have provoked terror, but actually have been relished.

It seems possible that for the greater part of the history of *Homo sapiens*, it has been this type of belief system, rather than belief in gods and deferential acts of worship, that has sustained people's spiritual needs – a system built on remembering and rationalizing dreams, and on other altered-consciousness experiences that seemed to access a supernatural world, a system whose common features may owe much to human neuropsychology. The inception of religion with anthropomorphic gods may have gone hand-in-hand with early state formation and the burgeoning power-base of the new leaders, something we may see appearing with dramatic speed and conflicting with the old religion at the remarkable sites of the early Neolithic – at Çatalhöyük, Göbekli Tepe, Nevali Çori, Çayönü – over nine thousand years ago. As more early sites are discovered and excavated – one day perhaps including submerged sites off the Black Sea coast of Turkey, even a real-life Atlantis – it may truly be possible to speak of archaeologists making the greatest discovery of all time, and revealing the birthplace of the gods.

★ ★ ★

The swirling vortex images from the Neolithic may be the origin of two ancient symbols that have come to have dark connotations, the swastika – first seen on Bronze Age pottery of Troy – and the *Sonnenrad*, the sun symbol that Heinrich Himmler incorporated in the decoration of his SS 'order-castle' at Wewelsburg. There, the symbol was placed in the floor as if it were at the apex of an *axis mundi*, an idea that would have been well within Himmler's mystical vision of Wewelsburg, and it was this that led me to imagine the Zoo flak tower in Berlin in similar terms.

The Zoo flak tower was one of the most terrifying German creations of the Second World War, a vast five-storey concrete bunker that rose like a castle keep out of the grounds of the Berlin Zoo. The tower provided shelter for thousands of civilians during bombing raids, and had its own power supply, water reservoir and hospital; in the final hours of the Russian onslaught, the defenders even dropped explosives off the parapet like medieval soldiers pouring burning oil on attackers. It was one of three flak towers in Berlin and was ready for action in April 1941, along with the adjacent L-Tower, which housed the radar that directed the flak (anti-aircraft) fire.

The main armament of the Zoo tower comprised four huge twin 128mm guns, each barrel capable of firing up to ten rounds a minute. The tower was designed with elasticity in the ferroconcrete to withstand the shock of the guns firing at high elevations, which drove the recoil force down into the structure; but damage was caused to the concrete as well as to the gun crews' hearing when the guns were fired at low elevations, at ground targets. The flak towers shot down many

British and American bombers, as well as Russian dive-bombers in the 1945 onslaught that were engaged by the 37mm and quadruple 20mm guns on the outer gallery below the parapet. During the final assault the big guns provided withering fire against infantry and tanks until the Soviets advanced below the minimum elevation of the guns, and the last German defenders outside the tower were overwhelmed.

Of great significance for this novel, the Zoo tower also provided safe storage for art and antiquities from numerous Berlin museums, held in special air-conditioned rooms on the third floor – among them the Egyptian bust of Nefertiti, the carved frieze from Pergamon in Turkey, Kaiser Wilhelm II's collection of coins and, most famously, the 'Treasure of Priam', excavated by Heinrich Schliemann at Troy in 1873, donated by him to the German people before his death in 1890, and held until the beginning of the Second World War in the Museum for Pre- and Proto-History in Berlin.

In March 1945, under orders from Hitler and overseen by Reichsleiter Martin Bormann, many of the treasures in the Zoo tower were removed to a salt mine at Merkers in Austria, where they were discovered soon after by soldiers of General Patton's US Third Army. Three crates were left behind; those containing the treasure of Priam. We know this because the Treasure disappeared after the war and for many years was thought lost. The true course of events has only recently been reconstructed, and much remains uncertain. The director of the Museum for Pre- and Proto-History, Dr Wilhelm Unverzagt, an ardent Nazi, is thought to have insisted that the crates remain in Berlin when the other treasures were removed in March 1945, though whether or not there was a higher authority behind that decision – Himmler would be a likely candidate, with his interest in prehistory – remains unknown. Unverzagt's words and actions in this novel are fictitious. However, he is thought to have stayed in the Zoo tower with the crates after the 2 May surrender to ensure that they were not looted by Russian soldiers but instead remained intact for transport to Moscow, where they remained hidden in the storerooms of the Pushkin Museum until they were rediscovered in 1987.

In the novel, I imagine the 'Schliemann Gallery' in the Museum for Pre- and Proto-History being presided over by a statue bust of Otto von Bismarck, the 'Iron Chancellor', who had been a friend of Schliemann's; my image of the broken statue in the Zoo tower is based on a real-life shattered statue of Bismarck photographed in 1945 in the town square of Rigorplatz, outside Berlin, and the fictional statue in turn inspires the fictional Hoffman to think of Ozymandias, the toppled statue of the king in Shelley's poem who seems to stand for all the crumbled dreams of power that Hoffman would have seen around him in those dark days of April 1945.

The Zoo tower provided a headquarters for Josef Goebbels in his final guise as Reich Commissioner for the Defence of Berlin, though he himself did not leave the Führerbunker in the days leading up to the murder of his children and his own suicide. The words and actions of Heinrich Himmler portrayed in this novel are fictional, including his appearance at the Zoo tower on the morning after Hitler's suicide on 30 April 1945. Nevertheless, Himmler's movements over the final days before the German surrender were secretive and shrouded in mystery, and allow the possibility of a clandestine visit to Berlin as suggested here. On 28 April 1945, the BBC had reported Himmler's attempt to negotiate with the Western Allies, and the following day Hitler declared him a traitor and ordered his arrest. Late on 1 May, Himmler attempted to negotiate with Grand Admiral Dönitz, Hitler's appointed successor, for a place in the new government, and over the next days he followed Dönitz and his puppet government from Plön to Flensburg on the Baltic. Despite being dismissed by Dönitz on 6 May, Himmler continued to retain the trappings of power, driving round with an SS escort and maintaining an aircraft. He was finally arrested in disguise – wearing an eye patch, with his moustache shaved off – by the British, and committed suicide in custody using a cyanide capsule on 23 May.

Oberstleutnant (Lieutenant-Colonel) Ernst Hoffman is fictional. In my story, Himmler promotes him two ranks higher to the SS equivalent of brigadier, SS-Brigadeführer. A real-life Stuka ace was closely associated with the Zoo tower: Oberst (Colonel) Hans-Ulrich Rudel, one of the most highly decorated German servicemen of the war, with over 2,500 combat missions to his credit. Rudel was a committed Nazi and much feted by the Nazi inner circle. On 8 February 1945, he was shot down and sent to the hospital in the Zoo tower to recover, spending over a month there and being visited by Goebbels and Göring. In a rare eyewitness account from inside the tower, Harry Schweitzer, a Hitler Youth flak auxiliary, described how Rudel was allowed on to the roof to see the 37mm guns in action, a matter of some interest to him as his Stuka mounted a version of the same weapon. Schweitzer was one of many Hitler Youth and Luftwaffe boy auxiliaries who manned the flak guns in Berlin, and he gives a vivid account of the final days in the Zoo tower: the terrible overcrowding, the asphyxiating conditions, attacks by dive-bombers, and the pulverizing effect of the 128mm guns when they were fired at low elevation into the city, causing shock waves so severe that they damaged the parapet of the tower. Colonel Hans-Oscar Wohlermann, a Panzer Corps artillery officer, described the horrific view from the gun platform: 'One had a panoramic view of the burning, smouldering and smoking great city, a scene which again and again shook one to the core.'

Harry Schweitzer also described the announcement that came through internal tannoys for a breakout from the Zoo tower at about 2300 hours on 1 May. The tower was surrendered to the Soviets about an hour and a half later. A Luftwaffe doctor present, Dr Walter Hagedorn, estimated the numbers inside at more than 30,000 – mostly civilians – including 1,500 wounded and 500 dead. Miraculously, most of the survivors were able to leave unharmed. The circumstances of the final day in the tower are hazy, but provide a basis for the fictional scenario in this novel. On the evening of 30 April, the Russians sent German prisoners to the tower to try to persuade the garrison to surrender, assuring them that there would be no executions. The following morning, the Russians received a reply, signed by Colonel Haller, garrison commander, saying that the surrender would take place at midnight. But Haller had not been the official garrison commander, suggesting that there had been a coup; the reason for the delay was apparently to allow time for a breakout, on the assumption that the Russian assurances were worthless. In the event the breakout never occurred and the Russians reached the tower and took the surrender from Haller, who apparently told a Russian officer that two high-ranking generals were hiding inside. The Russian writer Konstantin Simonov was led to a concrete room, where he found one of the generals lying dead, eyes wide open and clutching a pistol, a dead woman by his side, and between the general's legs 'a bottle of champagne, one third full'.

The idea that Hoffman could have flown out of Berlin in a Fieseler Storch is based on a true-life episode from those final days of Nazi power, when the celebrated Nazi aviator Hanna Reitsch (herself also treated in the Zoo tower hospital, in 1943) flew the wounded Luftwaffe general Ritter von Greim into Berlin and then out again after he had visited the Hitler bunker. They survived Russian anti-aircraft fire and landed on a Berlin street in a badly damaged Storch on 27 April, leaving two days later in an Arado Ar 96, hours before Hitler's suicide. Both aircraft types were lightweight, but the Storch in particular excelled at short take-off and landing.

After the surrender, the Zoo tower was used as a hospital and a shelter for the homeless, but in 1947 it was demolished by the British Royal Engineers, a huge job requiring a staggering thirty-five tons of dynamite. The resulting mountain of rubble – 412,000 cubic metres of it – was ground up and used for road construction during the 1950s, and in 1969 the foundations of the tower were removed. Today the site is occupied by the hippopotamus enclosure of the Berlin Zoo. To get a sense of its appearance, you can visit the remains of another of the three huge towers, the Humboldthain flak tower, which still survives on one side to its original height and has been converted into a memorial and viewing tower. Since 2004, the Berliner Underwelten Association has offered tours inside the ruins, and their efforts have revealed much that was previously buried. Whether or not more remains to be discovered at the site of the Zoo tower is unknown, but the enormous effort that went into its construction in the heart of Berlin suggests that more secrets of the Nazi period and those apocalyptic final days may yet be revealed beneath the modern city.

B-24 Liberator FK-856 is fictional, but is based on RAF Liberators that flew out of Nassau in the Bahamas as part of 111 Operational Training Unit until July 1945. The fictional pilot's experiences with Bomber Command are inspired by the wartime career of my great-uncle, Flight Lieutenant William Norman Cook, DFC and Bar, RAF, a Lancaster pathfinder pilot who flew 59 operations over Nazi Europe. 111 OTU also carried out anti-submarine patrols, and their losses over the 'Bermuda Triangle' – no greater than the losses in any other training unit anywhere – included one Liberator that disappeared without trace on a training mission in 1945. Whether U-boats entered the Caribbean after the German surrender in May 1945 may never be known; the possibility is suggested by the extraordinary voyages of U-977 and U-530, whose captains refused to surrender and did not finally give up until 10 July and 17 August respectively, at Mar del Plata in Argentina.

The Prologue invokes imagery from *The Epic of Gilgamesh*, the ancient Near Eastern poem also known in its Akkadian version by its first line, *Shanaqbaīmuru*, 'He who saw the deep' (in the Prologue I have imagined a similar meaning for the name Uta-napishtim, in a lost language). The passage quoted at the beginning of the book is my own rendering, though the translation of words and phrases owes much to previous scholarly versions including those of Reginald Campbell Thompson (1928), N. K. Sandars (1960 Penguin edition) and Andrew George (1999 Penguin edition). The modern poems referred to in this novel are Samuel Taylor Coleridge's 'Kubla Khan' (Chapter 7), Wilfred Owen's 'Strange Meeting' (Chapter 16) and Walter de la Mare's 'The Listeners' (Epilogue). The cover image is based on the Nazi *Sonnerod* symbol in the floor of the SS Generals' Hall at Wewelsburg Castle in Germany. Other images of sites and artefacts in this book are on my website www.davidgibbins.com

The Inspiration
for my Novels

I've been passionate about diving for as long as I can remember – the earliest photograph of me in diving gear was taken in New Zealand when I was three years old, equipped with rubber gloves for fins, a toy hollow-handled rake as a snorkel and an old copper laundry tub as a diving tank, all of my own devising. As a boy in the 1960s my greatest heroes were Captain Cousteau and his team on *Calypso*, and I was fortunate to dive early on in my career with some of the pioneers of underwater exploration who had first donned primitive aqualungs only a couple of decades earlier. When I trained to dive in the mid-1970s, we were still taught how to use old-fashioned twin-hose regulators, and much of the equipment of the modern diver was still on the drawing board. There were no dive computers – we worked out how much air we had left by a warning valve that cut off our air supply a few minutes before the tank became empty – buoyancy compensators were simple, mouth-inflated lifejackets and hardly anyone had a dry suit; my first dives under ice were in a wetsuit! Every dive was a huge adventure, particularly in the challenging waters of Canada and the North Atlantic where I did my first diving.

Even today I feel the same surge of adrenaline I felt when I first put on diving gear – for me the underwater world is still the fantastic new frontier I first saw in the pages of *National Geographic* magazine as a boy. It drives my own sense of excitement as I write my novels and I feel myself experiencing the same emotions that I know would be coursing through Jack and Costas as they contemplate another dive into the unknown.

My other great passion since childhood has been archaeology. I've always had a knack for finding artefacts – I still have the collection I amassed as a schoolboy, ranging from prehistoric stone tools to Roman pottery and coins to Victorian medicine bottles. I'm surrounded by ancient artefacts now as I write, and each of my novels has been associated with an artefact of particular significance for the story – for *The Last Gospel* it was a coin of the emperor Claudius, for *The Tiger Warrior* a lapis lazuli carving from the mines of Afghanistan, for *The Mask of Troy* a blackened sherd of pottery from Troy itself, and for *The Gods of Atlantis* a beautiful flint blade from the earliest period of civilisation. Handling artefacts has always been a great part of my inspiration as a novelist, and to me a simple sherd can be like gold. Even after finding real treasure as an archaeologist I've never lost the thrill I felt as a boy when I first picked up a potsherd or a flake of flint thousands of years old.

The stories in my novels have their roots in many years of adventure in my own life. I was born in 1962 in Saskatoon, Canada, to English parents, both academic scientists. We returned briefly to England and then went by sea to New Zealand, spending four years there before carrying on back to England in the same direction – so I'd circumnavigated the world by the age of six. I've no doubt that this helps to explain my early fascination with maritime exploration. I spent much of the remainder of my childhood in Canada, where my first experiences working on a formal excavation – and my first archaeological dives – were on colonial and prehistoric sites in Ontario. I was fascinated by the early history of the Americas, but yearned to return to Europe and immerse myself in the archaeology of the ancient world – and from

1980 I did so, studying at the Universities of Bristol and Cambridge. At Bristol I read Ancient Mediterranean Studies, graduating with a first-class honours degree, and I then took up a Research Scholarship at Corpus Christi College, Cambridge, where I completed a PhD in archaeology. After holding a research fellowship at Cambridge I spent almost a decade teaching archaeology, ancient history and art history as a university lecturer in England, before leaving my teaching career to write and carry out fieldwork full-time.

When I was growing up, not only was underwater archaeology in its infancy, but the science of archaeology itself was not far beyond its formative period – I was taught by scholars only a generation or two removed from the great pioneers of the late nineteenth and early twentieth centuries such as Heinrich Schliemann and Sir Arthur Evans. I've always felt close to that adventurous spirit of early archaeology. As an academic I enjoyed teaching wide-ranging courses, trying to infuse students with my passion for the past; writing archaeological thrillers represents a continuation of that passion. I grew up in a literary household surrounded by books, and have always written creatively. I began to see how I could write fiction with an underlying plausibility, and with the excitement that can only come from first-hand knowledge of what it's like to be there, to experience real-life adventure and discovery and danger.

I'd qualified as a diver in Canada at the age of fifteen with the Association of Canadian Underwater Councils and the Confédération Mondiale des Activités Subaquatiques. Later I did advanced training with the British Sub-Aqua Club. My first open-water dive was on a shipwreck in Lake Huron in Ontario, and I also dived under ice, in caves and in submerged mines. Afterwards I dived extensively in British waters, and in 1981 I joined my first underwater archaeological expedition to the Mediterranean, to spend the summer excavating a

Roman shipwreck off Sicily. Two years later I led my first expedition – the 1983 University of Bristol Sicily Expedition. Since then I've carried out numerous dives on ancient sites across the Mediterranean, from the waters of Italy and North Africa – where I led a Cambridge University team to excavate sunken remains at Carthage – to the Aegean and East Mediterranean. I took part in the first raising of a Roman hull in British waters off the Channel Islands, and in 1999–2000 I dived for two seasons off Turkey on the first wreck to be fully excavated from the classical Greek period, while I was an adjunct professor of the US-based Institute of Nautical Archaeology.

Along the way I've made many extraordinary discoveries underwater with my own hands – highlights for me include exquisite intact Greek painted pottery from the Etruscan period and the fifth century BC, and the unique medical kit of a Roman surgeon. Recently my diving has taken me to Australia, Hawaii and the Caribbean, and I've been drawn again to the cold waters of the Great Lakes in Canada – on my website www.davidgibbins.com you can see a short film of me enjoying diving under ice taken by my brother Alan off Tobermory, Ontario in April 2011.

In addition to diving and excavation projects I've travelled widely, and my experiences feed into my novels. As a student I undertook a tour of ancient acropolis sites, ranging from Cumae in Italy – where I first saw the Cave of the Sibyl (featured in my novel *The Last Gospel*) – to the remote mountain sites of ancient Crete, where I developed a fascination with the prehistoric Aegean (*Atlantis*, *The Mask of Troy*). A scholarship from the British Institute of Archaeology at Ankara allowed me to spend months in eastern Turkey just before the Kurdish uprising, which was when I first saw the Black Sea shore (*Atlantis*). As a Winston Churchill Travelling Fellow I was in Jerusalem in the weeks preceding the First

Gulf War, studying the archaeology of the Roman period (*The Last Gospel*). In recent years I've travelled to the Republic of Georgia, to Kyrgyzstan and the Lake of Issyk Kul (*The Tiger Warrior*), to Greenland and the Canadian High Arctic (*Crusader Gold*), and to Patagonia and Tierra del Fuego. My current projects in Egypt and on the trail of the first colonists in North America give some idea of the settings for my next novels!

When I'm not travelling I divide my time between a farm and wilderness tract in Canada and a sixteenth-century cottage beside a castle in England. My recreations include mountaineering – I've climbed in the Pyrenees, the Alps, the Caucasus and the Andes, and I often climb in North Wales. I love walking the hills and coasts of Britain, and wilderness canoeing and trekking in Canada. Other interests which figure in my novels include historic firearms, antiquarian books and maps, and eighteenth-century music.

I have an abiding interest in my own family history, and have used that in my novels – one of my ancestors, a Royal Engineers colonel who administered Baluchistan under British rule, was the basis for a character in *The Tiger Warrior*, and another inspired a character in *The Last Gospel*. My family history includes many threads through colonial British history, and many wars – from Culloden and the Napoleonic Wars to the Indian Mutiny and Afghanistan and the Boer War, and then the wars of the twentieth century. Hearing my grandfather talk of his experiences fighting on the Western Front in the First World War led to a fascination with the extremes of human endurance. My passion for the sea was fuelled by my other grandfather, a merchant navy captain who sailed for almost half a century with the Clan Line, the last of the great East Indies shipping companies. He came from a long line of army officers, sea captains and merchants whose activities took them to the Americas and India and the

Far East. My protagonist Jack Howard often has his best insights through the eyes of past explorers and adventurers, sometimes his own ancestors, and that reflects my own approach to historical fiction: seeing the past through lives that have so intrigued me.

My fictional characters draw on my experience of how expeditions work, of how people propel a quest forward. Diving expeditions can be like military operations – long periods of planning and preparation and waiting, followed by a short period of intense action. There's plenty of time for discussion; drawing in team members from widely varying backgrounds can sometimes provide the best insights into the archaeology, as in my novels. Expeditions are a great basis for fiction because they're an analogue of life itself – the voyage and the friendships made along the way can be as rewarding as the destination. Not all loose ends are tied up, and sometimes the treasure at the end remains elusive, just beyond reach – the thrill of the quest might be diminished otherwise. That's what makes the fiction come alive for me as I'm writing it, along with the adventure and the discoveries themselves.

I'm more enthused than ever about my real-life and fictional adventures ahead – every new shipwreck I dive on, every new archaeological site I explore, inspires me in some way. I feel only one step away from truly finding the treasures in my novels – the site of Atlantis, the lost golden menorah, an ancient text containing an astonishing revelation. These are real possibilities, not the stuff of fantasy. Every new novel I write excites me as much as the first one. I hope they do the same for you!

David Gibbins, August 2011